WATCH ME RISE

BY

KC KEAN

Watch Me Rise
Copyright © 2022 KC Kean

This book is licensed for your personal enjoyment only.
This book may not be re-sold or given away to other people. If you would like to share this book with another person, please purchase an additional copy for each recipient. If you're reading this book and did not purchase it, or it wasn't purchased for your use only, then please return to your favourite book retailer and purchase your own copy.
Thank you for respecting the hard work of this author.
All rights reserved.
This is a work of fiction. Names, characters, places, brands, media, and incidents are either the product of the authors imagination or are used fictitiously. The author acknowledges the trademark status and trademark owners of various products referred to in this work of fiction, which have been used without permission. The publication/use of these trademarks is not authorised, associated with, or sponsored by the trademark owners.

Cover Designer: Bellaluna Designs
Editor: Valerie Swope
Editor: Erica Colins
Proofreader: Sassi's Editing Services
Interior Design & Formatting: Sloane Murphy

Watch Me Rise/KC Kean – 1st ed.
ISBN-13 -

To Nicole, Tanya, and Jeni. You rock.

This one's for you.

There wouldn't be so much good peen in here if it wasn't for

you.

My kings may be monsters, but they're mine all the same.

*- **Luella Carter***

PROLOGUE

JAGGER
3 YEARS AGO

The sky is filled with thick, black clouds, a complete contrast to usual, but it seems to fit my mood exactly, and the mental hole I feel myself slipping into.

Anger rumbles under the surface of my skin as I walk up the path to my house. The whole yard is overgrown, and the actual pathway is barely visible, but it's not my problem. Especially not right now.

Jameson, Ezra, and Leo aren't far behind me, but I just need a minute to myself. I need to manage my own turmoil before I attempt to be a pillar of support to anyone else.

She's gone.

Luella has just fucking upped and disappeared into thin air, and none of it makes any goddamn motherfucking sense.

I should have known something was off when David came barreling over the other night, demanding she get downstairs immediately. But as usual, I was lost to the beautiful girl who had way too much sass for one person, yet has held my heart in her hands for as long as I can remember.

The fact she's gone refuses to settle in my mind as I continue to consider what the fuck has actually happened.

As I reach the front door, I notice it's slightly ajar, and it's only then that I hear the shouting coming from inside, before the sound of a smack rings out.

I'd been so wrapped up inside myself, trapped in my mind, I hadn't heard a single noise, not even my own breath as I marched back home from Luella's house. Or what *was* her house I should say.

I glance over my shoulder, spying my brothers at the end of the sidewalk as my brows knit together in confusion. I swipe a hand down my face, and I hold my finger up to the guys, telling them to stay here a minute while I go and check it out. They acknowledge the motion, but they're not close enough to hear what has my attention.

The hinges on the old and decaying green door squeak as I nudge it open, revealing the staircase to my right, and the open living room to the left. It's a huge step up from the trailer we lived in a couple of months ago, but it still needs more love and attention than anyone here will actually give it.

There's nothing in there except the basic furniture. A worn blue sofa, a brown armchair, a fake persian rug, and an old television.

I barely take two steps into the house when I pause, surprised to see my father standing with his arms folded over his chest on the rug in the middle of the room, with his gaze fixed on June, Luella's mother, who is sitting in the armchair. With her blonde hair and clothes a wrinkly mess, she looks even more disheveled than usual.

"You fucking did this to me, Robbie, you can't force me to do anything," she cries out, tears tracking down her face as she swipes at them angrily. The red mark on her cheek is a clear indicator where the smack that I heard landed while I was outside, and it instantly has me on high alert.

My father scoffs. "Bitch, watch your fucking tone. I didn't do anything, it's not my fault you're a fucking whore who spreads your legs for half of the fucking town for drugs," he growls, pacing in front of her with his hands on his hips. His cream pants, and off-white shirt look like they've seen better days, but it's the usual get up for this asshole. If it's not wrinkled or stained it's not his.

"Screw you, Robbie. If I go to the sheriff's office and explain, they'll say it's rape too. You. Raped. Me. A-a-and now I-I'm pregnant," June wails, her hands tangled in her pale blue floral dress, turning my blood to ice as my father steps forward and backhands her across her face. Again.

"That's enough," I bark, interrupting the chaos before he continues to beat her, and both of their heads whip around to face me in surprise as I remain frozen in place with my hands fisted at my sides.

I take the silence as a blessing, as I try to wrap my fucking brain around the information she just spewed. I've always known my father is a vile bastard, but admittedly, Luella's mother is a junkie piece of work too. It's all a fucking mess. Everything is a mess. More so than usual, and that's a shock. We don't live white picket fenced lives, and this is a stark reminder of the fact.

Together, they're my worst fucking nightmare.

Fuck.

"You stay out of this, boy, I have big plans coming for this family, and some little whore with a baby will *not* get in the way of that," my father spits, swiping his black hair back off his face in anger. "I'm shifting my direction toward politics, gaining power on a whole other level, and how would this look for me?" He points in disgust at the sobbing woman on the couch. "She isn't my wife and she will *never* be my wife so she has to be out of the picture." His face is red with anger as the veins pop on his forehead.

"I'm not aborting my child, Robbie. Over my dead body," Luella's mom hisses, her blonde hair pulled back off her face in a low hair tie as her fingers twitch. My gaze fixating on the dirt beneath her fingernails and the pick marks on her arms.

Addiction.

"If that's the only way, then so fucking be it," my father responds, producing a blade from his pocket with a devilish gleam in his brown eyes as June screams, and I know it's time to properly intervene.

With just a handful of steps, I'm quickly standing

between them as my father raises his eyebrow at me, but I raise my hands in surrender, trying to calm him by showing submission with the gesture.

"You're not going to be able to get into politics if you hurt someone, now are you?" I ask calmly, holding back all the snark and anger building inside me at this man's stupidity. "You were just complaining about her not being your wife and how that would look. Going down for murder won't work any better in your favor," I state, and he slowly lowers the blade, turning my words over in his head.

Dropping my hands, I run them over my jeans. I spy the guys hovering in the doorway to my left out of the corner of my eye, but I don't say or do anything to draw attention their way. Not when he seems this unhinged already.

Is this why Luella isn't here anymore?

Is this what's sent her away?

My heart pounds wildly in my chest as I try to calm the questions swirling in my mind.

I'd quite happily go down for murder right now.

Except… There's a baby involved.

My brother or sister is in her stomach.

Luella's brother or sister is in her stomach.

I can't let anything happen to them.

I can't.

I swallow past the lump of emotion forming in my throat, but before I can speak, my father beats me to it. "You're right, son, you're right," he says, pocketing his knife and patting my shoulder with a deep sigh. "It would look good for my image if I was married though, wouldn't it?" he adds, rubbing his chin as he stands deep in thought, and it's June's turn to scoff in response.

Whirling my head around, I glare at her before she can open her fucking mouth, and she thankfully clamps her lips together. She raises her trembling hand to cover her mouth too, the tell tale sign her twitching is getting worse.

"I don't think we need to go that far, Dad, but we can figure this shit out in a calmer, logical manner," I murmur, turning back to my dad as I run a hand through my hair. He looks at me, his eyes swirling with the overload of thoughts and emotions running through his mind as I wait for him to respond.

I have no idea what calmer actually looks like on his face, but I already know it deep within my soul; I will do whatever it takes to keep that baby safe, just like I will do whatever it takes for my Luella.

From this moment forward, I'll go to the ends of the

earth, with every breath and every inch of my being. I'm determined to be the savior in someone's story.

Some say I don't have a heart, that I'm cold and vicious, but that's because apart from my brothers, my heart has only ever beat for one person.

And now that's two.

WATCH ME RISE

CHAPTER ONE

Lou-Lou
PRESENT DAY

I hold the mug in my hand, the heat barely registering as I mindlessly tap my fingers on it. I don't know how I can feel so numb, yet fired up all at the same time.

There are four sets of eyes looking in my direction. I can feel them burning into the side of my head, but I can't bring myself to lift my gaze from the steaming coffee in my hand.

My mother has unexpectedly appeared in my life again. I didn't know how or when it would happen or if it even would. Half of me expected a phone call to say she had overdosed or something, but to find her there, at Lockwood, being half of the reason the boys are under Robbie's control, completely floors me.

It takes a lot to render me speechless, but this definitely has.

The second reason... well the second reason is likely why my mind is sinking in a mental quicksand.

I have a sister.

Technically a half-sister, but that's irrelevant. Lola shares my blood. She just also happens to share DNA with Jameson and Jagger too. The two men who I've loved since forever. How do I even think this through?

Fuck.

What does that even fucking mean for us?

I squeeze my eyes shut, taking a deep breath as I fight against the millions of questions rolling around in my mind. I don't even know where to fucking start.

Sadness. Anger. Regret. Despair. Happiness. It all storms around in a swirl of chaos.

Walking into Lockwood has left me with more questions than answers, which feels like the story of my life at the minute. I know I can't sit here for the rest of my life, hoping they'll remain silent and let me keep my head in the sand.

Pull your big girl panties on, Lou-Lou, and figure this shit out.

I've never backed down from anything or anyone, it's how David told me to be, how these motherfuckers taught me to be, so why can I not address any of this with them?

Does David know? Does he know about mom and Lola? I'm in no position to speak with him right now, there's far too much going on around me to bring him into the mix.

Three hours ago I was kneeing Leo in the balls, hijacking his SUV and racing to Lockwood demanding answers, and now I'm sitting tensely in my chair at the kitchen table back at home.

Home.

Is this my home? Or a shell? An illusion of what a home should look like, not necessarily *feel* like, but with skeletons falling out of every closet and more secrets unraveling with every breath I take, I know the answer to my own question. This is not a home but a *house*. A house built on lies and deception, nothing about this place screams family right now.

Someone clears their throat, pulling me from my jumbled mind, and I wet my lips as I scan my eyes around the table at them all. I'm sitting in my newly proclaimed seat that I've sat in every time I've been at the dining table with them; with Leo to my right, Ezra on the other side of him, and the twins sitting across the table.

Usually I would feel Jagger's scowl from the farthest seat, but even that seems to have disappeared.

Because I know. I *finally* know their little secret. Or one of them at least.

I take a few gulps of the scalding coffee, letting it burn down my throat, confirming that I'm not completely numb, before placing it on the wooden table before me. It must be after midnight by now, but I don't have the energy to pull my phone out to check.

Meeting their gazes, I pause on each set of eyes, finally seeing them as I try to get a read on them, and their reaction to the situation.

I look at Leo first, his blond hair sticking up in every direction like he's been raking his hands through it as guilt and uncertainty churns in his gray eyes.

Ezra sits beside him, with his unruly brown hair curling over his face as his glasses lay on the table and he swipes at his tired eyes.

Jameson looks wired, his hair is a mess, his brown eyes blown with what looks like adrenaline as he bounces his knee nervously under the table, jolting his entire body.

Jagger sits beside him, his tattooed hands tapping on the table nervously, as his long brown hair falls to his shoulders, and his brown eyes storm with anger.

It seems no one really knows what to say. After falling to the floor far too dramatically for my liking, I passed out for a couple of minutes, waking to find myself in the back of the SUV sprawled across Leo and Ezra with the twins up front. When I was able to lift myself up, I slipped into the empty middle seat and closed my eyes, letting my head fall into my hands as I put distance between us all. Silence consumed us as a feeling of detachment seeped through my body, and not one of the guys was able to find words to fill the thick air around us.

"Where do I even fucking start?" I ask with a sigh, folding my arms across my chest as I brace my elbows on the table, creating a physical and emotional barrier between us.

It takes a second for someone to respond, silence awkwardly continuing to stretch around us. "I mean, which part do you want to discuss first?" Jameson replies, making me scoff, my hackles instantly rising to the bait.

"Right? Like you've kept *so* much back, I have no idea where to even begin," I grumble, clenching my hands as I force myself to take another deep breath. Even though every fiber of my body wants to race back down to the basement, grab the crowbar, and go to fucking town on all of the shit down there. Again.

"We can start at the beginning," Ezra murmurs, swiping a hand down his face as I quirk an eyebrow at him.

"And where might that be, Ezra?" I retort, glancing around at the other three as well.

"How about when we realized you'd fucking left Nevada. I walked into my shitty living room to find my father and your mother yelling at each other," Jagger grunts, making my heart skip a beat when I become aware he's actually letting me in, and I force myself to keep my mouth shut so it doesn't stop him. His usually cold brown eyes seem warmer as he searches mine for a moment, before he reluctantly sighs. "A lot of shit was said, but ultimately, what mattered was your mom was pregnant because my father raped her."

His words turn my blood to ice as Leo's hand falls to

my shoulder in comfort. My jaw practically hits the floor in surprise at his words as my brows crinkle together in a mixture of pain and confusion.

I could enter a competition for world's shittiest mom any day of the week with mine, I'm fully aware of that, but rape? Holy shit.

"How… what… I—"

"He was threatening to *kill* her, Luella, and I couldn't let that happen to the unborn child. I couldn't. The only way it seemed to benefit him was if she became his wife, and we were completely caught off-guard at the time, agreeing to whatever possible."

So they're my… stepbrothers?

I fall back in my seat as Jagger continues to shine a light on just how fucking vile his father is. My mom and dad never married, not even a shotgun town hall job when they were pregnant with David. My parents were quite happy living a toxic lifestyle between themselves that revolved around drugs, sex, and fighting. Not necessarily just with each other either.

But to marry Robbie?

Did she even put up a fight?

Fuck.

Shaking my head, I focus my next question on the sweet little girl that was sleeping soundly as my world crumbled around me. "So you've known about her the whole time then? Knowing what relation we are to each other now?" I push for clarification, and the guilty look on all of their faces tells me they know I'm talking about Lola.

Motherfucking assholes.

"In our defense, how would you have liked us to broach the subject that we share a half sister?" Jameson asks, quirking his eyebrow at me, and my jaw tightens with agitation. I understand it's not that simple, but fuck, it's a huge goddamn piece of information that they've held back on.

Meeting his gaze head on, I put on my biggest, most condescending smile. "You say, hey, Lou-Lou, we've got something important—"

Jameson's eyes widen at my smart mouth as he shakes his head, throwing his hand up between us. "Let me stop you right there, I wouldn't call you Lou-Lou for one, and two—"

The sound of a hand slamming down on the table interrupts him, rattling my coffee mug enough for it to splash over the lip. We all turn to find Jagger with his fist planted firmly on the wood, a growl on his face and a tired look in his eyes.

"We're getting off topic," he grumbles, trying to soften his tone while running a hand down his face. The snarky comment on the tip of my tongue melts away when his pleading eyes meet mine. "If we didn't know about her, Luella, she would have never existed." His words are harsh, but true, and the reality of his statement washes over me in an almost calming manner, and my shoulders relax slightly.

"So why keep her a secret from me?"

"Because as much as we wanted you to stick around, we couldn't be sure that you wouldn't run the second you arrived," Jameson answers without blinking, the truth tumbling from his lips and hitting me square in the chest.

Wow.

I clear my throat as I shake my head in disappointment. "And when I didn't? Run, I mean. What then?"

No one answers me straight away, not like my last question. But I hold my ground, waiting for someone to take the floor.

"Then what if you ran because of it?"

Ezra's words cut me deep, so harshly that I feel like

I'm choking on air.

Would I really do that? Would I leave because of this secret and the ramification it could possibly have on our group dynamic?

Wetting my dry lips, I cast a glance around the table at the four of them, each looking as exhausted as the last, but Ezra's words shine in each of their eyes, even Jagger's, and it shocks me to my core.

Does it matter that I share a sibling with Jameson and Jagger? Well, it doesn't change my feelings, that's for sure, but would it be looked at funny to those outside of our little bubble?

I feel like that's an inconsequential question again because I'm in love with four fucking guys, people are already turning heads.

"That's not going to happen," I finally reply, watching as Leo's eyebrows rise at my words, and the corners of his mouth tilt up in a small relieved smile.

I try to organize the jumbled mess of questions in my head, wanting to set the conversation back on track, but I feel drained.

"Why are they at that place? At Lockwood?" I ask, folding my arms over my chest again, and it's Leo beside me who gains my attention as he squeezes my thigh in comfort.

"We're all in Emerson Grove because of Robbie's political aspirations. We're his bitches because it keeps Lola and your mom safe among other things. Like June being a complete publicity piece for him creates a fake and arrogant picture of him being a respectable man, but it's all about power and control on his end. We're trying to figure a way out of this mess, so they don't have to be locked away forever. We don't want you *anywhere* near him." His gentle touch on my thigh gets a little tighter as I try to decipher the emotion in his gray eyes, but it's gone too quickly.

"That's still so vague and didn't answer my questions. *Why* can't they live here? *Why* can't you just be out from under his thumb? *Why* do you think I can't protect myself among all of this mess?" My voice gets quieter as I ask each question, trying to wrap my head around the confusion, but it's no use. Why can't they see me for who I am? I understand protecting Lola and my mom, but I can take care of myself.

My chin falls to my chest as I try to figure out what I could be missing.

Why would Robbie come here for political reasons? Much less, *how* does Robbie even have political reasons? None of this makes any sense. I can't seem to silence the questions racing through my mind, but more than anything, I can sense there is something unspoken still in the air.

"What else aren't you saying?" I can feel it, I know there is another truth rippling beneath the surface, and the way they all cast their eyes at each other, but say nothing only confirms it.

As the silence stretches out between us, the air begins to thicken in anticipation.

"So, even after tonight, you're not willing to help me understand?" I state, swiping Leo's hand off my leg, and they continue to give me a blank expression.

"We should focus on your mom and Lola right now," Ezra says, and I scoff.

"Fuck you guys for telling me what I should and shouldn't be focusing on. I want the whole fucking picture, not just what the four of you deem suitable for me to know," I bite out, frustrated beyond words at the fucking audacity of them.

Planting my hands on the table, I rise to my feet, the scrape of the chair dragging across the floor echoing through the room as my shoulders sag with defeat.

"Lucy, don't leave yet, we need to talk about this," Jameson murmurs.

Is this guy fucking for real?

"I'm trying to talk, and you're giving me nothing but half ass answers. I guess even now, some things will never change," I hiss back, completely exhausted and drained with information overload, all from how much I've learned and yet how little I seem to know. Taking a deep breath, I step to the side, moving away from the table, and Jameson instantly reaches his hand out to grab my arm, but I bat him away.

"Luella—" Jagger starts, rising to his feet too. I raise my hand for him to stop, and to my surprise, he does.

"The fact that none of you see how huge this is, fucking breaks me even more than knowing we share a sibling. I spent three years *alone*, while you guys had each other. You got to continue being a team, I got… nothing. Now I finally learn some truth, yet you feel that's enough and still withhold information. I'm not some little bird who you can just feed dribs and drabs whenever you please." I drag my hands down my face, my body tense with the stress of today, with the stress of the last three years. "I need time,

I need to process what the fuck is going on, and as much as you might disagree, I deserve all the answers. It's not only because I'm asking you, it's also because this entire situation impacts *my life*. But since you're not going to give them to me out of respect, I need some time to myself. At least I know what I'm getting in *that* situation."

With that, I turn on my heel and head for my room, feeling the distance between us grow with every step I take.

WATCH ME RISE

CHAPTER TWO

Lou-Lou

I yawn, wiping the sleep from my eyes as I stretch out my legs, the warm sheets offering me no comfort as I glance at the window. I left the goddamn curtains open again like a fool, and now the sun is blinding me.

A glance at my phone tells me It's just past one in the afternoon, and I feel like I've barely slept. Thank god it's Friday. I left the guys downstairs last night at almost two in the morning, but it was easily five a.m. before my eyelids finally grew heavy.

Remembering the parting words I left them with,

instantly jogs my memory on all the fucking drama I'm juggling right now, and I cover my eyes with my hands, trying to hide myself from my own mental struggle that keeps repeating.

My long lost mother, who has apparently got herself clean, and a half sister who shares both mine and the twins blood.

God, as if I thought Emerson Grove couldn't get anymore fucked up than it already was, now I have more family shit to deal with than ever before. It seems my entire past is here to haunt me.

Maybe if I hide under the duvet, it'll all disappear and I'll never have to face the stark reality of the situation. But I know that's never going to happen.

With a sigh, I drop my hands down on the bed beside me, keeping my eyes squeezed shut as I try to magically fill myself with confidence.

As much as my mind wants me to hide away for the day, it's just not me, or the version of me I want to be. If I want the guys to see me for who I am, I have to prove that I am strong without them.

I hate the quietness that blankets me as I pry my eyes open and focus on the fairy lights on my wall. The frustration I managed to tamper down enough to fall asleep, is quickly rising to the surface again.

Dramatically pulling the duvet off my body, I swing my legs over the side of the bed and force myself to my feet before I change my mind. I head straight for the bathroom, switching on the shower to let it warm up while I take care of myself. As I brush my teeth, watching my reflection in the mirror, I instantly dislike the dark bags under my eyes and the dull skin on my face.

All of this stress is affecting my body as well as my mind now, and I need to figure out a way to adapt to the new twist in my life.

I either need to get over their lies and manipulation or bulldoze those four motherfuckers, and admittedly, the latter sounds far more enticing.

Pulling my nightshirt off, I drop it into the laundry basket before I step under the spray, my body relaxing a little as the warm water cascades over my body. I stand still for a moment, trying to let the shower wash all my problems away, but as usual, it doesn't happen.

It's quite obvious by their behavior that I still don't know everything that's going on. All the details, traits, and backbone that seem to make up this house and the people in it are still out of reach. Is it crazy of me to wish things were how they used to be three years ago?

Fuck, we had nothing and no one but each other, but that feels like more than I have now. Even in this fancy-ass house, surrounded by all the expensive cars and designer clothes, I would trade it all in a heartbeat. At least then I was fully aware of everything happening around me, or so I thought.

Stop letting this stupid shit pull you farther into the quick sand, Lou-Lou. I chastise myself as I swipe the hair off my face.

Instead, I focus on lathering the floral body wash all over myself, before running through my usual hair routine. As I step out of the shower and wrap a fluffy gray towel around my body, I feel more refreshed and lighter than when I first stepped inside.

Padding my way back into my bedroom, I hear my phone vibrate on my nightstand as I move into the closet to grab an outfit for today. I dry myself off quickly, before I step into my favorite lilac lace bra and panties set, a pair of leggings and an oversized, mint green, high-neck sweater. Letting my blonde hair loose, damp curls fall around my shoulders as I grab a pair of fluffy socks and head back to my bed.

Without even thinking, I grab my television remote and put an old series on in the background to block out the silence that would otherwise drive me crazy.

It feels so strange to be in all of these layers, but the temperature in Michigan is dropping quicker than I'm used to, and it's colder than I could have prepared for. Although I miss the heat from Nevada, Arizona and California, I can't deny how much I like feeling so snug though, and my new obsession with fluffy slipper socks will quickly be draining my newly obtained bank account, courtesy of Ryan. Let's hope he doesn't go through my statements and question my goddamn sanity.

Admittedly, the colder temperature has me excited for all things Fall. With pumpkin spice lattes, fallen leaves, and all of the things, including Halloween. The vision of being curled up in a blanket, with a mug of marshmallows and a side of hot chocolate while watching a christmassy movie. It's the only way to do it.

I wet my lips as I consider whether I should get back under the duvet again or make an appearance downstairs, and the sound of my stomach rumbling quickly makes the decision for me. Maybe I could grab some snacks and head back up here if I can't handle the tension downstairs.

Taking a deep breath, I stand tall and push my shoulders back, believing strongly in my *fake it til you make it* move. When I reach for my phone I frown slightly when I remember it vibrating earlier, but the text notification is from a number I'm not familiar with.

My brows knit together slightly as I use facial recognition to unlock the screen, only to find a text message from Robbie glaring back at me.

Unknown: Nice of you to make an appearance at the fight last night. Are you the reason Jagger fucked everything up? Maybe I should bring you fully into the fold, huh? Remind you, and those fuckers who is in charge here.

Unknown: And don't think I don't know about your late night trip to Lockwood. If you don't want to wind up there with them, you'd do well to fucking listen. Nobody gets away with ignoring Robbie Izaro, especially not you little fuckers.

What. In. The. Actual. Fuck?

I genuinely don't know if I'm more mad at him or

them. Maybe even myself since it irritates me that I let him affect me so much.

Fuck.

Robbie just about wins in my *most hated* department because he thinks he's God, and if this town actually gives him the chance at running in their political circles then they fucking deserve him.

But I'm mad at Jagger, Jameson, Leo, and Ezra for not seeing how keeping me in the dark leaves me at such a disadvantage. And now their shit decisions have officially bitten them in the ass.

Again.

Fuck.

I didn't even know Jagger won the fight last night, but I'm not sure we can count standing up to his father a victory just yet. Hell, I'm almost proud. But if I don't know that, along with the other secret or *secrets* hanging over my head, I don't know how they expect me to survive Robbie's wrath.

Glancing out of the window, I consider my next move, but the answer is obvious. They need to see this. They *need* to understand the position they're continuing to put me in and if Robbie's threats aren't enough to prove my case, then I'll figure this shit out on my own.

With determination, I march toward my bedroom door, swinging it open with force before pounding down the stairs with my phone firmly in my grip as my heart races with anger.

I pause as I hit the bottom step, trying to hear where they could be, but it's difficult over the pounding of my pulse in my ears. Swiping my hair back off my face, I stick my head in the game room, but I come up empty when only the huge beanbags, La-Z-Boy chairs, and gaming set up greets me.

Without pausing, I whirl around and rush for the living room to find it just as empty.

Where are these motherfuckers?

When I come up empty in the kitchen and yard as well, I plant my hands on my hips as I huff in frustration.

Think, Lou-Lou. Think.

My gaze searches around the table for some type of epiphany, and that's when I see the cupboard under the stairs slightly ajar. I could slap my forehead with irritation at myself for not considering the basement first.

I rush to the door, swinging it open the rest of the way, before rushing down the steps as quickly as possible. As soon as I reach the bottom, I brace my hand on the wall as I take the scene in before me.

Fuck.

As I slowly scan my eyes from left to right, my jaw drops more and more with every breath. Ezra is sitting in only a pair of gray sweats with his glasses firmly in place as he taps away on the computer, his brown curly hair sticking up in every direction. Instantly having my fingers desperate to run though it.

Jagger and Jameson are sparring on the mat in the far right corner, sweating, grunting and breathing heavily in only a pair of shorts each, and my mouth dries at the tattoos that are revealed. I really need to put exploring their ink higher on my priority list.

They're completely lost in each other, not noticing my arrival. Jagger's long hair is falling loose from his hair tie, and Jameson pulls at it like a child, which only makes Jagger growl as he chuckles in response. I have to bite my tongue to stop myself from joining in, reminding myself that I'm pissed.

What surprises me the most is Leo to my right, with his back to me, in a white cotton tee and black shorts as he tosses blades at a target on the fucking wall.

Blades. At a target. *On the fucking wall.*

This is not what I was expecting to walk into.

Not even a little bit.

How is he throwing them with such precision for one, and for two… why? Just why?

Seeing Leo in a t-shirt when the other three are topless instantly reminds me of the scars on his back that he covered up, making my heart break for him all over again when I don't even know *how* or *who* might have caused them.

I stand, frozen to the spot as I look over them all again, my heart aching and my throat dry as reality washes over me.

These guys, these *men*, are my fucking Kings. Always have been, always will be, and now I need to figure out how that will work going forward. They have me, even their arrogant, alpha, asshole versions of themselves, hold me tight in their grasp.

Fuck.

"Lou-Lou, hey," Ezra hollers, loud enough to gain everyone else's attention, and I instantly feel all of their eyes on me as I turn to face Ezra.

He rises from his seat, running his fingers through

his hair as my gaze trails over the subtle six-pack and V leading down to his sweatpants, and I have to shake my head to clear my thoughts.

Fuck, they distract me way too easily for my liking.

Pulling my head from the sexual gutter I had stumbled into, I hold my phone in the air, ready to talk about the message from Robbie, when Ezra plants his hands on his hips and quirks an eyebrow at me. This action tells me he's curious about something.

"Does any of this have to do with you? The twins are adamant they have no clue, but someone must have done it," Ezra asks, nodding at the dents in the side of the cabinet from where I attacked it with the crowbar.

Oh shit.

Clearing my throat, I chance a glance at the twins, both of which are looking at me with heat in their eyes like they're recalling exactly what happened when they got here, and I almost blush as I turn my gaze back to Ezra.

I really didn't consider the repercussions of my actions, but fuck, I can't deny that I enjoyed letting my rage and anger consume me as I attacked the cabinet.

"I was mad," I state calmly with a shrug, and his gray eyes widen in surprise.

"See, I told you it wasn't us," Jameson says with a grin as he wipes his face with a towel, and Ezra gives him the stink eye, before turning back to me with his facial expression transforming from shock to curiosity.

"I'm all for dealing with pent up rage, Lou-Lou, but can we do that on someone else's shit in future? Plus, I don't know what you three were doing, but I had to deep clean the fucking mats," he says with a sigh, and my cheeks instantly turn pink.

My gaze falls to my feet as Jameson cackles, and even Jagger barks out a short laugh. "We were getting rid of her pent up anger, just with a different method, right, Luella?" Jagger calls out, and I shake my head.

"Something like that," I murmur in response, rubbing my hand over my forehead as Leo appears at my side.

"Lucy, were you enjoying a threesome without me?" he asks with a pout as he opens a bottle of water, and I roll my eyes.

"Hell yeah she was. Took my cock so good, all while swallowing Jagger to the back of her throat like a fucking pro," Jameson announces, and I offer him a death glare as I look in his direction. Motherfucker and his big mouth doesn't know when to shut up.

"Will you stop," I grumble, completely lost in their banter, and I almost forget what it is I came down here for. I can see another remark ready to roll off Jagger's lips, but I hold my phone in the air, and utter one word, which instantly gains all of their attention. "Robbie."

CHAPTER THREE

Lou-Lou

I instantly feel the light atmosphere drop around us, tensions rising as the joking is put aside, and my protective alphas remember their roles.

"What the fuck did he do now?" Jagger grunts, storming toward me with purpose, and snatching my phone from my hands before I can stop him.

Alpha Asshole.

Jameson is hot on his heels as Jagger turns the phone to my face a moment, unlocking it before the message is front and center on the screen.

Leo's arm wraps around my shoulder in comfort. I don't need it, but my body clearly has different thoughts because I lean into him, appreciative of his touch as it calms and grounds me all at once.

As much as these assholes are fully aware of the shit that's causing me pain at the minute, they're also the only ones able to soothe me. And I hate how true that is.

They're my only balm to ease my mind, body, and soul. Which makes me desperate for them to stop putting barriers between us so they can keep their secrets hidden.

"What does it say?" Ezra asks, coming to stand to my left, and his fingers interlace with mine. "I've updated all the security feeds and changed every lock. That motherfucker can't get in here," he bites out, and I squeeze his hand in comfort, trying to calm the rage I feel radiating from him.

"He's asking if she's the reason Jagger knocked the fuck out of that guy, and threatening to bring her into the fold or placing her in Lockwood," Jameson bites out as he reads the message over Jagger's shoulder, and the reminder of Robbie's words has my hand clenching with anger again.

No one says a word for a moment, everyone reeling in the mind fuck that is Robbie Izaro. I hate feeling like this. I hate the effect Robbie seems to have, but most of all I hate that there are so many people caught in the crossfire.

"The four of you need to fucking realize that things *have* to change. I will not let this man use me as a pawn. Ever. But most importantly, I will not be locked away in an old abandoned mental institute. I will fight anyone who tries to put me there," I say with determination, looking each of them in the eye as I sweep my gaze around the room to make my point crystal clear.

"It won't come to that," Leo mutters as he pulls me in closer against his side, but this time, I push back and he lets me go. I can stand on my own two feet, and they need to see that.

"Don't patronize me by saying it won't come to that. I understand that there's a lot at play here, but I need to know what we're fighting for and against. I need that information now. Don't make me resort to going directly to Robbie for the answers."

Jameson curses under his breath at my threat as Jagger grinds his jaw. "The fuck you will. Soon, Luella. Okay? We're close, I promise," Jagger responds, reaching a hand out to me, but I take a step back, dodging his touch, even though it hurts me to do so.

"Let me know when that time is, and I'll be here," I say quietly, snatching my phone back out of his hand. I'm completely resigned to the fact they're not going to drop everything into my lap today.

Sometimes we have to hurt ourselves to protect ourselves, and this is one of those moments. I might long for their touch, their embrace, but I also know my worth, and how strong of a person I am.

It's about time they caught up.

"Everyone will find the Eco 101 assignment in their inboxes, you've got two weeks until the due date. Class dismissed."

I see the little mail icon on my laptop flash as the professor finishes speaking, and I want to fall flat on the table in front of me.

I've had four classes today, and every single one has had some form of assignment for me to do, and they've all got the same deadline. Two weeks. It's like the professors meet in the faculty room each week and conspire to have their assignments due around the same time to send us over the edge. It's barely October, and I'm already counting down until Thanksgiving break.

Fuck, I deserve a minute to breathe.

There's so much going on around me at the moment, I almost didn't wake up this morning for classes, but I had to remind myself what brought me here to begin with, and that is my education. I can't let that slip and put my future on the line. Although, if Robbie has anything to do with it, he'll either have me locked away from the world or doing his dirty work, and that doesn't align with my life goals at all.

"Hey, what are you up to now that classes are over for the day? We could go get some food if you like?" Naomi offers as she rises from her seat to my right, and I take a moment to consider her offer.

Closing my laptop, I slip it into my bag as I spy her in my peripheral vision. In a pair of leggings, a red tee, and a leather jacket, with a black cap covering her dark hair, she looks exactly like the girl I've known since I arrived. Admittedly, if I hadn't seen that text notification on her phone from Vince, I wouldn't see her any differently. But even though I don't know what the message said, she left swiftly after, and that's left an uneasy feeling in my stomach ever since.

It doesn't mean I can't do food though. I don't have to let her into my inner circle, telling her all my secrets and skip naked around a campfire. I can just go, talk trivial bullshit and eat, and that's tempting.

As if sensing my train of thought, an arm wraps around my shoulders as Leo comes to a stop between Naomi and me. He pulls me into his side, just like he has after every class today, and irritation itches under my skin again.

"Sorry, Naomi, I'm stealing her," he states, lifting the black baseball cap off his head, and flipping it in his hand before placing it back on his head backwards.

Show off.

Naomi's gaze flicks between the pair of us, her eyebrows raising slightly, and I force a smile to my face as I look at her. She must know something is off with the way Leo hasn't left my side all day.

Fuck. I even had Jameson sit with me at lunch.

They're taking this whole chaperoning me situation way too far, and it's getting on my last nerve. But if Leo is offering to make me some food, I could actually be persuaded to go with him. Although the petulant child within me wants to throw a tantrum, just to irritate him as much as he is irritating me.

"Are you feeding me too?" I ask, looking at him expectantly, and he grins.

"Of course, Lucy, we've spoken about my love language. I can show you what else I do with my tongue as well if you need a reminder," he states, and I roll my eyes, forcing the blush to remain at bay as I whack his chest.

"A reminder, huh?" Naomi says with a chuckle, the look in her eyes letting *me* know *she* knows I may have held back some details lately. It's obvious she wants to gossip about it with the way her eyes widen and her smile grows, but it seems jilted, awkward all of a sudden, and I know it's me. My gut feelings won't let me get past it.

I shrug, raking my teeth over my bottom lip as I slip from under Leo's arm, creating some much needed distance. "Raincheck?" I offer to Naomi, who nods instantly, and I shoot her a short smile as I move around her and head for the door.

Most of the students have dispersed already, but as I near the door, I feel another set of eyes on me that make me shudder. Flicking my gaze to the right, I find Vince standing with Tommy at the back of the class, and a cold shiver runs down my spine.

The leery look in his eyes, and the tightness of his jaw leaves me uncomfortable. How did this guy literally change over night? I was never besotted with him, but he seemed to have some positive qualities that were really appealing at the time. Although, saying that, so did Naomi, and there's clearly more to the pair of them than I originally thought if the text message is anything to go off.

Pushing them to the back of my mind, I head out of the door, and down the few steps of Michaelson Hall. The second I step outside, I wrap my coat tightly around my body. It's dry at least, but the chill in the air makes for a miserable day.

Even in my jeans, cream knitted sweater, heeled boots, and padded coat I shiver. I really need lessons on how to dress appropriately for the cold. And a car. I really need a new fucking car if Jameson isn't going to put the battery back in the Mustang over the winter.

"Wait up, Lucy," Leo hollers from behind me, and it annoys me that my body immediately slows at his command.

I've been attempting to give them all the cold shoulder since our conversation ended at an impasse yesterday, but it's fucking harder than expected. I think learning about my mom and sister, and them finally giving me the knowledge of their history has lowered my walls a little, but it's not enough.

Fuck, I only know because I took matters into my own hands and showed up at Lockwood to see what was there.

Leo falls into step beside me as I lift my backpack over my shoulder and fold my arms over my chest. "I'm not going to lie, I thought you would put up more of a fight with me over food with your friend," he murmurs, leaning in to speak in my ear, and his breath tickles my skin, making goosebumps rise in his wake.

God damn him for getting under my skin.

At the mention of Naomi, I glance back over my shoulder to see her stepping out of the main doors to Michaelson Hall, Vince not far behind her, with an angry look in his eyes and his hands clenched.

Fuck.

"Uh, I just wasn't feeling it," I mutter in response, not wanting to share my concerns with him when they don't share any of theirs with me.

"Well, I hope you're hungry, Luce, because I'm going to make clam chowder bread bowls," he says proudly as his arm finds its way back around my shoulders again, my stomach instantly grumbling at his words. "I'll take that as my answer then."

He steers us toward the parking lot, and I glance at the arch entryway, considering whether to be stubborn and walk or not, but the cold works in Leo's favor. It's not far at all, but the prospect of the heat in the car is calling to me.

I haven't seen any of the other guys today, except Jameson at lunch, so it catches me by surprise to find Ezra, Jagger, and Jameson all waiting around Leo's SUV.

Jagger is wearing jeans with a grey hoodie and a leather jacket, with the hood up, and god damn he looks fucking divine. Trouble. A whole heap of fucking trouble. But still divine.

Ezra has a heavy looking red flannel jacket on, with jeans and a white tee, and combined with his black, thick-rimmed glasses, he looks like Clark Kent on a casual day. Swoon.

Jameson on the other hand, has a pair of shorts on, and a thin black t-shirt. I watch as he twirls the switchblade in his hand, his eyes raking over me from head to toe as a grin spreads over his lips, and I have to bite my lip before I groan just from looking at them.

"What are you fuckers all doing here?" Leo asks, and

when I look up at him, I see genuine surprise in his eyes.

"They won't want to admit it, but we were waiting for Lou-Lou," Ezra states with a shrug, pocketing the phone he had just been looking at, and even though Jagger huffs at what Ezra said, he doesn't actually deny it.

My pulse quickens a little as I wet my lips. Could this be progress? Fuck, that's all I want, but I can't get my hopes up with these assholes which now leaves me suspicious.

They might be my kings, but they're not treating me like I'm their queen.

"Unlock the fucking car, man," Jagger says as we come to a stop before them, the parking lot filled with students ready to leave too, but thankfully, and for once, we don't have everyone's attention.

Jagger turns his back to me without a word and climbs into the passenger seat, while Jameson opens the rear passenger door with a flurry, bowing as he makes room for me, and I roll my eyes.

I slip from under Leo's arm as he heads for the driver's seat, and move for Jameson. The second I lift my leg to climb into the car, he pushes up behind me. The thin material of his shorts lets me feel the stiffness of his cock against my ass cheeks, and I gasp.

My gaze falls to Ezra's as he climbs in on the other side, a knowing smile on his face telling me he knows exactly what Jameson is doing.

With a shake of my head, I take the center seat. Between Ezra pulling my seatbelt around me and Jameson clipping it in, I don't do a single thing as Leo pulls out of the parking spot.

Silence descends over the car as we start to move, but I feel all of their gazes keep turning in my direction. It's as if they know I don't want to hear their voices and have a conversation unless they're going to give me something, and they seem to be stuck in their alpha ways over the situation still.

The silence bugs me, I hate it, and I refuse to let myself get lost in my head.

Needing a distraction, I pull my phone from my coat pocket, ready to mindlessly flip through social media, when I see I have a message from David.

It's like the universe really does want to piss me off today. Attacking me with far too many small inconveniences and triggering situations until I crumble. I reluctantly open the message, and a scoff instantly falls from my mouth. The nerve of this motherfucker.

David: Hey, can you loan me some money until Friday? I can pay you back then.

David: I need like five hundred. And don't tell me you haven't got it. Me and you both know Ryan set you up.

David: I'll send you the bank details now.

I can't even respond to him right now because I know it's just going to turn into an argument when I don't give him what he wants. How dare he think that he can just demand shit after everything he's done? What's the point in asking a question in the first message, to only continue like I gave him an answer.

Before I close the app and put my phone away so I can't see his shit anymore, I remember the last message he sent too.

"Fuck," Jameson mumbles to my left, and when I turn his way I find his gaze fixed on my phone. Ah, so someone was snooping. "Why do I feel like you don't care about the last three messages and are currently fixated on the one before them?" he says, and a grin spreads over my face as my eyes widen.

Thanks for the reminder, asshat.

"Look at you, Jameson, being all observant and shit," I say as the SUV comes to a stop, but nobody moves. Now is my time to wager for knowledge, I know it. I can feel it in my gut. Leo looks at me through the rearview mirror, while Ezra glances at me, and Jagger side-eyes me. "I think I have an excellent option for you guys to choose from."

I clap my hands once in anticipation, feeling the uncertainty float around all four of the guys, and I focus my gaze on all of them instead of just fixating on Jameson. Excitement bubbles beneath the surface of my skin as the nerves get their dose of adrenaline, but now I've thought of this idea, it's spiraling in my mind.

"Spit it out, Luella. I can hear the fucking cogs turning in your brain from here," Jagger grumbles, eyeing me through the mirror, but it doesn't deter me.

"You can either explain to me what my brother meant by the fact he said he 'saved my life,' or you can explain the entire situation here at Emerson Grove." I subconsciously nod as my teeth sink into my lip, and I watch as they all remain frozen in place. "Don't worry, I'm going to drop my things in my room and give you a few minutes to think it over while Leo makes me his promised clam chowder bread bowls."

With that being said, I unclip my seatbelt and lean over Ezra, opening the door before I slowly, and dramatically climb over him. Letting my ass drag over his lap slowly, I hear him inhale sharply, and I love being able to wield a tiny piece of power over them, even if it's only for a brief moment.

When my feet hit the ground, I quickly turn to look back in the car. It seems my little movement has everyone's attention. All four of them are watching me like hawks, and I smile sweetly as I lean over Ezra to grab my bag, my chest brushing ever so slightly against him.

"I'll even take a quick shower to freshen myself up and relax myself while you consider my options," I say with a wink, hearing Jameson groan as I turn on my heels and head for the door.

I hate ultimatums with a passion, but right now, it's the only way I'm getting through to these motherfuckers.

Please let them actually hear my unspoken plea. I don't know what I'll do if I have to push harder.

CHAPTER FOUR

LEO

I sit frozen in my seat as I watch Lucy sway her sweet ass while she makes her way to the house. None of us move, watching as she goes, and even when she steps inside, we remain exactly as we are.

That was an order if I ever heard one. She wasn't harsh, and if I'm being honest, she wasn't entirely out of place to do it either, but I don't think she truly understands the can of worms she would be opening. Which she obviously doesn't know because we've not given anything away previously. But as always, it's not as simple as black and white. We seem to spend all our time coasting in the gray area.

Dropping my hands from the steering wheel, I sigh. Casting my gaze to Jagger, I find him still staring at the door like she might magically reappear and say she was joking, but we all know she wasn't.

"How about we head inside and discuss our options while Leo makes food?" Ezra offers, and I glance at him the rear view mirror, nodding in agreement as the twins groan.

"Fine, but someone better turn on the fucking coffee machine too. I have a feeling this is going to be a long conversation," Jameson grumbles, like he's helpless and can't fucking do it himself. I shake my head as he jumps from the SUV with a pout and stalks toward the house.

I swing the door open, and quickly close it shut behind me as I follow after him, both Ezra and Jagger hot on my tail as we beeline to the house and out of the cool weather. The thought of the chill in the air makes me grin. I can see how much Lucy is struggling with the climate adjustment, and it reminds me of us last year when we first came to Emerson Grove.

Fuck, now Jameson walks around in shorts and a tee

like it's the middle of summer, but that's too much for me, the thought alone has my balls tightening.

Stepping into the house, all is quiet as I make my way straight to the kitchen. It's my favorite room in the house, where I find my peace, and the space provides sanctuary and nothing like anything else we've ever had. God, it used to be two burners on the side and a microwave, and I had the biggest house out of all of us. Didn't mean any of the appliances actually worked or we were better off. It just meant my parents didn't spend *quite* as much on drugs and liquor; they had other vices instead.

I hear the chairs scrape across the floor as Jagger and Ezra take a seat at the dining table, while I start pulling out the ingredients I need for dinner. To my surprise, when I hear the coffee machine turn on, it's actually Jameson taking care of himself. I almost make a smart ass comment, but think better of it with the serious discussion I know is coming.

As I get the stove going with the clam chowder for dinner, I pull five large bread rolls out of the cupboard that I made fresh last night. With all the cupboard space, counter tops, and fancy appliances, this kitchen has everything I could dream of and more.

Since we lived on ramen noodles and an occasional frozen pizza when we were younger, it's been my mission to learn about all the different foods of the world and try to make them myself. I want Lucy to eat like a queen. And to me, making meals from scratch is what that looks like. It's also my love language.

"So, what do we do?" Ezra asks, breaking the silence as the sound of the shower can be heard from Lucy's bathroom above us.

"We could boycott this whole conversation, and see if Ella is up there using one of her toys in the shower again," Jameson says with a sly grin, knowing *exactly* what that scene would look like. He casts his gaze up at the ceiling like he'll magically be able to see through it. The three of us instinctively following suit, hoping for the same.

"That sounds tempting," Jagger adds, and a grin which matches Jameson's spreads across his face.

The twins are so fucking hard for her it's hilarious. Ezra and I have come across barricades with them time and time again when it comes to Lucy, but they're just as obsessed with her as we are.

Fuckers just don't know when to leave their alpha personalities at the door.

"Or we could not piss her off even more and actually give her something for a change," I interject, glancing over my shoulder as I stir the ingredients in the pan, and Jagger gives me a death glare that could make a grown man fall to his knees, but I raise my eyebrows at him expectantly, and he sighs.

"I don't wanna," Jameson says with a pout, and I shake my head at him. I'm about to throw a clam at his damn head when Ezra responds, killing my chances.

"It's not about what we want anymore, and that's all this is; us telling her what *we* want her to know, not what Lou-Lou *needs* to know."

I couldn't have said it better myself. I almost want to give him a round of applause, but I turn my attention back to the pan so I don't burn the sauce. Setting everything to a low simmer, I quickly rinse my hands before finally remembering to take my jacket off.

Making my way to the dining table, I sling it over the back of my chair as I drop down into the seat, bracing my elbows on the table as I look around at the others.

"We're not telling her everything, not yet," Jagger states, his gaze stern as he glares at us. I hate to admit it, but I agree with him.

Fuck, after last weekend, she hasn't even mentioned her mom or Lola again. We need to finish addressing that situation before we drop everything in her lap. Even if she hates us for it, we're doing it for her.

"But…" Ezra goes to push back, but I quickly interrupt.

"I agree." Jameson drops down into the seat across from me, his eyes widen in surprise, but I simply shrug. "Don't get me wrong, I think she deserves to know everything, and soon, but right now she's still processing Lockwood. She hasn't uttered a word about June or Lola to any of us since the first night, and I hate that she's bottling it up. We need her to wrap her head around that before we overload her with all of the other shit."

Silence descends around us once more as Jameson swipes a hand down his face, Jagger unties his man bun and quickly goes through the motion of redoing it, and Ezra exhales sharply.

"You're right," the three of them say in unison, and I grin like a Cheshire Cat, even though the situation isn't great, I love it when someone tells me I'm right, so when the three of them say it at the same time, I feel like a kid in a fucking candy store.

"I think we have to give her something though," I say,

crossing my arms behind my head as I lean back, and Jagger throws his hands up in annoyance. He clearly thought I was going to be on his side with the whole situation, but I'm firmly in the middle. Give a little and withhold a lot more.

"She doesn't need to fucking know about the Arrows," Jagger grunts quietly, and my gaze quickly checks toward the doorway to make sure she isn't there. I can still hear the shower running above us, but Lucy is crafty as fuck so that means nothing.

"I'm not saying she does, but maybe we could explain the whole David situation to her?" I offer, and Jameson rolls his eyes.

"He's fucking exaggerating anyway," he mutters, pulling the closed switchblade from his pocket and instantly twirling it, and I can immediately see everyone is getting stressed out from trying to decide what information to share.

"How about we explain that to her then, let her see we're taking her request seriously. We want to make this work, all of us do, and if we don't start showing her that soon, she's going to fucking leave, and I refuse to let that happen," I state, my jaw tensing as I worry about the thought of her leaving us, and my hands clench on the table.

"What he said," Jameson chimes in, and my shoulders relax a little knowing someone still agrees with me.

In sync, the three of us turn our attention to Jagger, knowing he's the final one to make this a unanimous vote. I watch as he tilts his head back, running his tongue over his teeth as he considers our two sides, and the second he sighs I know we have him hooked.

He doesn't want Lucy to leave either, fuck, I don't think we could survive it happening again. But for once, Ezra's option isn't going to lead us to rainbows and sunshine. We need to appease her, and protect her. All at once.

A simple nod from him is all we get, and the tension we had been holding relaxes, silence surrounding us as the sound of the shower comes to a stop.

"I'm going to make her a coffee," Jameson says suddenly, jumping up from the table with excitement in his step, and I join him, checking the chowder while Ezra and Jagger mumble between themselves.

We're all changing, I can feel it happening. We're finding the people we used to be, under the shells of the people we had to become when she left.

The Arrows.

There's so much she doesn't know about what we had to do to survive. I'd much rather she hear the rambling of David's truth than any of that right now.

"Have you heard from June?" Ezra asks Jagger, Judith being Lucy's mom, and I hear Jagger exhale deeply before responding.

"She's called every day to ask about Luella, wanting to speak with her and explain, but Luella isn't ready for that. She wants her to meet Lola, but that has to be on Luella's terms and no one else's. She has to love Lola with her whole heart because she chooses to, and not just because it's expected." His voice is gruff as he taps on the table.

Any response is cut off as Lucy's footsteps can be heard coming down the stairs, and moments later she appears in the doorway looking every inch the queen that she is.

Her blonde hair is twisted up into a bun on top of her head, with a few tendrils loose around her face. In a pair of khaki green joggers, and a white cropped top, she looks like heaven.

When my eyes reach her face again, she's waiting expectantly with a quirked eyebrow, but I simply grin. I can't stop looking her over from head to toe all the time, and I'm not ashamed of staring.

"Had time to think, boys?" she asks, making her way to the dining table as I cut the inside of the bread bowls out, and I smirk at her sassiness.

She always wants to push buttons, get a rise out of us, and bring us to our knees, and without fail we fall every fucking time.

"Don't get mouthy, Luella. Sit your ass down," Jagger grumbles as I wipe my hands off, tossing the towel over my shoulder and going to join them. Jameson is a step in front of me as he places a mug down in front of her, and she smiles up at him like he's her king.

I can imagine her internal monologue now; *He's my favorite for the day*. I can see it in her eyes so much I can practically hear it rolling off her tongue.

"Thank you," she murmurs, taking her seat and giving Jagger the middle finger as I take my usual spot beside her. I love that she's naturally fallen into that same seat beside me. I'm sure the others will be trying to claim my spot soon enough.

A sense of awkwardness floats over the room as we wait for the next person to speak. Lucy glares at us all expectantly, clearly waiting for us to start spilling our secrets, while we don't even know where to begin and where to end.

"We'll tell you about David," Jameson says, leaning forward and bracing his arms on the table as she looks around at the four of us in surprise, but she doesn't utter a word as she holds her ground and waits for one of us to continue speaking.

I release a heavy sigh, turning my full attention to her as I speak. "The night when we were all at my house and David showed up," I start, waiting for her to nod in acknowledgment, and she smirks a little.

"You mean the night you took my virginity and David destroyed my life? Yeah, I remember." Her voice is too high pitched to be filled with sarcasm alone. The pain of how that night ended clearly had an unpleasant lasting impression on her.

"Well, apparently that night was when your mom found out she was pregnant. Your father found the pregnancy test and thought it was yours." I search her eyes, registering the confusion as she squints at me.

"How did that end up turning into David saving my life?" she asks, casting her eyes around at us all, and I clear my throat.

"Your dad was on the warpath, and you were the target," Jagger states, his words softer than I anticipated, and I swipe a hand down my face as I listen to a piece of our history I'd rather forget.

"So, what? My dad was going to come and kill me? That's fucking ridiculous. He might have been a completely shit dad, but he never laid a hand on me, so why would he want to kill me if I was pregnant? Why would he give a shit? And what's he going to do now?" Her brows crinkle together as she rapidly fires questions at us while she pieces two and two together. "Wait, wasn't that the night he was arrested?"

Bingo.

"It seems David planted a huge amount of cocaine on your dad and dropped an anonymous tip to the cops, before coming in search of you and getting you the fuck out of town. He thought if your dad somehow weaseled his way out of the charges he'd come after not only David but you too." Jameson releases a heavy sigh before continuing to share another truth. "You may not have realized it but you had three different people wanting David's head on a silver fucking platter. You were also at risk because of your association," Jameson answers as Lucy laces her fingers together on the table and looks down at her hands, trying to make sense of the story.

"Why did we have to leave town though? If my father was arrested, there would have been no need since the threat on my life was eliminated," she responds, rightfully confused with the entire situation, and thankfully Ezra takes over.

"For two reasons actually. One, because your brother stole the cocaine from the Sharks gang, which meant there was a target on his head and if you stayed, you could have been targeted as well. Two, your mother told David the baby was hers not yours, and who the father was. David didn't want to risk it, which makes sense since it led to Robbie putting a target on every Carter that held the chance of ruining, in his eyes, his ridiculous plans of world domination." He sighs as I watch Lucy's blue eyes darken. "If Jagger hadn't spoken to him, your mom and the baby wouldn't exist anymore and the bounty on every Carter would have remained," he adds, rounding off the story.

"I mean, I guess I understand why David thinks he's my savior but fucking hell, he just led me to another shit hole without filling me in. All he told me was mom was gone, again," Lucy murmurs, glancing at Jagger who nods, and I can't stop myself from reaching out to wrap my hand around hers.

I sag in relief when she doesn't pull away, and instead opens her palms up so I can hold her hand properly.

"So, if we're being technical, as much as he did some shit to get your father busted for possession, *I* protected you from Robbie which was more of a risk than your father coming after you," Jagger states, resuming his asshole ways, but Lucy just rolls her eyes at him. That makes no sense at all, but no one's entering that argument with him.

"None of this makes any actual sense. My father was a mean asshole, but wanting to kill me seems a little extreme," Lucy mumbles to herself as she scrubs a hand down her face. As if realizing she spoke out loud, she quickly sits tall again, hiding her feelings and emotions from us as she puts on a front. Hearing your dad wanted to kill you is not something you can digest in a few minutes. It doesn't even sound right to my own ears. "Whatever, I still hate the whole situation, and I'm sure my brother could have done many other things that night other than what he did," she responds, wetting her lips as I squeeze her hand in comfort.

"I agree, one hundred percent but that's the way things

went down, and we can only move forward now," I say, running my thumb over her knuckles, and she hums in response.

"So, tell me what else is happening in Emerson Grove that I don't know about," she probes, pulling her hand from mine as she tries to steer the conversation in a new direction, and I can't help but grin at the balls on this woman.

"No," Jagger grunts in response, and none of us step in, quite happy to leave the conversation there after our initial talk before she came down. The way she shakes her head at us and takes a deep breath, makes me think she knew she wouldn't get anything else out of us, but wanted to try her luck since it seems like we're open to giving her more truths.

"Fine, but if you're not going to fix my Mustang, I need something else to drive," she announces, folding her arms over her chest as she glares at us all. Changing the subject so abruptly I almost get whiplash.

A twinge of concern flickers in my chest, acknowledging the fact she's stepping away from the subject that is her father and the shit he tried to pull.

"I can take you car shopping tomorrow if you like,"

Jameson offers, twirling his switchblade in his hand as he leans further across the table toward her with a small smile on his lips, and I know for sure that fucker is definitely her favorite now.

Lucy eyes him, taking a sip of her coffee as she waits to see if there's a catch or if it's a joke, but when Jameson just continues to stare at her and none of us step in, she smiles.

"Perfect. Thank you," she responds, rising to her feet with the coffee in her hand, and I do the same, placing my hand at the base of her spine as I lean forward and place a kiss at her temple.

I love watching as her eyes close for the briefest moment as she basks in my touch, and it makes me desperate to do it again and again. But I don't want to overwhelm her, so instead I move back over to the stove to check on the food.

I hear Lucy clear her throat, and I glance over my shoulder at her as I stir the food in the pan. "After food, does anyone want to do their assignments with me? I got so many today I'm slightly freaking out, and as much as there's a lot of shit going on around me right now, my education and my future are far too important to me to let it all slip away."

Her words fill me with pride. I love knowing she has goals and aspirations. Fuck, it's a damn sight more than we ever dreamed of, and if it's important to her, it's important to me.

"I don't have anything to do at the minute, we can set up in the living room if you want, and I'll be beside you," I offer, and her brows knit together in confusion.

"But you were there with me in all of my classes today, which means we have the same pile of shit to get through," she states, placing her hands on her hips, and my mouth dries.

Ah, shit.

"About that..." I start, but Jagger interrupts me immediately.

"He's not actually taking any of the same classes as you, he's simply there *for* you," he says, rising from the table as he swipes his hair back off his face, and Lucy's eyes widen in surprise as she looks at me.

"Are you serious? What the hell are you doing sitting through all of those lectures? What are you even fucking learning? I don't understand. Do you even go to Emerson U?" Her questions shoot out of her mouth in succession as she tries to wrap her head around the situation, and I grin.

"He's serious. I'm protecting you, and yes, I do go to Emerson U but I'm going for a culinary degree. Nothing to stress yourself over," I respond quickly, mimicking her rambling as she glances around at the others.

"Wait, what are all of you majoring in at Emerson U? How have I not fucking asked this already?" Guilt washes over her features as she tucks a loose tendril of blonde hair behind her ear with a huff.

Jameson chuckles at her outburst as Ezra rises from his chair to move next to her.

"I'm studying game development," Ezra starts, pointing at himself, and she rolls her eyes.

"Well that makes sense, and what about these two?" she asks, waving her hand between Jagger and Jameson, and I grin, loving how natural this feels; her bossing us around while grilling us and caring about us all at the same time.

"Jameson is studying engineering, and Jagger is—"

"I'm majoring in business," Jagger interrupts with an eye roll of his own. "And actually, I do have a lot of shit to catch up on from last week too. So I'm game for overhauling the living room after we've eaten," he says with a shrug, leaving Lucy to nod with her jaw wide open.

"Look at us, we're acting like one big happy family, huh?" Jameson says, clapping his hands, and no one responds, happy to let those words settle around us.

That's the goal, that's what we're going to be, one big happy family. We just need to wade through the mess we're currently in to find the joy on the other side.

CHAPTER FIVE

Lou-Lou

I open the weather app on my phone, confirming it says there could be a chance of rain, and slip my arms into the sleeves of my coat before checking myself over in the mirror.

New car day.

I don't need a brand new car, but I need something to drive, and if it keeps the peace in this house, I'm all for it. I've never lived anywhere that would make my Mustang a safety hazard in the winter, and as much as I hate the way Jameson went about it, I don't want to put myself in any unnecessary danger.

Flicking my loose blonde curls over my shoulder, I fix my black coat which matches well with my skinny jeans and black sweater, with a cut out over the top of my breasts. I feel sexy as hell, even with the layers, and my heeled boots give me the little height that I love for an extra confidence boost.

I put my phone away in my coat, spritzing a few bursts of my favorite floral perfume over me before I head for the bedroom door.

Jameson didn't give me a time today for us to go, but I'm not spending the day waiting around. I checked, and the local car dealership opened at ten, and it's now ten thirty, so it's not like I had him up and ready to go at the ass crack of dawn even though I was.

Shutting my bedroom door behind me, I lock it, even though these motherfuckers seem to be able to get through it anyway, and turn to face the hallway. There are five more rooms out here; one for each of the guys, and a separate full bathroom.

I take a minute to figure out who's room is where since I've only actually been inside Ezra's, and by trial of elimination I work out Jameson's is to my right, closest to the staircase.

Yesterday was weird as fuck.

They *finally* offered me something. It's not everything I wanted to know, and realistically it doesn't actually affect the here and now, or my future, but it was *something*. I didn't realize David had framed our dad, and the main fact that's been playing on my mind this morning is that my father didn't go to prison for possession of class A drugs, even if that's what he was arrested for… he was sentenced to murder. Or that's what I've been told.

It all happened in the blink of an eye, and I was so numb to everything that didn't revolve around the loss of my kings, that I didn't pay enough attention.

Fuck, then there's the fact I haven't seen my dad since then either, not that I ever plan to change that.

Shaking out my hands, I focus on the present, not wanting to get lost inside my head again, before I raise my hand and rap my knuckles quickly against Jameson's door.

That's what knocking looks like, assholes, I sass internally, making a grin spread over my lips when I hear Jameson call out from the other side of the door.

"If that's Ella, you can come in, if it's not, fuck off."

I roll my eyes at him as I wrap my hand around the

door handle, and let the door swing open. Without pause I take a step onto the navy blue carpet, closing the door behind me as I glance around the space, not seeing Jameson anywhere.

Jameson's bed is on the far side of the room, nestled centrally beneath a large window. There are oak nightstands on either side, with a matching desk and drawer set lining the room, and a fifty inch television hanging on the wall beside me. There's a door to the left, and another to the right. With the steam billowing out of the door on the right, I'm going to assume that's the bathroom, and the other must be his closet.

The navy, gray, and off-white tones, actually feel cozy. Ridiculously manly, but still warm and welcoming.

Taking another step into the room, I notice a big chunk of metal on his desk, and when I take a closer look, it appears to be a part of an engine or something.

Completely Jameson.

Curiosity gets the better of me, and I reach out to run my finger over the steel rim.

"You always have to look with your hands, Ella," Jameson says, his voice catching me by surprise and making me jump like I've been caught doing something inappropriate.

I whirl around to give him a speech on surprising me like that, but when I look to face him, my brain short circuits, leaving me gaping at him.

Holy. Fucking. Shit.

Standing before me, with only a fluffy navy towel wrapped around his waist, I think I might have died and gone to hot guy heaven. His wet brown hair is swept back off his face, and his tattoos are on full display as water droplets run down his body.

My eyes skim over his entire body, then starting at his feet, they slowly make their way over his ripped abs, his pecks, then noticing his Adam's apple bob at my perusal before I reach his face. A smirk plays on his lips as his eyes sparkle knowingly, and I can't even defend myself or pretend I wasn't checking him out, because fuck, who wouldn't?

I wet my lips, willing my brain to give me something, *anything*, to say as he slowly prowls toward me. I remain frozen in place, tilting my head back slightly to keep my gaze fixed on his as he stops right in front of me.

Chest to chest like this has my heart pounding rapidly and my pulse booming in my ears, making the reaction he's getting from me more than obvious. I can practically feel myself tremble against him.

"Are you ready to go car shopping?" Jameson asks huskily, his dark, hooded eyes holding me captive as I focus on the intricate red mark shaped like a heart. The heat in his eyes lets me know he feels this too. The pull between us isn't just one sided. It never has been. He's right here feeling every miniscule touch right along with me.

I nod in response, still unable to make use of my tongue, and he grins, his pearly white teeth peeking through as he slowly lifts his hand to my face, tucking my blonde hair behind my ear, and I shiver at the light contact.

The room fades away around us, my gaze completely focused on Jameson as he fills my vision. A droplet of water drips from a strand of his hair that's flicked forward over his forehead, and it slowly trickles down his face, holding all of my attention as my mouth goes dry.

Jameson's hand tilts my chin back, forcing me to meet his gaze head on. My lids fall closed as my body instinctively moves toward his, and our lips delicately draw across each other's.

Every nerve in my body comes alive at the sweet touch

as he leaves me breathless. The fourth draw of his mouth across mine has him pulling back slightly, his nose still resting against mine as I blink my eyes open.

I can feel the unspoken question floating between us, but instead of answering with words, I use my mouth to take action. I lift up on my tiptoes, bringing my hand to the back of his neck as I crush my lips to his, and the kiss deepens.

The feel of his hands on my waist as he brings my chest flush against his floods my body with desire as we battle for control. The small droplets of water at the nape of his neck trickle over my fingers as I groan against his lips.

"I'm jealous as fuck right now," Leo hollers out, and we instinctively pull apart to glance at the door.

I hadn't left it open, so Leo must have done so when Jameson and I were lost in each other. The look in his eyes says he's a little bit jealous, but his grin says he's clearly taken joy in watching us jolt apart.

Asshole.

"Fuck off, Cooper. Don't cock block me again," Jameson grunts, bringing his gaze back to mine as he wets his lips, and a smile spreads across my face.

Reluctantly taking a step back, I rake my teeth over

my bottom lip as I look him over once more, while Leo chuckles all the way back downstairs.

"Meet you downstairs?" I ask, my voice raspier than usual, which makes Jameson groan in response.

"Fuck. Yes. But go quickly before I pin you to the bed and we don't leave it for the day," he purrs in response, making me catch my breath as his words ricochet around my body so much I almost consider doing just that.

Nope. I need a new car, plus a little delayed gratification never hurts anyone.

Although if the pulsing in my core is anything to go by, I just might fucking die from lack of dick.

I grip the armrest, my head thrown back against the headrest as Jameson speeds through town in his Nissan GTR.

Holy shit.

It feels amazing.

He's always had a love for cars, and the excitement that comes with the speed. He's an adrenaline junkie, but with cars, for the most part I guess, he is in control of the vehicle.

Looking him over, I can only guess the feel of his blood pumping and the grip on the steering wheel works fucking wonders, if the smile on his face is anything to go by.

Glancing at him, he looks just as hot now as he did earlier with a white tee, jeans, and a leather jacket on. The complete epitome of a bad boy, between him and his brother, I don't know who's worse at the moment.

He peers at me out of the corner of his eye, the grin on his lips widening as he winks and turns his attention back to the road.

I follow his line of sight, watching the town whiz by us as he slows, merging with the road to the left, and as we move around the bend, I see the straight road ahead.

Before I can even utter a word, he floors it again, and a squeal bursts from my lips as I'm thrown back in my seat.

"Ahh, Jameson," I yell with a laugh over the sound of the engine, and he laughs like a lunatic at my faux fear.

It leaves me speechless seeing him this carefree. Taking a moment to just be happy, having fun, and being crazy. It warms my soul, getting to be a witness to this side of him, but all too quickly the car slows, and we pull into the dealership on the right.

As we get closer, his smile weakens and I watch as his

mask slips firmly back in place. His neutral features make me gulp and a little sad, a stark reminder of the persona he has to those outside of our little bubble.

If I didn't still have butterflies swirling around in my stomach, I would have thought his smile and laughter were a figment of my imagination.

Catching my breath, I unclip my seatbelt as Jameson jumps from the car, slamming the door shut behind him and locking the doors. I gape in surprise as I watch him slowly walk around the front of the car, fixing his leather jacket as his gaze remains fixed on mine, until he comes to a stop at my door.

Just like the night he drove my Mustang, when he pulled it to a stop outside of our house, he unlocks the car again. I don't even have time to blink when he swings my door open and holds his hand out for me.

Well fuck.

Same motion, different setting, and this time, I feel the romantic side of the move. The feeling that was almost there that night, but was lost under the anger and secrets being held between us. Even more so than now.

I wet my lips as I place my hand in his, and before I can place a foot on the ground he's pulling me up and out of the car so we're chest to chest again, with my feet hanging just above the ground.

I don't know what's gotten into him today, and I've no idea how to react.

This is the Jameson I've always wanted, and it leaves me frozen, under his spell, and I don't want to move and break the connection. As I look straight into his brown eyes, I just want to melt into him.

Where is my fucking tongue around him all of a sudden? How have I forgotten how to use words? Jameson has officially caused my brain to short-circuit with his behavior.

"Ah, Mr. Izaro, we've been waiting for you. If you would like to follow me?"

Jameson glances to his right, offering a glare to whoever interrupted us, before returning his gaze to mine as he slowly lowers me back to my feet, dragging me over every single inch of his body as he goes.

I barely got over the jumbled mess he left me earlier, his nakedness leaving my brain and my body in a complete disarray before I practically ran from his room, so it doesn't take much to turn me all the way up again.

"I'll be there in a minute," Jameson grunts in response,

not turning to look at the guy again as he laces his fingers with mine and pulls me in the direction of the brand new shiny cars.

Excitement floods my system, but I can't stop the slight frown as I take in every single new car. "Jameson, how do you expect me to pay for this? I mean, I paid so much for my Mustang and that was used, but these all look like the kind that haven't left the lot yet," I murmur, glancing up at him. He doesn't need to know about the account Ryan set up for me. I would never use it. Not for this. He would be on the phone in seconds wanting to know what happened to the Mustang, and that's a can of worms I'm not ready to dive into.

He swipes a hand over his mouth as he looks down at me with a slight shake to his head. "That's not for you to worry about, Ella," he responds, squeezing my hand when he sees the next question in my eyes. "And no, it has *nothing* at all to do with Robbie. So, I promise, you don't need to worry about that."

It impresses me that he can read me so well, even after all this time, but I still feel uncertain. "I don't think I like this, Jameson," I mutter, rubbing my lips together nervously. I can't afford to pay him back for something like this.

"Ella, baby, this is a gift for having to deal with me going all macho on the 'stang, alright?" He releases my hand to wrap his arm around my shoulders, pulling me into his side as he continues to walk past all of the smaller hatchback cars. "Besides, it can be my apology to you, for believing David and Jagger," he adds, referring to the fact they believed I *chose* not to be with them, and a sad smile touches my lips as I avert my gaze.

"Okay," I say with a sigh, giving in to his reasoning. I just need a vehicle, and if it can't be my Mustang, then I need something as an alternative. "What are we looking at?" I ask, stepping out of his hold so I can think straight for a minute, and he pouts at me before rolling his eyes and pointing off in the distance toward the trucks.

"I may have already got one lined up for you," he answers with uncertainty, and my eyes widen in surprise.

"So I don't get a say?" I quirk my eyebrow at him, waiting for his response, and he just gives me a pointed look like the answer is obvious.

"Ella, I want you to be as safe as humanly possible. Which means I want you protected at all times."

Oh.

Well then.

Flicking my hair over my shoulder, I glance at him out of the corner of my eye. "Fine, I'll at least take a look at it," I respond, making him smother a grin as he places his palm at the base of my spine, directing me toward the main building where a guy stands waiting, nervously playing with his tie.

As we near, the small guy in his brown suit quickly steps inside for us to follow, opting not to speak to Jameson after their earlier interaction, and I'm almost envious of the power Jameson seems to hold, even with a single glance.

It's impressive.

The back of Jameson's hand brushes against mine as we follow the salesman, and my body clenches again, needy for his touch, and the motherfucker knows it. The entire place gives off an air of luxury and high-end brands, and I opt to focus on Jameson's proximity instead of feeling uncomfortable in here.

"Stop grinning, asshole. If I felt the front of your jeans right now, I know I'd find you hard," I murmur under my breath, and he throws me a casual wink, not denying it, which only leaves me even more frustrated.

Opting to focus on the salesman instead, I frown when

he comes to a stop beside a huge, charcoal gray Ford Raptor.

"I'll give you a few minutes, Mr. Izaro," he says quietly before quickly scurrying off, and I roll my eyes at his dramatics.

I stop at the hood of the truck as Jameson moves to the driver's side door and swings it open, nodding his head at me to follow.

"Jameson. It's a fucking beast, I don't need all of this," I say, waving my hand around as I join him by the driver's side, and the step up I'm definitely going to need to use because it's that high off the ground.

"I told you, I need you safe. I've had this customized and imported from some specialists located in Texas. So it'll be safe in the colder weather with all-wheel drive, but it's also bulletproof to protect you against the other dangers in our life," he states quietly, grabbing my waist and lifting me into the seat effortlessly.

What the fuck?

My hands instantly move to the steering wheel, but I keep my gaze fixed on his. "What *are* the other dangers, Jameson?" I almost shout in surprise as he rubs at the back of his neck in nervousness.

"I don't need to spell it out to you, Ella. Everything is so uncertain right now, with Robbie and... just stuff... nevermind, but please?" he responds, his eyes pleading with me just as much as his tone to accept his gift without any issues as I lean back in the seat to digest his words.

Averting my gaze, I take in the interior of the truck, impressed with all the luxuries in here, with the black leather seats, entertainment system, and the sleek dash. It's stunning, I won't deny it, but *bulletproof*?

That's either an exaggeration or there's far more going on in Emerson Grove than I know.

I can't imagine the need for a bulletproof vehicle, so I shake my head, choosing to believe the former. This is just Jameson going into overdrive with his protection, and if it means I get to drive this monster and keep the peace, then I'll take it.

"You can take it for a test drive if you want, I can—"

"That's pretty pointless, Jameson, when you've already organized it all for me. Let's be realistic about the situation and the position you've put me in, shall we?" I interrupt with a huff, and he surprisingly remains silent.

Yet again my head is at war with myself. If I say no to this car, wanting a smaller one or something else entirely, it won't change anything because it looks like he's already invested a lot of money and has it all ready to go.

Fuck.

Why does that annoy and impress me all at once?

"We'll just fucking take it," I grumble, closing my eyes as I sink farther into the seat.

God, give me strength to handle these damn men, and their overprotective and dominating ways.

CHAPTER SIX

JAGGER

I raise my wrapped fists to my face as my feet bounce, circling the punching bag that hangs from the ceiling in the basement. My blood pumps through my veins, sweat dripping over my brow and down my spine as I extend my arms repeatedly, connecting with the bag just right.

I go through the motions again and again, until my muscles scream for me to stop, but in fact, it only pushes me to go faster, harder, and be more precise. When my arms are on the brink of cramping, I switch to leg work until the pain subsides.

The red bag before me is my father in my mind, although Vince's face has popped up a time or two, and I'm not sure whether my movements got heavier in those moments, my punches harder as I connected with the bag. But either way, I definitely enjoyed pummeling his face too.

Heavy bass music booms through the speakers, while Ezra taps away on his computer, and Leo cleans the guns meticulously as always. Crazy motherfucker finds it therapeutic for some reason, but I take joy in beating the shit out of people, so I can't really say anything.

The only thing missing is Jameson fucking around with his blades, but that lucky asshole is with Luella right now. God, just the thought of her and my soul settles a little more, a complete contrast to only last week, but something has shifted inside of me. My vision keeps placing her here, on the mat with me too, the five of us finding our place among each other.

Now she knows about Lockwood, and Lola, there's one less thing hanging between us, and I can feel the change in our dynamics already. I'm sure we'll be competing for her attention and who will be her favorite of the day in no time.

Shit, the second Jameson left with Luella in his GTR, the three of us pulled fucking straws to see who got a chance to convince Luella to spend time with them.

I think the fact Leo won is why I've been beating at this goddamn punching bag for so long. The fucker is just lucky it's not *his* face I'm visualizing.

The music cuts out as my cell phone indicates an incoming text message, and I groan, forcing myself to stop as the music continues.

Taking a step back, I relax my shoulders and grab my towel at the edge of the mat, swiping at my face quickly, before pulling the hair tie at the back of my head out, and letting my hair fall to my shoulders.

I look over at Ezra who continues to tap on his keyboard with one hand, while the other holds my phone out in my direction as he pays me no attention. Grabbing it from him, I grunt in thanks while I grab a bottle of water from the mini fridge to the right of the table beside him.

Dropping down into the seat next to him, I completely forget that it has wheels, and I find myself gliding over the concrete floor for a second, spinning as I go. The moment I switch the music off on my phone, the room is filled with the sound of Ezra and Leo chuckling at me.

"Screw you, fuckers," I say with an uncontrollable smirk.

Without looking at either of them I flip them off, which only seems to please them more while I look who messaged me.

The second I open the app, my face drops and the atmosphere instantly takes a nosedive.

Robbie: Make sure you and your brother are ready, election rallies for Emerson councilmen starts next week.

Robbie: And if you think there won't be consequences for the shit you pulled at the warehouse, then you're sadly mistaken.

Robbie: Maybe I should take it out on your little queen?

That motherfucker.

My jaw tightens as my hand clenches around the phone, and I toss the bottle of water against the far wall, watching as it bounces off, but it does nothing to relieve the tension that's built up inside of me again.

"What's wrong?" Leo instantly asks, the sound of the gun he must have been cleaning clattering on the table as he makes his way over to us.

I feel Ezra's eyes on me too, wanting to know what my problem is as well, and I just don't have the strength to read this bullshit out loud, so instead, I pass my phone off to Leo who stands beside Ezra as they read through the messages.

How can I catch this man and either fucking kill him or make sure he finds his way into a never ending stint in prison? Especially when all his *friends* have jobs that make going to the authorities impossible.

I need him out of our lives, permanently gone, and I really don't give a fuck what or how that looks like. Shit the Arrows have—nope. I'm not going there with that right now.

"That cunt," Ezra bites out, and I scoff. Cunt doesn't even feel like a strong enough word for Robbie. I don't think any word will.

"Shit, we really need to see how Lucy actually shoots a gun after her little demonstration of unloading one the other week," Leo mumbles, handing my phone back, and I sigh.

"Luella does not need to be anywhere near a fucking gun, Leo," I grumble, raking my fingers through my hair as rage clings to me.

"I think we need to arm her with all sorts of skills instead of hiding her behind bulletproof cars and treating her like a damsel in distress," Ezra adds, and it only angers me.

Rising to my feet, my arms swing out wide as I try to contain my emotions. "She is ours to protect, Ezra. Ours. Luella has no need to defend herself when we will always be there to fucking do it," I bite out, feeling like a broken record as Ezra quirks his eyebrow at me. Leo waves a hand in front of his neck telling me to fucking stop, and I frown.

The sound of a throat clearing behind me is all the sound I need to understand the situation.

Luella is behind me.

Perfect.

I brush my hair back off my face as I glance over my shoulder, to find her standing side by side with Jameson.

She *always* looks beautiful, but with a frown on her face, her lips pursed, and her hands on her hips, Luella looks like a queen.

My queen.

Fuck, *our* queen.

"I can handle myself," she states firmly and confidently, making Jameson stand proudly next to her, while Ezra and Leo shuffle on their feet awkwardly waiting to see where this conversation will go.

"That's irrelevant, Luella, I—"

"No, no it fucking isn't irrelevant at all, it's far from it actually," she responds, taking a step toward me as she folds her arms over her chest, revealing the swell of her tits through the cut in the material, and it takes everything in me to pull my gaze to hers. "Do you know what it was like for me in White River, alone with David?" she asks, and my brows instantly knit together in confusion.

"What the fuck does that mean?" I grunt, taking a step toward her, and I don't miss the challenge in Jameson's eyes as he eyes me nearing her.

"It means it was rough, Jagger. It was like being back in Nevada, the Sharks weren't there, but fuck, neither were any of you guys. David was a sack of shit. He weaseled himself into a smaller gang which helped keep a roof over our head for sure, but I was the one to put the food on the table. I was the one that had to fight off guys twice my size when he didn't pay debts, or when one of his friends wanted to see what was beneath my clothes."

Her words are like daggers to my heart, every single one pushing the blades deeper and deeper as her poker face remains firmly in place.

Silence descends over the room as my hands clench at my sides. My heart feels like it's about to rip from my chest.

"I'm going to fucking kill him," I spit out, and I hear a few growls of approval, but Luella throws her arms out wide, just as I had done earlier, shaking her head at me with disappointment like I hadn't listened to a word she said.

"You're still focusing on the wrong shit, asshole. I know what dangers lurk out there, and I *know* how to defend myself. Do you need reminding of the fact I flipped you over my shoulder the other day?" she taunts, stepping toward me with her finger pointing in my direction.

My stomach turns, remembering the move that completely stunned me, and what followed has my cock twitching again. I can't deny how my body reacts to her being able to handle herself, but how can she not see that she shouldn't have to as long as we are here?

"Did that come before or after fucking on the mat?"

Leo asks, making Luella glare even more, not helping the situation, and I hear a grunt from behind me. I hope Ezra hit that fucker for having a big mouth.

"That's irrelevant," Jameson interjects, and I drag my hands down my face. "We're getting off topic again."

"You've said it yourself, Jagger. Robbie is dangling me like a carrot over you guys. That doesn't make me feel safe at all, especially when the first time I came face to face with him was right under your noses, when I was alone. You're trying to fit me into a box that suits you, but that just isn't me. Do I want you to protect me? Yeah. But I want us to feel like a team and right now, I'm not getting that vibe," Luella says, a heavy sigh on her lips like she knows her words won't sink in, but I hear her. I think. And she's right.

I don't want her to be anything but herself, and I need to accept that means she's tougher and stronger than she looks. Those three years apart impacted her differently than I hoped. I hate the thought of her going through any of that, but she still stands before me as the other half of my soul, and I need to remember that.

"Luella, I—"

"No, you don't get to keep dictating to me. How about

you call Robbie? Call him now. See where his threats lead to with regards to me. He's not playing games, Jagger, but it feels like we are," she states, folding her arms over her chest again as Jameson squeezes her shoulder in support.

Ignoring the other two murmuring under their breath behind me, I take a step toward her. We're toe to toe, and I tilt her chin up so she's looking deep into my eyes so she understands the point I'm about to make.

"Luella, I will never call him to see what he wants. He sends me shit to get a response out of me, and he won't get it, not when it's what he wants. Robbie doesn't get to see my wrath until I say so, when it's on my terms." I watch as she visibly swallows hard at my words, her tongue skimming over her bottom lip as I continue to speak. "If this is what you want, for me to see you as an equal, then you're going to have to prove to me you can handle yourself."

I quirk my eyebrow in challenge, watching as she searches my eyes for a hint of a lie, but she won't find it. I mean it.

Dropping my hand from her chin, I take a step back, maintaining eye contact, before I turn on my heels and make my way over to the mat in the corner. When I turn back around to face her, I find all four of them looking my way.

Each of the guys look at me like I'm a crazy motherfucker for propositioning her to spar, while Luella looks at me with excitement dancing in her eyes, and it makes me grin.

That's my girl.

Stretching my hand out, I give her the come get me signal, and before any of the guys can step in, she's pulling her coat off and placing it on the chair I just vacated.

She keeps her gaze fixed on mine as she lifts her feet up onto the seat and unties her laces, removing her heeled boots one at a time, before moving toward me barefoot in her sweater and leggings.

I almost offer for her to go and change, so she's in workout clothes, since I'm standing in only shorts, but fuck, if she wants to prove herself, we have to be realistic in this approach. In a real life situation, Robbie isn't going to give her that grace, so I'm not going to either.

"I think we need to put some prizes on the line if we're going to do this," Leo announces as he moves toward the edge of the mat, Ezra and Jameson hot on his heels as they watch Luella stretch her arms above her head.

Fuck.

She's so hot it's distracting.

"What do you have in mind?" Luella asks with confidence, entertaining Leo's idea, and I roll my eyes.

"Well, I'm just saying, if you were to knock this asshole to the mat, I would happily shower you with that good time I've been promising," Leo responds, moving close enough to stroke a finger down Luella's cheek, and she shivers under his touch.

I'm not sure what passes between them, their eyes doing all of the talking, but it feels important. Too important for any of us to interrupt, until she nods, agreeing with whatever prize he's offering, before turning to face me.

"Excellent. So we know what I get if I win, but what does Jagger get?" she asks, a grin on her lips, and I frown. But before I can even open my mouth, Ezra beats me to it.

"Wait, what is *it* you get?" He waves a hand between Luella and Leo, while Jameson and I track the movement too, just as intrigued, and Leo smiles so hard I think his jaw might lock in that position.

"I'm going to claim my girl. Then she knows she's mine forever," he states proudly, brushing Luella's hair over her shoulder as her teeth sink into her bottom lip, making me internally groan.

"The three of us have already claimed her, bro, if anything you're late to the party," Jameson retorts, shaking his head dismissively.

Luella scoffs as I shake out my shoulders. "Uh, no, no you fucking haven't," she states, and I take a step toward her, as does Jameson and Ezra, each of us scowling at her lie.

"Do I need to strip you bare and remind you how you felt beneath me?" I growl, and she tsks me with a wag of her finger.

"Actually, *you* were beneath *me*, and that wasn't claiming me, that was sex. Leo is the only one to have hinted at this being more, being official, and that is a huge difference. Now, shut the fuck up and fight me."

I can see her trying to change the subject as her cheeks redden a little, but I'm still stuck on what she said, and how glaringly fucking true it is.

Shit.

A quick glance at Ezra and Jameson, and I can see the realization on their faces too.

It's our own doing. For pulling her back into the fold while keeping her on the outside, we clearly didn't make our intentions known.

Fuck. Since the first night she showed up and watched Adele blow me, I haven't been near anyone since. Shit, as soon as she stormed out of the bathroom with her pussy exposed that night I pushed Adele off me.

That's probably why she's been a pissy little bitch, but that's not my issue. My issue is Luella not understanding how I feel.

"If I win, I get to show you just how fucking much I claim you," I state, keeping my gaze fixed on her, and I see the surprise dancing in her blue eyes.

"Wait, this isn't fucking fair, I claim her too," Jameson interjects, making her eyes widen further and Ezra huff as well.

"We all fucking claim her, jackass. But I want in the fucking loop too," Ezra grumbles, and instinctively we all move around her so she's practically in the middle of us.

Slowly turning on the spot, Luella looks each of us over with a hint of desire and sass in the quirk of her lips.

"Who says I want to be claimed by all of you? Most of you haven't been that nice to me, and you're all still keeping secrets," she says, her eyes settling on me, and I take the hint.

I know I've been the biggest asshole, but it's my way

of caring, she just doesn't see it like that anymore.

Shrugging my shoulders, I sigh. "You make it sound like you think you have a choice, Luella. You're ours, always. That's never going to change," I say, reaching forward to cup her cheek as she wets her lips. "We're all going to claim you, just how you want, and to prove I'm in it for the long haul, I'm going to let you leave this room right now with Leo."

"What the fuck?" Ezra and Jameson grumble in unison, but I keep my gaze locked on Luella's, trying to gauge her reaction to my comment.

"He's spent long enough without you, I can hold out another day until you're in my bed, Luella," I murmur, watching as she visibly swallows, shock and surprise in her eyes as Leo steps up behind her.

He bands his arms around her waist, lifting her against his chest as he grazes his lips over her neck, and I watch as her eyes roll back.

Fuck.

I'm instantly regretting my big boy decision right now.

"Thank fuck you said that, man. Because I have it all set up already," Leo responds, his breath cascading over her skin, and her eyes fall closed as her body reacts to his touch. A hint of jealousy courses through me when I watch her tighten her grip around his neck.

"Don't be an asshole, Leo. Go, before *I* change my fucking mind," Jameson grunts, lust in his voice too.

I need a cold shower. Maybe five.

Without a backward glance, Leo turns and rushes for the stairs, Luella chuckling in his arms as he carries her.

I haven't forgotten this moment though. I'm going to put her through her paces on the mat, whether she likes it or not, but for once, I see the bigger picture, and that's us.

I want us to be her kings again, just like she's our queen, and my Luella inspired tattoo burns in it's spot on my back.

She marked me long before that, and I refuse to not take the chance to be in her world forever, before it all fucking implodes around us.

WATCH ME RISE

CHAPTER SEVEN

Lou-Lou

Leo carries me up the stairs from the basement, and slowly lowers me to my feet when we reach the top. My heart feels like it's about to pound right out of my chest as my emotions swirl like crazy inside of me.

"Are you sure you want to follow me? I meant what I said last time, this is it, us, forever, no matter how bad the storm," he murmurs, looking down at me with heat burning in his eyes, and I find myself nodding in promise.

All I've wanted since I got here was for us to be a team, and I'll be the first to say these assholes have been a set of dickheads on more than one occasion, but *they're still mine*. Besides, I can handle some growing pains if it gets me where I want to be at the end of it; home.

That's what they are to me, my kings, and my home.

"Let me hear you say it, Luce. Out loud," he prods, reaching for both of my hands and I fucking swoon at his feet.

"I want it. I want you," I breathe, my body already tingling with anticipation as Leo grins down at me. "Now lead the way," I add, smirking at him, and I watch as his chest heaves with a heavy breath.

"Can we just stand still for a second? My dick is so hard I'm worried I'm going to cream my pants just walking up the stairs with you," he responds, and a burst of laughter falls from my lips as I shake my head at him and head for the stairs.

"Do I need to go and get one of my toys to take care of the need building inside of me?" I ask mockingly, making him growl as he laces his fingers through mine and takes the stairs with me.

"Don't you fucking dare," he groans, and I bite my bottom lip to stop another giggle from bursting out.

Leo's thumb strokes over my knuckles as he guides

me up the stairs, and between the four guys, I'm still reeling from the sudden need for each of them to claim me. Leo definitely started something here. I can't believe how quickly Jagger, Jameson, and Ezra realized how right I was.

It had been sex. Hot as fuck sex which meant something to me, but there was no talk of anything else, and I'm not just going to assume anything with these assholes. I love the idea of them claiming me. Individually, and all at once if I have it my way.

As we reach the top of the stairs, Leo's steps grow slow as he comes to a stop at the room on our left, next to mine. He turns his gaze to me, searching for something I'm not quite sure of, before releasing the breath he's holding.

"We may have drawn straws earlier to figure out who got to spend some time with you when you got home with Jameson, and I won! I got excited, went a little crazy and all that shit," he rambles, swiping a hand down his face as he looks to the ceiling for a moment. "Anyway, I just want magic with you, alright?"

My brows crinkle a little at his words, having no idea what in the hell he's talking about, but I smile all the same, because it's fucking adorable to see him all worked up like this.

The second he twists the door handle, revealing the inside of his bedroom, my jaw hits the floor in surprise. It definitely explains what had him all flustered moments ago.

My hand slips from his as I take a step inside, my feet carrying me on their own accord as I try to figure out where I should look first.

Candles line every surface. The window, the nightstands, his desk in the corner, damn, they're even on the floor. And I panic for a moment, until I realize they're all battery operated. Rose petals are scattered across the dark gray carpet, and over the mint green and gray comforter over his bed, leaving me in complete awe.

"Leo, I…"

My words trail off as I turn to face him, only to find him watching me take it all in. There are no words. We don't do love hearts, cutesy, romantic shit. We just love and care fiercely, which usually causes riots because we're all so pig headed in our ways.

But this, this is something else entirely.

"I said forever, remember? And I wanted it to be special. The real first time was abruptly ended by David and all the shit that happened, and I wanted a fresh start at that," he says, moving to stand toe to toe with me.

My hands instantly rise to his chest, feeling his heart beat beneath my palm as my own thunders inside of me.

I have no words to describe how I feel right now. Amidst all of the shit that keeps being thrown our way, this feels like hope, a beacon in the middle of it all.

Lifting up on my tiptoes, I press my lips to his, the sound of my pulse hammering in my ears as his hand touches the small of my back, holding me closer to him.

My lips tingle against his, and it almost feels like the room is spinning around us, yet he holds me tight, grounding me.

"This isn't everything," he mutters against my lips, making my eyebrows rise in question, and the grin on his lips makes him look sexy as hell. Since when could Leo fucking Cooper work a smoldering look? Fuck, but I won't complain.

Leo takes a step back, intertwining our fingers, he pulls me to the door beside us, and when he opens it wide, it reveals his private bathroom, and just when I thought I'd managed to pick my jaw up off the floor, it drops again.

First off, this motherfucker has a full-sized bathtub in

here, that's enough to make me melt into a puddle, but the additional battery-lit candles and rose petals that adorn every surface in here only makes it more serene. The smell of lavender gently floats around me as I step into the room and notice the bath almost filled already.

"Give me two minutes, and I'll have the water topped up so it's warm" he murmurs, breezing past me to turn the faucet on.

I remain quiet and in the exact spot as I try to process this whole situation right now, but it's not fully registering in my brain. I can barely see what his actual room looks like among all the little touches he's added to make our night special.

"What are you still doing in your clothes, Lucy? Strip down for me," Leo purrs as he glances over his shoulder and winks at me, and I can't help but roll my eyes at him.

It's on the tip of my tongue to ask him to strip first, but really, I want to reward him for making me feel like this.

Standing tall, I relax my shoulders back as I keep my gaze fixed on him. I slowly pull my arms out of the sleeves of my sweater, loving the feeling of his eyes all over me as I pull it over my head and drop the material at my feet.

The water behind him is long forgotten as I slip my

hands under the waistline of my leggings, and drag them down my legs.

When I stand back up, he's running his fingers over his mouth as he takes in my lilac lingerie set.

"I can't tell you how many cheesy lines are running through my head right now at the sight of you," he murmurs, and I grin.

"Don't spoil the moment," I answer, placing my hand in his as he reaches out for me, and guides me toward the huge bathtub.

I can't believe he's been hiding it in here for so long without saying a word. As if knowing what I'm thinking, he swirls me around to pull me in against his chest. With my back to his front, he props his chin on my shoulder and wraps his arms around my waist.

"When we first got the keys and moved in, we all hoped you would join us eventually, but none of us said it out loud. Hence why the last room at the end of the hall was left for you, we wanted to naturally protect you when you got here." Rocking us from side to side slightly, I let him lull me with his words. "But while the others were bickering about some shit downstairs, I glanced in all of the rooms, and I noticed this was the only one with a bathtub, so I called dibs before anyone else could. Knowing very well that when our queen did arrive, I could lure her with fancy bubbles and shit."

His lips brush over my skin as I let his words settle over me. Who knew he could be such a sweet talker?

"Well, consider me lured, Leo Cooper," I answer quietly, feeling my body relax as he trails a finger from my collarbone, down between my breasts, to circle around my belly button, leaving goosebumps in his wake.

"Look how responsive you are already, Lucy. Imagine what you're going to be like when I'm deep inside you," he whispers in my ear, before lifting me up off my feet, and placing me in the bathtub.

As he releases me to shut off the water, I stare at him with wide eyes as I stand with my lingerie still on, knee deep in the bath.

"Don't fucking touch a single inch of that material, Luce, it's for me," he states, leaning his hand behind his head to grab the material of his t-shirt, and pull it over his head.

Holy. Hot. Fuck.

It's like he knows what kind of a reaction that gives me as I watch his muscles flex.

The smirk on his lips coincides with my initial thought, and when he pulls his gray sweats down his legs, my knees almost buckle beneath me when I see he's not wearing anything underneath them.

"Fuck."

The word slips from my mouth before I can stop it, making his cock jut out at me in response. I want to feel him, and I want it all now, but I get the feeling he's going to drag this all out to make up for lost time.

His muscles flex before my eyes, his six pack calling for my tongue to skin in the ridges and dips.

"Sit down in the water, Lucy," he says, slowly making his way toward me, making my body and mind battle internally.

My body wants to jump at his command, while my mind wants to sass the fuck out of him. It's no surprise when my mind gives in, my legs colliding with the water as I drop to my knees.

Leo's eyes darken as the water laps around me, but it doesn't go over the sides since the bathtub is big enough for four easily. It's practically a jacuzzi.

"Good girl. Now, move over so I can join you," he purrs again, his long, thick length screaming for attention as I move to the left.

Why does hearing the words 'good girl' from his lips feel so damn good?

He wastes no time climbing in beside me, and I turn to face him, pressing my back against the tub as I extend my legs in his direction, and he silently grins.

It feels foreign being in the tub with my bra and panties on, the lace clinging to me just like I want to cling to him, but I don't show the discomfort. I want him to strip me bare, and if this is what that looks like, I'm here for it.

"I think it's cute that *you* think I'm going to fuck you in the bathtub, Lucy," he murmurs, lying back in the water until his shoulders are covered, before pulling my legs over his, and my back arches instantly with the move.

"You're teasing, Leo, and it really doesn't suit you," I say with a pout, making his grin spread wider.

Screw this.

I move to stand, but the second I move my leg from his thigh he grabs my ankle, holding me in place. The challenge is clear in his eyes as I glare at him. Frustration mingles with the previous excitement that bubbled inside of me. I can fall into this little submissive role and have some fun, but fuck, don't ask me to be patient.

"It's not going to be a memorable first time for the right reasons if you tease me and make me wait an eternity, Leo," I grumble, and his eyebrows raise at my words.

"Is that so?" he breathes, grabbing my other ankle too so he can pull me toward him. When I perch in his lap, my knees on either side of him, he circles his arms around my waist, pressing my chest to his as he eyes my cleavage. "You look stunning in this lilac lace, Lucy, it makes you look delicate and fierce all at once," he states, dragging his lips over my collarbone, and I shiver at the contact.

"*Show me* how that makes you feel then," I whisper in response, my skin prickling with desire as the water laps around my waist.

"I thought I already told you, I'm trying to hold it together so I don't cream my pants too soon," he says with a grin, and I roll my eyes, pressing down against his cock beneath me and he groans. "Fuck, Lucy," he hisses, and I love it.

I want to watch this man fall apart easily, simply because it's me touching him. I want to make him fall, just like I do for them.

"You need to decide quickly where you want this to happen, before I make that decision for you," I say as I rake my fingers through his hair, pulling slightly at the back, forcing him to look up at me, and his hands tighten on my waist.

Tugging at his blond hair, I pause when I see a patch of black ink behind his ear, and I frown. I push up on my knees slightly, tilting his head to the side as I go, and he moves willingly.

Leo doesn't say a word as my eyes zero in on exactly what the black ink is that caught my attention.

My name.

It's my name.

Designed into a crown, just like Ezra's is. But instead of saying Lou-Lou like Ezra's, it says Lucy.

Holy fuck.

Goosebumps rise all over my skin as I stare at it with wide eyes.

There's no need for me to claim them, *they* already did it for me.

My hips move of their own accord, grinding my lace covered pussy against his length, and we both moan.

"Do you like it, Lucy?" he asks, and I lean forward, brushing my lips over the marked skin in response, and I hear him catch his breath.

"I'm done dancing around each other slowly, I want you, and I want you now."

Reaching a hand between us, I pull my panties to the side as I pull his head back with the other hand, his gaze colliding with mine in an instant.

The gray pits lead straight to his soul, making my heart pound in my chest as he looks at me like I hung the fucking moon.

"Do it, Lucy. Fuck, I need you to ruin me for everyone else," he breathes. I can tell there is more he wants to say, but he's holding back. My own emotions and feelings are frazzled right now, and I don't want to delve any deeper into them myself.

Releasing his hair, I grip his shoulder for balance as I line his cock up at my entrance, and slowly sink down. I feel the stretch instantly as I work myself down his length. My mouth falls further open with each little nudge as he fills me, and a silent cry pleads to burst from my lips.

I don't stop until he's fully seated inside of me. My nipples are tight against my lace bra as they brush against his chest, and I watch as his eyes roll back in his head.

"Fuck," I groan, rising slowly back up as Leo strokes his hands up my back, releasing my bra in one swift move before I swoop back down, the water swishing around us, but neither of us care as we get lost in each other.

Leo pulls the straps of my bra down my arms, and tosses it aside, before ghosting his hands over my skin, down my spine, and over the globes of my ass. My skin tingles at his touch as I grind against him.

"Holy shit, Lucy," he rasps, tightening his grip on my ass as he pulls me toward him, encouraging the movement.

My pussy clenches around him as his voice goes straight to my core, making his thighs tense beneath me.

Dragging his hands up my sides, he moves them to cup my breasts, my nipples tightening under his grip before his mouth descends on the taut peak, and a moan falls from my lips as my head tilts back.

I can't stop my nails from biting into his skin as I cling to him, continuing to work my body over his as he swirls his tongue and nips his teeth across my breasts.

"God, Leo," I groan, feeling his lips rise in a smile as my clit rubs slightly against his length as I rock against him, his cock filling me so much I'm breathless.

"You feel like heaven, Lucy, fucking divine heaven," he grunts, his hips lifting slightly to meet my thrusts, and the added motion only heightens how intense this feels right now. "Fuck this," he adds, hissing against my nipple, before I'm suddenly being moved backward.

The water whooshes around me as Leo grabs me around the waist and rises up to his feet in one move, leaving me gasping for breath in surprise. Wrapping my arms and legs around him instinctively, he steps out of the bathtub effortlessly, water dripping down our bodies, and places me on the vanity. The marble beneath my thighs is cool against my skin, but I'm too focused on the man in front of me to care.

Done with the tension that still continues to rise around us, I cup the back of his neck and pull him closer to me, and our mouths collide.

Gone are the gentle touches and heated gazes, we're a frenzied mess of need, sizzling against each other. I hear the sound of a tear, and it takes me a moment to realize it's my panties, or what's left of them as Leo grabs my thighs, pulling me to the edge of the vanity to tilt my hips.

In one swift motion, with our lips still pressed together, and my arms around his neck, clinging to him like my life depends on it, he lines his cock up at my entrance and slams all the way home.

"Oh fuck," I cry against his lips as he fills me up once

more.

I'm not going to be able to take much more before I explode. I want to feel it all, and I want it to be at his hands, *finally*.

His eyes shimmer with heat as I glance up at him, and he leans back, pulling his lips from mine as he lifts my thighs, forcing me back on to my elbows as I prop myself up.

The slight move makes him hit even deeper as he fucks me harder, faster, and so fucking sweet, my hand moves for my clit without me even realizing.

"Touch yourself, Lucy, be a good little girl for me," he breathes, not relenting on his movement as he speaks.

I roll my eyes as I ghost my fingertips on my swollen nub, desperate for attention. "I'm older than you by two months, asshole, don't call me little," I grumble, and he grins down at me.

"Shut the fuck up, Lucy, and let me hear you scream." His fingers dig into my thighs as his cock thrusts into me with precision, and he leans forward to capture my nipple in his mouth again.

I feel my body begin to tingle as I circle my clit, which combined with his touch all over me is all I need. It's too much, it's all too much.

I've never felt like this with anyone but my guys, my kings, and being here with Leo only solidifies our connection.

This is it. He is mine, and I am his.

That knowledge settles over my soul, and it's like the final touch I needed for my body to explode.

A scream bursts from my lips as ecstasy ricochets through my body, wave after wave of pleasure pouring through my body as Leo slams into me again and again, dragging out every touch. As his movements stutter, and his own orgasm washes over him, he sinks his teeth into my nipple, and a fresh scream rips from my lungs as my core spasms around his pulsing cock again.

My pulse pounds in my ears as my body goes limp beneath him. As we both remain in place, a complete tangled mess of limbs, I feel Leo stroke his hand through my hair, which is wet from the bath, and clinging to my face and neck.

"Lucy?" he murmurs, running his thumb over my cheek, and I realize my eyes are closed. Blinking them open, I instantly meet his gaze, the raw emotion in his eyes holding me captive.

"Leo," I murmur, stroking my hand up his chest and over his neck until I find the spot where I know my name is inked into his skin.

"I fucking love you, Lucy. Always have, always will. This isn't some post sex shit, this is me, telling you, that I will always be yours."

My heart beats rapidly in my chest as I search his eyes, but all I see is the truth.

"I love you too, Leo, with everything that I am, but this only works if we're a team. I'm not a damsel in distress. You guys once treated me like a queen, this ink proves that, I need that again for this to work," I respond truthfully as Leo rests his forehead against mine.

"You're my queen, my Lucy, and I'll find a way to make it right. All of it."

WATCH ME RISE

CHAPTER EIGHT

Lou-Lou

I grip the steering wheel tightly as I navigate the huge fucking truck through the turn leading onto our street. It might be bulky as fuck, but it is divine to drive. All roomy, luxurious, and shiny, but more importantly, it's freaking *bulletproof*. It's so bizarre and a bit worrisome, but I'm rolling with it.

Maybe Leo's magic dick has made me soften over the past twenty-four hours, but I'm trying to avoid all aspects of drama for a minute. There's more than enough going on around me already, so I'm not going to purposely add to the pile by pitching a fit over a brand new, bulletproof, truck.

A hand brushes against my thigh as I pull the truck over outside of the house, and I turn to glance at Ezra. His thumb strokes over my jeans, sending a shiver through my body, and I raise an eyebrow in question at him.

Ever since Leo announced he was claiming me last night, it has set the others in motion too. My day has been filled with small touches, distant glances, and smoldering eyes.

It has been everything, it's just a shame we were on campus, otherwise I would have done something about it. I'm glad tomorrow is a half day, and I have Friday off, although I did take yesterday off, but missing one day of classes doesn't mean I've failed the class.

"What's going on in that pretty little head of yours, Lou-Lou Carter?" Ezra asks, and I offer a soft smile as I shake my head slightly.

"What *isn't* going on in there should be the question," I respond, only half joking as I slump back in my seat, turning the engine off as I release a sigh.

He doesn't answer me back, offer to help or make it better, because he fucking knows I'll demand to know all the other shit they're keeping from me.

"Well, I suggest clearing your mind before you step in there," he murmurs, lacing his fingers with mine as I frown in confusion. "There's an Izaro waiting for you in the basement," he adds dubiously, before leaning across the center console to kiss the corner of my lips.

Just as I'm about to turn my head to capture a real kiss, the fucker is jumping out of the truck with a wink over his shoulder, and I scream internally.

Asshole.

My heart is pounding with a mixture of emotions, the fact that Ezra has been giving me hot glances all day, but then suddenly bails when we have a moment alone, just makes me want to nut punch him.

Well, maybe not the dick, that'd only make me more sexually frustrated if a peen was ruled out because of my own actions.

With a sigh, I grab my bag from the backseat, and climb down from the truck. Shutting the door behind me, I lock it and head inside.

Ezra hovers by the door, not completely leaving me on my own as is my new norm now, and I hold back the eye roll. All Ezra, Jameson, and Leo have done today is follow me around school. Leo actually attended his culinary class this afternoon, which is why Ezra drove home with me. He mentioned the class is called Global à la Carte, sounds fancy and he was animated talking about it. But now that I know Leo has a completely different major and shouldn't attend my classes, I feel bad that he's there all the time.

This morning he mentioned it was more for his peace of mind, but I'm still not sold on that being the only reason.

Naomi and Vince were nowhere to be seen today, just another layer of confusion as I wonder what kind of connection they have. Maybe I should be straight up and just ask her, but something is holding me back.

I step inside the house, my teeth sinking into my bottom lip when Ezra follows behind me, closing the door as he grazes his hand over my ass. But that fucker teased me earlier, so he can have a taste of his own medicine.

"Thanks," I murmur, glancing over my shoulder to find him right behind me. I move slightly, so my mouth is a fraction away from his, and I watch as his mouth morphs, ready for me to kiss him, but I pull away, turning quickly on my heels and sashaying toward the basement.

"Fuck," he mumbles, clearly to himself, but loud enough for me to hear, and I force myself not to react as I drop my bag at the bottom of the stairs, and continue to the basement door.

It's funny how I didn't know this place existed a few weeks ago, and now I'm almost down here working out as much as I'm in my room.

Hopefully it means they'll start to trust me with the other secrets they're holding back.

Heavy bass dance music pumps through the speakers as I make my way downstairs, and when I reach the bottom, my eyes instantly fixate on Jagger working over the punching bag in the far corner.

Yes. Please.

In just a pair of loose fitted shorts, his muscles tense, his body slick with sweat as he lands move after move, I think I may orgasm just from watching. Tearing my eyes from his body, I glance around to see if Jameson is here too, but it's just the two of us.

Pulling my coat off, I lay it over the seat by Ezra's computer setup, before fixing my ponytail.

I consider sneaking up on him since his back is to me, and he's clearly not heard my arrival over the noise, but I remember the way I reacted to him doing the exact same thing to me, and decide against it.

Looking around for where the music is coming from, I spy a phone on the desk, and when I swipe my finger over the screen, the music app comes to life.

I hit the pause button, which even startles me with how quiet the room suddenly becomes, and when I look over my shoulder I find Jagger looking at me with wild eyes, clearly making him jump with the sudden silence that now surrounds him.

"The fuck, Luella? Don't fucking do that," he grunts, swiping at the loose pieces of hair flopping over his face, and I roll my eyes at him.

"I either had to pause the music or approach you, and I'm quite happy with option one thanks," I retort, with my arms folded over my chest, and he shakes his head at me while reaching for the bottle of water laying on the mat. "Ezra said you wanted me," I continue, and he nods as he chugs the rest of the bottle in one go.

"Yup."

That's all he says for a moment, leaving me to watch and wait for him to continue, and a part of me thinks he's doing it just to piss me off as he unties his hair, running his fingers through the wavy brown ends, before retying it.

There's a smart ass comment on the tip of my tongue

ready to go, but as I take a step toward him, he *finally* fucking speaks. "Don't just stand there, Luella. You said you wanted to prove yourself, now's your chance. You. Me. Mat. Now," he states with a challenge flashing in his brown eyes, but he really must have forgotten the kind of person I am over the past three years, because this sounds like fun.

As much as I loved leaving in Leo's arms yesterday when Jagger surrendered me to him, and what subsequently followed, I was a little regretful that I didn't get to put this man through his paces on the mat. It's a shame there's not an audience this time, but I'll take what I can get.

"Oh, I'm ready," I say with a smile, kicking my Vans off, and removing my oversized hoodie, tossing it aside and leaving me in a black cropped top and my black leggings.

Game on, fucker.

"What made you change your mind?" I ask as I step onto the mat, and quickly slip my socks off too. I love the feel of the mat beneath my feet, it helps make me feel more grounded, and I want to show him what I've learned. It's a shame he is underestimating me but I'll make him pay.

Jagger stares me down for a moment, his hands on his hips like he's weighing his words, and he sighs. "Well, if

I'm going to fucking claim you, I need you to have no doubt over the fact that I *see* you, Luella. And you're right. If something happens and we can't protect you, I need to know you can handle yourself."

His confession makes my heart soar, and a grin spreads across my face as I rise up on my tiptoes. Bracing my hands on his shoulders, I lick the end of his nose, before quickly jumping back.

The frown instantly appears on his face at my giggle, bending my knees slightly as I lift my hands up high to protect my jaw, keeping my hands fisted, readying myself.

"You're playing dirty," he gripes, swiping at the end of his nose in disgust, and I stick my tongue out tauntingly again, which makes him growl. "Have it your way," he mumbles, falling into his fighting stance too, and suddenly the silence that surrounds us feels tense as hell. It looks like we're finally going to do this.

Maybe I should have insisted on him watching me fight someone else, because his Adonis body is a fucking distraction.

"Who's going to make the first move, Luella?" he goads as he bounces on the balls of his feet, slowly beginning to circle around me.

I shrug in response, taking a step back so I can move with him. I refuse to let him trap me in the center, like he's the predator and I'm the prey.

Keeping my gaze fixed on his, I focus, ignoring how hot he looks, the fact that we're in the basement, I forget about all of it. In my mind, I'm back in White River, in the rundown gym where I trained my heart out to make myself as brutal as the gang members who had their eyes on me.

It meant spending hours upon hours at the gym, getting lost in the pain and anger, before quickly losing myself in the parties that followed on my block.

A wave of calmness washes over me as I squint in Jagger's direction, and he must be able to see the shift as I change before his eyes.

There's no laughter on my lips, no humor in my eyes, my face morphing into cold and calculated as I lock my arms closer together and take deep breaths.

I center myself, keep my cool, and like I hope, he makes the first move almost as if he can't help it, his right hand extending to make contact with my stomach, but I quickly move out of his reach. It's not escaped my attention that we're not wearing any form of protective wear, but that's exactly how I like it. I want to feel my skin press against his and my fists meeting bare flesh.

Jagger raises his eyebrow at me as he considers his next move, and I don't want him to think I'm too scared to attack, so I crouch, extending my left hand which he avoids, before I rise to my full height again.

Continuing around the mat, repeating the same motion a few times, neither of us make a connection as we block each move. There's something in the air, something stopping us from pushing and taking like we usually would, and I want to eliminate it.

Just as I'm about to make a move, I notice he takes a deep breath, an instant sign he's about to come at me, and this time he moves toward me, cutting the distance in a matter of seconds. His hand is just about to skin my arm, when I drop to the floor, my ass hitting the mat with a thud, before I swing my legs out to the left, colliding with his ankle, and he stumbles, but manages to remain on his feet.

Fucker.

He immediately whips his head around to look down at me, the surprise clear in his eyes, and I plant my feet on the mat and remain in a crouched position as I look up at him for a moment.

Using the slight distraction, I lunge for him, shoving

my shoulder straight into his stomach before he can stop me, and we both fall to the mat. I manage to place the palms of my hands on the ground before they get trapped behind him, but I land directly above Jagger, and he uses that to his advantage.

His thick arm bands around my waist as he wraps his legs around mine and rolls us so he comes out on top. Our eyes crash together as he keeps my arms pinned at my side, but his legs around mine are slack enough for me to pull out of the hold quickly.

I offer a sickly sweet smile up at him as his chest heaves above me, before straightening my right leg out, and sharply raising my knee to connect with the back of his thigh. The grunt from above lets me know he felt it, but it's not enough to shift him off me, and moments later he's shuffling up my body so his ass is firmly pinning my thighs to the mat as his hands wrap around my arms, keeping me locked in place.

Motherfucker.

"Shake me off, Luella," he grunts, a loose piece of hair flopping over his forehead, and I grind my teeth together in anger.

Arrogant shithead.

I need to change tactics because there's no way I can buck him off of me, so I need to improvise and do it quickly.

I never really expected to out maneuver him on the ground or stand-up, fuck, it's Jagger for Christ's sake, the best fighter I've ever seen, but I don't want him to win so easily. If I tapped now, he'd see it as being weak.

I know what I have to do to use his momentum against him.

If I have to play dirty, then I fucking will.

Batting my eyelashes, I look up at him innocently. "Why would I shake you off, Jagger, when I have you right where I want you?" I purr, attempting to lift my hips up off the mat to grind against him, but he makes it very difficult with his hold on me.

"You think I'm going to fall for some sweet pussy, Luella? Please," he responds with a roll of his eyes and a pointed glare, and I grin.

"Jagger, I'm not just *any* sweet pussy and we both know it. I've seen you in your element, and it's here, on the mat, just where I love to watch you. I always wondered what it would be like beneath you, feeling you press up against me, and it doesn't disappoint," I state, running my tongue over my bottom lip, and his eyes turn to slits as he stares down at me.

As he digests my words, he doesn't realize it, but his grip on my arms loosens, and I try to remain casual and unaware that he's slowly lowering his guard.

"You can't tell me you've never wanted to feel this here with me," I continue, watching as a bead of sweat trails down his temple, and he lifts his thighs off me so I can't tell if he's sporting wood or not.

I'm playing with fire, I know I am, but it's so fucking worth it.

With him lifted off me slightly, I plant my feet on the floor, bending my knees as he frowns, but I lift my core up toward him, and the friction is delicious as I drag across his thigh, but I focus on the task at hand, and not what my body desires. I may be speaking the truth, but winning right now exceeds my sexual frustration.

His guard lowers slightly as he rubs his lips together, but I have him exactly where I need him. In one swift move, I lower my hips to the mat before thrusting them back in the air, harder this time, while swiping my hands down toward my waist. He doesn't release my wrists in time, and the movement has him face planting the mat above me, with his hips now dangerously close to my face, and before he can come at me with anything else, I wrap my hands tightly around his waist, and use all my core strength to spin us. My muscles are screaming as we move.

In seconds I'm back on top, my body between his thighs as my head remains nestled against his abs, and neither of us move for a moment. Jagger is not fighting back like I expected, but I'm too nervous to lift my head up to check his facial expression as my heart pounds. The moment continues to drag out, until a bark of laughter booms around us, and I realize it's Jagger.

Turning to face him, with my hands planted on either side of his hips, I find him looking up at the ceiling yet his eyes are closed and a huge grin is on his face.

He laughs to himself for what feels like an eternity as I stare at him like he's lost his goddamn mind, until he blinks his eyes open and stares down at me.

His dark eyes instantly heat as they connect with mine, making me shiver without even being touched.

"What's so funny?" I manage to ask, still breathing heavily as I await his next move, but he continues to relax more and more beneath me, which only has me even more on edge.

"Nothing, nothing at all," he says with a smile, and

I quirk an eyebrow at him. "I'm just laughing at how I underestimated your fierceness again, and I apologize." The smile on his face is genuine as he places his hands under my arms and drags me up the length of him.

My legs instantly fall to either side of him as I sit back on his thighs, and place my hands on my hips.

"Lesson one for me, was always that ninety nine percent of men will be bigger than me, so I either put them in a spot to disarm them enough to use their momentum against them, or go for the most debilitating spots. Luckily for you, I love your dick far too much to hit it with a swift knee," I retort, which only makes another bout of laughter pass his lips.

I like seeing him like this, it's addictive.

"You love my dick, huh?" he responds, his already deep voice dropping further as his hands move to my thighs, squeezing them as he tilts his hips up so I can feel his steel cock beneath me.

Fuck.

My breath catches in my throat as he effortlessly lifts to a sitting position, his chest pressing against mine as my gaze remains locked with his.

"Of course that's what you took away from everything

I said," I murmur in response as my mouth dries, and he grins.

"I heard love and I heard dick in the same sentence, of course my brain short circuited there and focused on the important stuff," he says quietly, and it's my turn to roll my eyes at him.

My hands rise to his shoulders, his skin hot beneath my touch as he strokes his fingers down my spine, and I find myself leaning closer instinctively, needing my lips to press against his again, but a throat clears behind me, breaking our moment.

"With the position you're in, I'm going to assume you didn't tell her." I turn to find Jameson in jeans and a t-shirt, both completely covered in oil and dirt, and it's crazy how much it fucking suits him, but my brain is too busy replaying his words to fully enjoy his messy look.

"Tell me what?" I ask, glancing between them both, and Jagger sighs, resting his forehead on my shoulder for a moment before looking up at me.

All the fun and jokes are long gone as he searches my eyes. "Robbie has an election rally next week. He's going for a seat on the Emerson Grove Town Council," he states, his voice devoid of any emotion, and my eyebrows knit together in confusion.

"What does that have to do with me? With us?" I ask, glancing over my shoulder at Jameson too, but he's already looking down at his feet because they know what Jagger says next will send me into a spiral.

"Honestly, I don't know, but it means your mom and Lola will be put on parade." My heart lurches at the mention of the both of them, my brain still unable to process how I feel about everything.

"What he's trying to say, Ella, is we never leave them alone with him. So, we'll have to put on a public display of unity to keep June and Lola safe, and as far away from his post-event rage as possible," Jameson says, and the reality of the situation settles in.

They're going to pretend everything is all sunshine and rainbows for the public. Like Robbie isn't the vile creature that he is. But if I do this with them, it'll look like we're siblings to the world, when we're *so* far from it it's unreal.

"What is my role in all of this? Do I get to dodge it all, or am I expected to be paraded around like my mom and Lola," I mutter, not wanting to hear the response as Jagger strokes his hand down my spine soothingly.

"I don't know, Luella, I really don't know. But I think

we need to go and see your mom, she's always given the run down from Robbie before any of this shit."

Fuck.

I already get the feeling that no isn't really an option. Not when there seems to be so much at play here, including the lives of my family, and it makes sense for her to pass on everything she knows so we can figure out how to handle it on our end too. I've learned to hope for the best but prepare for the worst.

It doesn't ease the pain in my chest though. It doesn't help me forget the information I've tried to leave back at Lockwood.

I guess I'm going to have to face the fact my mom is here and I have a sibling far sooner than I planned.

WATCH ME RISE

CHAPTER NINE

Lou-Lou

I feel sick to my stomach as the truck rolls to a stop outside Lockwood.

Jameson is behind the wheel, I was not ready to drive us here, but even sitting shotgun, looking up at the rundown building still gives me chills.

It's Friday morning, and the overcast sky and rain aren't helping paint the setting in a better light.

Jagger, Ezra, and Leo are all in the back, but everyone is now silent, watching and waiting for my reaction. If my mind wasn't all over the place I'm sure I'd give them something, anything, to indicate how I feel, but my brain is mush.

I remain frozen in my seat, my eyes focusing on the nearest window as I try to take a deep breath. It's crazy how derelict and run down it is from the outside, with the overgrown shrubs and bushes surrounding the entire building. While inside the one story building, with the small windows lining the entire level, is more modernized than you would initially think.

I don't mind stepping inside.

I don't mind the suffocating temperature from the central heating blasting on high.

I don't mind the older woman who sat at the reception desk.

What I *do* mind is June Carter, or whatever her last name is now.

She was once in the running for world's worst mother—prioritizing alcohol and drugs over your children will do that.

So how has she been able to stay here with the little girl?

Not just any little girl; Lola.

My sister.

Jagger and Jameson's sister.

The memory of her light blonde hair fanned out across the pillow as she slept is what kicks me into motion, and without a word, I unclip my seatbelt, swing the door open, and jump down from the truck.

I hear the guys rushing to keep up with me, but I don't look back until I reach the revolving door. Leo is the closest to me, with Ezra, Jagger, and Jameson hot on his heels, each of them looking at me with concern flashing in their eyes.

I try to muster a smile, but it's pointless when I feel so confused, and the guys attempting to baby me doesn't help.

Leo comes to a stop beside me, fixing the cap on his head, before wrapping his arm around my shoulders.

Leo must sense I need strength from them all, and waits for the other three to catch up before he turns to me, waiting for me to take the lead.

I'm not embarrassed or ashamed to say I need them to walk through these doors again.

"It's something we need to do, Luella. But we'll do it at your pace, okay?"

Jagger's words repeat in my mind, and my eyes fall

to him. With his long wavy hair tied back in a bun on top of his head, and the stubble on his chin a little longer than usual, he looks like a member of a motorcycle club or something with a rugged side. Especially with his leather jacket, black tee, combat pants and matching boots. The tattoos on his hands remind me I still haven't explored his ink like I want to.

I'm letting myself down.

As I move my focus to Ezra, I rub my lips together as he fixes his black-rimmed glasses, his messy brown hair curling in every direction as he tightens his jacket around himself to keep out the chill in the air. There's always something slightly innocent about Ezra, and that could be because I've been there to see the pain he's felt, especially with his sister. It resonates in my soul, making me want to grab the waist of his sweatpants and tug him closer, before enveloping him in my arms.

Remembering the tattoo on his chest, the one that matches the crown tattoo behind Leo's ear, I flick my gaze at Jameson, wondering if he or Jagger have something similar. It would take an extra minute to find it among the other tattoos on his skin, but I'm *all* for searching. His brown eyes are fixed on mine, silently asking if I'm okay, but I catch sight of the switchblade spinning in his hand, and I can tell he's stressing because of me.

My uncertainty over this entire situation is rubbing off on him, most likely all of them, for sure.

Taking a deep breath, I wet my lips, relax my shoulders back, and turn for the revolving doors, not wanting any of us to get any wetter from the rain than we already are.

Leo grabs my hand as we step through the doors, the heat engulfs me instantly as it did the last time I was here, and I'm already itching to take my coat off.

As we move into the lobby, I recognize the woman as she looks up at us, her gaze casting over the guys filtering in behind us too, and to my surprise, she smiles wide.

"Boys, it's good to see you," she says as she stands, her eyes falling back to mine with her smile still fixed in place as she exhales. "You too, Luella."

The pleasantries feel awkward, which doesn't help when I remain silent. Jameson approaches her, and to my surprise he gives her a side hug while muttering something about cupcakes. But I'm too focused on the hallway I know led to my mother the last time I was here.

"Want to get this first part over with?" Leo murmurs in my ear, his hand squeezing my shoulder as I glance up at him and nod.

Standing here is just making it worse, allowing my emotions to continue on with the internal. With heightened senses I can feel them beginning to bubble at the surface. I need to nip it in the bud and address this crazy shit that is now my life.

Leo places his arm around my shoulders again, steering me to the hallway, and I instinctively reach my hand under his t-shirt, running my fingers over his back. The skin on skin contact immediately settles my soul a little with each step we take.

I don't turn to check if the others are following, and I know if they're not, I'm still okay. With Leo comforting and guiding me, I feel like I can manage the situation.

We slowly make our way down the long corridor, approaching the door I remember from last time, and just as I move to knock, a giggle echoes from the other side, melting my heart as I assume it's Lola's.

I feel like I can't breathe as I try to take a deep breath, my lungs acting like they can't expand but I know it's my reaction. I can recognize the moment my whole mind softens to the situation as Leo knocks on the door for me. My pulse pounds in my ears as I wait for it to open.

Moments later, the door swings open to reveal my mom, her brown eyes widening in surprise when she sees me, and it feels like an eternity as we both simply stand and stare at each other.

"Mom," I finally murmur, looking her over from head to toe. In a pair of jeans and a loose necked cashmere sweater, she looks nothing like I remember. She was always in skimpy outfits, trying to use her body to pay for drugs. Not that my dad ever cared what she did since he reaped the benefits too.

With her blonde hair scooped back off her face, completely make-up free, she looks like a soccer mom, and the thought almost makes me burst into hysterics of tears and laughter.

Who'd have thought? Not me, that's for fucking sure.

I was nearly positive this woman was dead in a ditch somewhere.

"Mama! Mama! Who here?" the sweet voice sings from behind her, making my heart pound faster in my chest, before she appears at my mom's side.

Lola.

Her blonde hair is in pigtails, her brown eyes sparkling as she looks up at us, and with her pink jean dress and tights on, she looks like the sweetest damn angel I've ever seen.

"Leo, it's Leo," she shouts gleefully, before launching herself at him.

In one swift move, he collects her in his arm as the other remains tightly around my shoulder. It feels surreal looking at her up close.

Jagger said he was instantly protective of the unborn child three years ago, which I thought was a bag of bull shit. Before knowing the gender or their personality, he knew he wanted to protect them with everything he had.

While I practically ran from this room the last time we were here, irrelevant of who was inside. But now, standing before her, with her rosy cheeks and animated smile, I know she's just slayed my heart.

I want to bundle her in my arms and take her away from my mom immediately, but the guys mentioned that would only make the situation worse, and for now, I have to trust them at their word.

They've dealt with this whole fucked up mess much longer than me, so I have to look for their guidance so I don't ruin this whole thing all together.

"You look well, Luella," my mom says casually,

drawing my attention to her, and I almost smile instinctively at the compliment until she continues. "I mean, you could do with bigger tits still, but not much has changed, huh?"

This fucking woman.

No, things definitely haven't changed. Not when she has the ability to tear me to shreds with one single line. But fuck her, I've lived the past three years without her crap, I'm not about to get all hurt over her mind games again.

With a roll of my eyes, I slip out of Leo's hold and take a step forward so I'm toe to toe with my mom. We're the same height now, and the annoyed look in my eyes has clearly been noticed with the way she edges back slightly.

"You better not say any of that shit to Lola or I'll bury you my fucking self," I bite, begging for her to have some retort for me, so I can release some of the pent up anger brimming inside of me.

Her mouth opens, her eyes wide in surprise, but before she can speak, Jagger interrupts.

"She wouldn't fucking dare, and she's lucky to still be breathing after doing it to you." The venom in his words is undeniable, and when I turn to find him a couple of steps back, with his arms folded over his chest and his red face filled with rage, I almost smile at how protective he is, not only of me but Lola as well.

"I'm sorry, I just—"

"Save it," I interrupt, not needing to hear her excuses. She must be doing something right, otherwise the guys wouldn't be so happy to leave Lola with her, do all of this for them. It must just be me she has an issue with.

Jameson and Ezra flank him on each side, a cupcake in each hand, and I roll my eyes. Of course they snuck off for the sweet stuff.

"How about we move this inside so Lola can play with her toys instead of having to listen to all this grown-up stuff," Leo suggests, nodding at the room my mom is currently blocking, and I reluctantly agree.

My mom steps back, and I step farther into the room, surprised by how big it actually is.

It's like a studio apartment. A bed set up to the right, a kitchen in the far right corner, with a dining table and sofa set up to our left. The walls are a fresh off-white, and the furniture looks like it's new too, and something tells me that has everything to do with the four guys here with me now, and nothing at all to do with Robbie fucking Izaro.

Awkwardly hovering in the open space by the beds, a cupcake is offered out and I look to find Ezra smiling at me. I take the cupcake with the pink frosting, letting him grab my other hand as he pulls me over to the sofa, where a children's show called Bluey plays on the television and a box of toys are scattered across the rug in front of it. I remember the show from Cody watching it back at Ryan and Beth's.

Moments later, like a hurricane, Lola races back to her toys, and I watch in silence as she jumps from one toy to another. Hugging and rocking a baby doll, before grabbing a car and racing it around the swirl patterns on the rug.

Fuck.

She's as scatterbrained as I am right now.

Mindlessly nibbling on the cupcake, I take a few minutes to watch her play, basking in her innocence, and it makes my heart soar to know the guys cared so much about her that they've ensured she's safe and protected even from her own mother.

But they're right, we need to get her out of this situation.

"So, June, did my father say anything about the upcoming election rally?" Jameson asks, taking a seat on the sofa to my left, and Lola instantly runs at him, diving into his lap with a little book.

A grin transforms on his lips as he nestles back in his

seat, adjusting her so she can see the book as he turns the first page.

Who the fuck are these guys?

I never thought I'd see them like this, and it's sweet as hell.

"He wants to get out there, put his name on every building, on every park bench, hear it on everyone's lips," my mom responds, walking around to pull a chair from the dining table over, and I squint at her in curiosity.

I wonder what makes her tick these days? I can't see her doing drugs or having too much liquor, the guys wouldn't allow Lola near her if that was the case.

"What does that look like to him? What does he plan for us to do?" Jagger asks, pulling me from my thoughts as Ezra strokes his hand over my thigh.

"He wants you to go door to door campaigning. He wants to really go for the *family man* appeal, which means he'll likely want a family lunch, and to do something charitable," she answers. It all sounds simple, almost casual, but we all know it's much more than that.

"Did he specify what he wants from us?" Jagger repeats, since she talked as a whole, and she shrugs.

"He hasn't been here this past week or so. He only

called to give me his general plans, but there was nothing specific, not yet at least," she murmurs, rubbing a hand down her face, and I sigh.

What a waste of fucking time this was then if she has no concrete answers.

Well, maybe not where Lola is concerned. Seeing her again only solidified that she's important to me now too.

"Do you still have the cell phone I gave you?" Ezra asks, and my mom nods in response. "Good, any updates, you call us straight away," he orders, not putting it out there as a question, and I have to hold back a smile.

I love it when Ezra gets bossy.

My mom murmurs her agreement, and my gaze shifts back to Jameson and Lola, only to find Jameson whispering in her ear, and Lola staring straight at me.

What's going on?

"If that's all, then we'll be out of your hair. The nanny will be here for Lola soon, and we don't want to mess with her routine," Leo announces, and my heart sinks at having to leave her here.

A nanny? Why?

As if sensing my question, Ezra leans closer and whispers in my ear, "Your mom can't leave the grounds.

We have a nanny come in to take Lola to the park and stuff since Robbie won't allow us to do it."

His words rip my heart from my chest and smash it to pieces at the revelation.

Have I mentioned Robbie Izaro is a cunt yet today?

I don't really care about my mom, but the memories Lola and the guys are missing out on because they can only see her here breaks my heart.

Looking back at her on Jameson's lap, I stall when I don't see her there. A small hand falls to my knee, and a lump instantly lodges in my throat as I look down to see her looking up at me with the twins' matching eyes.

I'm a fucking goner.

"It's Le-La," she says with a gentle smile and wide eyes, and I can't help but match it as I look down at her.

"We've tried every nickname with her, but she keeps coming back to Le-La," Jameson says, but I don't move my gaze from Lola's.

"How does she—"

"She knows all about her bestest big sister in the whole wide world, Luella," Jagger states from somewhere behind me, and tears instantly prick my eyes as she casually climbs up into my lap and wraps her arms around my neck.

Holy fuck.

I don't ever want to let go.

Ever.

It's right here, in this moment, that I promise with all of my soul, that one day, I will leave this run down piece of shit building with Lola in my arms.

And we will never look back.

CHAPTER TEN

Lou-Lou

I tap my finger on the back of my phone case as I stare at the text flashing on my screen.

Naomi: Hey, girl. It's been forever. Are you partying tonight?

I've been looking at it for the past ten minutes, wondering how I should respond, and I still haven't come up with a definitive answer.

Today has been a complete tsunami of emotions. My brain, heart, and overall mental state have been crashing against me relentlessly, and it all circles around to one thing. No, one *person*.

Lola.

Fuck, if I had walked in that room and just seen my mom, I would have lasted two seconds before quickly giving her a piece of my mind and turning my back on her, just like she has always done to me.

I wish I could have said more, pushed back at her more, but the second Lola stepped up beside her, all of those negative thoughts were pushed aside and I was officially a goner.

Now, there's something in this fucked up situation that matters to me, more than myself.

All of my arguments with the guys circled around the fact *I* was being left in the dark, *I* didn't know shit, and *I* felt vulnerable. But as much as all of that still matters, Lola's safety is paramount to me.

I want her to feel safe. To have the life we never did. To be nurtured, cared for, and protected. All of which instantly reminds me of Ryan and Bethany with their son Cody. That's exactly how they treat him, and I want that for her too.

I almost close the text message I'm still idly staring

at to call Ryan for help, but my stomach clenches with worry. I don't want to burden him with this shit, not when he is handling so much already. But, if it comes to a point where I can't figure this all out with the guys, then I'll call him in an instant because this is important to me. *Lola* is important to me.

Dropping the phone on the bed beside me, I sigh as I throw my arms out wide in frustration. I wish, just for a minute, that I could shut all of this off. I feel so much responsibility and pressure all of a sudden, that it's hard to breathe.

I swipe my loose hair back off my face, my eyes falling to the phone again as *Superstore* plays on my television in the background, and I consider Naomi's message again.

Maybe I could do with some girl time, and there's still a possibility everything that's had me concerned with her and Vince is all in my head.

Maybe... I don't know. She's technically not done anything to make me specifically not trust her, but fuck, the guys bought be a bulletproof truck for a reason. I have to be cautious.

What would she even gain from lying to me? Nothing, absolutely nothing.

Fuck it.

Pushing myself up to sit on the edge of the bed, I swing my legs over the side and unlock my cell, quickly tapping out a message in response.

Me: Hey, yeah I'm down for some fun. The guys are throwing a party as always. Let me know when you're here.

I flick the phone off silent, before placing it on my nightstand and rising from the bed.

There's no fucking reason for there to be a party tonight, but here we are. The guys talked some shit about appearances, but none of it made any sense to me, so I just nodded in agreement.

I was all ready to hide out in my room, letting the boom of the music vibrate the floor beneath my feet, but now I want to let loose, forget about my life for a few minutes, and have some fun.

Getting lost to the music and the sweet taste of a cocktail or two sounds like perfection.

I head for the walk-in closet, opting for a black mini skirt and tights combo, with a cropped white tee and my leather jacket. I feel good, and the boots I pair it all with make my legs look longer than usual. It's enough of an effort to say I've arrived, but nowhere near as attention grabbing as my prior outfits.

Quickly changing, I pull my blonde hair into a loose bun on top of my head, letting a few tendrils fall down around my face, before I add an extra layer of mascara to my lashes.

Done.

As if sensing I was ready, my phone pings with an incoming message, and a quick glance at the screen again tells me Naomi has arrived.

Naomi: Girl, I'm here. You already partying or upstairs?

Not wanting her to come upstairs, I quickly shoot off a response, before pocketing my phone and heading for the door.

Me: On my way down now.

I might be relaxed enough to have fun with her, but I don't want her up in my personal space again. Not yet anyway.

Making sure the door is locked behind me, I pocket the key and head downstairs. I'm not surprised to see the two guys and the red rope blocking off the stairs from the partygoers, and as usual they somehow manage to know I'm on my way down without glancing in my direction, opening the rope without even making eye contact with me.

Again.

The music is louder down here, some new drill track that instantly has my hips swaying a little as I search for Naomi.

There's a few people hovering around the open entryway, but I still manage to find her jet black hair instantly. It falls sleek down her back as she pulls her denim jacket tight around her waist. With black skinny jeans and doc martens on her feet, she looks as edgy as ever.

Squeezing between the two guys laughing and yelling over the music to my left, she catches sight of me as I near, a smile spreading across her face as she instantly links her arm through mine.

"Hey, it's been forever. I thought you were mad at me or something," she says in my ear so I can hear her over all the noise, and I shake my head.

Clearly my sudden uncertainty hadn't gone unnoticed, but I don't say anything since my head shake seems to satisfy her concern.

"What do you want to drink?" I ask, guiding us toward the kitchen, where I find Jameson, my eyes locking with his as soon as I step through the door.

His gaze drifts over me from head to toe, and I don't miss the question in his eyes since I'd mentioned earlier that I wouldn't be making an appearance.

I shrug my shoulders, and he smirks, raising a bottle of tequila in one hand, and a bottle of vodka in the other. I can't stop the smile spreading across my face as I drag Naomi toward him through the few people milling around. I just fucking love that he's instantly on my wave length.

"I will take a vodka and orange juice if you're offering," I state as I stop at the kitchen island beside him, and he nods.

"Whatever my girl wants, she can have," he replies with a wink, making me roll my eyes at his cheesy response, but it doesn't stop the butterflies swarming in my stomach at his words. My body is officially a cliché.

"I see a few things have changed around here, huh?" Naomi asks, unlinking our arms as she leans against the countertop with raised eyebrows and a short smile on her face.

"Something like that," I mutter, taking the glass from Jameson's hand, before he offers the other to Naomi.

As I turn to face the back door, I notice the garden is packed with people, Jameson manages to plant himself at my side and wrap his arm around my shoulders. "Jagger and Leo are outside, and Ezra is in the living room. I'm happy to give you the space you need to relax with your friend and have some fun, but if you need any of us, you know where we are," he whispers against my earlobe, and I nod subtly in response.

One thing that worried me about being here for the party was who would be hanging off the guys. I know they're all about laying their claim now, but I haven't been to a single one of these parties that hasn't ended up a disaster. Most of which involved the perky fucking redhead with her claws in Jagger.

I can only fucking pray that she isn't here tonight because I don't think I can handle that again.

"Okay, thanks," I respond, looking up at him as his fingers stroke over my collarbone, and I feel my skin heat under his touch. Wetting my lips I force myself to take a step forward, making his arm drop from my side as I turn to Naomi, who is already looking at us with curiosity.

It's not a secret, and I don't plan for it to be, that these guys are mine, and I'm not embarrassed about it. I'm sure there's going to be catcalls and slurs in my direction, but I'd take them all on for the end goal, and that's them.

But tonight is about me letting my hair down and taking a breather from all the stressful situations that've been going on around us.

"Will you be outside at some point too?" I ask, looking back over my shoulder at him, and he shakes his head.

"That's not my job for the night, babe. But if anything changes, I'll let you know," he answers, and I don't miss the subtle way he readjusts himself through his joggers as he moves back around to the other side of the kitchen island.

Fuck I wish I could take care of that for him right now.

Reluctantly, I offer a simple nod, and head for the backyard, falling in step with Naomi as we head out into the night air. It's a little after ten, and it's cold as hell, but with all the bodies here it's not as overbearing as I was expecting. I'm still glad I wore tights though.

There's a couple of people to our right playing beer

pong, and I spot Leo among them, but I'm not really feeling up to it, so I opt to walk the long way around the people dancing in the middle of the grass, to find an empty table and chairs.

The music isn't as loud back here, but there's still a good view over the entire space. Although it takes me a second to find Jagger at the very back of the yard with a couple of guys I don't recognize. I don't know what he's saying to them, but they look completely invested in whatever it is.

"So, what's been going on with you?" Naomi asks as I drop down into the white plastic chair and place my glass on the matching table. I turn my attention her way, rubbing my lips together as I remind myself to be careful about what I say around her.

As much as it might all be in my head, I know to trust my gut on some level.

"Nothing much, I've just had a lot of assignments and some family stuff going on, but otherwise I've been relaxing," I respond, lifting my glass to my lips and tasting the delicious drink as she quirks an eyebrow at me.

"And by relaxing do you mean fucking?" she asks with a wag of her eyebrows, pointing back over her shoulder toward the kitchen so I know she's referring to Jameson.

I can't stop the grin from running across my lips, even as I tell myself to keep my mouth shut internally. "I don't kiss and tell, Naomi, but I've definitely kept my activity levels up," I respond casually, making her chuckle as she surveys everyone out here.

"Fair enough. I thought I had done something to piss you off, but if I had, you would talk to me about it, right?" she circles her finger around the rim of her glass, her gaze not quite meeting mine, and the whole thing feels off.

I squint at her, really taking her in, from her bone straight hair to her doc martens, my gaze flicking over the corner of a tattoo peeking out under the collar of her t-shirt that catches me by surprise. I can't make out what it is, but it kind of looks like part of a Celtic sign.

I didn't know she had a tattoo, but to be fair, there's no reason for me to know, and it's never really come up in conversation. The clearing of a throat catches my attention, and I rush to meet her gaze. Adjusting her t-shirt she covers the ink as she stares at me expectantly, and it takes me a second to remember she asked me a question.

"Oh, no, everything's fine, I'm just used to my own company, and sometimes I prefer it. It's no offense to anyone else, just me taking care of myself," I finally answer with a smile. It's not a lie, but it's not the full truth either.

I do like my own company, it's my fucking safe place, but no, not everything is completely fine between us.

"For sure, I get that. But I'm glad you decided to have some fun tonight, and I say cheers to that," she responds seamlessly, offering her glass up for me to clink mine against, which I do, and we both down a couple of gulps before I place it back down on the table.

"How's everything with you?" I ask, wanting to be polite since she asked me, but also intrigued to see if she says anything out of the ordinary.

She looks up at the stars for a moment, her eyes closing briefly, before she looks back at me with an almost sad smile on her lips. "I'm okay. Stressed, a lot of family drama, and a never ending to do list, but I'm still breathing, so it can't all be bad, right?"

Her words make me pause as she quickly distracts herself with more of her vodka, and a rock settles in my stomach.

But I'm still breathing?

I don't know whether to take that figuratively or literally. I can't help but jump to the worst conclusions at the minute.

Opting not to over analyze everything, I reach my hand out, ready to distract us both with some dancing, when her phone goes off in her pocket, and she rushes to pull it out.

"I'm so sorry, I have to take this. I won't be a minute," she says, rising to her feet and dashing back inside before I can respond. I remain seated, and a little surprised for a moment, before I slump back in my seat and gulp down the rest of my drink, letting the vodka warm my veins.

Good luck trying to have a conversation in there with the music so loud.

I spy Leo over by the beer pong table still, his fitted black jeans and pale blue henley making him look like a fucking greek god as he runs his fingers though his hair, laughing and joking with someone. Seeing him smile instantly makes me grin too, and it's crazy how we all seem to have such an effect on one another.

My gaze automatically sweeps across the yard, until it lands on Jagger still at the back in the shadows talking with five or six guys, but he seems a little more heated than he did earlier. With his jaw tight and his hands fisted at his sides, it has me slightly concerned.

I'm on my feet and making my way toward him before

I even realize what I'm doing. The vodka clearly overriding my brain, but I can't complain since the foggy head I had earlier has faded with it.

Jagger is standing off to the side, so he doesn't see me coming, and I use the time to really take him in as I approach. With his black jeans, black tee, and black leather jacket, he looks like a remodeled biker version of an avatar from the Matrix. He looks delicious, especially with his hair twisted into a bun. It makes me want to snap the hair tie to release his wavy hair and run my fingers through it.

I wonder if I could add to the deal that he doesn't get to open his mouth and say something asshole-ish, that way there's no chance of the moment being ruined.

Slowing my pace as I get within a few feet of them all, I immediately feel the tension rise and the atmosphere cloud as Jagger growls. "I don't give a fuck what the Vulture's crew say or fucking do. If you want to be onboard with the Arrows, then this is what we do. Put up, shut up, and get the fuck on with it. I have plenty of other guys desperate to swear allegiance to the Arrows and proudly wear the mark if you don't want to."

I pause, gaping at him as I try to process his words, and ever so slowly, it's like everything clicks into place in my brain.

This is their secret.

This is what they've not been telling me.

The Arrows?

I don't know who or what the fuck they are for sure, but my gut tells me they are another gang. I thought this shit had all been left behind in Nevada, I'd prayed for it to be forever a distant memory. For all of us.

"The Arrows?" I ask, loud enough to be heard above the music as I watch Jagger's body language. If I thought he was tense before, I was mistaken.

The sound of my voice saying those two words makes him practically turn to stone as he grinds his jaw. "Get the fuck out of here, report back by two, no later, or you're gone," he finishes, ignoring me as he addresses the little bitches that stumble over their own feet to adhere to his words. His order.

Fuck.

I fold my arms over my chest as my heart pounds rapidly, for what feels like an eternity as I wait for him to turn and face me.

With every passing second I get angrier, and it pisses me off even more when he waves his hand at someone first before he turns around, finally giving me his attention.

His brown eyes are like black pits as he glares at me, his eyebrows knitted together as he works his jaw, but he flicks his gaze away for a split second before focusing back on me.

"Cat got your tongue, Jagger Izaro? Or are you trying to think of an excuse for what I just heard?" I say sarcastically, quirking an eyebrow at him as he plants his hands on his hips.

I barely restrain myself from tapping my foot like a petulant child as he continues to glare at me for a moment longer. I'm about to ask the question again, when an arm slings around my shoulders, and I look to my right to find Leo beside me with a wide grin on his face.

"Hey, Lucy, do you want to—"

"No. Whatever it is, the answer is no," I interrupt, my blood simmering with red hot anger below the surface.

Jagger clearly fucking waved Leo over here as a distraction. That's what he was doing.

Motherfucker.

Glancing between them, I see the uncertainty, and it makes my hands ball into fists as I tighten my arms around myself. Taking a deep breath, I look up at Leo with a forced smile on my lips. "If you want to do anything with me, Leo, maybe you could explain who or what the Arrows are."

The color drains from his face as he looks between Jagger and I, his mouth falling open in surprise as he tries to find something to say since Jagger left Leo to flounder all on his own.

"I… well we could, uh—"

"Oh fucking save it," I hiss, shoving my elbow back into his stomach so he releases his hold on me, and he bends forward slightly as he grunts in pain. "The fuck, Luce," he gasps, looking up at me like I'm crazy, and it takes everything I have not to knee them both in the dick right now.

"Look, Luella," Jagger starts, pulling my attention toward him, but I can tell by the stern look on his face that he's not going to tell me anything, and it only infuriates me more.

"Let me stop you right there. I don't want to hear your shit, I really fucking don't. If *the Arrows* are what I think they are, then you have a lot of fucking explaining to do. If that's the big secret you've been hiding from me, then you deserve a swift fucking throat punch for being a bunch of lying assholes." My chest heaves as my hands fall to my sides and I look at both of them in desperation, but all I see in response is guilt.

"Lucy, it's—"

"No, you don't get to speak, neither of you do," I interrupt again, but I really don't fucking care. "You've all done enough talking without saying anything that matters, and I'm fucking sick of it. I've been patient, allowed you to drip feed me information, but enough is enough," I shout, taking a few steps forward so I can turn and face them better. Brushing the loose tendrils of hair back off my face, I try to take a calming breath, but it's useless. "If you want to claim me, be with me, make this all a fucking thing, then you need to be open, honest, and truthful with me. You can't keep gangs and shit like that a secret from me, not after our history. This is a fucking hard limit for me."

They both stare at me, trying to anticipate my next move or what I may say next, and that irritates me too.

"Luella, you're being ridiculous," Jagger growls, rubbing the back of his neck as I laugh at his words.

"No, no I'm really fucking not. You make me act like a petulant fucking child. Making me want to stomp my foot in a tantrum with frustration. I'm not this bitch. I'm not fucking hot and cold all the time. I'm Luella Carter, confident and badass to the bone, and you turn me into this," I respond, throwing my arms out wide, looking at Leo for his insight too, but he just runs his hands through his hair like he's still thinking everything over. I'm obviously not going to get what I want out of these two, not right now anyway. "Fuck you both," I state, my voice laced with venom as I turn on my heels and head for the back door, trying not to bump into anyone or make eye contact as I go.

Fuck. Fuck. Fuck. Fuck. Fuck.

I'm doing it again, letting them get the better of me, but I don't know how to control all of the fucking emotions swirling around inside of me. It's infuriating. Which only makes me mad at myself as well as them too.

Swiping a hand down my face, I pull my phone to message Naomi and see where she is, but there's already a message on my phone waiting from her.

Naomi: I'm so sorry, girl, I had to bail. Family issue as always. Speak soon.

I sigh as I slip my phone back into my pocket, and step inside the kitchen where my eyes instantly fall to Jameson.

The way his eyebrows scrunch together tells me he can sense something is wrong, and he's moving toward me instantly.

"Hey, what's wrong, Ella?" he asks, bracing his hands on my shoulders as he stops in front of me, but it does nothing to stop the scathing look I give him.

"Nothing would be wrong if you'd like to explain the Arrows to me," I state as calmly as possible, and his hands instantly drop from my body as he curses under his breath.

Typical.

His pleading eyes do nothing to calm my anger, and I hate myself even more for expecting anything different from any of them.

Screw them all.

I need to get my head on straight and start remembering the strong-ass woman that I am. Back in White River I would never let anyone get away with shit like this, I guess that's because no one there was actually *them*. But still, I know my fucking worth, and if gangs are involved, I deserve to know the ins and outs. Living here, with them, puts me at the heart of it all, and I refuse to be blindsided by both Robbie and gang life.

Fuck that.

"When one or all of you are ready to explain, I'll be fucking waiting," I growl, and with that, I turn for the stairs. The people part down the center like they can feel my fucking rage and don't want to be in the way of my war path.

At least they can acknowledge my fucking feelings. It's just a pity the guys who *really* need to take note, seem to see me as a child.

No more.

No fucking more.

CHAPTER ELEVEN

Lou-Lou

*L**ift, extend, protect, repeat.*
Crouch, lean, kick, swipe.
Lift, extend, protect, repeat.
Crouch, lean, kick, swipe.

Going through the motions of alternating between my arm and leg movements, I repeatedly pound into Keith as he holds the protective pads in front of him. He doesn't say a word, the smile on his face letting me know he's more than happy to feel the power of my strength through the cushioning.

He's an OG pro, this is nothing to him, and he loves to use me as an example to the other trainees in times like these. Showing my strength, stamina, and determination over and over again.

Fuck, I can already feel their eyes tearing me to shreds as I continuously hit the pads with precision. My back and temple are dripping with sweat, but that's all worth it as my muscles scream.

I'm so angry, so fucking annoyed with the guys and their bullshit. I was restless all night as I tried to sleep, having this hanging over me. Even Leo didn't attempt to slip into my room last night, it's clear a line has been drawn. The kings versus their queen and now it is up to them whether they cross it or not.

The Arrows.

It's a gang. I fucking know it, and the fact they didn't immediately tell me I was wrong is all pretty close to admitting the truth. I know the secret now, but if I want details, it's only going to come from their mouths.

"Look at the form of her leg extension. We've been at this for over twenty minutes, and it hasn't faltered once," Keith says, his voice booming around me and pulling me from my thoughts as I don't stop the repeated action.

I can hear a few guys grumbling among the small audience we have going on, but I pay them no attention. I don't care whether they're interested or not, I don't care if they learn anything from me or not, I just want to hit something without consequence, so here I am.

"Can we get back to our own shit now?" someone hollers back, a few murmuring their agreement throughout the gym, making Keith shake his head.

"One thing you need to understand, boys, is I'm the fucking boss. If you want to learn, you do it the way I say. If your masculinity hinders you from being able to see raw talent right in front of you, then this isn't the sport for you," he shouts, and the room falls back into silence again, everyone shutting the fuck up while the quiet R&B song plays in the background.

"Two more rounds, old man, then I'm done," I mutter, my body aching from head to toe, but at least my brain isn't in overdrive anymore. I feel calmer, my head feels clearer, and I know what I want. It might not make the guys happy, but fuck, that's not a priority in this situation right now.

"Girlie, you've lasted longer than even I thought you would. It seemed like you had a little chip on your shoulder when you walked in here today, so I thought I would give you the space to do what you needed to do," Keith replies, making my eyes widen in surprise as I continue to kick and punch at his pads.

I'm beginning to learn that Keith is damn good at reading people, including my stormy mood. It's still a pity the guys can't fucking see the change in my attitude for themselves.

I have no idea what time it is. I snuck out of the house at seven this morning, knowing full well if I happened to run into one of them, then they'd likely make me go down into the basement to train. I just don't want to give them the opportunity to gloss over shit. I want every drop of information. All of it.

If I jumped on the mat with one of them, they'd think they had managed to shut me up, and I'm far from being ready to quieten down.

As I reach out with the last leg extension, I plant my foot firmly on the ground and brace my hands on my knees as I suck in every ounce of air I can.

"Thanks, Keith," I manage to murmur as he tosses the pads down on the mat, and turns to address the crowd of wannabe fighters.

I don't wait for his response, I don't expect there to be one, so I quickly slip out of the ring on the other side as Keith starts handing out orders.

Grabbing my towel and bottle of water, I pat the sweat from my face as I make my way to the locker room.

I feel a couple of glares in my direction from the guys on the weights at the far right of the room, but I just stand taller, pushing my shoulders back as I walk with confidence.

Cringing at the location of the gross girls locker room where I stored my bag, I push against the door and step inside. The quicker I can grab my shit, the quicker I can get back to the house and shower because there's not a chance I'm doing it here.

I let the door swing shut behind me as I take a deep breath, but the clearing of someone's throat instantly has me freezing in place. Flicking my gaze toward the bench area, I find myself face to face with the current villain in my life.

Robbie Izaro.

Fucking perfect.

A sneer transforms his lips the second he realizes I've spotted him, and he stretches his legs out, crossing them at the ankle as he links his hands together. It's still so strange seeing him in a suit, tailored perfectly too, and sitting in a grimy as fuck locker room, but he's still the same man underneath. My hatred toward him is even worse now I know he sexually assaulted my mom all those years ago.

It makes my blood boil. Knowing he has a connection to Lola as well only deepens my anger. He shouldn't get to be in her life, I'd prefer him as far away as possible.

"Any reason you're in the girls locker room, Robbie?" I ask casually, keeping to the right side of the room where I left my belongings.

He scoffs, his eyes roaming over me from head to toe as he runs his tongue over his teeth, and it makes my skin crawl.

"I wanted to see how my Luella was doing now that she's been to see her mother and meet her baby sister," he says with a fake smile, rubbing his hands over his knees as I clench mine at my side in anger.

My adrenaline spikes as my heart starts to beat faster in my chest, and my pulse rings in my ears. I'm desperate to lay into him, rip him to shreds for even thinking about Lola, let alone acknowledging her to me, but I know that's what he wants. It's what he always wants. A reaction. It instantly reminds me of Jagger's words a few days ago.

"Robbie doesn't get to see my wrath until I say so, when it's on my terms."

Fuck.

That makes a hell of a lot more sense right now because I feel the exact same way.

"I'm doing just fine, Robbie. Is there anything else? I have things to do," I respond casually with a shrug as I lift my backpack over my shoulder and look at him expectantly.

He taps his fingers on the wooden bench beneath him a few times as he eyes me, but he doesn't say a word until he rises to his feet, taking a step toward me, and my defenses immediately rise.

Come at me, motherfucker, I'm ready to take you down.

My muscles scream with every slight move I make since I overworked myself in the ring with Keith, but I'd push through it all to cause this man physical pain. I actually hate that he's here, that he likely saw me in the ring, and knows I can move. I would have appreciated catching this asshole by surprise when it suited me.

Dammit.

"I'm trying to decide where you fit in the grand scheme

of things in Emerson Grove," he says, tapping his finger against his lip as his eyes continue to burn my skin with each passing gaze.

"You don't need to worry about me in the grand scheme, Robbie. I don't fit in it, and that's absolutely fine with me," I respond, pulling my other arm through the strap of my backpack so it sits perfectly against my back, in case I have to block any advances from him.

"Ah, but that's where you're wrong, as always." He takes another step toward me, and I force myself to remain looking unfazed on the spot, but if he reaches his hand out now he'll be able to touch me, and that thought alone has my skin crawling with disgust and anger. "You see, everybody serves a purpose for me, for my advantage. For you, I have two options, be a member of our perfect little family, or run jobs for the family business. I couldn't give a shit if the boys have you doing something for the Arrows, that's inconsequential to me. I'm the boss around here, I'll be on the council soon enough, and will have enough power to influence what happens in this town. So, it would work in your favor to be an asset and not an enemy," he states proudly, just as his hand reaches out to touch my shoulder.

I want to snap his fucking fingers off first, stop him from fucking touching me, and I make a mental note of that for when the time comes and he *does* get to see and feel my wrath.

"I really don't care to have any part of it. Not your perfect little family or your family business. Really, you are not my family, so I'll politely decline," I say, forcing a smile to my lips as I try to unclench my hands at my side, but this guy really riles me up by trying to control me.

"Tut, tut, tut, tut, tut," he starts, taking another step closer so we're toe to toe as he wags his finger at me. "You see, that's where you're completely mistaken because you don't get a fucking choice, just like the boys don't. They brought you into the fold, it's only fair I treat you the same as them." His fingers tug on a loose piece of my hair as he sneers down at me, and my mouth dries with anger and annoyance.

I stall a moment, my response unsure on my lips as I consider whether or not I should just fucking pacify him so I can get out of here, or stand my goddamn ground like I want to do. The second he starts trailing his fingers down my arm, I know I've had enough and my decision has been made.

Grabbing his wrist, I meet his gaze with a fiery glare, and when he lifts the other hand in surrender I push the one in my hand away.

"This conversation is done. Don't fucking touch me. Ever," I bite, taking a step away from him, maintaining eye contact the entire time as I head for the door behind me. I refuse to turn my back on this asshole.

"But I thought we were getting along so well. I could bump you up in the family picture to be my wife if you like? You'd look excellent in place of your mother," he purrs, licking his lips, and I scoff.

"I'd rather fucking die," I grind out, wrapping my hand around the door handle as he instantly drops the smarmy look from his face and glares at me.

"You think you get a say? I can have you do whatever I please. I can *make* you my bitch however I please. *Make* you jump whenever I say, have you ask how high ever so politely so I don't crush what you love. I could *make* you work a pole in some shitty strip club making peanuts while I got all your tips if that's what I fucking wanted," he hisses, his face getting redder with each word. "There still needs to be repercussions for the fact you made Jagger go against my orders at the fight too, let's not forget about that," he adds, his eyes getting darker as my pulse rings so loud in my ears I barely fucking hear him.

"I'm sure you'll stay true to your cuntish ways, Robbie, you always do," I say, my voice far too sarcastic for my own liking as I swing the door open, temporarily blocking him from view, and I use the distraction to get the fuck out of there.

Moving as fast as I can without running like a bitch, I cut through the distance between me and the exit in record time, bursting through the main doors in a flurry as I try to catch my breath.

I need to get back, and finally talk this out with the guys. Having Robbie show up at the gym, even mentioning the Arrows so casually like he assumes I fucking know, along with my mom and Lola, I'm ready to gut him alive.

I hate feeling like this, like my skin is itching on the inside, and it's because I don't know how to resolve the situation.

Brushing my hair back off my face, I head straight for my truck, the huge thing sticking out for miles in the parking lot. Everything else is a random piece of metal in comparison.

As I near, my heart rate spikes further when I notice

someone leaning against the driver's side door, but when I round the rear of the truck, I find Ezra.

Fuck.

Thank god.

He looks up as I near, a soft smile starting to spread across his face, until he realizes I'm far from happy right now, and he instantly stands tall with his eyes narrowed to slits behind his glasses.

"What's wrong?" he asks, looking me over from head to toe like I'm injured, and I almost fucking cackle.

"What's not wrong, should be the question we use here," I retort, swiping a hand down my face in exasperation. "I just had the pleasure of another visit from Robbie," I murmur, trying to contain all of the emotions swirling inside of me.

I came here to calm myself and gain some control back, and it lasted all of five fucking seconds.

Ezra absorbs my words, going on high alert as he scans the area behind me. "What the fuck did he have to say?"

I'd rather go through all of that with them together because I know if I start here I'll only have to repeat myself back at the house, and I haven't forgotten how mad I am still about last night. They've got some fucking explaining to do.

"I am driving myself home, right now. I want *every* answer to my questions, without interrupting me or deflecting. You no longer have the right to hold any details back now," I state, grabbing his arm as he tries to walk around me, and he pauses at my side.

"But, Lou-Lou, it's—"

Fuck. Fine. "He threatened to put me on a fucking pole," I growl, my face heating with anger as I glare at Ezra, watching as the color drains from his face and his jaw tightens with rage at my words.

"Over my dead fucking body," he bites, and I roll my eyes.

"That won't be necessary if you let me in, and help me understand the bigger picture," I respond, as I drop my hold on his arm. Silence surrounds us for what feels like an eternity, until he finally sighs.

"If that's what it takes."

CHAPTER TWELVE

Lou-Lou

I step into the house as Ezra holds the door open for me, and as he closes it behind me, I remain frozen in place for a moment. I already know it's going to get heated in here. It always fucking does. It's never going to be as simple as them just explaining. It's like drawing blood from a stone, but it'll be worth it though, once I have the knowledge I need to survive this fucking town and it's people.

Ezra runs his hand down my back in what seems like a silent touch of support, but I can't be sure since we spent the entire car ride home not speaking. We were both lost in our thoughts, and it irritates the hell out of me that Robbie can do this to us. If he knew, I bet he'd fucking love it too.

Asshole.

Wetting my lips, I look to my left to see Ezra already glancing down at me. "Have you told them?" I ask, dropping my backpack at the bottom of the stairs as I wait for him to respond.

He shakes his head with a sigh. "No, I thought it would be best to explain in person. The house was kind of in uproar this morning when we realized you had left," he states quietly, pushing his glasses up his nose as he raises an eyebrow at me, and I roll my eyes.

Oh boo fucking hoo.

They still found me easily enough it seems. They're either really good at guessing or they have a tracker on me somewhere. If Ezra has anything to do with it, it'll likely be the latter, but I will address that once I've had answers to everything else.

Baby steps, Lou-Lou, baby steps.

With a deep breath, I head for the kitchen where I can hear the other guys talking. I can't piece together what they're saying, their voices only just loud enough to help guide me in their direction.

The second I step through the open doorway, I find three sets of eyes on me, and they don't look happy.

Just wait until they realize Ezra agreed to tell me everything.

Leo is by the stove, making what looks like eggs and bacon as he stands shirtless with a dish cloth thrown over his shoulder. In a pair of gray sweats, with bare feet, his blond hair is damp and swept back off his face, he looks like sin.

Jagger is sitting at the table, glaring at me like even my breathing pisses him off, and I quirk an eyebrow at him. His hands are clenched as he runs his eyes over me from head to toe. In a baggy tee and a pair of shorts, he looks far more relaxed and casual than he does in his usual black on black get up. His hair is loose around his face, and if he wasn't scowling, he'd look like a dark fucking angel.

Jameson is sitting right beside him, twirling his switchblade in his hand mindlessly as he looks over his shoulder at me. His brown hair is sticking up in every direction as he yawns, likely the last one to have woken up. His tight-fitted navy t-shirt and skinny jeans enhance the outline of every muscle on his body, making me desperate to fuck this all to hell and just drag him up to my room.

Ezra clears his throat, breaking the stare off around the room as I side eye him. Rubbing the back of his neck, his mouth opens, but before he can speak, the others all start at once.

"Where the fuck were you, Luella?"

"Why do you seem to think you can just suddenly leave in the morning when there's clearly threats out there, Ella?"

"Do you know how damn scared I was when I snuck into your room this morning to find you not there, Lucy?"

Wow. Ezra was right, their minds were clearly in utter chaos this morning.

"Hi, good morning. How are you feeling today after we continued to leave you in the dark last night, Lou-Lou? Oh me? I'm barely holding it together by a thread, so I thought I'd go somewhere to kick some ass to try and settle the stress inside of me. Did it work, Lou-Lou? Well, it definitely did for the first five seconds, but my joy was short-lived when Robbie was waiting for me in the locker room, far too excited to bring me into the family business in one way or another." I smile sweetly at them as I talk higher and louder the more sarcastic I get.

It takes a moment for my words to register, and the

second they process that I've had another run in with Robbie, Jagger is on his feet and storming toward me, while Leo curses loudly, and Jameson tosses his switchblade in anger at the far wall, and I watch as it lodges into the sheetrock effortlessly.

Well then.

"This is why you don't fucking go anywhere alone. Are you stupid, Luella?" Jagger growls as he approaches, but before he can stop right in front of me, Ezra steps between us with his hand raised and halting Jagger in his tracks. "Don't stand in the way, Ezra, she needs to fucking learn that her actions have consequences. Preferably before Robbie takes her right from under our noses," he bites, glaring between us both, and to my surprise Ezra scoffs at him.

"Jagger, she's my girl too. I'll defend her against anyone and everyone, even you, now back the fuck off," his voice is harsher than usual, his body tense as he stares Jagger down, leaving me to gape at him in utter surprise.

I glance at Leo and Jameson too, who are watching the pair of them in just as much shock as I am, which tells me Ezra never usually stands his ground.

Sighing, I place my hand on Ezra's shoulder, not

wanting him to get into an argument with Jagger over me. Especially when deep down, they're right.

Obviously if I hadn't been there, I never would have had a run in with Robbie, that's fact, but I also wouldn't have been able to beat the anger out of my body either, and I was too mad to ask one of them to go with me.

Not that I'm willing to admit any of that right now. Priority number one is having the information I deserve, for the sake of my safety and sanity.

"Ezra, it's fine. He can be a baby about it all he wants, but we're going to sit at the table and hash this all out. No more secrets, no more lies, and no more thinking that leaving me in the dark is good for me because it definitely fucking isn't," I say, rubbing my thumb over the bare skin of his neck as I talk, and I feel him physically relax beneath my touch.

"That's hilarious, but I didn't agree to do shit, Luella," Jagger grunts, and I shake my head. He's always stuck in his own ways, never seeing past the end of his goddamn nose to notice how his choices and decisions impact others.

"Open your eyes, Jagger, keeping secrets isn't working, not even a little bit," I shout back as I drag my hand down the length of Ezra's arm until our fingers are laced together.

"Ezra can fucking see that, he also saw the state of me after Robbie threw a couple of threats around. I'm not safe without the knowledge, Jagger, and I refuse to live like fucking Rapunzel, trapped in this ivory tower." My chest heaves as I get more and more angry, trying to catch my breath, but it's pretty pointless.

Ezra tugs my hand, pulling me from an angry Jagger as he walks me toward the table. "Leo, Lou-Lou needs to eat. While she's devouring a plate of eggs and bacon, we can fill her in. Like I said the last time, she's right, this isn't working," he states loud and firmly as we pass Jameson, and Ezra pulls my chair out for me to take a seat. Only it's Leo's usual spot. I glance in confusion at Ezra, but he shakes his head. "It's fine, I want you near me too," he murmurs, and I drop into the seat without further question, to find Jameson already sitting directly opposite me, but he still doesn't say another word.

Moments later, a plate of steaming hot eggs and bacon is placed in front of me, and I glance to my left to find Leo taking the seat beside me, with his own plate in front of him, but his gaze remains fixed on mine.

"Things must have gone to shit if Ezra's *that* mad," he states, offering a fork out to me, and I take it with a nod. "Then we'll tell you everything you need to know," he states as Jagger scrapes his chair across the floor and takes his seat facing Ezra on my right.

"Are you not feeding us too, Leo?" Jameson asks with a pout, and it's only then that I notice none of the guys have food except Leo. I look back at him with my eyebrows raised and he shrugs with a half smile on his lips.

"I'm not your fucking lap dog, assholes. Plates are made up on the counter ready for you, get them yourselves," he grumbles, before scooping a forkful of eggs and shoveling it into his mouth.

I press my lips together firmly as I try to hold back the smile threatening to take over, but it's hard, so I quickly do the same, distracting myself with the food in front of me.

Both Ezra and Leo are willing to explain everything to me, without much question in it. Maybe it was something from last night, or the clear state of me this morning, but I'm not complaining.

The other two grumble under their breaths as they go to get their own food, and the second Jameson sits back down across from me, I know there's a question on his tongue. The way he squints at me and works his jaw like he's trying to find the right words makes it clear as day.

"Spit it out, Jameson," I murmur before taking a bite of bacon, and groaning at the deliciousness as it touches my lips.

"I wish you groaned like that when you took a bite of me," Jameson says, making a chuckle fall from my lips before I can stop it as I eye him across the table.

"If your dick went anywhere near my mouth right now, I'd likely bite the fucking thing off," I say sweetly, batting my eyes at him, which makes him gape at me and Leo laugh beside me.

"You're mad enough, Ella, that you would threaten my golden jewels?" Jameson asks wearily, and I quirk my eyebrow at him.

"After being threatened by Robbie to work a pole at his pleasure, then yeah, I'm feeling feisty today. I refuse to be a puppet on a string for him," I respond, and the fun atmosphere that had descended over us for a moment quickly disappears as they hear my words.

"He said what now?" Leo growls from beside me, and I exhale, letting the weight of the situation actually wash over me, but before I can respond, Jameson jumps in.

"How about you explain what went down with Robbie first, and then we can discuss last night and everything else," he offers, and when I meet his gaze all I see is sincerity, which makes me instantly nod in agreement. If he's willing to sound reasonable, I'm willing to play along.

Swallowing the food in my mouth, I offer a tight smile as Ezra places a bottle of water in front of me, and I busy myself opening it as I try to give them an overview of my fantastic catch up with Robbie.

"He was waiting for me in the locker room after I'd been in the ring with Keith. He wanted to 'see how my Luella was doing now that she'd been to see her mother and meet her baby sister.'" Repeating his words makes me feel sick, and I haven't even gotten to the worst part yet. "He said some shit to try and rile me up, which made me remember Jagger's words." I meet Jagger's questioning gaze as I wet my lips. "I agree, Robbie doesn't get to see my wrath until I say so, when it's on my terms."

His eyebrows raise as he nods along with me, a slight smile on his mouth as he takes a bite of bacon, and I clear my throat, focusing back on the details.

"Then he went on about trying to decide where I fit in the grand scheme of things. Saying everyone serves a purpose to him, for his advantage, and he couldn't decide if it was playing the perfect role in the perfect little family in front of the camera, or running jobs for the family business—"

"Like fuck," Jameson grunts, his eyebrows knitting together as his hands clench on top of the table, and I raise my hand to calm him down.

"He expected me to know the entire picture since he assumes I'm an Arrow," I continue, casting my gaze over the four of them with an expectant look, but none of them utter a word. "When I politely declined all options he told me I must be fucking mistaken because I didn't get a choice. You guys brought me into the fold, it's only fitting he treated me the same as he treats you."

I can feel the strain of my words affecting the room, making them angrier as I still have more to say, but if that makes them mad, I know the next bit is going to cause riots. I instinctively look to my right, finding Ezra already looking at me, and he offers a subtle nod, encouraging me to continue.

"Then when he tried to touch me—"

"The Fuck!" Leo growls, interrupting me as his chair drags across the floor when he jumps to his feet, planting his palms flat on the table.

"I grabbed his hand and told him we were done talking,

which is when he changed tactics and offered to bump me up in the family photos to his wife—"

"Over my dead fucking body," Jagger grinds out, slamming his fist down on the table and making the plates wobble.

Fuck.

I knew they wouldn't react well, but if we're going to figure this out, I need to get this over with so we can move on to the more important facts.

The Arrows.

"He stated some bullshit about me being his bitch in whatever way he saw fit, and before I got out of there he mentioned that there were still consequences for Jagger not following orders at the last fight." All that can be heard is our breathing as we all take deep lungfuls of air, but it does nothing to calm the environment. They all remain silent, continuing to stare at me, willing me to go on. I sigh, slouching back in my seat. "So, now that part is out of the way, how about you do your part and expand on everything relating to the Arrows," I say, pushing my plate away because I know I'm too amped up to eat. If they try to swing this conversation back around to Robbie, I think I might scream. I spoke first against my better judgment so we could get to this.

I fold my arms over my chest, glancing at Leo as he stays standing, but when I quirk an eyebrow he drops down beside me. Looking over at Jameson, he scrubs his hands down his face in frustration. Jagger stares off toward the back door as he grinds his jaw in anger, and when I turn to Ezra, I find him fidgeting with his hands as he tries to process everything I hadn't mentioned earlier.

"I'm sure you've assumed already, but the Arrows are a gang. Our gang," Jameson starts, and my eyes widen at his openness, and it makes my heart pound in my chest as I frantically search his gaze for more. I'm not sure what exactly, but I'm desperate to find it.

"I'll know if you don't tell me everything," I state, sitting taller, and Jameson nods in understanding as Jagger's jaw only grows tighter. I don't ask any questions or push for more information. Instead I sit and wait patiently.

This is bigger than I thought.

"When you left Nevada, and everything with Robbie and June came to light, he quickly moved them out to Lockwood, and we scrambled to follow them to Emerson Grove for Lola's sake, but she was still pregnant so we had a little time," Ezra says, folding his arms as he leans on the table. "When we couldn't find you anywhere, we focused our attention in that direction too," he admits, and it makes my heart stutter in my chest.

I wet my dry lips as I try to focus on the new information they're giving me, but my heart remains stuck on that fact. I know they eventually found me, and Jagger lied about talking to me, but to know they spent a long time searching for me? Since day one? Fuck that squeezes my icy heart.

"To get out of the tangled mess out there we had to take care of business with the locals gangs, and to do so, we had to create our own, be our own people, and run our own shit so we no longer fell under someone else's control," Leo adds as he taps his fingers on the table, and I nod along. "So when we came here, we arrived as the Arrows, just as we left Nevada. We expected it all to dissolve when we got to Emerson Grove, but somehow our reputation had traveled and all we've done is grow since then. Everything happens for a reason, and we clearly needed this to combat against Robbie. Have something he couldn't touch."

So they left the Wolves, the gang they were a part of when we were teens, to do what… start their own?

Fuck.

Searching his gaze, I see a mixture of pride and

disappointment in his eyes, and it saddens me that they were yet again forced into a lifestyle out of their control.

"Now we have people running drugs, weapons, and taking care of shit when things go south. But we're most popular for our clean up crew. Is that what you wanted to hear, Luella? How fucking criminal we are? How we fuck the law and do what needs to be done? Is that going to help you sleep at night?" Jagger grinds out, his eyes darkening as they search mine, and I swallow past the lump in my throat as I force myself not to crumble under his harsh gaze.

"What Jagger is trying to say is we protected you when we were kids, and that's not stopped since you got here either," Leo murmurs, trying a softer approach, but I just shake my head.

"Not specifically, but the shit you just listed off isn't rainbows and sunshine, which you know. I deserve to understand what's going on around us, what troubles we could face. How can you think I can continue living here without all the information?"

Ezra squeezes my thigh, but I keep my gaze fixed on Jagger, and I gape in surprise when he breaks eye contact and glances down at his lap.

"You're right," Jameson interjects as my eyebrows rise in surprise.

Fuck.

I mean, I know I am, but for one of them to admit it feels good.

"The main concerns are with the rival gang on the other side of town called the Vultures. When we arrived and realized we couldn't just slip into normal life, where we focused on June and the baby, we overran the gang that used to cover this side of town, which only pissed the Vultures off because they'd been trying to do it for years. But instead they ended up with a harder competitor," Leo states with a shrug, like it's nothing, and my eyes continue to widen.

"Are there any active issues with them right now?" I ask, relaxing into my seat as I try to get the full picture.

"Well, there's a lot of controlled fights, street races, and other organized shit for money, but things have been escalating with the—"

"That's enough, Jameson, she doesn't need to know all of that shit right now," Jagger interrupts, and the twins stare each other down in a silent argument.

Right now. I've listened to enough to have a better

understanding of everything, and if I'm honest, Jagger put the brakes on things much later than I actually expected. I need to choose my battles, and wrap my head around everything they've just said.

"I'm not a toddler you're trying to teach to eat from a spoon. If you want all of me, all of this that we're tiptoeing around, then you have to compromise too. You keep giving me a little and I keep accepting it like a love sick puppy, but I deserve more than that, and I can't keep doing it to myself." No one says a word, the stilted energy sitting heavy around us. Shaking my head in disappointment I sigh. "Is there a tracker on my phone or truck or something?" I ask, ignoring the guys glaring at each other across the table as I look to Ezra who instantly sits back in his seat and clears his throat.

"How about both," Jagger barks, clearly taking his anger out on me as Jameson slams his fist down on the table.

Of course it's both, and of course he finds the words to respond when I change the fucking subject.

My fight or flight mode is in full swing, and to my surprise, I need space.

I'm done with this shit right now. I can't even bring

myself to grill them over somehow tracking my phone.

Motherfuckers.

"Is there anything else you'd like to share with me?" I ask, looking each one of them in the eye as they shake their heads in response. "Good, then I'm taking a fucking shower," I add, rising from the table, but I barely take two steps when Jagger's voice booms around the room again.

"We haven't finished talking about the fact you hightailed it out of here this morning. Alone," he states, and I glance over my shoulder to see him staring at me expectantly, and I roll my eyes.

"You can either shut the fuck up and get over it, or follow me, but either way I'm washing the grime of the day off of me right now," I respond, puckering my lips at him sarcastically, before dismissing them all and marching for the door.

It isn't until I'm halfway up the stairs that I hear the scrape of a chair, and heavy footsteps heading my direction.

Fuck.

Picking up my pace I fucking run the rest of the way, but as my hand wraps around my bedroom door handle, and I turn the key in the lock with the other, a body presses up against my back, pinning me to my door.

"Have it your way, Luella, let me in."

CHAPTER THIRTEEN

JAGGER

My heart pounds as she rises from the table, knowing my father had Luella in his grasp earlier is playing havoc with my mind.

"We haven't finished talking about the fact you hightailed it out of here this morning. Alone," I blurt out, needing something, anything, to keep her with me for just a little longer. I may be selfish, but fuck her alone time. She doesn't get to think or whatever it is she does.

I need her in my company. *I* need to feel her presence, and *I* want to hold her close, out of harm's way. Forever.

I can feel the guys glaring at me as I make her pause, probably not liking my choice of words, but fuck them too. Luella knows I'm an asshole, that has never changed so why pretend I'm anything but?

She glances over her shoulder at me with a dramatic roll of her eyes, and I instantly see the sass on her face as her mouth opens. "You can either shut the fuck up and get over it, or follow me, but either way I'm washing the grime of the day off of me right now." She puckers her lips at me, before waving her hand dismissively and heading for the stairs.

I remain frozen in place, my hands clenched in my lap as I stare at the empty spot she was just in. Leo clears his throat, giving me the immediate feeling that he's going to chase after her, and I'm going to nip that in the bud before he starts to steal my idea.

Abruptly standing from my seat, the chair scrapes along the floor as I flip the other guys the bird, and storm after her. I don't slow my pace or the determination in each step, and a grin begins to transform my lips when I hear her starting to run.

I love a little game of cat and mouse, and my cock *definitely* does as it strains against my waistband, desperate for her.

Reaching the top of the stairs, I see her fumbling with the door handle, but before she can swing it open, I press up against her back, pinning her sweet body between the door and me.

Fuck.

Tilting forward, I brush my lips against her ear as I murmur to her. "Have it your way, Luella, let me in."

Silence falls over us as her shoulders rise and fall with every breath she takes, trapped in this moment with me as she tries to decide whether to let me in or not.

I don't utter another word, letting her make the decision all on her own, and when I hear the sound of the lock clicking my heart starts to beat faster, my body thrumming with need as my pulse rings in my ears.

She's either going to swing the door open wide and let me in, or she's going to squeeze through the smallest gap so she can slam the wood in my face. But she knows I'm not like the others either. So if she chooses the latter option, I won't stand here and try to worm my way in, no matter how much I need her right now. But if she does let me in, it's not going to be pretty. We're both too amped up for that. The way we both control our anger and rage isn't all that different, which will only make us even more explosive.

All at once Luella swings the door open wide, letting it slam against the wall dramatically, as always. That's my cue, my sign, and when she takes a step forward, I'm hot on her heels. As the door slowly swings back in the other direction again, I hook my foot around the back of it, kicking it all the way closed with a bang, loving the way it echoes around the room before silence descends on us again.

I stop where I am, planting my feet shoulder width apart as I fold my arms over my chest, when she whirls around to face me. Her eyes have turned to slits, her face red with fury as she clenches and unclenches her hands, trying to find the right words.

Wetting my lips, I quirk an eyebrow at her as I wait for her to make the first move.

"What do you want, Jagger?" she finally bites out, placing her hands on her hips.

My lip turns up at the corners as I give her a pointed stare. "I thought that would be obvious, Luella. I want you."

No dodging the truth, no sweetening my words, just

straight to the fucking point.

Her eyes widen slightly as she taps her fingers on her waist, drawing my attention down, and it has me desperate to have my fingers wrapped around her too.

"Do you think you fucking deserve me when you treat me like a child?" she hisses, nipping at her bottom lip as she searches my gaze.

Rolling my eyes, I brush my loose hair back off my face. "Luella, there's a huge difference between wanting to protect you and treating you like a child," I respond, making her scoff.

"You seem to keep forgetting the fact I was all on my own because of something *you* did for the past three years."

Her words confuse me for a moment, making my brows knit together as I look her over, until I realize she's talking about the lie I told the guys.

Fuck.

I still haven't given her the whole truth.

"Luella, you may have thought you were on your own, but ever since the first time we spoke to David and I came looking for you, I made it my personal mission to make the trip every other week to White River to check on you. I just… I could never get too close, for your own safety," I reply, another truth seamlessly falling from my lips again.

She takes a step toward me, her finger raised and pointed in my direction as she shakes her head. "Don't feed me bullshit now, Jagger." Her finger jabs against my chest as her blue eyes swirl with a whirlwind of emotions that I can't separate to understand right now.

"I'm not, Luella. The reason I fucking ran, leaving you there with that cunt of a brother of yours, was because Robbie was already watching *me* watch *you*. He threatened me with you, so I did what I always do and protected this fucking family." My tone is harsh, my words real as I watch her gape at me, trying to process what I just said.

"You're lying," she grinds out, pushing both hands against my chest in annoyance, but I don't move an inch as I let her unleash the emotions overspilling from her body. "I'm sick of you locking me in a fucking box and tossing away the key. I'm not a toy to be played with whenever you see fit," she continues, loose tendrils of hair falling around her face as she keeps pushing me, but I just raise my eyebrows at her.

"I'm not lying about this, it's the truth whether you can believe it or not. And you're not a toy. Fuck, Luella, we both know I'm a cunt, it's not a secret, but when it comes to you, you make it all worth living for. So I will *always* do whatever it takes to keep you safe."

My heart races in my chest, my body desperate to reach out and touch her, knowing the feel of her skin against mine will instantly calm my soul.

"I hate you," she hisses, pushing harder against me with her palms flat against my chest, and hearing those words slip past her lips burns me.

Fuck this.

If she wants to hate me, I'll give her something to hate me for.

Reaching my hand out, my fingers wrap around the front of her neck, I flex my grip, watching the surprise wash over her face as I wrap my other hand around her waist. Her hands remain pressed against my chest as I turn on the spot, spinning her with me, and plaster her against the door.

The thud that sounds as her back hits the wood has a wave of pleasure rippling through my body, and the way her mouth is wide open and her pupils dilate makes my cock twitch.

She liked that.

Before she gets the chance to tear me to shreds with her

sharp tongue, I move in closer, towering over her as I keep my hand around her throat, but I don't choke her. I simply lean forward, searching her gaze before I press my lips to hers, kissing her so hard she doesn't know whose air she's breathing.

Her lips mold to mine as her fingers curl into my t-shirt, pulling me in closer against her, before one hand finds its way to my hair.

We're a complete mess, starved for each other's lips as we fight for control between the two of us.

We might be angry, we might be pent up with fury, but unlike the last time I was in this room, this isn't a rage fuck. This is desperation. This is need. This is us.

Reluctantly releasing my grip on her throat, I feel her whimper against my mouth in protest, which makes me smile against her lips as I wrap both hands around her thighs and lift her off the ground.

Luella's legs instantly wrap around my waist, her arms tightening around my neck as she tugs on my hair, and my cock grinds against her core.

Subconsciously I want to take my girl downstairs, spread her out on the dining room table and fuck her while my brothers watch, just like Jameson did when he locked us outside. But truthfully, at this moment, I just need her, pressed against my body and consuming my mind.

If we were in my room, I could use my...

Fuck yeah.

Blindly searching for the door handle, I hold her against my body as I take a step back and let the door fall open. I reluctantly pull my lips from hers so I can see where I'm going, and she doesn't seem to mind as her lips trail down my neck, nipping and sucking as I go.

I don't stop her, not when she's fucking marking me, claiming me right back, even if she doesn't realize it.

Moving to the farthest door on the left, I push my bedroom door open and slip inside, slamming the door shut behind us. Luella's onslaught on my neck is quickly cut short as she lifts her gaze to look around the room.

I watch as she wets her lips, twisting her head around to see the whole room, and I try to see it through her eyes. With the pale gray walls, it's likely much lighter than she expects for me, but the deep emerald green balances the room in the furnishings. Apart from the bed that sits central on the right wall, there's access to my en-suite and walk-in closet to the left, with the window brightening the room straight ahead.

My desk to my left sits tidy and organized with all my college work, but other than that, there's not much in here that says this room belongs to me. It never really has. I don't need my own space, I just need hers, so why waste time making this room out to be something it's not?

As her gaze swings back to mine, I can see the question in her eyes and the hint of sadness at the lack of personality here, but I take two steps toward the bed, tossing her down on the mattress before she can speak.

"Ahh, Jagger," she squeals as she bounces a few times on the bed, her blonde hair becoming even more loose on her head as her sports bra restricts the bounce of her tits, and I almost pout at missing out on the motion.

I don't respond as I take slow, measured steps toward the bottom of the bed, pleased when she shuffles around until her head is up by the pillows. She props herself up on her elbows, tracking my every movement, and I waste no time pulling my t-shirt over my head, making my intentions more than clear as a smile breaks out across her lips.

Turning around, I discard the t-shirt on my desk chair, before pulling my shorts down quickly and tossing them in the same direction. As I glance back at Luella, I find her sitting on her knees at the end of the bed and leaning in my direction.

What the fuck?

Her mouth is wide open in surprise as she raises a trembling finger in my direction, and I frown in confusion.

"What's wrong?" I ask, worry and concern seeping into my skin as I take a step toward her.

Her hand falls to my chest as I reach her, but she shakes her head. "Turn around," she says, barely more than a whisper, and I slowly follow her order.

This is not the interaction I was expecting when I dropped my pants and revealed my thick, pulsing cock.

I hear her intake of breath before her fingers stroke over my back, and it takes a second for me to realize what's caught her attention.

Shit.

"Luella, it's—"

"Beautiful," she finishes, interrupting my excuse and making me pause as she continues to glide her fingers across my skin. "It's just like Leo's and Ezra's. I can't believe I haven't paid closer attention to the tattoos on your back before," she adds, her fingers brushing against my skin as she leans in close, making me shiver and my cock jump.

My shoulders sag a little in relief, knowing she's seen some of the other tattoos before mine, which I think helps her remain so calm.

The vision of Leo's and Ezra's ink flashes in my mind, but I almost scoff at the comparison. Leo has a crown behind his ear with the word Lucy intertwined, while Ezra has a tattoo on his chest with Lou-Lou scrawled in it too.

But mine… fuck, mine's not quite that small.

At all.

I can recall every inch of ink etched into my skin, but this one takes pride of place. The majority of my back is covered in red roses, one for each of my brothers, Luella, and one for Lola. But in the center of it all sits my own crown with Luella engraved into it too.

You can't really see it unless you get up close and really look, to the outside I look like a long-haired, meathead, tattooed asshole, but they hold meaning, and all the roses protect the crown.

"Jagger, I don't know what to say," she murmurs, making me frown, and I quickly turn to face her, leaving her hand floating in the air between us as I tilt her chin back, forcing her to meet my gaze.

"I don't want you to say anything, Luella."

Looking deep into her eyes like this, with her neck exposed and still sitting on her knees, she almost looks vulnerable. But I see the strength, the pain, and the determination to let the world feel her wrath if they underestimate her.

Like I've underestimated her.

"You're the delicate petals of the rose, Luella. Stunning, exquisite, and awe-inspiring. While we are the thorns. We make up a part of the rose, we're important to the rose, we make up the darkest and harshest parts of it, and we will defend it to our last breath."

My heart burns in my chest as the words leave my mouth, watching as Luella's cheeks redden. I drop my hand from her chin, pulling my hair back off my face as her eyes cast over me from head to toe.

On the move back up my body, her gaze zones in on my cock, and she drags her tongue along her bottom lip. The zipper up the center of her sports bra beckons me closer, and my fingers wrap around the cold metal before I slowly drag it down.

The noise reverberates around us until it falls loose, revealing her perky tits and tight nipples. She shrugs the scrap of material down her arms, before rising up onto her feet to stand on the bed. Her fingers dip into the waistband of her leggings, but I beat her to it, slowly dragging them down her legs along with her panties, revealing her pretty pink pussy.

I want to lay her bare on the bed, and take my time tasting every inch of her skin against my tongue. There's no need for words anymore, our bodies are happy to do the talking.

I'm ready to grab her ankles and toss her back on the bed, but she drops to her knees lightning fast, wrapping her hand around my dick and dragging her tongue over the engorged head before I can even blink.

"Fuck," I hiss as she circles the tip of my cock with her tongue, teasing the length with her dainty fingers. My hands instantly find her ponytail, and I wrap my fingers in the ends. I don't force her movement, just hold on for the ride.

Her other hand moves to cup my balls, rolling them in her palms as she works the length and swallows me to the back of her throat in one swift move.

"Shit, Luella," I grind out as she hums, only enhancing the pleasure rippling through my body right now, and I know if I don't change this up, I'm going to be coming much quicker than either one of us would like.

Tightening my grip in her hair, I pull my cock from her lips reluctantly, and she pouts up at me with a glare, making me smirk.

"Let me see your tight pussy, Luella, I've fucking missed it," I murmur, and she immediately grins up at me as she lays back on the bed.

She pulls her hair tie out as she rests her head on the pillow, and my cock tenses as her hair fans out around her, making her look every inch the angel that she is. But when she plants her feet on the bed, bending her knees as she spreads her legs for me, I know I've struck gold.

Wrapping my hands around her ankles, I pull her closer, making her gasp as I stop when her feet reach the end of the bed, and I grin. Luella quirks her eyebrow at me, but I quickly bend down, blindly feeling around under the bed until I find what I need, before locking the first cuff around her left leg.

"What the—" her words are cut off as the second cuff effortlessly slips into place, and I check the bindings before looking up at her.

With her mouth wide open, her body on display, and her ankles strapped to the spreader bar, I think I could come from the vision alone.

"Jagger, I—"

"I can undo it if you'd prefer," I offer immediately, interrupting whatever it is she was about to say, but she's already shaking her head before I finish my sentence.

"No, n-no, I want it," she mutters, testing the pull of the bar as I hold it in the middle, and I watch as her eyes darken with desire too.

That's my girl.

Not wanting to wait any longer, I pull the bar up to my shoulder height, watching as her legs lift with the movement, forcing her flat on her back and giving me a better view of her core.

Swiping a finger through her folds from her clit to her entrance, she shivers beneath my touch as I feel just how wet she is. But I want more.

I sink two fingers deep into her pussy, watching as her eyes roll back in her head. I lower the bar slightly, but lift it toward her. When she opens her eyes, I nudge the bar a little closer to her. "Hold this, and don't let go," I order, watching as she tentatively takes a hold of it. "If you let go, I stop," I state, gripping the end of my cock as I really take her in.

Seeing her lay completely naked on my bed, holding the bar as it spreads her wide, I have to force myself to slow down and take a deep breath, before I simply plow straight into her without thought.

Crouching down with my knees on the floor, I grab her thighs, watching as her eyes widen, before I lean forward and run my tongue over the same path I did moments ago with my finger.

"Ahh."

The moan falls effortlessly from her lips as her legs quiver, and I almost think she's going to release the bar already, but she tightens her hold, her knuckles turning white with the pressure.

I love how she squirms beneath me as I circle her clit with my tongue, and thrust two fingers into her tight cunt. Her moans get longer, deeper as I play with her body like it was made for me.

Raking my teeth over her sensitive nub, her body tenses, and I love how my body instinctively knows how to heighten her pleasure. Swirling my fingers slowly inside of her, I repeat the motion over and over again as I dedicate all of my attention to her clit.

I can tell it's taking everything she has to keep a hold

of the bar as she braces it against my shoulder blades, and I dig my hands into her thighs.

"Fuck, Jagger. Fuck."

Any other words she was about to say are cut off as a groan passes her lips, and her pussy clenches around my fingers. Riding wave after wave of pleasure, she manages to pull the bar a little higher so it rests at my neck, allowing her to grind her pussy up against my face, making every cell in my body feel more alive.

When her body is spent beneath me, her breathing calming down as she takes lungfuls of air at a time, I lift the bar over my head, and she releases her grip, peering up at me through half-mast eyes as she grins.

"I need you inside, now," she demands, making my cock twitch at her confidence and certainty.

"Let me grab a—"

"No. There's no time for that. I need you now," she pleads, looking up at me, desperate to taste another orgasm like she didn't just ride the waves moments ago.

I just haven't… I've never…

I don't say the words out loud, but it's like she can sense them running around in my head as she nods at me. "Please, Jagger. I'm on the shot, and I need to feel you. I'm clean, I swear."

My cock loves the sound of all that, jutting out toward her as I wet my lips. She holds her hand out, and I take it immediately, letting her pull me forward slightly, before she releases my hand and swings her legs over my head so the bar is behind me again.

I thought this was a sex toy for my pleasure first? My control?

How have I surrendered control to her with the damn thing?

She taps it against my back, drawing me closer as she tilts her hips up, nudging my cock at her entrance, and I hiss at the contact.

"You're the fucking devil dressed as an angel," I grunt, her heat engulfing my tip as I sink into her core. My thighs burn as I strain, pulling back slightly against the bar as her eyes blaze into mine.

"I never said I was an angel, that's the role you four opted to place me in," she purrs, grinning up at me. "But red is definitely more my color," she adds, using much more strength as she pulls her legs in, making the bar push against my back, and my cock drags against every inch of her pussy as I find myself fully seated at her center.

My cock aches with need, desperate to thrust as I fall forward, bracing my hands on either side of her. The grin that was on her lips moments ago has gone, and is replaced by a silent moan desperate to fall from her lips as her head tilts back and her hands grip the comforter beneath her.

Fuck.

Testing the movement, I thrust a little, coming to grips with how hot she feels.

"Fuck."

"Jagger, leave your mark." Her sultry words rattle around in my mind, and I grin, more than happy to rise to the occasion.

"As you wish, Luella."

I grip her waist, lifting her ass in the air as I stand tall again, and the feel of the bar as it hits the bottom of my spine actually sends tingles down my back.

Making eye contact with her, I don't wait for any kind of words as I slam into her again and again, the sound of her moans echoing around the room and filling me with far too much joy. Her tits bounce as I pound into her repeatedly, her blazing hot pussy only getting hotter and tighter with every move.

The bed jolts, and the bar continues to smack into the

bottom of my back. I know it's going to leave marks too, but fuck, it'll be worth it.

I want to hear my girl scream one more time before I find my own release.

Moving my right hand to the small of her back, keeping her propped up in the air, I use the other to tease her clit in time with my thrusts. "Come for me one more time, Luella," I bite out, my body tingling from head to toe as I pinch her clit, and like my words were a magic switch she screams, bucking beneath me as another orgasm races through her.

If I thought her cunt squeezed my fingers hard earlier, that was nothing in comparison to the tightness I feel around my cock now. Her pleasure makes my movements slow as my pleasure ripples through my body, and I fill her with my cum.

"Holy fuck," I groan, sweat beading over my temple as I find the perfect dose of ecstasy only Luella can supply me with.

Slumping forward, we both try to catch our breaths as I blindly feel around behind me to undo the cuffs at her ankles. When I get the second one undone, the bar falls to the floor with a bang, but I pay it no mind as I focus on the beauty beneath me.

"Are you okay?" I murmur, brushing her damp hair back as she smiles wistfully up at me, and she nods. "Good, give me a second and I'll clean you up," I add, slowly slipping my cock from her core as I stand up, but mid-move I freeze, my jaw hitting the floor as I watch my cum drip out of her.

What. A. Fucking. Sight.

"Jagger!" Luella's voice cuts through the thrumming in my ears, dragging my gaze up to hers, only to find her shaking her head at me. "I can tell by the look in your eyes you love the scene before you, but could you get a fucking towel? Please," she gripes, and I nod dumbly, twirling around and looking for the bathroom like this isn't my room and I haven't used the damn thing hundreds of times.

Quickly rushing to grab a cloth, I run it under the warm water before I step back into the bedroom. Luella's hands are thrown over her head, her knees touching as she covers herself slightly. Likely to make sure I don't get distracted again, and as I lean closer she peers up at me, taking the cloth from my hands before I can assist.

I'm not saying the clean up isn't harder without a condom, but fuck me, it's totally worth it.

She shakes her head at me as she rises from the bed, taking the cloth with her as she moves to the bathroom, and I slip into a pair of black boxers. When she steps back out completely naked, I almost consider grabbing her by the waist and going again, but I can see a slight wince in her steps and bruises from my fingers on her hips are already appearing.

Fuck.

Pulling the comforter back on the bed, I grab one of my hair ties off the nightstand, twisting my hair up into a bun on top of my head, before I lay down, looking up at Luella expectantly.

"What is this?" she asks, a hint of uncertainty in her tone as she eyes me and the bed.

I roll my eyes. "Get in the fucking bed, Luella," I grumble, reaching for the remote as I turn the television on and flick to the movies section.

Without uttering a word, she grabs the t-shirt I was wearing earlier and slips it over her head, before climbing into bed beside me. As she tentatively moves to lay back on the bed, I throw my arm out, catching her neck and pulling her into my side.

Neither of us speak for a moment, trapped in this

foreign situation together as we keep our eyes fixed on the television.

"So, are we snuggling now or something?" she asks, propping her chin on my chest, and I glance down at her with a grin.

"I'm not fucking sure if I'm honest, I've never done it before, but if that's what we're calling it, then yeah, we are." She bites her lip, holding back a smile before she settles back down against my chest.

"Who the fuck are you?" she mutters under her breath, making me roll my eyes even though she can't see.

"Don't make me change my mind," I grouch, searching through the action movies, trying to act like my heart isn't pounding like crazy in my chest at the feel of her.

"Don't tell me you're trying to be nice, Jagger," she taunts, peering up at me, and I raise my eyebrows.

Nice? Maybe.

Selfish? Fuck yeah.

"Maybe. I'm not nice, Luella. I want to feel you pressed against me. I don't want you sleeping alone anymore, I don't like the distance I feel when you close your bedroom door and shut us out," I start, and she lifts to her elbow as she glares at me.

"I'm not the one—"

I wave my hand, cutting her off as I clear my throat. "From now on, if you're not sleeping with me, you're with one of the others. I don't want you on your own anymore," I state, ready for the argument that's sure to follow, and she scoffs.

"I need my space, Jagger," she rebuffs. Is that the only argument she's got?

"You can have your space, just not at nighttime when we need you. But your space no longer counts at Keith's gym. You can't go there alone when Robbie can just show up like that. Okay?"

I can't stop myself from holding my breath, preparing for her response as she stares into my eyes for what feels like an eternity.

"Okay," she finally mutters, turning back to face the television casually, and my brows knit together in confusion.

"Okay?" I ask, repeating her words in utter amazement.

"Don't make me change my mind," she retorts, echoing my own words back at me.

I keep my fucking mouth shut.

For once, even if it's only for today, I have my girl

tucked under my arm, in my room, and it feels like the world is at our feet.

If only every day could feel like this.

We have problems to address, shit to organize, but fuck all that to hell. It can wait.

WATCH ME RISE

CHAPTER FOURTEEN

Lou-Lou

"Fuck Monday mornings," I grumble to myself as I try to adjust to the lighting in Jagger's bathroom so I can do my make-up. Apparently stepping into my room to paint my face is too far away right now.

He's been like this since Saturday. That's the last time I left the fucking room. I haven't even crossed paths with Ezra, Jameson, or Leo because we've been holed up in bed. A single touch, a sharp inhale, a lingering glance, and we were diving beneath the covers and exploring each other again.

It seems like we were both happy to hide away from all the shit happening around us for a minute, and I can't deny that I didn't enjoy it. But staying locked in Jagger's room can't last forever. Not when we're juggling so much.

Twisting the lid on my mascara back in place, I place it back in my make-up bag before taking a step away from the mirror. I've kept my make-up light, my big-ass hoop earrings doing all the talking along with my cream turtleneck and leather pants.

The turtle neck is to hide the marks Jagger left, but I've seen what he's wearing today, and every motherfucker is going to see the bruises all over his neck from my mouth. The thought makes me smirk, adding an extra bounce to my step as I move back into the bedroom.

My eyes instantly fall to a naked Jagger and the crumpled sheets beneath him as he fixes his hair, grinning wide at me as I roll my eyes.

"Luella, don't tell me it isn't tempting," he murmurs, making my body tingle with all the memories.

"I'm going before you make me late for school," I declare, widening my eyes at him, which only makes him smile wider. He wets his lips, reaching his hand out for me to take, but I dodge him, running for the door. I hear him chuckle behind me as I step out into the hall, only to find my bag propped against the wall.

I giggle to myself as I grab it and make my way downstairs. I don't know if he hears my footsteps, but before I reach the bottom, Jameson appears, his eyes wide and his mouth open until he spots me. With his fitted jeans, white tee, and black jacket, he looks hot as fuck, and I hate to admit it, but watching him swirl the switchblade in his hand only excites me more.

"Fuck me, Ella. You don't get to go back in that room again. He doesn't know how to share," he says with a pout, and I shake my head. I couldn't agree more. I'm *definitely* stepping in his space again, and soon.

Coming to a stop in front of him, I squeeze his shoulder as I bat my lashes at him. "Well, that wonderful brother of yours said I was no longer allowed to sleep alone. So, I'm excited to find out who's next," I say with a wink, releasing my hold on him as I brush past.

"Wait, what? I call dibs!" he hollers, and I glance over my shoulder to find Leo and Ezra racing from the kitchen to see what he's shouting at like giddy kids.

"What are you calling dibs on?" Leo asks as Ezra smiles softly at me, and my soul feels complete having seen all of them this morning.

"Having Ella in my bed tonight, or me in hers. I'm not fucking picky," Jameson responds excitedly, a wicked gleam in his eyes as Jagger appears at the top of the stairs too.

"I want dibs too," Ezra adds, stepping closer toward me, and I almost feel embarrassed with all the attention and fighting over where I'm sleeping and with who, but shit, I fucking love it.

This is what I live for.

Fight away, boys.

Casting my gaze over them all, I wet my bottom lip, considering how this is going to go, then a thought occurs to me, making me smile even more as I clear my throat and pull all of their eyes to mine again.

"Jameson, I want to see something. If it's there and you show me, I'll stay with you tonight," I offer, lifting my bag over my shoulder as I stare him down, watching as he nods eagerly like a puppy.

"Whatever you need, Ella," he responds, moving to step toward me so we're toe to toe, and the other guys follow behind him, hovering just a step away.

"Show me your ink."

Four random words, a completely short and ominous sentence, but the second I utter them, his eyes widen and a smile spreads across his face as he holds his hand out to me.

I frown down at it in confusion, noticing the rose tattooed on his hand, similar to the ones covering Jagger's back, but when he wiggles his fingers too, my heart almost falls out of my chest.

Holy. Fuck.

There. In black ink is the crown, with Ella, scrawled into it. On. His. Motherfucking. Ring. Finger.

My mouth goes dry as my eyes flick between his and the tattoo, completely in shock and amazed all at the same time.

My brain short circuits as I try to find something to say in response, and when I lift my gaze back to his, he's smirking like a goddamn Cheshire Cat.

"Ah fuck, of course he wins," Leo grumbles, swiping a hand down his face as Ezra rolls his eyes while fixing his glasses, and Jagger chuckles.

"Such an asshole," Jagger mutters, passing the other guys to plant a kiss on my forehead and head out of the front door without another word, and if he didn't seem to be in a good mood I would have been worried something was wrong.

"Oh, he's not bothered because he kept you holed up for over twenty-four hours," Leo grumbles as Jameson laces his fingers with mine, drawing my attention back to him.

"I'm claiming you tonight, Ella," he states, and I nod, still in too much shock to respond properly as Ezra breaks the moment.

"Dibs on tomorrow," he shouts, clapping his hands.

"What the fuck? This isn't fair!" Leo exclaims, glancing around at the three of us, which only makes Jameson and Ezra laugh.

Fuck. How am I supposed to choose a favorite when they're like this?

"How about you ride to school with me?" I offer, my heart pounding in my chest as he sighs with relief and grins at me.

This feeling, with the four of them, this is what I've been desperate for. Just the five of us, out here living our best life without a care in the world and enjoying each other's company. I only wish it could last, without the outside world getting in.

Leo wraps his arm around my shoulder, pulling me away from Jameson as he heads toward the door, taking me with him.

"Bye," I call out over my shoulder, letting him take me so we're not late for school.

When I pull my truck key from my pocket, unlocking my truck, I almost expect him to tell me to get in his car, but he happily climbs into the passenger seat without a word. As I climb in, I realize it's because mine is bulletproof, so it'll always be the best option.

At least it worked in my favor.

It's only a few minutes drive away, but it's cold outside again, which I still haven't got used to. I like getting to college in comfort, it helps me start the day better.

As I start the engine, Leo turns the radio on quietly in the background, some country song coming on, but I don't mind since it's quiet.

Pulling out onto the street, Leo's hand finds my thigh, making me bite back another smile from bursting out over my lips. My jaw is going to be aching by the end of the day if this continues.

"So, you seem calmer than I expected after Saturday. Apparently Jagger really does have a magic dick, huh?"

Leo says, breaking the ice as his hand flexes against my leather pants.

"I have a lot of questions still, but after you guys finished talking on Saturday, I could feel the tension and atmosphere lift around us because you weren't holding as much back anymore," I respond honestly, glancing at him out of the corner of my eye to see him smile, relaxing back into the seat with relief. "I know there are Arrow details I won't pick up until I'm in the middle of it all, and you have no choice now but to let me in."

"Agreed."

Silence settles comfortably around us for a moment as I consider if I can ask any more questions now before class, tapping my fingers on the steering wheel as I take the next turn toward the college parking lot.

"Is there anything glaringly obvious that's related to the Arrows that I should know?" I ask, keeping my tone light so he knows I'm not bitching or grilling him for details.

"Uh, we've kept a lot away from you on purpose. I guess the main thing around you that's related to the Arrows is the Friday night parties. We have to make deals, organize business, and they give us an alibi if anything goes wrong on a run," he answers honestly, filling me with a feeling I can't quite decipher, but I know it's because he's being open with me.

That actually makes a lot of sense, and now that he's said it, I can't believe I hadn't seen it before. It's literally what we would do back in Nevada every time.

"So they're not going to end anytime soon. Noted. I can adapt to that," I respond with a soft smile as I flick my gaze his way before I turn into the parking lot, driving around until I can get the closest spot to the Augustine building where my first class is.

"You're taking this far better than I thought," he says, releasing my thigh as I pull the truck to a stop, and when I shut off the engine I turn to face him.

"I don't care what you do, or have to do, to survive. I just want to be there with you. Did I think I'd managed to get away from gang life by coming to Emerson Grove? Hell yeah I did, but it doesn't matter that we're back in the thick of it, not at all, especially when Lola is involved too, and I'm willing to do whatever it takes," I answer honestly, watching as he secures a gray hat on his head, hiding his blond hair, and I almost whimper.

"This is why I fucking love you, Lucy," he murmurs, stroking a thumb over my cheek as I look up at him.

"Always wanting to be a unit, and never wanting to be treated like a damn princess when you're so clearly a queen. I'm sorry I forgot that."

My heart pounds at his words as I wet my lips and swallow past the lump in my throat. I can't believe I'm the same girl, surrounded by the same four guys like I was last week. I hope they can see the shift in us now since they've been much more open with me.

"Are you ready to spend the next two hours in a class you don't need to be in?" I ask with a grin, leaning forward to press my lips against his before I open the truck door and step down.

I leave him to adjust himself as he climbs down too, meeting me at the front of the truck and instantly lacing his fingers with mine, making me smile.

I feel like I'm walking on cloud nine. I wonder how long this can last for?

Leaving the first class, Leo right behind me, I spent the entire time feeling Vince's death glare burning into the back of my head, but I refused to acknowledge it. The need to use the bathroom is far more important right now. We've already had enough public situations involving him, and I'd like to avoid any in the future.

As we reach the bottom step, I consider my options. I can either use the restroom here, or wait until we get to the next class, but either way it needs to happen.

Rubbing my lips together as my steps slow, I grab Leo's arm as I turn to face him. "Hey, I'm just going to run to the restroom. I'll only be a minute, alright?" I murmur, trying to not stand in everyone else's way as they pass us, but it's as if Leo stands taller, wider, purposely being an inconvenience to people.

"Wait, on your own?" he asks, his eyebrows knitting together with concern, and I roll my eyes at him.

"Stop being so dramatic, Leo. I'll be quick, and you'll be right outside," I answer, before turning on my heels and heading for the women's restroom.

As I step inside, I don't see anyone else in here as I make my way to the first stall on my left, facing the sinks across the room. Just as I reach my hand out to push the door open, I hear someone talking in a stall a few doors down, and it makes me pause.

It's not just someone, it's *Naomi*.

"What do you mean, Dax? No, that's not fair. I've already missed classes today. Get someone else to do it. How are you wanting me to work for the family business in a high position if you keep stopping my education to run stupid errands like a rat boy?" she hisses quietly.

Naomi wasn't in class this morning, I've only just realized that now, but why is she still in this building instead of going to her next one? I know she said she had a lot of family drama, but fuck, this sounds harsh.

"No, Dax, fuck that. Haven't I done enough for the Vultures?"

The Vultures?

Remaining poised by the stall in front of me, I try to remain as silent as possible, not wanting to alert her to my presence, and feeling the need to hear her conversation. I'm not usually one for snooping, but my gut tells me to remain in place. The instinct to stay was right once she said *Vultures*.

A few moments pass as the person on the other end of the phone talks to her, and I find my eyes glossing over as I stare at the white tiles that decorate the room until she speaks again.

"I'm trying, I swear, but I'm telling you, Dax, she

knows nothing about the Arrows. I'm sure of it."

My blood runs cold at her words. I fucking *know* she's talking about me.

I should have listened to my gut with her. I knew something was off with the whole Vince shit, but this? This is something else entirely. With my heart lodged in my throat, I know I need to get out of here before her call ends because I won't confront the bitch until I know the whole situation. My mood swings and rage bursts have gotten me into enough trouble in the past, and I need to learn from those situations at this moment.

Tiptoeing back out into the hall, I expect to find Leo outside by the steps leading down to the court, but to my surprise, he's waiting to my right. It catches me by surprise, making me jump as I reach out to grab him at the same time.

"We need to get out of here," I whisper, pulling him close to my chest, ready to run for it, but his brows knit together as he grips my arm, holding me still.

"What's wrong?" His voice is blunt as his tone comes across short, but I know it's because he's lost all the pleasantries and just wants to get to the point of what's upsetting me.

Here just isn't the place for this conversation. Not when she's on the other side of the door.

"Leo, not here, we need to—"

"No, Luce, whatever it is, you tell me, and you tell me now," he grinds out, his body tensing as he prepares for the worst.

I can hear the telltale sign of the restroom door being opened before I see it, and I think fast on my feet, pushing my lips against Leo's as his back hits the wall behind him. I pray with everything that I am that he takes the hint and goes with it as I sense Naomi step out.

Thankfully, Leo crushes his mouth against mine, running his tongue along my bottom lip as he consumes me, and I let him. My body thrums with desire like I've been starved for him as he cups my face with both hands, turning me to putty with his touch.

I can't physically swoon anymore.

I've lost all sense of where or if Naomi is still nearby as I melt into Leo, until he separates our lips, and I have to pry my eyes open to get a sense of my surroundings again. My heart pounds like crazy in my chest as my pulse throbs, ringing in my ears, blocking out all of the noise until he finally speaks.

"Not that I mind at all, but would you care to explain to me why you pressed your lips against mine as Naomi came out of there?" he asks, just as breathless as me, and I take a second to try and catch my breath before I even consider piecing together what happened.

My mind is a mess, and part of that is due to the world-spinning kiss from Leo, which is all my fault, but fuck it was worth it.

Peering back over my shoulder, I make sure she's definitely gone which makes Leo scoff.

"Lucy, she left at least two minutes ago," he mutters, tucking a loose piece of hair behind my ear as I try to figure out how long we were kissing for.

Fuck. That's not important right now.

Shaking my head, I look up at him. "I've had a bad feeling in my gut for a little while about Naomi, something seemed really off. But then I just overheard a conversation and I think I need to speak to you all about it," I state, taking a step back from him so I can think straight. His spicy scent is enveloping me and making my head spin when I need to focus on some serious and important shit.

"Okay. Let's get to the library now, then we can call the guys and you can fill us in. If that's alright?" he offers, and

I nod eagerly. I love that he doesn't demand to know right now when he can sense I need a minute to process, and I'm going to have to repeat myself again as well.

Lacing our fingers together with one hand, he grabs his phone in the other, tapping out a message in some group chat with the guys that I spy looking over his shoulder as he leads me out of the building and down the steps.

"Is it embarrassing that I have no idea where the library is?" I ask, huddling in close against his side as we step out into the cold, while also looking for Naomi, but she's nowhere in sight.

Leo offers a tight chuckle in response as he pockets his phone, picking up our pace as he walks toward the building to our left, a little farther around the court. His thumb runs over my knuckles in an attempt at comfort or support, I'm not quite sure, but either way, I'm still tense as hell.

Rushing up the few steps into Centennial Library, I shiver as the contrast from cold to warm washes over me. Leo holds the second set of doors open as I move inside.

It's huge. Like the entire building is the library. It looks like it's three stories high, completely open in the middle with open staircases leading off in different directions. The atmosphere feels calm and relaxing, which is the complete contrast to us right now, and I'm hoping it might be able to seep into my bones.

Leo's grip on my hand tightens as he walks us to the desk, and before we even reach it, the librarian is holding out a key for him to take, which he does, without a single word exchanged between them. Trying to hide my surprise, I follow Leo's lead as he pulls me toward the stairs on the right. He takes the steps so quickly I'm practically running beside him, until we reach the top. Doors lead off around the outskirts of the hallways, while the banister looks down over the ground floor of the library.

Letting Leo lead me to a Study Room on the far right hand side, he slips the key in the lock and swings the door open. It's only when we're fully in the room that he releases my hand. As he draws the blinds closed, I blink at how serious he's taking this, but I don't complain, it really is that important.

Crossing my arms over my chest, I glance around the room, which is simply made up of a large conference table in the middle with five black cushioned seats perfectly placed around it. It doesn't pass my observation that there's five seats for specifically the five of us, but my eyes are drawn to the filing cabinets nestled in the corner.

"Do you want to call the guys, or—"

My words are cut off as I turn to glance at Leo, only to see Ezra, Jagger, and Jameson piling in through the door.

What the fuck?

They must be able to sense the confusion infusing my brain as I space out staring at them when Leo clears his throat. "They were all on campus, and they didn't want to handle whatever this was over the phone instead of in person," he explains, and I shake my head as I wet my lips.

Now I'm doubting how serious and important this actually is.

"Hey, Lou-Lou, whatever this is, it's clearly shaken something inside of you, so even if it does wind up being nothing, at least we left no stone unturned, alright?" Ezra's calming words make a gentle smile ghost my lips as I nod.

He places his laptop down on the table while Jameson moves straight to me, moving around to my back so his chest is flush against my spine as he wraps his arms around me. "We've got you, Ella." His words make my heart soar as he kisses the crown of my head. "Whatever you're holding in, lets get it out and sorted, okay?"

Overreaction much? God, these men.

Jagger nods gruffly along with his brother as he takes a

seat at the table, and I follow suit, reluctantly slipping out of Jameson's hold to fall down into the seat across from Jagger.

Jameson takes the seat to my left, while Leo and Ezra flank Jagger's sides, giving me the space they clearly think I need. No one says a word, waiting patiently for me to figure out where to start with the whole shitshow that I can feel brewing.

Pulling a hair tie from my wrist, I run my fingers through my hair and quickly tie it on top of my head in a bun as if it's going to help me concentrate better.

"I'm sorry in advance, I'm venting, but I need to start at the beginning to try and figure it out," I ramble, and they all smile softly at me in understanding as I tap my fingers nervously on the table.

"I'm assuming it's about Naomi?" Ezra clarifies, and I nod.

"Yeah. She stayed over a few weeks ago, and everything was chill, but the next day, I thought my phone notification went off, but when I glanced it was a message from Vince to *her* phone," I start, watching as each of them sit taller and scowl, but don't interrupt me. "I thought it was a bit odd, so I put a little distance between us until the party on

Friday night. I assumed it was all in my head and I was overreacting, so when she showed up, we barely shared a drink before she took off and the whole Arrow shit went down," I state, my eyes instinctively going to Jagger's who rolls his back at me.

A hand lays on top of mine, stopping the tapping I hadn't even realized I was doing, and I glance to my left to find Jameson smiling sympathetically at me.

"What happened today, Luce?" Leo murmurs, and I take a deep breath as I look at him.

"I needed to use the bathroom before the next class, none of which I've actually done, and when I walked in I heard her talking on the phone. She mentioned something about Vultures?" My words come out like more of a question as I squint at the guys, and they all instantly glare like my words offended them.

"Fuck, fuck, fuck," Jagger chants as he rakes his hands through his hair.

"But the main thing I caught was her saying she was adamant *she* didn't know anything about the Arrows, and I think that *she* is me."

The room falls silent, but I can feel the chaos rumbling beneath the surface as Jameson squeezes my hand tighter.

"If she is a Vulture, she would have a tattoo of a Celtic symbol," Ezra murmurs, almost to himself as he whips his laptop open and starts tapping away, when a memory from Friday night dawns on me.

"Guys, on Friday, her top fell loose a little, and I saw like a quarter of a tattoo on her neck, and my first thought was that it resembled a Celtic kind of sign," my words get quieter as the reality of the situation sinks in.

Naomi is our enemy.

I let her into our house, into our *home*, and I dread to think what damage she could have possibly done behind the scenes already.

"I want concrete fucking evidence," Jagger bites, slamming his fist on the table in anger as the rest of us nod, my heart pounding in my ears as anger courses through me.

"Then we run tonight's job instead of letting the newbies do it, then we can drive by their pad on the way home," Jameson states, one hand gripping mine while the other has his switchblade flicked open as he carves into the wooden table top.

"You can't leave me out, I'm coming too," I declare, staring them all dead in the eye, ready for an argument.

"Agreed," Jagger mutters.

One word. One *single* word, and I've never felt acceptance like I do at this moment.

Nerves vibrate through my body as I rub my lips together.

I have no idea what I'm getting into, or where any of it may lead, but you can bet your ass I'm determined to be worthy of walking at their side.

WATCH ME RISE

CHAPTER FIFTEEN

JAMESON

I slow the truck, pulling in against the usual shipping container as Adele blasts through the stereo. Apparently whatever Ella wants, she gets, including control of the damn music.

It's a little after eight in the evening, making it the perfect time for us to hide in the darkness to get through the weapon exchange without anyone seeing. The shipyard is always quiet at this time, but over the summer it was difficult trying to organize everything in broad daylight, which meant we had to opt for four a.m. trips instead.

Releasing my hold on the steering wheel, I ignore Jagger sitting beside me as I look in the rear view mirror to spy Ella. With Leo to her left and Ezra to her right, she's nestled perfectly in the back seat.

When I suggested using her truck for safety purposes, she was more than happy to oblige. I really thought I was going to get a huge argument from her when I said I would be driving and she would most definitely not be riding shotgun. Again, I was wrong.

It seems she's far more level headed with this shit than I gave her credit for. Than we *all* gave her credit for.

She offers me a soft smile as she catches my gaze in the mirror, before clearing her throat. "So, what now?" she asks, rubbing her hands on her thighs as Jagger turns in his seat to respond.

"The container is dropped with goods bi-weekly, and we opt to have it collected on different dates and at different times to seem less obvious. It's usually the errand boys who do this, but since we're going to take a trip out toward the Vultures turf, it seemed fitting to give everything a quick glance over here since it's been a hot minute," he explains. It baffles me how the two of them are suddenly able to hold a calming conversation without ripping each other's heads off, but I'm glad they're finally at an understanding.

For now at least.

"So you're saying the container is filled with different weapons?" Ella clarifies, glancing around at us all as Leo turns on the overhead light so she can see better, and we all nod. "And where do they go from here?"

"That can change all the time," Ezra responds, tucking a loose piece of hair behind her ear as he smiles at her. "If we're supplying ourselves we'll take them to the safe house. If they're for Robbie, they'll go to the gym, and if we're selling them, then they go to the auction house out on Fairclough's Road."

I watch as Ella nods along with him, like the rest of us do, as I dim the headlights and Jagger gets out to do a quick sweep of the exterior before we go anywhere near the container.

"I didn't realize there is a safe house," she murmurs, looking at Leo who rolls his eyes. Of course she got stuck on that part.

"Yeah, it's a little closer to Lockwood in case we need to grab June and Lola as well, but it's never needed to be much more than a safety net," he explains, making her smile. I can feel how different it is now that we're opening up with her. It truly is making a difference now there are fewer secrets. It's like the air is clearer between us all.

I spot Jagger give the signal, and I nod, even though he likely can't see me, and I step out of the truck, leaving the other two to occupy her while we focus on loading the trunk bed. Approaching the blue steel container coded KCK, I glance through the peephole we had installed before Jagger pulls the key from his pocket, stopping at my side and quickly unlocking the padlock.

Within moments, we're prying open the steel doors and looking at two wooden crates sitting in the center of the space. Always two. Always small orders, and one is always alcohol, while the other is alcohol on top and weapons on the bottom.

Or drugs depending on what day of the week it is, but we are slowly trying to step further and further away from that. It never brings good memories from our childhoods.

The shipments are usually a two man job per crate for the errand boys, but Jagger lifts one up with ease, slowly walking back to the truck without a word as I do the same.

Fuck.

It's times like this I can admit to myself that Jagger is a little bit more built than me. It must be all that fucking hair giving him extra strength, but I'd rather die than admit it out loud.

Controlling my breathing, I follow after him, hyper aware of my surroundings, paying close attention to any sudden noises or movements as I round the back of the truck. The crate slips in perfectly beside Jagger's, who is already rushing back to the container to lock it up as quickly as possible. Leaving me to secure the truck bed cover back in place.

We always work in sync, ninety-nine percent of the time in fucking silence because our brains already know what the other is thinking. The remaining one percent usually centers around Ella, which is exactly why she is our kryptonite.

Sliding back into the driver's seat, I instinctively flick my gaze to Ella's first, to find her already looking directly at the rearview mirror in preparation. Jagger swiftly follows, grumbling some shit about getting on with it, but I don't hear him properly since I'm so absorbed by her.

With a nod, I put the truck in drive and get the fuck out of here. It's not the best thing we have to do, but it's important for us to continuously oversee what's happening with the business side.

We remain quiet as Ella continues to play the new Adele album, which we've been warned will be followed immediately with the new *Red* album by Taylor Swift whether we like it or not.

I've already decided I'm buying my girl headphones for Christmas because I don't know if I can survive listening to this sappy love or man hater music. Either that or I'm subconsciously worried I'm going to start fucking singing them.

"Have you heard anything today from Robbie?" Jagger asks, pulling my attention his way, and I quickly shake my head. Let's be real, Jagger's two minute age advantage on me has always made him the apple of my father's eye, not that I would ever wish to trade places, but I don't think Robbie has contacted me directly in years.

"We both know he'll blow up your phone when he's ready," I murmur, not wanting to interrupt the casual conversation going on in the back between Ella, Leo, and Ezra. She deserves a minute to let her hair down and chat about inconsequential shit. Especially after Saturday.

"That's what concerns me. I've heard nothing from him, and there's been no backlash over the fight, and then with all the councilman shit coming up, I thought he would be down our throats by now. Especially after his little visit with Luella too." I can see the slight touch of concern crinkling his eyes as he tries to remain as impassive as ever, but living with a cunt of a father like Robbie for all our lives makes it hard for us to react to his shit.

My fingers itch to pull my switchblade from my pocket, twirl it in my hand, feel the weight in my grip, but that'll have to wait until I finish driving. So for now, I'll just have to make do with the steering wheel. My other love, and I gain some calm from knowing my knuckles are white from gripping it so damn hard.

"It's a mind game, Jag. It always is with him. We just need to stay alert, be prepared for the worst, and protect Ella and Lola at all costs," I answer, turning the corner as I see the drop spot up ahead.

Jagger doesn't respond as he too sees where we are. Tonight, we're selling, which is always the hardest drop since money is involved, but it made sense since we are on the edge of the Vulture's turf. We're about thirty-five minutes from home, but only ten minutes from their main house.

The thought alone makes me want to break Naomi, piece by piece, for breaking my girl's trust.

Slowing down along the road, it always catches me by surprise how much this area screams the American Dream. All picket fences, two story homes, with perfectly trimmed lawns and the whole two point five kid ratio.

It just shows you that no matter where you are in the world, no matter what luxuries you think you have, you still have darkness lurking in your shadows.

The olive green house sticks out like a beacon to me as we come to a stop, and Jagger sends the usual message alerting them to our arrival. Not a moment passes before a response comes in, and Jagger shows me the screen.

Unknown: Use the garage.

I squint at the words. None of the runners had explained this change to us, so we definitely need to raise it with them when we get back, but for now I simply nod, turning the car onto the driveway which has a slope down to the garage. Nothing down there is visible unless you're specifically looking, and I want to see which motherfuckers are there, so I opt to drive head on so I can shine my lights in their faces.

"Something feels off," Ella murmurs as she sits forward in her seat, and my eyebrows knit together. I don't respond, but how the fuck can something feel off if she's never even done this with us before?

The question lingers in my mind as we sit and wait, watching as the garage door slowly opens, and when I see it three quarters of the way up, I instantly see the *off* Ella was talking about.

The owner of the house is sitting strapped to a chair with a gag in his mouth as he sobs in the corner of the room, while the leader of the Vultures, and six of his men, stand facing us, dressed in black, with their arms folded across their chest.

"Shit," Leo murmurs, pulling Ella back in her seat to try and obstruct her from view, and my hand instantly wraps around my blade like it's so desperately been waiting for.

"The fuck is this?" Jagger grunts, not moving from his seat, none of us do. We'll climb out when we're ready, not when they think they've scared us into doing so.

"We're about to find out," I respond, racking my brain for a plan as I consider Ella's presence.

Fuck.

"Does someone want to explain what's going on? Because your reaction is clearly saying this is *not* normal," Ella asks, her voice tight, but I can tell she's trying to not overreact.

"Standing dead center is the leader of the Vultures, Dax Brent," Ezra starts to explain, and Ella quickly raises her hand to pause him.

"Guys, when Naomi was on the phone she said the name Dax multiple times, I swear."

Another piece to the puzzle falls into place, only solidifying the fact that Naomi really has tried to fuck her over.

Shit.

"I don't want him to see you, Luella. We could use this to our advantage if she truly thinks you don't know anything, then we can continue to act that way, and we can find out what it is they're fucking after," Jagger bites out, not turning to face her because that would only draw attention her way.

"Whatever it takes," she responds immediately, slipping further down into her seat. I'm sure that they can barely see me and Jagger upfront, never mind the three in the back since I'm shining the light in their faces.

"Good girl, Luella," Jagger almost purrs in response, and I don't miss the way she rubs her thighs together at the gruff tone of his voice.

"Fuck me, we've created monsters," Leo grumbles, making me bite back a smile. I can't let these fuckers see me smiling when it's supposed to be serious right now.

"The four of us climb out, and I'll lock the truck instantly. I'm not worried about you remaining in here, Ella, not with all the customizations I had done to this thing. But I need you to stay as low as possible, no matter how curious you are or if you think things are going south, okay?"

The back windows are tinted and I had the rest of the windows done as much as legally possible, but I just want to be sure.

"Whatever it takes, Jameson," she repeats, and I nod in acknowledgment, before taking the lead and swinging open the driver's side door.

Jagger quickly follows suit, the two of us standing by the truck with the open doors in front of us as we wait for Leo and Ezra to pile out too. Like a set of fucking synchronized swimmers, all four of our doors shut at once, and as we make our way forward, the slight nervous jitters visible in Dax's men as we approach, I make sure to lock the truck.

It takes everything I have not to glance back, to check

on my girl, *my life*, but I know acting this way, ignoring the fact she's even here, is what will protect her.

"Well, if it isn't my lucky day," Dax declares, swinging his arms out wide, with his men flanking his sides as we come to a stop facing them. With his black hat and tracksuit firmly in place, you can't see the scars and tattoos that mark his body, but the ones on his face, the teardrops for all his little fallen soldiers are as visible as ever. "I thought I was going to have some little runner boys to fuck up, and you've gone and spoiled my fun," he says with a sneer, and I scoff.

"I didn't realize you wanted me to bring my violin and play you a little tune, boo. But if you give me twenty minutes I can at least try and find someone who gives a shit."

Every single one of them glare at me as I eye them, the two on either end holding baseball bats behind them like I can't fucking see. Pocketing my switchblade, I go to step forward, but Jagger beats me to it.

"What do you want, Dax?"

"I want you to stop fucking pushing on my territory, this is far too fucking close for my liking," he hisses, his emotions getting the better of him as the cords in his neck tighten and he loses his cool a little.

"Lines are there for a reason, Dax. Do I need to send you a fresh copy? Just because something is *close* to your side of town, doesn't mean we can't fucking operate. You're on our side of town right now. Territories haven't moved overnight," Ezra states in a bored tone, and I watch as Dax grinds his teeth in anger.

He's always going to be one of those fucking rats that wants more, to be more, to have more.

Fuck.

He's a baby Robbie in the making.

"Don't fucking patronize me, I—"

"Do you even know what that fucking word means?" Leo interrupts, pissing him off even more, and I have to rub my lips together so I don't fucking laugh. He always makes it so easy.

One of his little goons takes a step toward Leo, who instantly starts laughing as if the challenge excites him, and to my surprise, Dax throws his arm out to stop him in his tracks.

Good choice.

"How about we have a wager on who gets to have this side of town, huh? Fuck, I'll even make it a street race for you, if ya like?"

I can't stop my eyes from widening, loving the sound of getting behind a wheel the second the words leave his mouth, but it also doesn't escape me that he's trying to make it all too easy for us.

"You let me know where and when, and I'm in," I respond with a shrug, not wanting to air my concerns or seem put off. Regardless, I'll beat this fucker in a heartbeat along with whatever plan he has concocted.

I can practically hear Jagger's muscles clenching as he tightens his fists with annoyance over the whole situation as the question still lingers in the air; what the fuck are we doing with the shipment we just brought over?

"Your buy in can be the little gift you brought with you tonight," Dax announces, answering my question, before clapping his hands and taking a step back, which in turn has his men taking a step forward, practically charging at us, ready to fight.

Yes. Fucking. Please.

The guy who was standing to his left makes his way toward me, and I crouch down a little, ready for his attack as he goes to swing his fist at my face. Capturing his clenched knuckles, I pull him toward me as I thrust my fist into his face, the sound of the crunch as his nose breaks is like ecstasy to my ears.

I can hear grunts and moans around me as hit after hit is landed, but I have no idea from who or where as I focus on the other guy now coming toward me, and I drop him like a bag of shit at my feet.

All too late, I spot that he's one with a bat, and he smashes it into my rib cage before I can stop him. "Motherfucker," I grind out, rage pumping through my veins as I stand bent over, hugging my body as I try to catch my breath. Out of the corner of my eye I spy Dax sneaking up the staircase that leads directly into the house as the owner still whimpers in the corner.

Shit. I was really hoping I was going to be able to get my hands on him.

"Jameson!" Ezra shouts, gaining my attention as I look over my shoulder, watching as the guy with the bat prepares to swing for my face this time. Who knows what damage that could do, but I refuse to find out.

These cunts clearly have a death wish, and I'm more than happy to send them to their grave.

He sneers down at me, almost taunting like he has the entire world in his hands, glory at his feet, but he underestimates me. I had hoped it wouldn't come down to this, but here we are. Tucking my hand into my pocket, I have my switchblade out and open before he can even take a step toward me. Before he can even get the bat to half swing, I lunge forward, my blade exposed as I aim for his gut.

The sound of the sharp end, ripping through the material of his jacket, then his skin gives me goosebumps as he freezes in place, his mouth wide open as he realizes he actually doesn't have the upper fucking hand.

His face pales as he looks down at me, my knuckles brushing against his jacket as I hold the blade in place, and the bat falls from his hand in shock. Pulling the blade out, I watch as he scans his eyes from the bloodied knife to the blood oozing from his core.

My heart pounds wildly in my chest as I stand alert, my eyes wide as I ready myself to pounce again if needed, but to my surprise he takes a step back, then another, followed by another, before he's racing up the sloped driveway, past the truck, and out into the dead of night.

"Jameson, are you alright?" Leo asks as he comes to a stop before me, his hands on my shoulders as I slowly move to stand tall again.

I don't know what I am.

Always a mixture of numb and alive, but never sad, never guilty. Even if I have another man's blood on my hands.

Taking in the scene around me, all of Dax's men are either gone, or crumpled on the ground in pain, and a tiny part of my mind begs me to step forward and finish off the remaining. That would really send a fucking message to Dax and the Vultures.

But the only thing that holds me back is the knowledge of Ella in the truck.

Ella is in the truck.

I repeat it over and over again in my head as I continue to take deep breaths, watching as Ezra does the same, while Jagger steps around each guy, checking their pockets for anything that might be useful, but he comes up short with a shake of his head.

Wetting my lips, I can't stop my eyes from zoning in on the truck, and I'm sure I can see a hint of Ella's eye from here, but it must be my imagination because the entire interior of the car is blacked out.

"Jagger, get the crates while Ezra unties this guy. We'll wait in the truck," Leo orders, likely feeling the tremble running through my body as adrenaline continues to pulsate through me, begging for me to do something.

No one argues over his command as I let him nudge me toward the driver's side door, pulling his jacket off and offering it out to me, and it takes me a second to understand, until I remember I still have a blade dripping with blood in my hand.

"Get in the back, I've got this," Leo murmurs, holding his hand out for the key, and I nod numbly, unlocking the truck before I give them over. I wrap my hand around the door handle, but I've barely got a grip when it swings open, and a wide-eyed Ella is staring up at me.

She instantly moves back, making space for me as I fall into the seat, wincing as my ribs jolt, while mindlessly wiping the jacket over the blade. Looking her over from head to toe, I can tell she saw me, saw what I had to do to protect myself, and I wait on bated breath for the response I'm sure is to follow.

I knew this was all too good to be true with her, I knew I'd blow it in seconds.

"Give me the switchblade, Jameson," she murmurs, reaching her hand out as Leo climbs into the driver's seat, and I offer it to her without question, watching as she takes it in her hand and folds it away, placing it in the other door pocket before looking back at me nervously.

The reality is, things are only going to get tougher before we finally see the light at the end of the tunnel. Lord fucking knows I can only dream to see the day. I don't have a death wish, but I find myself on the cusp of a one way ticket to hell daily. Sometimes because of my own doing, but mostly it's situational.

I can't pretend this hasn't happened before, and I won't lie and say it won't happen again. I ready myself for the brutally honest and soul destroying words that are ready to fly out of her mouth as she lifts her hands to my face.

"When we get home, we're stealing Leo's bathtub," she states, placing a kiss at the corner of my lips as I stare at her in shock, waiting for her wrath, but nothing comes.

Not a single thing, and as the others climb in the truck too, Leo puts the vehicle in drive, heading toward home without a word, I realize it's because she accepts us.

Accepts me.

In every way, shape, and form.

That's why she's our fucking glue.

CHAPTER SIXTEEN

Lou-Lou

Will I ever stop feeling guilty that Leo has to sit through my classes when he really doesn't need to know all of this shit? No, I don't think I will, but there's no arguing with any of them over the situation. They don't want me alone, especially not at the moment, and most definitely not after last night.

Professor Forbes is going through the assignment she has set, and I feel my insides die just a little at the expectation again. I feel like I've got homework pouring out of my ears at the minute, and the struggle to keep up is real. But it just reminds me no matter how much I may get swept up in the shitshow happening around me, this is still just as important.

In the same breath, I slouch down in my seat a little more as I keep my gaze focused on the front, while remembering exactly what I saw last night. Pulling up to that house to drop off the weapons and alcohol was already surreal, but for the Vultures to be there too… fuck, I definitely felt the heat growing worse around us. It seems we're meant to sink further into the swamps of darkness before we see the light.

Dax, their leader, looks kind of like a fucking vulture. I wonder if that's where they came up with the name? He looked a bit like a weasel too. A slimy, weasley Vulture who had been dipped in grease and definitely needed burning at the stake. Even the tattoos covering his face couldn't hide that about him.

With his slick brown hair and piercing green eyes, he looked like the murderer in a horror movie. Everything about him was just… wrong.

I sat helplessly as I watched them fighting and brawling, trying to keep my head as low as possible. Then Ezra yelled Jameson's name, making my heart freeze as he gained his attention, and I wanted to scream too when I saw the guy hovering above him with the bat poised, ready to smash into his head.

All too quickly, Jameson saw the advantage he needed, and moments later, his switchblade was out and wedged into the guy. The scene before me felt like it had been put in slow motion, the array of emotions that filtered over Jameson's face left me stunned.

I repeatedly chanted over and over again that he did what he had to do, but the more I watched him, the more I realized he had no issue stabbing his blade into that man's flesh. None at all. If anything, it was like the darkness was begging to creep over him and do it again, and again, and again, until the Vulture was a bloody mess pierced with holes.

To my surprise though, he let the guy run, and when he moved up past the truck I sank further down in my seat, making sure to not be seen. What felt like an eternity passed before Leo finally walked Jameson up to the truck.

I could have sobbed when the truck door was opened and I could finally touch him, but I saw the fear in his eyes first. The fear that said he was worried I had seen what had happened, and I was going to run from him.

His eyes were tight and his jaw tense, and I knew at that moment I had to make sure he knew I was still here.

This asshole had clearly forgotten who I was, *again*, because that's not how I operate, how *any* of us here operate. With my heart thundering in my chest, I took the bloodied blade from his hand, placed a gentle kiss to the corner of his mouth and told him what I wanted to happen when we got home. When I saw the surprise in his eyes, followed swiftly by relief, it made my heart soar.

My kings may be monsters, but they're mine all the same.

If anything, watching what happened last night only cemented that truth.

"This is all for today, there's a two week turn around on the paper," Professor Forbes announces, shaking me from my thoughts as I blink rapidly and glance around.

Fuck, I zoned out so hard it felt like I was back in the truck.

Wetting my lips, I glance to my right to see Leo staring at me with concern, but I shake my head, offering a gentle smile, and he immediately relaxes.

He looks like sin today, with his hat backwards on his head, his jeans molding to his body perfectly, and the way his jacket sits over his shoulders, making them look even broader, I could melt into a puddle at his feet.

When he rises from the table, offering his hand out to me, I take it instantly. The second I'm on my feet, he pulls me into his chest as his mouth descends on mine. I reach for his neck, running my fingers over his pulse as I kiss him back.

There are a few murmurs about getting a room and even some girls crying that he's wasting his time on me instead of being with them, but it only urges me on.

Nobody gets to claim what's already mine.

Reluctantly pulling our lips apart, I catch my breath as I turn on the spot and quickly pack everything away into my bag. I can feel Leo standing barely an inch away from me, his body heat mingling with mine before I turn back to face him.

"Want to get some lunch with us today in the cafeteria?" he asks, repeating the same question he has asked most days since I learned about my mom and Lola, and for the first time, I sink my teeth into my bottom lip and nod. I've been making excuses to go home or the library, avoiding the food hall altogether.

The smile that spreads across his face is infectious,

like he just won the fucking lottery, and I can't help but match it as he intertwines our fingers and pulls me to the exit. We rush past everyone in a blur, and I pay them no attention as I focus on Leo. In a matter of minutes we're out of the lecture hall, down the steps, and moving out into the courtyard with ease while still bundled together.

Stepping out into the cold air, I take a deep breath, inhaling the fresh, crisp scent that surrounds us, and for the first time, I appreciate it. It's taking some getting used to, but I'm falling in love with the weather. Autumn in Michigan is breathtaking, especially as the yellow, orange, and red leaves start to color the ground from the nearby trees.

Leo slows our pace now that we're outside, and I fall comfortably into step with him as we cut through the courtyard. One thing I've started to notice when walking with one of the guys around campus, is how the other students react to them, which inevitably then relates to *how* they know them. I mentioned the observation to Leo the other day, and he laughed me off, but as I glance up into his eyes, I can see the realization reflected too.

There are four categories, and I can see an example of them all from my spot beside him right now. To our left, are a group of people glaring daggers at me while simultaneously wanting to fuck the ever loving hell out of my man. Straight ahead, are the guys that clearly work for the Arrows, the subtle nod they offer as they otherwise act inconspicuously makes it more than obvious.

Then there is the group of guys to the right, who stand with their hands in their pockets, their spines straight with sneers on their lips as we pass. From my new knowledge, I would bet in a heartbeat that they have some connection to the Vultures.

As we approach the food hall, I spy my fourth and final group of people, and when I look up at Leo with my eyebrows raised, he chuckles, clearly seeing it too. These are the wannabes. They dress like them, they try to walk, talk, and act like them, but most of all, they brown nose them.

Fully grown men push and shove each other as they try to open the door for us, grumbling about whose turn it is. I have to bite back the laugh desperate to break free as we pass.

"Thanks," Leo murmurs, keeping his gaze fixed ahead, which is quickly followed by the guys stumbling over themselves to explain it's *no problem at all*.

The second the door closed behind us, we both snort, unable to contain our laughter any longer. When I finally calm myself, I glance around the room looking for the others before my eyes fall to the table in the center of the room.

Fuck, I remember the first day I showed up here, and avoided that table all together. Now I'm finally giving in and joining them. Ezra and Jameson sit on one side of the bench, laughing about something as Jagger sits across from them. Then my heart sinks when I see who is sitting beside him.

Any laughter or joy is short lived as I glare at the red headed bitch sitting beside Jagger. Leo's hold on my fingers tightens as he clearly senses the change in me, and I know the second he sees what I see too when he curses under his breath.

"Fuck her, Lucy, she's not you. No one ever will be, and maybe you showing up today to sit together as a unit will be the reminder that's needed," he murmurs in my ear, and I nod, taking a deep breath as I try to calm the rage inside of me.

I hate feeling like I'm spiraling with anger, like I have no power, no control, but I'll be sure to remind this bitch

I'm here.

"You're right," I answer, forcing a smile to my face as I point at the pizza zone. "But I need pizza first to make me feel better."

He chuckles at my response, placing a gentle kiss on my forehead before turning us in that direction. I force myself to keep my anger contained and the red head out of my mind. It's not something I can control right this very moment, but I will be able to handle it in the next few minutes. The knowledge, that reminder, that I haven't lost all of my control, settles my soul a little.

Maybe this part of me is what resonates with Jameson. Understanding the need to survive, the craving for control. This is my control.

As we join the back of the line for pizzas, Leo releases my hand to stand with his chest to my back, wrapping his arms around me in a protective and comforting stance all at once. My heart leaps in my chest as I smile up at him, far too happy to be like this in public with him.

Lowering my gaze back to the front as the line moves, I catch sight of Naomi in my peripheral vision, and when I glance to my right so I can see her properly, I find Vince hovering above her. His demeanor looks tense, his jaw tight, and his brows knitted together as they argue. I can't hear what they're saying, they're too far away, but whatever it is only seems to piss Naomi off more and more as her eyebrows raise with anger.

My hands instantly wrap around Leo's arm, clenching as I look her over for the first time since yesterday. She was in classes earlier, but I managed to keep my head down and avoid her gaze.

Wait… what if…

"Leo—"

"Do you think their connection could be what I think it could be?" he whispers against my ear, clearly having seen the pair of them together just like me, and I nod subtly in response.

I don't want to be overheard by anyone else since we have no idea who we are up against in this school. The reality of that was made clear yesterday, and Ezra is determined to run some background checks to see if we can get a clearer picture of who is mingled among us.

"Don't mention anything here, but I'll add it to Ezra's radar. I can't believe we didn't consider it yesterday," he states, kissing my temple before releasing me as we reach the front of the line.

Ordering two meat feast pizzas, we quickly grab them and pay, before making our way to the table, where I remember the whore is.

I would love to just have a minute to catch my fucking breath with all the drama going on around me. I really can't be bothered with this bitch, but Leo is right, I need to make a point with her, otherwise she'll never back off or other girls will try to replace her.

As if sensing the fact that I'm getting tenser with every step we take toward the table, Leo speeds up so he's in front, trying to block my view, but the way she just rubbed Jagger's arm is seared into my brain. And why the fuck isn't he removing her?

Leo moves to take a seat on the bench beside Jameson, and there's room beside him, but I have my sights set on her instead.

"When will you just fuck off, Julia? You're starting to really piss me off," Jagger bites, and my shoulders relax a little when I realize he's *not* encouraging her at all, it's just the opposite. He's just trying to not cause a scene to get rid of her.

Unfortunately for her, I'm not that fucking polite.

Slamming my tray harder than necessary down on the

table, I thank God when the pizza doesn't go flying, but my bottle of water topples over, rolling across the table, and someone manages to catch it before it hits the ground. I don't see who though, my focus really zoned in on this bitch.

She looks up at me with her red lips turned up in a sneer as she eyeballs me, and I really just want to jab her in the eyes, make this skank regret she ever laid eyes on Jagger to begin with. Instead, I plaster a smile on my face as I brace my hands on the table and tower over her.

"What the fuck do you want?" she grunts, moving to touch Jagger's arm again, but he brushes her off this time, so she turns all her attention to me.

"I want you to fuck off," I respond with a shrug, parroting Jagger's words. Not beating around the bush as I raise my eyebrows at her expectantly, and she scoffs, looking over her shoulder to Jagger for reassurance, but his eyes are fixed on me.

Clearing her throat, she clasps her hands together as she offers me a sympathetic smile. "Listen, Luella, right? Why don't you move along and let the adults sit in peace, okay?"

Fuck.

I've changed my mind.

I want to throat punch this bitch so I don't have to listen to her shrill voice. I would rather have someone scrape nails on a chalkboard or hear a cat meowing all night. Anything else at all but the sound of her.

Bending my elbows, I lower myself so we're eye to eye, offering her my own sympathetic smile as I feel the guys across the table watching my every move too. "Don't make me ask Jameson for his switchblade so I can slit your throat for touching what is *mine*."

My skin prickles as anger simmers beneath the surface, my cheeks heating as rage tries to get the better of me. My ears prick up at the sound of metal hitting the tabletop, and I know for a fact it'll be Jameson placing his blade on the table in warning.

I pause, waiting to see what her next move will be, but no surprise at all, she laughs me off. This girl really doesn't know who she's fucking with. "Please, I saw you with Leo, you can't have them all," she bites, the sweet side of her diminishing as her eyes widen and she stares at me like I'm crazy.

"You see, that's where you're wrong," I say with a smile, flashing my teeth as I hold my hand out, feeling the cool metal of Jameson's blade moments later. Pressing the little button to release the blade, I aim it in her direction, the tip of the blade mere inches from her chin as I squint my eyes at her. "They're all mine. Leo, Ezra, Jameson, *and* Jagger. Now I won't repeat myself again, bitch. Back. The. Fuck. Off. Before I make you."

Even through her thick layer of make-up I can see the color draining from her face as her eyes flick between me and the blade. I can sense the attention of other people around the food court, the murmurs not loud enough for me to decipher, but I don't give a shit.

I watch her throat bob as she tries to swallow, and the slight tremble in her hands makes me grin. "Y-you can't fucking speak to me or threaten me like that," she mumbles in response, but the confident bitch from earlier is long gone.

She thought I was weak when she cornered me at the party a few weeks ago, clearly thinking the same again today, but she's wrong.

"I can do what the fuck I like. Please, try me," I snap, my fingers clenching around the handle as my heart pounds in my chest. "Give me a reason to fucking hurt you, please."

"I suggest you do as our lady says or be prepared for

the consequences," Ezra announces, his voice sounding far too smug as I keep my eyes on her, watching as she slowly tries to stand from the table.

"We're not done here," she mutters, brushing her hair back off her face as I keep the blade poised in her direction. I know I look like a crazy bitch right now, but for my guys, I don't mind letting my crazy show if need be.

"Excellent, I'll be waiting," I state, calling out to her retreating form as she cuts across the food court as quickly as possible. Folding the blade away, I blindly hand it back to Jameson as I eye everyone ballsy enough to meet my gaze right now, which isn't many.

I worry if Naomi or Vince saw me, but I don't see them right now. Making such a big show won't help us in trying to play things calm around them. This is clearly me *not* being oblivious to the gang life.

Finally falling into my seat, I want to sag with relief, but I keep my face impassive as I stare at my kings, each of them wearing smug as fuck grins.

Assholes.

"You are hot as fuck when you're claiming us, Lucy," Leo declares, before taking a bite of his pizza casually, and I roll my eyes at him.

"I don't know what you're talking about," I reply, playing up my innocence, which makes them all laugh at me.

"You're definitely something else, Luella, and that's what makes you ours," Jagger murmurs, as he leans toward me, pulling his cell from his jeans pocket, and I watch as the lightness dies in his eyes as he scans the screen.

"What? What is it?" I ask, trying to remain quiet, but feeling the tension rising from him. His bleak eyes look across the table first as if silently portraying what's going on, before turning the screen to me so I can see, and my heart drops right along with his.

Robbie: Friday. Family lunch. It'll be televised so make a fucking effort. Bring the bitch.

WATCH ME RISE

CHAPTER SEVENTEEN

Lou-Lou

My eyes widen as I step out of the SUV, the sight of Robbie's 'home' catching me by complete surprise, and yet it's somehow still a classic Robbie move.

To start with, the gates had to be opened by security to let us in, then we drove down a long stone driveway where a water fountain sits in the center, creating a rounded entrance way to the house.

Well, not so much a house, more a mansion, or a stately home, there's that much to it.

Painted yellow, and standing four stories tall, it looks

like something imported from Italy, with the arched windows and vines growing up the side. The entrance is double doors, giving an even grander feel, and I dread to think what's going to greet us inside. But the fact that it's so big, so grand, makes it so Robbie too. Always running around, finding new ways to project his little dick syndrome.

"You ready?" Leo asks as he steps up beside me, and I shake my head instantly.

I hate Robbie on the best of days, but in the presence of my mom and Lola, with a camera crew on us? I'm not prepared for that at all. "Not even a little bit," I admit, not wanting to have my 'all is fine and I'm a badass bitch' mask on with the guys, I'm going to need all my energy to wear it inside.

Focusing my attention on him instead of the oversized house, I can't stop the quirk of my lips as I take him in again. Every single one of my men are suited and booted, and I couldn't find the scene any more delicious.

I take a step forward, turning so my back is to the house. I get a good picture of my guys as Jameson and Ezra walk around from the other side of the SUV and Jagger climbs out before me, rolling his eyes because he knows exactly what I'm doing.

Imagining what every piece of their suits would look like on my bedroom floor. Not that it would really make a difference whose suit it was since they opted to wear matching. The only difference is the design pattern on their goddamn shoes, and I love it.

With crisp white shirts, and a tailored navy suit, the tie matching perfectly, they look fucking lickable, and their tan, leather shoes completely finish off the entire look.

H.O.T.

I wet my lips, smirking as I continue to drag my eyes over them, watching their little quirks that they always do. Leo stands before me with a hat in his hand, desperate to put it on backwards, but knowing it'll cause issues if he does. Ezra fixes his glasses as he wrinkles his nose, looking up at the house with disappointment. While Jameson swirls the switchblade around in his palm like it's any other day. Which leaves Jagger to pull the hair tie from his wrist and twist his hair up into a bun on top of his head.

"I can feel my clothes burning off under your gaze, Luella," Jagger states, raising an eyebrow at me, and I shrug my shoulders.

"If it was up to me we would be at home, those clothes

strewn all over the floor, and... well, you can imagine the rest, I'm sure," I murmur, winking at him as his eyes widen in surprise, before turning back to face the house.

I catch a glimpse of my own dress as I move, a grin fixing on my lips as my words from days ago to Jagger rattle in my head. In a body hugging red dress, with a chiffon overlay over one shoulder, I feel hot as fuck, and I stand by the fact that red is most definitely my color.

Pairing the eye-catching dress with black studded heels and a matching clutch, I went a little heavier on the make-up, making sure my red lips complimented the dress too. My hair is coiled up on top of my head, with a few tendrils framing my face.

We look like a badass unit, the five of us together, and I've never loved it more.

With the confidence boost in my mind, I clear my throat and set my shoulders back. "Let's go," I announce quietly, heading for the door as carefully as I can since it's still fucking stone here and it's difficult to maneuver in my heels. I hear the guys follow after me immediately, and only a moment later, I find myself being whisked off my feet and carried toward the house.

I glance over my shoulder to see who's chest is pressed

against my back, to find Jameson already smirking down at me. I'm not usually appreciative of being manhandled, but fuck if I'm not relieved for it right now.

When he reaches the bottom step, leading up to the house, he slowly places me back on my feet, and I shiver when I feel the telltale sign of his cock pressing against my ass cheeks. Fuck. Later, *definitely* later.

I gulp as I look back up at the house, but my mask is firmly in place now, especially since I know Lola is in there too. She's going to need me to have my shit together.

"No one goes off alone, especially Lou-Lou, remember that," Ezra states, coming to a stop on my left as Jagger hovers to my right, leaving Leo to walk around to my front. The four of them boxing me in as they wait to make sure I remember the rule.

I nod, wiggling my fingers to calm the uncertainty pulsating through me. "If I need to leave, I'll excuse myself to the bathroom upstairs, and someone will follow me," I repeat the words from earlier, and they all give a sharp nod in response.

Leo opens his mouth to say something as he lifts his hand to my face, his knuckles grazing my cheek, when a voice booms from above.

"We're fucking waiting, you imbeciles. I enjoy these little games." I look past Leo to see Robbie glaring down at us in a cream suit, with his hands clenched at his sides like a petulant child.

Fuck. Me.

I'm ready to have this over with.

None of us reply as we move in sync, taking the steps up to him, and I don't miss the slight stumble in his steps as he moves back. He doesn't like us all together, he definitely doesn't like me in their grasp instead of his, and he most certainly doesn't like what he knows we'll be capable of one day when his time comes.

Stepping into the house, I almost roll my eyes at how grand, traditional, and… gold everything is. The foyer has four large open archways leading into different parts of the house, with two sets of stairs wrapping around the outside, leading up to the second floor, where the banister wraps around, offering a full view from above. Each archway is painted gold, the walls are filled with art from another era, while what I would imagine is a Persian rug is laying at our feet.

I bite my lip, holding back the snark on my tongue as Jagger continues to move toward the middle archway, and the rest of us follow suit.

The second we step through, I find myself in an ultra modern and sleek kitchen, a complete contrast to the lobby. All glossy whites with stainless steel, it's *almost* fucking nice, but we walk through in a blur before I can decide whether to truly like it or hate it.

Following Jagger, with Ezra and Leo firmly at my sides now, and Jameson remaining close behind me, we step into a dining room just off to the right of the kitchen.

The first thing I notice is the camera crew. There are at least six of them here, all ready to film Robbie being a complete fucking phony, but I try to take a deep breath and not get stuck on that again. As much as it annoys the fuck out of me, I have to do whatever it takes to protect Lola. Screw the fucking town.

Sensing our approach, the six men all move off to the left so they're not in the way of the room. The second they step out to the side, my eyes fall on Lola's little brown ones, and I'm brushing past Jagger, with my hand on his arm before anyone can stop me.

My mom acknowledges me first, a soft smile on her lips which looks foreign, but I don't miss her leaning in to whisper in Lola's ear, who suddenly whips her head around in my direction, a grin spreading across her sweet face.

I expect her to zone in on one of the guys first, but when she claps her hands and shouts, "Le-La, it's Le-La." My heart almost bursts from my chest.

I can't help but match her smile, picking up my pace until I'm stopping at the seat beside her highchair. Quickly pulling out the chair, I lean down to place a soft kiss on her forehead, trying not to cover her in my lipstick, before dropping down into the seat.

"How's my best girl doing?" I ask, loving how her smile widens at my words, but she doesn't respond, and the fact one of the guys is stepping up behind me has her completely distracted now.

As each of the guys come to say hello to her, I take in the rest of the room. The table is solid oak, and there are chairs for twelve people in total, but with the food serving trays laid out, you would think we were feeding twelve hundred.

I can see this for what it really is; a show. The meats, potatoes, and side dishes are sprawled across the entire length of the table like it's Thanksgiving or something, but I am certainly not fucking thankful for being here today.

Not enough pumpkin pie in the world could make

being in Robbie's presence fucking tolerable.

We hadn't really discussed seating arrangements, but there's no way I'm leaving Lola's side now, no way in hell. But the guys must be okay with where I've placed myself because they continue to find their seats.

With my mom at the end, and Lola between us, Leo takes the seat to my right, squeezing my thigh under the table as Jagger, Jameson, and Ezra sit across from us, leaving the end seat free. Which tells me Robbie is going to sit at the end like king of the world, and Jagger doesn't want to be too close to him. Good call.

As if sensing his name in my mind, the man of the hour arrives, his eyes wide with excitement as he rubs his hands together.

"Excellent, everyone's taken their places. Let's get this lunch going shall we?" Gone is the man who only moments ago was a cunt at the front door, and in his place stands a man who looks like he enjoys being present in his children's lives.

He rounds the table, thankfully walking behind the guys across from me. As he takes his seat he makes sure to plant a kiss on my mom's forehead while maintaining eye contact with me, and I think I'm going to be sick.

I watch as my mom's eyes fall closed and she bites her bottom lip, clearly uncomfortable, and it makes me pause. She's a cunt too, and always has been. But regardless of her shitty comment about my appearance the last time I saw her, she doesn't deserve this. To be touched and treated a certain way to stay alive. It makes me sick.

She's a fucking prisoner, my sister too, and I won't allow it.

I bite my tongue, sure I'm going to draw blood as I swallow back the rage wanting to burst from my lips.

Now isn't the time, but his motherfucking time *is* coming.

Leo squeezes my leg tighter, pulling my attention to him, and I see the question in his eyes, but I force a smile to my lips as I lace my fingers with his.

"And three… two… one…"

A cameraman counts down quietly, and the moment he says one, I know the filming is going to start. How am I supposed to get through this fake shit? I thought I could, but now that I'm here, I don't know how I'm supposed to keep my mouth shut.

Needing a distraction, I turn to Lola, stroking her fair hair behind her ear as I smile down at her. I spy a few servers entering the room, beginning to serve our meal, but I occupy myself with Lola so I don't get snappy at the whole situation. Robbie would have me painted as the bad guy, the black sheep, in fucking moments, and even if it takes everything I have, I won't let that happen. I will never understand how this guy operates. It makes no sense for me to be here, a new addition to his campaign front, but how will he even explain that?

"How about you explain to us the new addition to the table," one of the men behind the camera offers to get the conversation going. I can't tell which one, but either way it catches Robbie by surprise. I watch him fight with his initial reaction before he settles his eyes on me.

"I haven't yet decided what best suits her."

His words make my skin crawl, but I force myself to keep my features neutral.

The silence feels deafening around us, but the second Robbie opens his mouth again, I wish we could slip straight back into it.

"So, Luella, how has Emerson Grove been treating you so far?" he asks, sounding like he gives a shit, but I remember what we're here for, and play along.

"It's been wonderful," I murmur in response, a smile

on my face as I meet his gaze, the sparkle of approval clear in his eyes.

I can sense that he sees this as a 'jump when I say' challenge, and me answering the questions he throws my way is his way of controlling me, making sure I'm onboard and aware of what's at stake for us.

"Excellent, I'm glad to hear it, and you've been studying at Emerson U, correct?" He continues, and I have to bite the inside of my cheek. Of course he's pressuring me with more.

Before I can respond, a server clinks a wine glass, and announces to the room, "Lunch is served." Without another word or a backward glance he exits the room, and when I look down at my plate I find a small portion of food, smothered in gravy. It's barely more than the food they've given, Lola.

A quick glance around the other plates in front of everyone and I see them all with food piled high, like normal fucking people portions, and I know this is another power play. Especially when I chance a look at Robbie out of the corner of my eye and see him smirking at me.

Fucking creeper.

Joke's on him, because I don't plan to eat shit here

anyway.

Remembering his question, I remain unfazed with the food situation as I respond. "I am studying at Emerson U, yes."

His eyes fucking gleam when he sees me keep my mouth shut, and when I glance across the table to Ezra, Jameson, and Jagger, I find them all grinding their jaws as they see the power play too. I don't need to look at Leo to see if he's noticed, the grip on my thigh is likely going to leave bruises with how angry he is.

"And what might you be studying?" he asks, singing into his food as he waits for me to answer, and I relax back into my seat, not even lifting my fork as I stare him down.

"I'm currently studying Psychology and Political Science, with a set plan to proceed to Law School once I've received my Bachelors," I say with a smile, pride in myself warms my soul as he nods in response.

"Excellent, excellent," he says, repeating that same goddamn fucking word again, and it starts to irritate the hell out of me. "Who knows, when that's all done, you could be my lawyer," he states, not asking, then takes a sip of the wine in front of him as I scoff uncontrollably.

Fuck.

"Uh, I haven't decided what specific field I want to go into yet, so the Jury's still out on that," I mutter, clearing my throat as I reach in front of me for a drink, only to find a glass of water.

It'll have to fucking do.

"Don't be ridiculous, we have to stick together as a family, so of course you'll take the route best suited to that," he pushes back, disguising it with a chuckle that makes my body tense.

Wetting my lips, I glance around the table, watching as my mother's cheeks turn pink as she looks firmly at her food, while Lola plays with the vegetables on her little dish, and every single one of my guys sits tensely.

We already fucking look ridiculous, it's clear no one wants to be here with this man. I can feel the camera men circling the table in silence, trying to keep out of the next person's shot, but it still leaves me on edge.

"It's funny that you say that, because I've been leaning toward family and children's Law. Supporting children who need it, helping families mediate peacefully so the situation isn't overrun by one singular person," I state, quirking my eyebrow at him as I watch his Adam's apple bob.

Oh, he didn't like that response. Not one bit.

Excellent.

"That would be no use to us as a unit, Luella," Robbie says, shaking his head dismissively at me.

He's fucking pushing me to admit on camera that I would work with him, be a part of this bullshit family for years to come, and I just can't do it. I won't submit to his will on this, ever. Fury bubbles through my veins, and I struggle to contain it.

"Please forgive me, everyone. I just need to take a moment, I'm not feeling too well." My chair scrapes across the floor as I rise from my seat, keeping a smile plastered on my face as I exit the room, moving swiftly through the kitchen and back into the foyer.

Remembering Jameson's directions, I take the left set of stairs, and the first door on my left would be a bathroom. Taking slow, measured steps I continue to follow his guidance, not wanting to be caught on camera looking like I'm running away.

The cream carpet on the stairs looks like it's barely been stepped on as I take my time in my heels, holding onto the banister for dear life, and when I reach the top, I spy the door to the bathroom just like Jameson said.

Moving inside, I close the door behind me and quickly lock it. I won't open it again until one of the guys gets here, which I hope will be in a minute or two because I just need a second to fucking breathe.

There's just a sink and a toilet in here, nothing oversized, and that helps calm me a little because it's so *normal*. I can't deal with all of this fake shit.

How do they do this?

Over and over again?

Be in his presence like you don't want to slaughter him? Act like things are okay when they're so far from it? I feel like we're in an alternate dimension.

Bracing my hands on the sink, I look at myself in the mirror as I try to get a hold of myself, and I can already see the strain around my eyes. I hate that I have to lie, pretend that this is all happy shit, but I'm even more fearful that I won't be able to sell it enough to get his approval and he'll do something to Lola.

Fuck.

Taking another deep breath, I freeze as a knock sounds on the door, but it's followed moments later by Ezra's voice. "Lou-Lou? Everything okay? Let me in."

I reach for the door handle before I even realize it, and

the second the door swings open and I see his concerned face, I calm a little more. "I'm okay, I could just feel him pushing me, seeing how far I would go, and as much as I expected him to be an asshole, I wasn't expecting *this*."

He steps forward, stroking his thumb down my face as he offers me a comforting smile. "I know. It doesn't help with the cameras either. I've spent every second at that table, considering whether I can slip the blade from Jameson's possession and just be done with him," he mutters, referring to Robbie, and I *really* fucking get it.

We both sigh as I plant my hands on his chest and he holds my waist. "I just feel antsy, I can't stop my anger from instantly rising the second he opens his goddamn mouth. I feel jittery as fuck."

"We need to relieve some of the tension building inside of you, Lou-Lou," he murmurs, stroking his fingers over the globes of my ass, and I shiver under his touch.

Shit.

That would definitely help release some of the tension, but there's nowhere for us to go right now.

Running my fingers through his curly brown hair, I grin back at him. "I fucking wish, Ezra," I practically purr as his hands move to the hem of my dress, stroking the bare skin of my thighs.

With my heels on, we're the same height, and I love being able to reach for his mouth without tilting my head, so I do, without a second thought, I crush my lips to his.

If I can't have him fucking the tension out of me right now, then I can try to smother it down with his lips.

I wrap my hands around the back of his head, my fingers curling into his hair as he pulls me in tighter against his chest.

My heart is pounding wildly for a completely different reason now. A reason I'm more than happy to get behind, or under, either way, my arousal is spiked thanks to Ezra. I can't tell where he ends and I begin as he consumes my mouth, tangling our tongues together as the rest of the world falls away.

I release his lips, only for a moment, trying to catch my breath, and when I look into his darkened gray eyes, I know he feels the same way.

"I need you, Lou-Lou. I need you now," he murmurs against my lips, sending goosebumps all over my body as I nod eagerly in response.

"I need you too, but where? In here?" I ask, pointing over my shoulder to the small bathroom as we still remain standing in the doorway.

He leans back, his eyes scanning around like crazy as he gazes over his shoulder too, and when he turns back to me, I'm shocked by the menacing smile that has taken over his lips.

"Do you trust me?" he asks quietly, stroking his fingers down my face before tilting my chin up, exposing my throat.

"Yes." My response is instant, there's no question or time to consider what I already know to be true.

The smile spreads even farther across his face, running from ear to ear as his gray eyes appear almost black. Placing my hand in his outstretched palm, his fingers wrap around mine as he takes a step back, guiding me back into the open hallway.

Now that I'm paying a little more attention, eager to see where he might be taking me, I really notice the layout up here compared to when I walked up in a blind hurry earlier. Doors lead off to different rooms on the left as the banister runs in a semi circle wrapping around the whole area and offering a perfect view of the floor below.

When Ezra comes to a stop, I bump into him a little as I take an extra step, and when I meet his gaze, he quickly brushes his lips against mine, before placing my hands on the wooden bannister. Staring around in confusion, it takes a minute for me to register that we're standing overlooking the foyer area, my hands braced on the rail as Ezra strokes a finger down my spine.

Here? He thinks here is a good place?

Glancing over my shoulder at him, I find him staring at me intently. "I want to fuck you like this, with them below, knowing that you'll always be my strong, independent, and fierce woman, that will never bow at anyone's feet. Especially not Robbie Izaro's."

I nibble at my bottom lip, his words only turning me on more as I nod in agreement. "I want that too," I murmur, purposely tilting my hips slightly so my ass glosses against the outline of his rigid cock through his pants.

His breath hitches as he grips my hips, holding me in place, and I stifle a moan. "Are you going to be able to keep quiet, Lou-Lou? There's a lot of people down there that could hear us, and we wouldn't want the press to catch you mid-orgasm now would we? Or am I going to need to gag you?"

My eyes fall closed of their own accord, his words going straight to my core as I consider what he's asking.

I'm a fucking moaner, and he knows that. If he plans to fuck me here, there's going to be a need for a gag or we're likely to find ourselves on the cover of the local newspaper tomorrow morning. Fuck, imagine that headline?

"Gag me."

Uttering those two little words has him groaning under his breath as he releases my hold for a moment. I have no idea what he's going to use, but seconds later the silk of his navy tie appears in front of my face, and my mouth gapes open in surprise.

This motherfucker thinks of everything.

Everything.

Thank God.

As if waiting for me to truly comply, I widen my mouth and he brings the material closer, wrapping it around my mouth and the back of my head twice, before securing it at my left side.

"If you need to release it, just pull here," he murmurs, indicating where he tied it off, while kissing my temple. "It should be slack enough now though, right?" he adds, making sure I'm alright, and I nod feebly as I stand still, my body tightly strung and desperate for release.

Anticipation tingles through me as I titter on my heels,

and it feels surreal.

This is all foreplay I've never dabbled in before, but I swear to god I can feel how wet I am already. Moments ago I wasn't sure if I was going to like this or not, now I think I might be obsessed.

Ezra stands pressed against me as he runs his fingers over my bare thighs, and tantalizingly slowly he drags the material up my thighs as he reveals my core.

"Fuck," he curses under his breath, when he realizes I have no panties on, revealing my glistening core as my grip tightens on the bannister.

If anyone was to look up here now, they'd be able to see my pussy through the spindles and that instantly heightens my nerves, while adding a layer of excitement to it all at once.

As Ezra drags his fingers over my folds, my back arches, my eyes rolling to the back of my head as he tries to untangle the tension building inside of me. I buck as he drags his fingers from my clit to my core, teasing a finger at my entrance, before slotting two inside of me in one swift move, making me bite down on the tie as I stifle a moan.

Holy fuck.

My gaze is fixed on the entryway into the kitchen, where I know everyone is sitting on the other side, likely waiting on our return. Well fuck them.

"Stretch me with your cock, please," I plead, muffled around the tie as his hot breath breezes over my neck.

"Fuck, you're just a handful of sin, aren't you?" he mutters into my hair, making my lips attempt to break into a smile as I preen under his words.

The sound of his zipper rings in my ears as I clench my teeth, desperate for what's to come. The nudge of his cock at my entrance makes my body stiffen at first contact, but I quickly push back, arching away from the banister as he slowly enters my center.

There's no condom again, so I can feel every vein as he drags along the insides of my pussy, making me throb with need. Once he is fully seated, he pauses, and my walls tighten around him, needy for more.

My gaze is still honed in on the entryway below, my chest heaving with every breath I take in case someone sees, while my body is pleading for release.

Ezra retreats, pulling out until only his tip remains, before slamming back inside me in one fluid motion, and my muffled moan rings out around us.

"I thought I gagged you to make you quiet?" he chuckles in my ear as I try to swallow around the tie. "But imagine how loud you would have been if I hadn't," he adds, before repeating the exact same motion.

It's like he's taunting me. Pushing me to make a noise and draw attention to us, while knowing that would cause a shit storm, so actually needing me to get control of my mouth.

Sweat beads down my spine as his fingers dig into my hips and his thrusts grow harder, faster, needier, and I fight to keep my voice hushed.

I match Ezra thrust for thrust as the banister remains steady in my grip, but I startle when I see the glow of the kitchen light flick on.

Shit.

I don't know if Ezra notices it too, but if he does, it only increases his thrusts as he slams into me repeatedly. I try to listen to see if I can hear anyone, but my pulse is ringing too loudly in my ears for me to focus.

"Fuck," he hisses, unable to contain his own moans as the hushed growl of Robbie's voice can be heard.

"I don't give a shit what you have to fucking do, go and fucking find them. If that bitch and your little rat boy are gone too long then they'll start to get suspicious," he bites out, making it very clear he's talking about the two of us.

"We're not going anywhere until you come for me, Lou-Lou," Ezra whispers as the shadow of someone standing in the entryway registers in my brain, all while Ezra wraps his hand around my thigh so he can stroke my raging clit.

Holy sweet fuck.

My body is in overdrive, dancing to the tune Ezra has set as the sound of Jagger's grunt reverberates around us.

"Watch your fucking tongue. I'll go and take care of it," he bites, only to step out into the foyer. Instantly his eyes land on us, like he knew exactly what we would be up to and where.

His eyes widen and his jaw slackens as he stares at us, and it's all too much for me. With one final swipe over my clit as Ezra rams inside of me, I come apart. Slamming my lips together as best as I can, I hum my pleasure as I explode at the seams. My gaze fixed on Jagger's.

My core tightens around Ezra as I pulsate from head to toe, feeling his movements fall out of sync as he too reaches his climax.

Ezra's lips graze my neck as we ride through the waves,

his fingers still teasing my clit as we sag against each other.

I watch as Jagger wets his lips, clearing his throat as he rubs at the back of his neck, before turning around to face his father again, who thankfully still remains in the kitchen.

"Nevermind. It seems Ezra knew exactly what to do. Take a seat, *Father*, they'll be joining us in a minute." I don't miss the sarcasm as he speaks, but I'm too busy whimpering as Ezra slips from my body, and pulls me back to the bathroom.

I feel completely relaxed and dazed as I hear him shut the door behind us, before the sound of the tap comes on. He delicately pulls on the tie, releasing it from my mouth as I work my jaw and slowly start to focus.

I'm not prepared for the warm, damp cloth between my legs as Ezra tries to clean me up, and I jump a little in surprise, before smiling down at him in appreciation.

"Thank you," I murmur, finally glancing up to take a look at myself in the mirror.

Holy fuck. I look flushed as hell. My pupils are blown, my hair has fallen from my clips, and my cheeks are pink. There is no way we're going back down there without them realizing what we just did.

As Ezra stands, the tie draped over his shoulders without being tied up, I notice the slight wet spots from my mouth.

Yup.

"We're definitely fucked," I state, meeting Ezra's gaze in the mirror, and he chuckles.

"I mean, one hundred percent. I could definitely fucking nap about now," he says in response with a pleased grin on his lips, and I roll my eyes.

"That's *not* the type of fucked I was talking about," I grumble, and he winks at me.

"I know, but it's the only one I'll accept."

I wet my lips, my red lipstick smudged to hell, and I smile. I really do feel like I could take on the goddamn world right now.

Who knew a killer orgasm could make me feel so fresh and energized?

"You ready?" he asks, offering me his hand with a satisfied grin on his lips, and I nod.

Stepping into battle with my four kings? I'm ready for war.

CHAPTER EIGHTEEN

Lou-Lou

I stretch my spine as I lean back on the sofa, groaning as my muscles ache from being hunched over the coffee table.

"If you keep moaning like that, we're going to get very distracted," Leo announces, making me pause, but I can't stop the grin that spreads over my face when I glance around the room to see the four of them all looking at me with heated gazes.

"That almost sounds like a fun idea right now," I respond with a pout on my lips. Knowing full well I would love nothing more than being stripped bare by my kings, except for the fact this assignment is due on Monday and I'm still going to need tomorrow to finish too. I'd still be a nice distraction though.

I managed to hide out from the Friday night party ritual yesterday, but instead of getting any work done, I was tucked into Leo's side as we started watching the entire Marvel collection in release order.

"It can be your reward once you've finally caught up on your class work," Ezra adds, nudging his glasses up his nose as he smirks at me, and my eyes light up with excitement when I realize he's not joking.

Yes. Please.

With Ezra to my left, Jameson to my right, Jagger on the armchair next to Ezra, and Leo taking up the other half of the coffee table, I am truly surrounded by my favorites. It's so strange that no one is specifically sticking out as a firm favorite for the day so far, they're all just making me happy with little effort, and I'm totally here for it.

We've all been working on homework for what feels like an eternity, but in reality it's only been about the last six hours. At least Leo's homework involved food, otherwise we'd have never eaten. But now I'm really starting to lag.

I think I'm still on a mental brain dump from yesterday at Robbie's. All the mind games with him fucked my head, but then Ezra *literally* fucked me, and I was a lot more calm.

When we reentered the dining room, not much was said, and to my surprise, Robbie remained the complete persona of what America believes a good man should look and act like. An attentive husband, touching my mom every so often and engaging her in conversations. A loving father by joking around with the guys and talking sweetly to Lola. And a shrewd businessman explaining his goals for Emerson Grove and how he wants to change the town. *We* all know it was all a fucking facade, but whatever. Other than sweet talking Lola a few times, he pretty much left her alone and she brightened my day, and that's all that matters.

Apart from furthering my determination to bring Robbie down, the only other notion I took away from the day was that I really want to be able to see Lola more. As much as she knew who I was and smiled up at me like a little ray of sunshine, I wanted to learn everything there was to know about her. Not from the guys, but from seeing it for myself.

"Jameson doesn't get to be in charge of the group fun, not after he fucked her against the patio glass while we were all locked outside last time," Jagger grumbles, startling me from my thoughts as I gape at him, but when the others chuckle, including Jameson, I can't help but join in.

My teeth sink into my bottom lip, remembering how hot it was when Leo pressed his hand against the glass where my breast was pushed up, while Jagger took Ezra in his mouth.

A thought occurs to me, and I consider whether it's a good idea to mention it, but fuck it, I'm never going to be someone who holds back. "Jagger took dick like a pro that day," I state, flashing my gaze toward him, watching as he rolls his eyes at me.

"What can I say? I'm a natural," he responds, acting bored as he shrugs and flicks the page of his text book.

"What he means to say is he'd never sucked cock until then, but you made for the perfect audience," Ezra murmurs beside me, but it's loud enough for everyone to hear.

Holy fuck.

It's like he just pressed a button to stimulate my clit

with his damn words as my pussy comes alive, thrumming with need.

"I just… I thought…" My words trail off as I glance between the two of them, making Jagger shake his head as Ezra clears his throat, clearly knowing what I was going to say.

"We have, very, very rarely. When I was so down because you weren't with us anymore, and I was uncontrollably stressed that my insomnia was at it's worst, he would fuck me. It wasn't all that sweet, and there was no deep underlying love involved, but it helped release the tension in me to help me sleep for just a little while afterward."

I gape at the two of them, completely surprised by that answer as both Leo and Jameson say nothing. I've always been stuck on the fact that I was on my own these past three years, when they all got to be together. I didn't realize, as one person, I could have such an effect on them while I was gone. Maybe there was a reason I was meant to be alone, to get stronger, braver, and more resilient, while they needed to remain together, so they would have the ability to pick each other up and strengthen their bond.

Wetting my lips, I can feel both Jagger and Ezra waiting

for a response from me as I lean my elbow on the back of the sofa, resting my head on my hand as I turn to face them. "And since I've been here, have you—"

"No," they both respond in sync, shaking their heads. If it was anyone else, I'd be worried they answered too quickly or something, but I can see the sincerity in their eyes.

"So I'm never going to get a chance to see any of that?" I clarify, a tinge of disappointment washing over me as they both stare at me in surprise. "What? That would be the hottest fucking thing in the history of peen," I add with a shrug as Jameson chuckles beside me, pulling my gaze away from them for a moment.

"Well fuck, now I'm feeling salty. I didn't think to be there for Ezra because I sure as fuck would put on a show for you, baby," he states, tucking my hair behind my ear all sweet, not matching his words at all as he grins.

"If she's lucky, she still might if the way they're both looking at her makes any difference," Leo sings, winking at me as I look at him, before I turn to see what he means.

There are two pairs of heated eyes staring deep into my soul to see if I am joking, and when I lean closer, practically sprawling over Ezra's lap, I grin. "Imagine if you were fucking him, Jagger, while Ezra was fucking me, and—"

"Shit."

Jameson's sharp tone interrupts my teasing as I turn to see what's wrong. This motherfucker better have a good reason to disturb the visual I had going on just now.

"What? What's going on?" I ask, feeling the tension rise throughout the room as we all seem to edge closer, waiting for him to respond.

"You better get yourselves ready," Jameson says with a smirk, his eyes darkening as his hand slips into his pocket, and I know he's just wrapped his fingers around his switchblade. "The details have been confirmed. It's time to go racing."

I have never in my life had to get changed so quickly, before being bundled into my truck, and rushing it out of the house. It still feels like my heart is pounding in my chest, but I know that's a mixture of excitement and adrenaline, tinged with nerves over what's about to happen tonight. With the exception of Jameson's reputation to maintain, there's also a part of the town up for grabs that the Arrows need to keep.

There's only Jagger and Leo here with me, while Ezra helps Jameson, and they'll arrive after us in Jameson's Nissan GTR that he'll be racing.

It's no surprise that I wasn't able to drive us, but it did surprise me that Jagger opted to sit in the back with me instead of calling shotgun. Leo even let me be in charge of the music again, but I decided on some more upbeat songs this time. It feels like we need to arrive pumped and ready for a wild time.

Lacing my fingers together with Jagger's, I watch as the world goes by, the street lamps getting fewer and farther between as I see a huge group of car lights ahead. My instincts tell me we're here and I have no idea what to expect.

Back when we were kids, I never saw street races, and Jameson spent more time hijacking cars than actually participating in anything. Sure, this is illegal too, but I'm fucking excited to watch him in action.

When I came down the stairs earlier, in my tight black jeans, heeled boots, fitted black sweater, large hooped earrings, with my hair piled on top of my head, and my black puffer coat, he grabbed me by the waist, lifting me off the ground slightly, before crushing his lips to mine. My feet had barely touched the ground before he was heading for the door, leaving me to look longingly after him.

Motherfucking tease.

"We're here," Leo announces, glancing back at me through the rearview mirror, and I feel Jagger's hand tighten around mine.

"Whatever you do, don't go anywhere on your own. Do you understand? Besides for some of the Arrows, we don't know exactly who is here, and we want to keep it that way, alright?" he grumbles, rubbing at his face like the whole thing has exhausted him already.

"I won't," I agree, leaning over to place a kiss at the corner of his mouth as the truck comes to a stop.

Glancing out of the windows, we're surrounded by lights, it looks like complete mayhem as we're swarmed with people excitedly running past us, and people flexing over their cars.

Fuck, I'm excited.

Please let there be no issues tonight so I can actually enjoy myself.

Leo climbs out first, putting his hat backward on his

head as always, while moving to my door. He seems to search around first, I have no idea what for, but when he seems happy, the door opens. I take his outstretched hand, letting him guide me down from the jacked up seat, and I'm instantly overwhelmed by the blasting music.

I have no idea where it's coming from, but it's made worse with how loud everyone is shouting over it too. Fuck me, this is a night out for the senses for sure.

Blinded by the lights. Deafened by the music. Sick with the smell of gasoline.

Wait, am I getting old or something? Fuck.

Shaking my head, I let Leo tighten his grip on my hand and pull me into his side as Jagger climbs out of the truck too. Before Jagger can reach our side, Leo pulls me away, flipping his hat around to cover his face and almost act inconspicuous, while the crowd around Jagger instantly parts at his arrival.

It takes me a second to understand, but they're trying to keep me in the shadows. The one difficulty we have with attempting to hide me in a crowd like this, is the guys, my guys, or technically the *Arrows* right now, are like gods.

People watch Jagger's every move, some in awe of him, others in fear, while a few are scowling like little bitches, and again that's our clue that they're likely a Vulture.

Leo moves us around the group of people to the left, over by some boulders as he stops to the right of them, leaning against one as he pulls me in front of him. It's a nice vantage point at the back of the open space, and my eyes widen in surprise with how many people are actually here.

We're not far from the shipyard we were at the other day, but this is a long track off road, curving to our left, and pretty much derelict. There must be close to one hundred cars, trucks, SUV's, and motorcycles here, and triple that in people.

The energy feels electric as I look around the crowd again.

Fuck me, I get the hype of being a car girl. I love a beasty engine, the growl as the RPMs get higher, and there's some pretty sights to see here. I can see a few Audi R8s, a couple of older Mustangs, and even an Aston Martin close by.

"The start line is over there," Leo murmurs in my ear, pointing to our right where I see a few people standing by, one holding a checkered flag, and behind them are people taking bets. This is a bigger deal than I originally thought.

Just as I think I catch a glimpse of Dax across the road, two cars come zooming from the left, around the bend, careening for the line Leo just mentioned, before an additional three cars appear behind them.

The crowd roars as the Corvette wins, and Leo pulls me in close, taking a step back as everyone jumps around like crazy in front of us. I hate that the Vulture's are spoiling this experience for me. I want to go wild with the other people here.

Before I can ask when Jameson's race is, Leo shuffles around to pull his phone from his pocket, Ezra's name flashing across the front in their group chat.

Something is wrong. If he's called the group chat, needing everyone's attention, there must be an issue, I can feel it.

He lifts the phone to his ear, releasing his hold on me slightly so he can focus on the call, and yells into the speaker.

"What's up?" He listens, focusing on their words, and I hate that I have no idea what's going on. "Fuck… Are you sure?… Shit… Yeah, yeah, I can do that… Those motherfuckers!"

He pockets his phone again, his jaw tight and his

body stiff as he looks down at me. "Leo, what's going on?" I demand, hating only having heard one side of the conversation.

"Jameson was supposed to race the Nissan GTR tonight, but what I guess people don't fucking know, is Ezra goes with him to run a diagnostic test on it every time, and when they scanned over it, there was a fucking brakes error."

A what? Wait… what the fuck? Someone messed with his brakes?

My heart pounds in my chest as anger races through my body. Who the fuck had the balls to do that? The Vultures, it had to be.

"But how did someone get their hands on his car without him knowing?" I ask, confusion laced in my words.

"We have a few spots around town where we park the cars, so it's not noticeable and if anything does get taken, they don't have access to all the vehicles," Leo answers, and I nod in understanding, unsure whether he means taken by other people or by the police, but either way, it makes sense.

"So he'll be here in two minutes, in a different car, which will hopefully fucking spook whoever did it. But

Ezra was calling because Jameson is adamant he'll only do the race if you're beside him." He reaches out, squeezing my shoulder in comfort as my eyes widen in surprise. "You don't have to if you don't want to. He's never going to fucking force you, but—"

"Are you joking? Count me the fuck in," I interrupt, excitement quickly buzzing through me too, toning my anger down a little. "But how are we going to get away with people not seeing me?" I ask, not wanting to blow everything because of this, and Leo grins in response.

"You'll see. Of course Jameson thought of it all when he had to make a last minute car change," he says with a wink, wrapping his arm around my shoulder, pulling me to his chest and leading me away from the crowd.

Keeping to the outskirts, he moves us toward the curve in the road, the last corner before the finish line, and the number of people hovering around dwindles significantly.

"I swear to God, if this fucker does something crazy with you in the car, I'll kill him," he grumbles, and I raise my head to face him, barely able to see him since it's a little darker over here, but I still quirk my eyebrow all the same.

"Do you really not trust him with me in the car?" I ask,

watching as he immediately nods.

Someone doesn't like the lack of control he has over the situation, and I can understand that.

Just as I'm about to respond, I notice a car driving toward us with no lights on, and it slowly rolls to a stop in front of us. My body tense as my pulse rings in my ears, preparing to fight however is necessary, when Leo squeezes me tight. "Don't worry, Luce, it's Jameson and Ezra," he murmurs into my ear, and I instantly relax.

Thank fuck.

Wetting my lips, I watch as Ezra climbs out, leaving the passenger door open as he approaches us, but my focus is on the car.

A blacked out Toyota Supra MK IV, with even the front windscreen tinted, it looks hot as fuck.

"He's going to be living his best life in there if your eyes are already glistening with excitement, Lou-Lou," Ezra states, pulling me in for a quick hug before pressing his lips to my forehead.

I'm grinning from ear to ear as I slip out of his hold and head for the car, propping my hand on the roof as I lean the other on the corner of the door, I bend to look inside, finding Jameson grinning just as wide as me right now.

"If this baby doesn't have an iconic 2JZ-GTE engine, then I'm not getting in," I say, raising my eyebrows at him, and a burst of laughter breaks through his lips.

"You bet your sweet ass it does. It's even been modified to have two-thousand horse-power," he states, and I slip into the car seamlessly at the confirmation.

This is going be one hell of a fucking ride.

Jameson leans over me, grabbing the seatbelt before I can even reach for it myself, and he plants a kiss at my temple as he clips me in.

"Are you excited?" I ask, watching as he finally flicks the lights on, and heads for the start line.

"Hell yeah I am," he responds with a grin, but I don't miss the anger still sizzling beneath the surface over the fact that someone fucked with his GTR and for trying to hurt or kill him.

"Are you sure no one will see me here?" I ask, wanting to be sure, and he nods, slowing at the white line beside a Honda Civic to our left, and a Mitsubishi Lancer Evo to our right. I think I can spot a Camaro on the other side of it too.

"They don't need facial confirmation from me, Ella. My personalized registration plate does the talking for me.

So unless I need to roll the window down, we're good," he states, leaning across the center console to squeeze my thigh.

I nibble at my bottom lip as I try to remain still, but also attempting to take it all in at once. I watch as some girl with a green flag moves to stand between our car and the Evo, in a pair of denim shorts, and a mini tee, and I fucking shiver for her. Maybe back in Cali I could have done that, but not here. Definitely fucking not. It's too cold for that shit.

"Are you ready?" Jameson asks as the girl lifts her hands in the air, and he revs the engine, making the seat beneath me rumble, and a giggle falls from my lips.

"I was born ready, baby," I purr in response, keeping my eyes trained forward as two sets of headlights flash from the side, and on the third flash, the girl drops the green flag, and I'm thrown back in my seat as Jameson hits the gas.

I feel like I can't breathe as my heart is left back at the start line, and we power forward at a high speed. My mouth falls open on a silent scream, my hands clutching the bucket seat as the blaring lights disappear into the background.

"Holy fuck," I blurt, but it's barely audible over the sound of the engine, and when I chance a glance to my side, I spy Jameson grinning like a maniac as he takes the first corner. We're in the lead, but the Camaro is hot on our tail, and when I look over my shoulder, I can spot the Evo and Civic battling it out.

This isn't going to be a clean race, everyone's fighting with all they've got.

The tires screech as Jameson brakes late, and I grab onto the oh-shit bar as we're thrown around the car.

Holy fucking shit. This is the best. Moment. Ever.

Jameson Izaro is officially my favorite of the day.

I squeal like I'm on a rollercoaster, watching as Jameson's knuckles tighten around the steering wheel, his muscles tensing as the veins in his arms pop, which only adds to my racing car driver fantasies.

Fuck.

Imagine his hand around my throat like that.

I can't focus on anything important right now. With the vibrations beneath us, the adrenaline coursing through my veins, and my hot man beside me, I'm melting into a goddamn puddle.

The car lurches forward a little, making me jump as

I glance back over my shoulder again, to see the Camaro nudging at our rear bumper.

Motherfucker.

"He better not scratch the paint work," I grunt, glaring at the driver like he can actually fucking see me, and Jameson grunts.

"Let's not give him a chance. What do you say?" Jameson says with a grin, somehow managing to gain more speed as we continue down a barely lit straight road. I can't see a single fucking thing, but Jameson seems to know exactly what he's doing. "Get ready for the last corner, Ella. It's tighter than it looks," he shouts, and I tighten my grip on the handle. The quicker we get over that finish line, the quicker I get my heart back in my chest.

Glancing over my shoulder again, I find the Evo almost side by side with the Camaro, the Civic long forgotten, but I start to panic when I notice them both creeping around to either side of us.

"Jameson!" I holler, concern in my voice as I watch them edging in closer and closer.

They must be working together to box us in and sweep us off the road.

"Hold on, Ella," Jameson growls, his face etched with

anger as he slams on the brakes, steering the car to the left as he drags short around the corner, and in slow motion the Camaro and the Evo crash into each other with a huge bang as we just manage to circle around them.

I'm clinging on to my seat for dear life as we whizz past the checkered flag at lightning speed, the lights from the cars spectating dazzling me as we continue down the road.

We won.

We fucking won.

"Woohoo!" I cheer, giddiness getting the better of me as I grin wildly at Jameson, who smirks back at me.

When I expect him to slow down, and join the celebration back at the car meet, he just continues on, barely lifting his foot off the throttle, and I frown in confusion.

"Where are we going? What about the others? What about your prize?" I ramble, asking him all of the questions running through my mind right now.

"The prize is money, money that is immediately transferred to Robbie so we don't claim anything, and the fact Dax backs the fuck off," he says with a shrug as I gape at him. "We're going home because I never stay around to get caught up in all of that bullshit. It's unchartered territory, so anything could go down, and after someone fucked with my car, I'm not about to wander into no mans land," he grunts as I nod along. "And the others can meet us back at home. Leo will drive them, besides we deserve a couple of minutes of peace and quiet before Jagger finds us anyway," he mumbles at the end, and I squint at him.

"What does that mean? Why would we need a couple of minutes of peace and quiet before Jagger gets home?" I try to rack my brain for whatever this issue is, but I come up short. He was fine when I last saw him.

Jameson rubs at the back of his neck nervously as he peers across at me. "Uh, well, he was definitely not onboard with you being in the car with me," he states, and my stomach drops.

Ah, fuck.

"On a scale of one to nuclear, how mad is he going to be?" I ask, nibbling my bottom lip as Jameson slows the car, and we drive through town.

"Nuclear," he admits, and I bite back a grin.

"I wasn't aware there was any other type with him," I respond.

It's cute that Jagger thinks he gets the overall vote on what I do and don't get to do, but nothing brings me more joy than bringing that motherfucker down a peg or two.

Bring it on, Izaro, I'm not backing down, and he sure as fuck better believe I'll be doing this again.

WATCH ME RISE

CHAPTER NINETEEN

EZRA

Jagger slams the truck door behind him quicker than I can even jump down from the vehicle. He storms for the house in a fit of anger as Leo and I glance at each other.

Since Lou-Lou made her own choice that went against what he thought, that put us on his shit list too, so he hadn't uttered a word on the ride home, just simply growled the entire time as his anger rose within him.

Quickly shutting my door behind me, Leo catches up as we quicken our pace, to remain only a couple of steps behind Jagger as the door to the house swings open and bounces off the wall. There's nothing like a slamming door to announce, 'Honey, I'm home.'

He pauses for a moment, his chest heaving as he seems to strain his ears to guess which direction of the house they're in, and moments later he's moving again as we silently follow, closing the front door behind us.

Ah, fuck.

Why do I feel like this is not going to end well for Jagger?

"He needs to calm down," Leo murmurs as Jagger steps into the living room, and I nod my agreement. At least this time we have his soothing balm here. Lou-Lou. Even if he denies it until he's blue in the face.

I watch in surprise as Jagger's eyes fixate on something, his jaw clenching along with his fists contracting at his side, before he starts charging across the room. I quickly break into a run, my glasses nearly falling from my face as I struggle to keep up, but as I step into the living room too, I realize he's gunning straight for Jameson.

Curled up on the sofa together, Lou-Lou in Jameson's lap, her eyes widen in surprise as Jameson grips the arm in an attempt to rise to his feet. As if sensing the same issue as me, Lou-Lou places herself between the twins as I manage to wrap my hands around Jagger's arms.

He growls as he pauses, very able to break free of my hold if he truly wants to, but he manages to restrain himself since Lou-Lou has placed herself in harm's way.

"Do you have a fucking death wish?" he growls, turning his anger to Lou-Lou. He leans forward a little as I still hold him back, and with wide eyes I glance toward Leo, who also has the same 'we're fucked' look on his face.

"What the fuck, Jagger? Do you? Get a fucking grip on yourself," Lou-Lou hisses, placing her hand over Jameson's on the arm of the sofa. "I don't know who you think you are, but I'm a grown-ass woman who gets to make her own fucking choices. I don't need your permission to do anything. I'm standing here right now, in front of you, showing you everything is okay, and you still act like a grouchy, pain in my fucking ass," she adds, folding her arms over her chest as she meets Jagger's stare.

Her gaze flicks to mine, only for a split second, but I see the words shining in them, and I reluctantly release Jagger's arms and take a step back. We all watch as he rolls his shoulders, his gaze fixed on Lou-Lou's as we wait for the next one to speak.

"I'm not trying to be a controlling asshole, but you continuously put yourself in harm's way. When is it going to be the wrong time or a freak accident? Then what? We'll—"

"You're trying to wrap me in bubble wrap. I'm not delicate, and I *don't* need a babysitter, those were *your* exact words."

They're both practically vibrating with rage as neither of them want to back down. Sometimes they can be so alike they can butt heads like this, but it'll take a miracle to make one of them, never mind both of them calm the fuck down and see the other person's point of view.

Jameson clears his throat as he sits forward, placing his hand on Lou-Lou's hip. "Listen, Jagger, I—"

"Shut the fuck up Jameson, I'll deal with *you* later," Jagger bites out, interrupting whatever he was going to say, making Lou-Lou shove against his chest in Jameson's defense.

"Or maybe you need dealing with first," she states, quirking her eyebrow at him.

"Maybe I need to go and grab the popcorn because it looks like it's going to be a lengthy show," Leo interjects, a grin on his lips as I hold back a smile, while the other three glare at him, not seeing the humor in his tone.

Fuck me.

We need to step up and get involved before this continues to go south and we're left with none of them speaking to each other.

Focusing my gaze back on Lou-Lou, I fix my glasses as she meets my gaze. Her chest is heaving with every breath she takes, her knuckles are white as she keeps her arms folded tightly across her chest with her hands clenched, and her pupils aren't just dilated; they're completely fucking blown.

Ah, I see it now.

"Jagger, back the fuck off, man," I state, feeling four sets of eyes turn my way in surprise as I rub the back of my neck. I can feel him ready to respond in anger to me as well, but I shake my head, flicking my gaze from Lou-Lou's to his. "She's not really all that angry, Jagger. If you just look beneath the surface a little you'd see she's edgy as fuck, and needy after her first race."

His head slowly turns back to the woman in question as she fidgets from foot to foot, trying to swallow past the lump in her throat as she skittishly glances around at us, unable to deny my observation.

"The conversation you guys were having before we had to rush out of the house wouldn't have helped either," Leo adds, dropping down on the opposite end of the sofa to Jameson as he takes his hat off and places it on the coffee table.

It takes me a second to remember what he's talking about, but my dick twitches as the memory comes to life.

"Imagine if you were fucking him, Jagger, while he was fucking me, and—"

Her little fantasy had been cut off right as Jameson got the text.

I watch as she wets her lips, remembering her words too, but that's not what she needs right now. That little bubble of fantasy was her imagining what it would be like to bring me all the pleasure in the world, and right now this needs to be *all* about her.

She needs us all. Just like the very first time. Only more if we plan to take the edge off her adrenaline rush.

"Jagger, how are we going to calm her down?" Jameson asks, rubbing his hands over her waist as he rests his forehead on the base of her spine. He's clearly on the same wavelength as me, we just need the other two on board.

Leo will be zero issue, but we need to pacify Jagger if

we expect him to climb down off his high horse.

Ever so slowly, Jagger's gaze scans to each of us, silently communicating that he wants to rock her world, and when none of us protest, he swipes a hand down his face, and turns his gaze back to our girl.

"Is that right, Luella? Are you needy right now? Do we need to take the edge off?" he practically purrs as he takes a step toward her, watching as she nods, nibbling on her bottom lip at the same time. "I can't hear you," he says when she doesn't respond, placing his hand under her chin as he tilts her head back.

Now that she doesn't have her heeled boots on, she's back down to her normal size, but she rises up on her tiptoes and presses her lips to his, hard, stoking the beast as he wraps his arms around her waist, pulling her out of Jameson's hold.

My cock presses against my sweatpants, desperate for me to give it some much needed attention, but I fight against it. Although Leo quite happily rearranges himself without any concern.

Jameson grumbles about Jagger taking his girl from his arms, but he doesn't protest further. If anyone here knows the need of taking the edge off after an adrenaline rush, it's him, so he knows how much she needs this.

If letting Jagger set the tone also stops him growling, then it's a win-win situation.

Shrugging my jacket off, I throw it over the arm of the sofa by Leo, the three of us eagerly watching as Jagger and Lou-Lou battle for control.

When Jagger can't take it anymore, he tightens his hold on Lou-Lou's hips and twirls her around so her back is now pressed against his front.

I bite back a groan as I take her in, with her swollen lips, pitch black eyes, and messy blonde hair, she looks like a fucking wet dream.

My eyes zero in on Jagger's hands as he drags them around the waistband of her jeans, before popping the button, and slowly pulling down her zipper. None of us utter a word, completely enraptured as Lou-Lou tilts her head up at the ceiling, her hands curve around her own neck as she tries to play the submissive, completely wrapped up in her own need and desire.

Jagger falls back into the armchair behind him, dragging her jeans down her legs as he goes, and when they pool at her feet she manages to step out of them effortlessly.

"Sit, Luella," Jagger orders, making my own cock

pulsate as she falls into his lap with her back still pressed against his front. "Good girl," he breathes against her neck as he trails kisses over her skin, and her hands fall to the arms of the chair, gripping the material like her life depends on it.

Lou-Lou rests her head back on Jagger's shoulder as he lifts the material of her turtleneck sweater up, revealing her pretty pale pink lingerie set underneath.

Fuck, I'm losing my cool, and my cock is going to explode without being touched at this rate from this little peep show.

Without a word, Jagger places his knees in-between hers, effortlessly spreading her legs wide as he simultaneously pulls at the thin material covering her pussy, completely exposing her to us.

Shit.

My hand slips inside my joggers before I can stop myself, squeezing my engorged cock as I watch Jagger trail his fingers through her folds as her perky nipples press against the lacy material of her bra.

A groan to my left catches my attention as I glimpse to see both Jameson and Leo gripping their cocks too, only Leo has somehow dropped his pants to his ankles, his dick on full display.

"Look what you do to them, Luella," Jagger murmurs, making her blink her eyes open and her jaw drops, as she squirms in his lap. "They're all jealous that I get to touch you right now. They all want to be me, with you spread across them, begging to be fucked."

"I-I... I need that," she stutters, desperate to find her high in the form of release, hoping to satisfy the adrenaline coursing through her veins.

"Are you going to let me be in charge?" he asks, waiting on bated breath for her response. Her eyes swirl with a mixture of need and determination. She won't want to hand the reins over to him so easily, not when she's this worked up, but deep down she knows she's also going to get everything she wants.

He circles her swollen clit gently, waiting on her response as I take a long, tight pull of my cock, trying to relieve my own tension as her teeth sink into her bottom lip.

"Yes," she says with a sigh, reluctant to hand over control, but the second she agrees he thrusts two fingers inside of her, making her back arch and a groan fall from her lips, and she knows she made the right choice.

"Good girl," he murmurs again, and she preens under his praise. "Now, do you want to hear what I have planned?" he asks, continuing to fuck her with his fingers as she nods eagerly, and he finally switches his gaze to look at us. "Ezra is going to fuck your sweet little pussy, while Leo is going to fill your ass. Then we might let you taste Jameson's cock on your tongue, and give you a little show of Ezra taking my cock in his mouth," he states, his eyes meeting mine in question, and I nod.

Fuck. Lou-Lou is my everything, but I can't deny that I've always wanted to feel a cock on my tongue, and the fact she's so open and eager for us to explore only makes my feelings for her intensify. I was jealous as fuck when Jagger got to do it the last time, even though it was my dick in his mouth.

Her eyes find mine immediately, and widen with excitement as she envisions what it all might look like.

"Fuck, has anyone ever taken you from behind before?" Leo asks, squeezing his cock as he searches her gaze.

"No. That would take too much trust, and the only people I trust enough are in this room," she admits, making my fucking heart soar as Leo's eyes darken in response, pleased with the words that slipped from her mouth.

"Then we need to get you ready, baby," Jameson states, rising from the sofa and dragging the coffee table to the side of the room quickly, leaving the fluffy cream rug where it is, as a perfect space for us to lose ourselves on.

Jameson offers out his hand as Jagger stalls a moment, not releasing his grip on her, clearly still pissed at his brother, but reluctantly lets her go as Jameson drags her to her feet. Their lips crush together, leaving me desperate to taste her too, before he pulls her sweater over her head and discards it, along with her bra that he unclips and tosses aside too.

"You motherfuckers better get on this level. If you think I'm just going to stand around naked while—"

Her words are cut off when she watches Leo kick his pants the rest of the way off, and I follow suit. Whatever she wants, she can have.

"Fuck," she groans, her hands falling to Jameson's shoulders as he drops to his knees before her, dragging his tongue over her clit.

Pulling my hoodie off too, I move toward them, loving how her eyes roam over my body as I squeeze my cock.

"Get on your knees on the center of the rug, Luella," Jagger mutters, pulling his own clothes off just as swiftly as the rest of us, leaving Jameson the only one to catch up.

Jameson drags his tongue through her folds once more, before letting Lou-Lou follow his order. She falls to her knees right by me, looking up at my round, needy eyes as she wets her lips, and I find myself dropping to my knees right along with her.

"We're going to make you feel so good, Lou-Lou. It's going to be euphoric," I murmur, leaning in to press my lips against hers, and her hands instantly find their way into my hair.

Stroking my hands down her sides, she shivers under my touch as I hear Jagger tell Jameson to get some lube, and excitement bubbles in my chest at just how good we're going to make her feel.

We've obviously never done this before, or we haven't as a group at least, but I know we're going to overwhelm all of her senses.

Dragging my lips from her mouth, I kiss over her collarbone as I sense the others moving in closer. Peering up, I see Leo drop to his knees behind her, trailing his fingers down her spine as Jameson comes rushing back into the room.

"Ezra, you need to sit flat on your ass, so Luella can

straddle you. She'll adjust better to the stretching with you deep inside of her," Jagger states, making my cock jut toward her in need, and when I turn my eyes back to her, I find her grinning with excitement too.

I drop back, getting comfortable on the rug, with my knees slightly bent as she places her thighs on either side of my legs, her silky pussy gliding over my dick, and I hiss at the contact, my ass clenching with need to thrust up into her center.

Leaning back on my palms, Lou-Lou places her delicate hands on my shoulders as she looks into my eyes, while Jagger leans forward, wrapping his thick knuckles around my length, making me grunt as he lines me up perfectly with her entrance.

His calloused fingers, combined with the softness of her folds in a complete contrast, like night and day. "Fuck," I grunt as Lou-Lou slowly slips down my cock, her pussy walls clenching tight as she takes me all the way.

Once she is fully seated, and Jagger has removed his hand, he lifts his fingers to stroke down Lou-Lou's face, and her eyes almost close as she shivers between our touch.

"Ride him, Luella," he demands, and never one to back down from a challenge, Lou-Lou does just that.

I groan as she rises up on her knees, before swiftly slamming back down, impaling herself on my cock. The moan that falls from her lips in ecstasy rings out around us, kicking everyone into action.

Jameson steps back to undress in record time, before moving in to crush his lips with Lou-Lou's as she continues to ride me. I instantly sense the moment Leo teases her ass, when she stiffens against me for a moment.

Leaning forward a little, I stroke her hair back off her face. "Relax, Lou-Lou. Relax, and when you're ready, push back, I promise you it'll be worth it," I murmur, watching as she nods, her lips falling from Jameson's as she takes a deep breath and does as I say.

She tentatively rises and slams back down onto my cock again, relaxing her body as Leo grins over at me. I feel the moment he slips a finger inside her, slowly stretching her entrance, his tip stroking against the wall separating us both, and Lou-Lou's pussy strangles my cock as she screams.

"Ah, oh my god." Her words are strangled as she climaxes all over my cock, her body trembling above mine as Jameson moves to hold her up.

Leo doesn't stop, letting her ride wave after wave of

her orgasm as she continues to move her hips. "More, please, I need more," she begs, looking up with needy eyes at Jagger and I hold still. As much as I want to thrust up into her core, we need to take this slow.

"She's as ready as she'll ever be," Leo mutters, drizzling lube in his hand as he slowly works his cock over. Lou-Lou's skin is blotchy and flush from her orgasm, but she's not ready for this to end yet.

"Luella, take Jameson's cock in your mouth before Leo fills you up. And because he's such a cunt, if you feel the need to bite down, by all means do so," Jagger says with a wicked grin as Jameson grunts.

Positioning himself perfectly so his cock is the right height for Lou-Lou's mouth without her straining too much, she slowly teases her tongue over the end, before swallowing him halfway in one go.

Her moan is muffled as I feel Leo's cock press into her entrance. She's about to be consumed beyond words.

Jagger stands right beside Lou-Lou, his thick cock clenched between his fist as he looks down at her, before turning his gaze to me. "She wants something to watch too, Ezra," he says, heat in his gaze from watching our girl follow his orders seamlessly, and I nod, wetting my lips as

I feel Lou-Lou gazing out of the corner of her eye at us.

"Make my eyes burn," I mutter as he teases the tip of his cock along my lips, at the same time Leo pushes deep inside of her.

Fuck.

This is almost too much for me, nevermind Lou-Lou.

Sweat beads along my brow as I try to catch my breath, my pulse throbbing at my throat. Opening my mouth wide, Jagger places the head of his cock on my tongue, letting me test the weight, and the mere sound of Lou-Lou moaning has him slamming right to the back of my throat.

I splutter and gag around his length, but I don't stop from wrapping my lips around his cock as Lou-Lou moves closer, her chest almost flush against mine as Leo sets the pace.

His cock continues to rub against mine through the thin wall separating us, while Lou-Lou's pussy squeezes my length, and Jagger pounds my mouth.

I hear a small pop from Lou-Lou's mouth, drawing my gaze her way as she pants. "Holy fucking shit," she hisses, tears welling in her eyes, and I panic for a moment before she scoffs. "It's too much and not enough all at once. My body is going to detonate," she cries, before wrapping her lips back around Jameson's cock, and his head falls back with pleasure.

Grunts, groans, and moans fill the air as everyone becomes lost in the ecstasy around us. But one thing's for certain, all of our eyes are fixed on Lou-Lou as she holds us all captive with her intoxicating body. Her gaze skims across the three of us when she can pry her lids open, like a beacon luring us further into her web of desire.

Jagger's hands tighten in my hair as his thrusts increase, watching as Lou-Lou falls apart between us.

"Fuck, you're so tight, Lucy. I'm not going to last," Leo grunts, his movements becoming much shorter and faster as he uses my knee to brace himself, while his other arm wraps around Lou-Lou's waist.

"Nobody comes until Luella does," Jagger bites out, clearly holding his own release back as my body tightens.

The second I know I can't come, the more I fucking want to, and the harder it is to hold back.

Lou-Lou moans long and hard around Jameson's cock, making him grunt. "Come on, Ella, we want to watch you shatter," he begs as she takes his cock to the back of her throat.

Like his words were all she needed, her body tenses,

her back arching as she tilts back, and I raise a hand to pinch her nipple, feeling her tighten around us as a scream fills the room. Even muffled by Jameson's cock, it resonates around us all, a siren drawing us closer as we all desperately chase after our own climaxes with her.

My eyes burn, tears welling in my eyes as Jagger's thrusts become almost unbearable, until he suddenly releases me, encasing his cock in his thick hand while turning to Lou-Lou, before the first rope of cum lands on her face.

With Jameson's length still in her mouth, Leo and I inside of her, and Jagger's cum painting her face as he continues to explode, I can't take it anymore either.

My thighs tense as I uncontrollably jut up inside of her, battling against Leo's pace as I lean forward, clamping my mouth around her other nipple and finding my release. Lou-Lou continues to spasm around me as I fill her over and over again, riding the wave of ecstasy running through my body.

"Shit," Jameson grunts, before he too releases from her mouth, and quickly aims his cock in her direction, his cum mixing with his brother's as her mouth remains wide open.

"Holy fuck, holy fuck, holy fuck," Leo chants as he

falls off the cliff too, and I feel his cock pulse inside of Lou-Lou, which only makes her body tense more.

Trying to catch my breath, I catch Lou-Lou as she slumps forward, her body a pile of limbs as she basks in the aftermath of what just happened.

Jameson and Jagger wordlessly disappear for a moment, before coming back in with fresh towels and a cleaning cloth for our girl as Leo slowly slips from her body, making her whimper.

Wrapping my arms around her tight, I tentatively roll us, until she is beneath me and gently lay her on the soft rug. A soft smile plays on her lips, a clear sign that whatever adrenaline was causing havoc in her body has been released, and she looks the most relaxed I've ever seen her.

"Message received. If you're acting as crazy as Jagger, you just need a good dicking, huh," I murmur against her lips before I slowly pull out of her, and she giggles.

"I would expect Leo to say that shit," she responds with a grin, peering her eyes open, and I shrug.

"Well, his dick was just rubbing against mine, maybe some of his personality came with it," I say with a wink, kissing her one more time before I move out of the way so she can be cleaned up.

Nothing has ever been clearer than this moment.

We are truly nothing without her.

Nothing.

With every beat of my heart, I know she's the reason it started to work again, and I'm going to do whatever it takes to help get us all out in one piece.

She deserves a future like this. The four of us doting on her, and being exactly what she needs. Now we just need to make sure *we* deserve her.

CHAPTER TWENTY

Lou-Lou

As I step down from my truck, I lean over to grab my backpack, but just when my fingers gloss over the strap, Leo pulls it from me. He effortlessly lifts it over his shoulder with a wink, before shutting his door, and I quickly do the same, racing him around to the front of the truck.

We're both grinning from ear to ear, and there's no particular reason why.

After a *long-ass* day at Emerson U, we now have a *long-ass* evening of trying to get on top of assignments.

Not that I'm complaining really. We were supposed to do all of this on Sunday, but after mind blowing sex the night before, I practically zombied in a pure state of bliss the next day.

But now it's Tuesday, and I really need to get my shit together because I fell asleep way too early last night too.

Leo's arm wraps around my shoulder as we head for the front door, my mind a little preoccupied as I remember just how full I felt with Leo and Ezra fucking me, Jameson on my tongue, while watching Jagger fuck Ezra's mouth. I can still feel the aches throughout my body, but they only serve to remind me just how fucking phenomenal it was. I am beyond ready to ask to go again, but they've all been treating me delicately since then, so I know if I asked, I would be greeted with a resounding *no*. For now, at least.

I need to time my request well, because I *have* to feel all of that again, and soon. We've never been more connected than we were at that moment.

The press of a pair of lips at my temple jolts me from my internal thoughts, pulling me back to the present as Leo grins down at me.

"When you're ready to come back to the land of the living, Lucy, you let me know," he murmurs against my ear, making me blush as I realize we're simply standing at the front door, but I've halted us in our tracks.

Tilting my head down as I try to hide my slight blush, I can't help but grin. "Sorry, I was just… thinking about… stuff," I mutter, making Leo's chest vibrate as he chuckles beside me.

"Uh-huh, I bet I can guess exactly what was running through your mind too. I would love to be able to see it through your eyes, piece together how you felt," he admits, encouraging me inside and out of the cold while keeping his arm firmly wrapped around me.

"Like a goddamn queen," I respond. I've already thought long and hard over this, and there really is no other way to describe it. Except maybe switching queen for goddess, but either way, they fucking worshipped me, and that's the part that still sends shivers down my spine.

"I like that," he responds, squeezing me to his side before leading me into the living room to place both of our bags down on the floor. "We'll come back to those later. Want to help me organize food for everyone? Then once we've eaten you can dive into all your homework," he offers, and I nod eagerly.

I'm not above admitting I love watching this man work

in the kitchen, it's hot as fuck when he's in his element, and the food is always delicious.

Lacing our fingers together, Leo pulls me into the kitchen, leaving me to obsess over the way they always want to touch me in some way, and it makes me smile. Apparently we all need touch as part of our love language, and I'm here for it.

I shrug out of my coat, placing it on the back of a chair at the dining table, before I roll the sleeves to my sweater up, wiggling my fingers in Leo's direction in a flash of jazz hands. "Tell me where you want me," I say with a smile, and I watch as his eyes rake me over from head to toe.

"On the dining table? Across the kitchen island? Bent over the stove? Basically on every surface in here," he says with a grin, winking at me as his eyes darken. "But not today, Luce. Today I would love for you to help cut the veggies up for the lasagna I'm going to make if that's okay?"

I almost pout at his teasing, my body tingling at his words until he leaves me hanging. I feel like there's a joint agreement between the guys that they're not allowed to be intimate with me until they think I'm no longer sore.

Taking a deep breath, I raise my eyebrows at him. "I'll

help however you like, but trust me when I say, if you keep teasing me without touching me and following through on your sexy taunts, then I am going to turn into a mean bitch and take matters into my own hands. Understand what I'm saying, Leo Cooper?"

His teeth rake over his bottom lip as he nods. "Definitely, sure," he rambles in response, and I roll my eyes, this fucker's listening but not actually hearing me.

Fucking men.

Just… fucking men.

There's no other way to describe it.

I brush past him, opening the fridge to take control, but in all honesty I have no idea what I'm doing, so I quirk an eyebrow at him, and wave my hand in front of me, signaling for him to tell me what veggies to actually pull out.

Realization washes over his face as he quickly moves toward me and grabs what we need, before setting me up to the right of the stove with a chopping board and a sharp chef's knife, along with peppers, onions, tomatoes, garlic, and some fresh Italian herbs.

Fuck, for a moment, I forgot who I was dealing with, forgetting that he would obviously make everything from scratch. My mind was ready to get the sauces from the cupboard and chuck it all together in less than five minutes flat. But it fills me with butterflies that he's happy to let me be a part of his whole process.

We seamlessly fall into sync with each other, while I take an eternity to chop and dice all of the things, but he's patient as hell, and if the love I can see in his eyes is anything to go by, then I think he likes me being here just as much as I'm enjoying it.

I wet my lips as I think of something that has been playing on my mind a lot lately, and I instantly feel antsy as I consider whether I should bring it up. We're almost like different people now we've eradicated most of the secrets between us. This isn't like that, not really, but it's something I don't know, and I'm desperate to understand. I just don't want to make things worse for him.

"I can practically hear the wheels turning in your mind from here, Luce, what's going on?" He asks, standing on the other side of the stove as he joins in with dicing the veggies with me, otherwise we might not eat tonight.

Pausing, I glance in his direction. Searching his gray eyes, I have no idea what I'm looking for, but I just don't know how to start.

I place the knife down as I clear my throat, and wipe my hands on the side of my jeans nervously. "I, uh, I was just… I… you know what? It really doesn't matter," I ramble, moving to pick the knife back up, when he moves to my side instantly, his fingers curling around my wrist as he glances down at me.

"Lucy, whatever it is, you can talk to me. You know that, right?" His voice is soft, filled with concern as he uses his other hand to tuck a loose strand of hair behind my ear.

"Yeah. Yeah, I know that, but it's more about me wanting *you* to talk to me."

As I stare up at him, his eyes widen in understanding and his Adam's apple bobs when he tries to swallow past the lump in his throat.

"You mean my back," he states, not asking for clarification because he already knows.

I offer one simple nod in confirmation, and he rubs his lips together, stepping back from me a little, and I don't take offense. I clearly just touched on a sore subject, and he needs a little bit of space to handle that.

"You don't have to tell me, not at all. It just plays on my mind sometimes ever since I saw the scars," I admit, wanting to be open with him about my thought process, and he swipes a hand down his face.

"No, I understand. It's just not something, I uh…"

"Ella, Ella, Ella! Your favorite of the day has arrived," Jameson hollers as the sound of the front door swinging open vibrates throughout the house, killing the intense moment between Leo and I as he quickly steps back to his chopping board, busying himself. But I don't miss his quick glance in my direction as an apologetic look flashes across his face.

He has no reason to be sorry at all, I just want to understand, and that can be on his terms. I don't remember the scars being there three years ago, and they're not something I would easily forget.

Taking a deep breath, I shake my hands out, before reaching for the knife again. "I don't have a favorite yet today, so I have no idea who's here," I shout back, and I see Leo's shoulders sag in relief as I don't try and push the conversation with the guys around.

"That's mean," Jameson says with a pout as he comes to a stop in the doorway, his chin pressed against his chest as he looks up at me through his lashes.

"You're being annoying as fuck," Jagger grunts as he appears behind him, and I shake my head at the pair of them as Ezra opts to come in from the living room, running his fingers through his unruly brown curls as he smiles at me.

"Shut the fuck up," Jameson grumbles back, throwing his elbow back into Jagger's gut, before walking toward me. "I'm about to be your favorite when you see what Halloween costume I picked out for you," he says, waggling his eyebrows, and I frown in confusion.

"Halloween?" I mumble, racking my brain to try and catch up with what fucking day it is never mind what month it is.

"Don't tell me you've forgotten about Halloween, babe," Jameson says as he stops in front of me, grabbing the knife from my hand and placing it on the side of the cutting board, before turning me to face him head on. His arms wrap around me, pulling me in close so I have to tilt my head right back to see his face.

"I've been so busy lately, I honestly forgot we were even in October," I admit, trying to mentally figure out my life right now, but Jameson's chuckle breaks through the surface.

"Well, we're making this Friday's party a Halloween party, and I have a surprise costume for you. I'm not going to let you see it until that night though." His smile is wide as he looks down at me, overly pleased with himself, and it's infectious as I grin along with him.

"Sure, I'm cool with that," I respond, glad I don't have to rush around in a blind panic to figure it all out. "What are you guys going to dress as?" I ask, but Jameson places his finger over my lips as he shakes his head.

"You're just going to have to wait and see, aren't you?" he says with a wink, before pressing his lips to mine.

My fingers instantly stroke over his shoulders as I deepen the kiss, my fingers itching to touch his hair, but he's suddenly pulled from my grasp.

"Stop hogging her," Jagger grunts, shoving Jameson aside before he grabs my hips, but I instantly place my hand under his chin, forcing his head back with all my strength, and he pauses.

"What the fuck, Luella?" He grunts, making me chuckle as I drop my hand, and he doesn't lift me off my feet like I expect him to.

"I'm not a possession that is passed around from one to the other," I state, not angry, but loving to make a point with him when he's being a bossy asshole, and he glares down at me. "Now, I'm helping Leo with the food, so how about you either take a seat at the table or even better, turn the coffee machine on, while you tell me what you've found, if anything, on who fucked with Jameson's car."

I keep my back straight, and my shoulders pressed back as I stare him down, and to my surprise, he grumbles under his breath as he moves to my right and flicks the coffee machine on.

Well then.

"Ezra's better at explaining what he's found in the car," Jagger states, looking at me in his peripheral vision, and I don't miss the slight grin that graces his lips as he spies me gaping at him in surprise for being so... compliant.

"Which is a sweet old pile of nothing," Ezra admits, and I turn to glance at him over my shoulder. "The security system set up at that specific location cut out twenty minutes before we arrived, and there's nothing on the cloud drive that I can see prior to that either. So whoever it was, seemed to know what they were doing. I'm trying to test for fingerprints on anything in the garage at the minute."

Wait, what?

"You can do that?" I ask, my eyes widening in surprise, and he chuckles at me as he drops down into his seat at the table.

"I can. Not that anything's coming up, and as much as I want to test every inch of the garage to find something, it's likely not there. And this isn't an episode of *NCIS* where I'm going to find one loose strand of hair that belongs to the motherfucker who did it," Ezra states, lifting his glasses off his face as he swipes a hand over his tired eyes.

Fuck. We're all run down and drained at the minute, and it's understandable.

Maybe we need to just *be* tonight. We deserve a minute to *be* ourselves and do nothing. And I need Ezra to sleep too. Those are my two goals for the evening.

"We need to de-stress, and since no one is touching me at the minute, how about we relax? I have some assignments to do, but we could kick back with some movies on in the living room, do a little bit of nothing to try and unwind. Again," I offer, and all four of my guys nod in agreement.

"That sounds like a plan," Jagger says beside me, and I grin up at him. I know he takes the weight of the world on his shoulders for everyone else sometimes, so if I can ease some of that strain, even just a little, with a movie and some down time, then I'm all in.

"I'm sleeping with Ezra tonight," I announce, turning my gaze to the man in question as the other three grumble their displeasure at my statement. "You need to sleep tonight," I demand, trying to be gentle with him, and he smiles sweetly at me as he nods.

Pleased I've been heard, I turn back to carry on with my task, to find Leo has already finished everything, and a tinge of guilt zips through me, but when I meet his gaze, I know he's not mad.

"Soon," he mouths, clearly talking about our conversation from earlier, and I offer him a soft smile.

I can take soon, it's closer than never, and I want to be his rock as much as he is mine.

This is my family, my unit, my everything, and I'm going to show them that they're my kings, just like they worship me as their queen.

CHAPTER TWENTY ONE

LEO

The front door opens again as more people join the party, and as much as I wish there was no one here but the five of us, I roll my shoulders back and plaster a smile on my face.

I think this is the part of the Arrows that annoys me the most. I wish business was actually about transactions or fighting only. Like, I would rather have a brawl in the middle of nowhere and walk away with a few bruises than continue to hold parties as a cover for discreet transactions.

That's why I said I would handle the runners tonight.

I'm not making sure there's plenty of Halloween punch in the kitchen for everyone, and I'm *definitely* not making sure the Halloween themed tunes continue to fill the air.

Socializing is a hard no from me today.

Turning my back on the new guests, I head for the kitchen so I can step outside into the yard and wait for work to begin.

As I pass through the kitchen, I catch sight of Jameson's handiwork in arranging our costumes.

Fuck.

I mash my lips together as I force myself to keep my mouth shut, but it's a little hard when your usually quiet friend is dressed head to toe as a purple striped cat. The *Cheshire Cat* to be precise.

As if sensing my gaze on him, Ezra glares in my direction, fixing the glasses on his nose as he tries to avoid smudging the black circle painted on the end. With his cat ears, purple striped pants, matching body paint on his upper half, and a tail hanging from his ass, he looks awesome. I just thank my lucky stars that Jameson gave that outfit to him.

Although, being the Mad Hatter doesn't feel much safer.

Stepping out into the yard, I run my hands over my dusty blue blazer, straightening the lapels before I fix my matching top hat. With a white, ruffled cravat, blue pants that stop just above the ankle, and a pair of black dress shoes, I look ridiculous too. But at least I don't have a fucking tail.

There are a few groups out here already, laughing, dancing, and getting wasted. A part of me almost wishes I was one of them, just a random person among the fray, without any concerns or worries. But then I remember the life I just dreamed of also comes without being the ones on top, the ones in control of everything. And that thought alone has the scars on my back burning as a reminder.

The four of us always be the ones on top, there's no other way. Now I just need to man up and explain to Lucy what the fuck happened to me. I fucking stumbled the other day, completely caught off guard by her request. Then Jameson charged in, unaware of what he was walking into, and I lost my nerve.

Shaking my head, I focus on the here and now, and notice the beer pong table hasn't been organized yet, so I head in that direction to give myself a distraction. Pulling the red cups from the stack stored beneath the foldaway table, I go through the motions of placing them into triangles.

My mind is in overdrive tonight, and I can't figure out why. Maybe because after the incident with Dax on the run the other week, the street race Jameson won after his other car was tampered with, and the fact that Robbie hasn't retaliated since Jagger disobeyed his orders in the fight last month, it's been quiet. Far too fucking quiet.

Our lifestyle has never been like this.

The Vulture's must be biding their time to attack again, but fuck, I want it over and done with already. We're caught in a situation where we can't be proactive and instead, have to be reactive.

Placing the last cup, I glance up to see the twins step out into the garden, Jameson grinning like a maniac while Jagger looks about ready to beat the fuck out of someone.

Perfect.

It's barely even ten o'clock, and he's already growly. Although his outfit might be the cause of it. With matching blue and red hats, black shorts, and red t-shirts, it's instantly obvious that they're tweedle-dee and tweedle-dum.

Fuck.

None of us got a choice in this decision, but my dick

twitches at the thought of what Lucy will look like.

As if the mere thought in my mind summons her, Lucy steps through the door after them. It takes a second for me to recognize it's her with the bright red hair and smoky make-up, but as I trail my eyes over her from head to toe, I know going with this whole Alice in Wonderland theme was totally fucking worth it.

I half expected her to appear in a little blue dress as our little Alice, but instead, she stands before me in black platform boots, white tights, and a deep red dress. Finished off with a white shawl over her shoulders with red love hearts scattered along the hem.

She's our Queen of Hearts.

Fuck, I'm definitely impressed, and as I adjust my cock in my pants, I know he's eager to impress her in this little get up.

Lucy Carter is fucking stunning, there's no doubt about it, and she's all ours.

That thought alone makes a smile spread across my face, and before I even realize it, I'm halfway across the yard, making my way toward her.

As I near the three of them, I hear Jameson and Jagger grumbling at each other, but my focus is on my girl as her eyes find mine. I watch as they widen in surprise as she takes in my outfit, and wanting to see her smile, I tip my hat and bow. I hear the giggle fall from her lips before I lift my head back up, and when I spy her bright red lips grinning at me, I feel like a fucking king.

"Jameson Izaro, excellent choice on our Queen of Hearts here, but did we really have to look like dickheads?" I say, before leaning in to place a small, lingering kiss on the corner of her mouth, and her hands instantly land on my chest as I pull her in closer by her hips.

"Right? My point exactly, this is stupid as fuck," Jagger grunts, making me smile as I look down at Lucy, who rolls her eyes at him.

"Excuse me, motherfucker, I found a way for there to be twins while representing the fact that our girl is our queen. I did excellent, thank you very much," Jameson responds, folding his arms over his chest as he raises his eyebrows at us all, and deep down, I can't argue with that.

Turning my attention back to Lucy, I run my hands through the red wig, before thinking better of it. It doesn't hold the same connection when it's not her real hair, and it feels weird as shit.

"What is your plan this evening? I have a few things to

arrange, but I was hoping this hot redhead dressed as the Queen of Hearts might save me a dance later," I purr into her ear, feeling her shiver in my arms, and my needy cock juts out in her direction again.

I've been uncontrollable like this since I took her ass. Now my cock just can't calm down around her. It's like we need to repeatedly claim her over and over again.

"Naomi messaged, she's making an appearance and I need to keep up the whole fucking charade, but you can bet your ass I'm in the mood to dance with the Mad Hatter tonight," she responds, her breath hot against my ear as she whispers back.

My gut clenches for her. I hate that she has to act like everything is okay with the two-faced bitch, when it's really not, but I understand that it'll help us in the long run.

"Perfect. Stay safe. I'm going to be out here the entire time so if you need me, just give me a glance and I'll know, alright?" I squeeze her tight in my arms, and when she looks up at me with a soft smile on her lips, I can't help but lean in and brush mine against hers.

Fuck her red lipstick, I hope it smears. I want everyone to know she's off limits. I love how she matches me with force, the battle for control, demanding to take the lead over our lips, and for once, I let her. The second I relax, letting her guide her mouth over mine, she instantly softens, turning the kiss sweet but intoxicating, leaving me even more needy than before.

As her lips fall from mine, I reluctantly take a step back, pleased to see a little of her lipstick has faded, and I hope it's pasted over my mouth. If it is, I won't wipe it off.

"Save me that dance," I repeat, tilting her chin up and staring into her blue eyes before she nods. With a wink, I turn on my heel, patting Jagger's tense arm as he grumbles some shit about hogging his girl, again, and I move toward the back of the yard where the six runners are waiting for me.

I slow my pace as I approach the guys dressed casually in black jeans and matching tees, not taking part in the Halloween party at all. "Boys, how have things been this week?" I ask, flipping my hat off as I come to a stop before them. These are the main group of guys who run our shit, the rest we tend to alterate, but I have a feeling it could all do with a shift.

I can see the question in their eyes over my choice of outfit, but they don't get to understand the inside joke and meaning to it, that's not their place and they know it.

"We've had no issues at all," the guy to my right responds, holding out the backpack, but I nod to the floor for him to drop it at my feet. No direct switch. Ever. I stare him down a moment making sure his fuck up is known, then nod slowly before I cast my gaze over the others.

"Is that right?" I ask, wanting clarity on this guy's answer as he nods eagerly in response.

"Yep, not a single issue with the distributions at all," he states, meaning the drugs were distributed like normal, and it always makes me fucking cringe, but we have to do whatever it takes to survive, and right now, it includes that.

Slipping my hand into my pants pocket, I take a step forward, placing myself in the center as they almost circle around me.

I give them a moment, to let them feel like the predator, let them feel what it's like to always have prey in their hands, and it's no surprise when they all stand a little taller as I slightly hunch my shoulders and turn on the spot, looking down at their feet.

When I come back to face the guy who answered me, I can see the twitch of a smile on his lips, a smug ass look pleading to take over his face, and I almost want to laugh.

In one swift move, I pull a knife from my pocket and

press the blade against his throat. His eyes widen in surprise as I grin at him. I fucking love catching people off guard.

Jameson is known for his switchblade, which is why I'm usually the one to step in when it comes time to actually using one, because no one fucking expects me, but I know my way around the heavy metal in my hand too.

"Now I know you're a lying cunt," I spit out, going toe to toe with him as I tower slightly above him, pressing the tip of my blade into his throat so it mildly pierces the skin, and I hear small gasps from the guys around us. "Now, do you want to try again, or would you prefer that I make an example of you?"

His back is to the crowd in the yard so I have the advantage to see who is watching, but everyone is too distracted by the music pumping through the speakers and the alcohol to even notice us back here.

Except Lucy of course.

She stands beside Naomi, who must have only just arrived, and I can feel her trying to decipher what's happening over here.

Always wanting to be in the know, just like I would right now.

Turning my focus back on this asshole, I quirk an

eyebrow, which will be barely visible at this end of the yard, but he must get the message as I nudge the blade a millimeter and he starts to scramble.

"They fucking had us, man, what were we supposed to do?" He yells as his hands clench at his sides, and I shake my head.

We'd got word earlier today that last night's shipment went wrong, but we knew it would be better to approach them here to see how things panned out first, and it looks like not a single one of these men are loyal.

Pity.

"You were supposed to get a message straight to us, asshole. I'm going to assume it was the Vulture's," I say in a bored tone, and he nods ever so slightly, not wanting to move the blade too much as I keep it pressed against his neck. "Use your voice, motherfucker, tell me what went down," I bite, getting annoyed at the situation, and it's the guy to his left that caves first.

"When we went to make the drop over on Sycamore, some of Dax's men were waiting for us. They took all the goods, and then Dax appeared, demanding we keep our mouths shut or they'd rip out our tongues," he rambles, his hands flying around as he tries to explain. He doesn't know the first thing about threats, and he wouldn't handle a single second under interrogation it seems.

A chuckle falls from my lips as I shake my head. These motherfucking idiots. "What's to say I won't rip your tongues out now? Maybe I should make you permanently silent because you *chose* silence," I taunt, flicking my gaze to the left and the right as I watch each of them swallow at my words. "Luckily for you, your story checks out and it seems you have people that might miss you. But you're done here. Fucking done."

"Wait, what? But we need our cut," the guy beneath my blade grunts, and I laugh.

"You lost your cut when you let them take the drugs and fuck knows, probably the money too," I bite back in response. "We don't allow traitors into the circle. Now, you have approximately ten seconds to get the fuck out of my house before I let Jagger and Jameson have free rein on you all," I growl, done with their shit as I pocket the blade and stare them all down.

"Don't you want to know who was there?" One of the guys behind me asks, his hands out wide as he scrambles to find a way to get on our good graces again. I simply raise my eyebrows at him, waiting for him to continue.

He shakes his hands out, glancing at the others, and I see one of them slightly shake his head.

"If you're not talking, then your ten seconds are almost up," I announce, and all but the guy standing before me make a run for it.

Cowardly rat bastards.

They'll probably try to join the Vulture's in retaliation, that's if they haven't already. But fortunately, Dax seems to hate rats more than we do, so I'm not worried about their attempted role in our demise.

"Cat got your tongue?" I state, tucking both hands in my pockets as I look him over. It's funny how, even dressed as the fucking Mad Hatter, I can make assholes quiver in their boots.

"Vince was there, Vince Monroe." Without another word he rushes after the other guys, likely knowing the twins are watching and ready to pounce.

My heart pounds in my chest as I stare after him, before catching sight of Lucy as she looks at me in concern. We'd had our doubts about him, but there was nothing we could pinpoint.

Fuck.

They're definitely trying to come at us through Lucy if

this is the case. Things have definitely been shifting lately.

One hundred fucking percent.

We need to come up with a plan, and now. I won't risk Lucy getting caught in the crossfire. Not ever. Swiping a hand down my face, I sigh. There goes my dance later with my girl.

There are unfortunately now more pressing matters to attend to.

You can come for me, fuck, you can even come for my brothers, but coming for our girl? Fuck, that's suicide.

WATCH ME RISE

CHAPTER TWENTY TWO

Lou-Lou

I tap my fingers on the steering wheel as I wait for Jagger to lock the front door and climb in. Apparently we're all going to campus together this morning, piled into my truck, which is fine, except I've been sitting here waiting for almost twenty minutes for them all to get in. I've got about fifteen minutes to get to class, and I hate being late, it makes me antsy.

Jagger climbs into the back with Ezra and Leo, and the second the door shuts behind him, I start to move the truck.

"Wow, can a guy not get his seatbelt on?" he grumbles,

and I roll my eyes.

"Please, it'll take you two seconds, although with the amount of time I just had to wait for you, we could still be sitting there until next year," I sass back, raising my eyebrow at him in the rearview mirror, and he shakes his head at me.

I want to stick my tongue out at him, but I somehow manage to refrain.

Everyone seems a little tense and on edge since Friday's Halloween party. Having Dax and the Vulture's fuck with another part of the Arrow's set up, doesn't sit well with any of us, but the mention of Vince's name had my gut dropping as we attempt to piece it all together.

There's a mole, there has to be, but I have no idea where to begin with that. Although it seems Ezra has made it his personal mission.

It's all just a fucking nightmare.

Even a little Halloween party fun was short-lived. But I had to pretend like I couldn't see there was trouble since I was entertaining Naomi all night. Which was harder than I thought it would be since she was her usual chirpy self.

Shaking my head, I focus on the issue of today, and the topic of conversation before Jagger got in the car. "Have you got your sensible and reasonable head on today or are you in typical asshole mode?" I ask, flicking my eyes to him in the mirror before taking the left turning off our street.

"What kind of question is that? Asshole. Always asshole, I thought we already discussed this?" he responds, swiping his hand down his face, and I have to bite back the smile. I love that he can't even see himself, how soft he can be with me sometimes. But if he wants to live by the asshole code, then I'll go along with it.

"We're trying to figure out the logistics for the day because I have a culinary exam this morning, and I don't want to leave Lucy on her own," Leo says to Jagger, and I refrain from rolling my eyes as he continues. "I don't want her on her own in class with Naomi and Vince, especially if the information we got the other day proves to be true."

Jameson and Ezra remain quiet, waiting for Jagger to respond, but it's only fair that I get to explain my thought process too.

"I think I should be able to attend class on my own. I have a list of reasons, care to hear them?" I ask, but even if he says no I'm going to push. When I take a chance and glance in the mirror, I find a knowing look in his eyes, like he can tell I won't take no for an answer.

"Fire away," he mumbles, relaxing back in his seat as he stares me down, leaving me to picture his jeans stretching across his thighs as he gets comfortable.

Fuck.

What was I saying?

Clearing my throat, I wet my lips as Jameson's hand squeezes my leg. "Okay. Reason number one is I'm an adult who can take care of herself, examples of this can be linked back to the past three years," I start as I slow at the traffic light, but I keep my gaze forward so I don't stop my flow. "Reason number two would be the fact that it would look suspicious because they likely assume Leo just takes the class with us, while someone else suddenly appearing would make them take notice. Reason number three is I refuse to cower to these motherfuckers. Reason number four—"

"You've made your point, Luella," Jagger interrupts, making me glare at him through the mirror as the lights turn to green and I have to focus back on driving. "Jameson?" He says his name as a question, wanting his input on the situation, which catches me by surprise because he usually just steam rolls us all.

Jameson's grip on my thigh tightens as I turn into the campus parking lot. "I think she actually has a point, Jag. If we're supposed to be letting them think they have the upper hand then it would be too obvious if one of us rocked up with her." I smile at his words since he's agreeing with me. "But I also don't like her being alone on the other side of campus," he adds, and my smile instantly drops.

Asshole.

They're twin assholes and not my favorites of the day.

Jagger nods in understanding, before turning to look at the guys beside him. "I can already tell by the look on Leo's face that he doesn't want to leave you on your own so I'm not even going to ask, but Ezra?"

Is this going to a fucking vote or something?

How ridiculous.

"I'm with Jameson, it's a difficult situation, but ultimately we have to hear what Lou-Lou's saying."

"Thank you!" I exclaim, looking over my shoulder to smile wide at him once the truck is in park. "Figuring out all of this shit with the Vulture's is important, and I don't want to ruin it all because of my *safety* which isn't even an issue," I state, clasping my hands together in front of me. "You guys could still walk me over there, your presence, even for five seconds, would set the tone. Then once the lesson is over, I can meet the nearest one of you, or my class is in the building next to the library, and I could meet you there," I offer, trying to show I'm being flexible and not a brat. Compromise, it is a thing that they've clearly forgotten about.

Silence fills the car, leaving me even more antsy as I glance at the time. I really don't have time for this to take all week. My class starts in five minutes, but if I push it'll probably work against me, so I take a deep breath, waiting as patiently as I can for a response.

After what feels like an eternity, Jagger finally speaks.

"She's right." My heart just about stops as I process his words, my jaw hanging open slightly as I turn to look at him, but I quickly slam my mouth shut before I piss him off and he changes his mind. "But we don't fuck around with this shit, Luella. Your safety is paramount. As soon as your class is over, you go straight to the library, up to the room where you went with Leo last time, and you don't leave until one of us gets there, understood?"

His growly voice does nothing but make me smile wider. Victory at last.

"Understood. Now, can we go before I'm late?" I ask,

quirking an eyebrow, before I climb out of the truck.

The guys quickly follow, falling into step with me as I start toward the courtyard. Flanked by Ezra and Jameson on my left, and Leo and Jagger on my right, I feel all eyes on us, or them, as always.

Ezra's arm drops over my shoulders, and I can feel the stares from a group of girls as they watch me. They've likely been taking note of me appearing with the guys, and there's always a different one of my kings with his hands on me at any given moment.

Glancing at them out of the corner of my eye and I find them glaring at me, but I shrug it off. People are either going to be offended by our setup or jealous. Either way, I'm good with just doing whatever makes us happy.

Fuck the rest of the world.

As we approach the Salvatore building, my steps slow and Ezra pulls me in tight to his chest as he whispers in my ear. "Be careful, Lou. If you feel unsure at any time, send a text, make a call, whatever it is, and we'll come running alright?" I nod in response as he presses his lips to my forehead and takes a step back.

Jameson wastes no time filling the spot Ezra just vacated, his hands landing straight on my waist as he pulls me against his chest. "I think my class is the closest. The second I'm out I'll be at the library, baby," he murmurs, before placing his lips on mine, and I melt into him as his fingers run through my wavy hair.

When he reluctantly pulls away, I pout a little, but he seamlessly hands me off to Leo, who tucks my hair behind my ear as he looks into my eyes. "I'm not trying to be suffocating, Lucy. I just don't want—"

I cut him off by pressing my lips to his, trying to portray that I'm not mad at him for wanting someone to replace him for the class. I get the need to protect each other, fuck I feel it too, but I love the fact that he's willing to hear me and the others without arguing and making me feel like my opinion doesn't matter.

Prying my lips from his, I run my thumb across his bottom lip as his gray eyes burn into mine, and I grin, reaching up on my tiptoes once more, kissing the corner of his mouth before he steps back.

Which just leaves Jagger.

Of course it does.

Before I can consider whether he's going to make a scene or not, I'm being lifted off the ground effortlessly, my back pressed to his front as he walks us the short distance to the steps leading into the hall. As he comes to a stop, he slowly lowers me to stand on one of the steps, before turning me to face him.

I'm the same height as him on this step, and as I look him over, I can feel every pair of eyes in the court on us, but I don't pull my gaze from his. Out of all of the guys he's the least into public displays of affection, so I think that little show, plus the fact I've had the other three claiming me on the spot too, could make us top gossip for the day.

I don't mind being campus gossip if it makes everyone aware they're mine.

Jagger places his fingers under my chin, tilting my head back even though we're eye to eye, he leans in closer so I can feel his breath brush against my cheek.

"Don't make me regret it, Luella," he murmurs, referring to letting me go in there alone, and I try to nod in understanding, but his grip tightens making it difficult. "You're precious to me, I refuse to let anyone fuck with that. So if that means I have to keep you locked in an ivory tower to ensure your safety, then I will."

His words wash over me as I try to swallow past the lump in my throat, but before I can respond, he crushes his lips to mine, and my hands rise to his chest. My fingers grip his white tee as I fight him for control, but it's futile, and within moments I submit, letting him suck the air from my body.

All too quickly the professor begins speaking to the class, and I jolt back, a little light headed as I turn to go up the steps and his hand falls away. Raking my teeth over my bottom lip, I feel my cheeks heat as I desperately want to take them all home, but I have to remember how important college is. Graduating has always been the goal but now they're a part of that end-game too.

With that, I offer a half smile, that's all I can manage as I try to contain my raging hormones, before turning on my heels and racing inside. Once in, I take the staircase two steps at a time until I reach my row, and drop into my seat effortlessly before the professor can begin the class. Only then do I release the breath I was holding.

"Hey, no Leo today?" Naomi whispers from beside me, startling me a little since I'm still in a daze from my kings, and I quickly shake my head.

"Not today," I answer as relaxed as I can, not wanting to add any more to the conversation as I shoot her a smile, and she offers me a tight one in response, before glancing over her shoulder.

Weird.

Shaking my head, I focus on the professor as she begins to address the class, and I'm instantly sucked into the work. The more I focus in class and absorb everything I can, the easier everything else in my life will be.

There's a niggling feeling at the back of my mind throughout the entire class, and I can't seem to wipe the frown from my face as I take notes on my laptop, something is off. I just don't know what.

I can't message Ezra like he said. Imagine? What would I even say? Oh, I feel like someone's looking at me? That's ridiculous, and not a reason to interrupt any of their classes, so I buckle down and just get the work done while keeping to myself.

As the class draws to an end, the professor reminds everyone of the paper due next week, and I make a reminder to check if I've finished that one as I put away my things.

"Hey, uh, do you want to run to the bathroom with me before lunch?" Naomi asks, and I instantly go on high alert. Is that why she was asking if Leo was here or not? What's going to happen once I get in there? Is it a setup?

Fuck.

I can feel myself spiraling a little as I scramble for a

logical response. As I look her over from head to toe, she seems unsure, fidgety, and a little skittish while she nibbles on her lip, all of which are huge red flags for me.

Maybe that's what's been giving me the icky feeling throughout the entire class then? I don't know.

Clearing my throat as she continues to stare at me, waiting for an answer, I offer a subtle head shake. "Sorry, I'm meeting one of the guys today for a little one on one, but we should definitely do something one night after school soon if you're game?" I offer, and her eyes widen. I can't quite decipher if it's in desperation or agitation, but I don't stick around to find out as I lift my bag over my shoulder and head for the door.

I can feel eyes drilling into the back of my head as I follow the crowd of students out into the hallway and down the steps. As I near the bottom, I pull my phone from my pocket to find a new group chat started.

Ezra added you to the Wonderland group chat.

Fucking Wonderland. I knew Jameson's option for Halloween would have a lasting impression, but I have no issues being their queen in every sense of the word; even in fairytales.

As I continue reading, I can't contain my smile.

Ezra renamed Jagger: Tweedle-Dum
Ezra renamed Jameson: Tweedle-Dee
Ezra renamed Leo: Mad Hatter
Ezra renamed himself: Cheshire Cat
Ezra renamed Lou-Lou: Queen of Hearts

We are never changing these. Not ever.

Tweedle-Dum: Is this a fucking joke, Ezra? Change my name back.

Tweedle-Dum: I'm serious, Ez!

Cheshire Cat: I don't know how.

Tweedle-Dum: Don't fuck with me. Besides who chose me to be the Dum one? At least switch me out for Dee.

Tweedle Dee: Nope, I paid him to make sure I didn't get the shitty one, bro. Get over it.

Oh fuck. I don't know whether I already regret

everyone in one spot, but we're definitely going to have some fun winding Jagger up, that's for sure.

The blast of cool air catches me off guard as I step outside, and I quickly pocket my phone so I can focus on getting to the library. I can read the rest of the messages when I get there.

I can't seem to shake the icky feeling that continues to wash over me as I put as much distance between me and the building as possible, hopefully leaving Naomi and Vince behind, but I don't want to turn back and look. The last thing I want is to appear startled and unsure.

Rushing up the steps to the library, I try to subtly look over my shoulder as I step inside, but I can't focus on anything to notice if something is wrong or out of place.

Once I'm in the room with the door lock firmly in place, I'll be fine. I reassure myself, even if I am overreacting.

As I step into the library, I recognize the woman behind the desk as the same lady who was here the last time I came in with Leo. Brushing my hair back over my face, I panic over what I'm supposed to say to her, but as I near the desk, her eyes reach mine, and she instantly rises, and by the time I get to her, she's already holding a key out for me.

"Thank you," I mumble, and she offers a sharp nod in response before retaking her seat, dismissing me instantly, but I don't mind. Nothing would have made the situation worse than her trying to talk with me when I really just wanted to get upstairs.

Making my way to the same stairs I took with Leo, I try to keep my steps relaxed and casual, but the hairs on the back of my neck are standing at attention, unpleasant goosebumps appearing on my skin and the icky feeling I felt earlier, only feels more intense now.

The second I reach the top of the steps, I up my pace, kicking my casual attitude in the ass as uncertainty swirls in my stomach. I spot the room up ahead, and I keep the key poised and ready in my hand as I race toward it.

I refuse to look back over my shoulder, even as I reach the door to the room the key slips into the lock seamlessly. The second I hear the click of the lock, I sag in relief, pushing the door open in a flurry, before whirling around to slam it shut, ready to lock it and wait for one of the guys. But just as the door is about to hit the frame, a foot stops the door in its tracks. Like a fucking scene from a horror movie, I look up with wide eyes to find Vince standing before me.

Fuck.

His usually blond, well-kept hair is sticking up in every direction as he stares down at me with wide eyes, his pupils blown as he taps his fingers on the door.

"Uh, can I help you?" I ask, my voice firm as I look him over, and he scoffs.

"Yeah, you really fucking could, Luella Carter." He says my name slowly, like the two words are heavy on his tongue.

Is he high? Or drunk? Fuck, he could be both.

"Sorry, that must have come out wrong. I have no interest in helping you with shit, so please, fuck all the way off," I rephrase, batting my eyelashes with a sickly sweet smile as I push at the door again, but he just shakes his head, not moving an inch as he eyes me.

I almost consider sucker punching this motherfucker but he starts to speak before I get a chance, interrupting my thoughts.

"It's almost funny that you think you get a choice," he bites back, almost bearing his teeth at me. It's surreal to compare him to the guy I met when I first got here because right now, they're lightyears apart. But this version of him seems erratic, and I don't know how to handle that. His fist slams into the door, and I feel it rattle beneath my touch as I stare at him with wide eyes. "Why couldn't you just—"

"Is everything okay here?" Jameson spits out, cutting Vince off before he can finish his sentence, and I'm both thankful and eager to know what he was about to say.

Vince stumbles back a step or two, flicking his gaze between Jameson and I as he runs his hand through his hair.

"I asked a fucking question, is everything okay here?" Jameson bites, the cords in his neck straining as he repeats himself, but he seems a little more satisfied now that there's space between Vince and me.

"We're good. Vince was *just* leaving," I state, still holding the door handle tightly as I barely keep the door open.

"Fuck this shit," Vince hisses, before moving to brush past Jameson, but of course Jameson refuses to let him go easily. He growls something in Vince's ear that I can't quite make out, but then pushes him toward the stairs before I can even blink, and in the next moment I'm wrapped up in Jameson's arms.

"Are you okay, Ella? I can chase that motherfucker down and chop him into tiny pieces if that will make you feel better," he offers, and I almost consider it since the creepy motherfucker was obviously following me, but I think better of it.

"We have bigger problems to be dealing with than fucking Vince. He seems like a small fish in a big pond," I mutter in response as Jameson leans back to glance down at me, searching my eyes to make sure I'm telling the truth. I try to hide the tremble in my fingers, but I know he sees right through me, attempting to cover up how shaken I actually am.

"You're right, but you know this means you can never be left alone again, right? Although we respect your opinion, clearly it wasn't the right call to make. At least not right now." He tucks my hair behind my ear as I roll my eyes.

Even with my heart pounding wildly in my chest and my pulse ringing in my ears, I still shake my head at him. "Please, this was nothing, I could have taken that fucker if I needed to," I say with a shrug. "I was more concerned about Naomi in class than him," I add, and he widens his eyes at me like I just proved his point.

Fuck.

Taking a step back, I shake my hands out, trying to

release some of the adrenaline pumping through my system right now, but it's useless.

It's on the tip of my tongue to ask him to sneak home and spar with me, but he opens his mouth before I get the chance, and I like his suggestion far better.

"Get your shit, you're coming with me. If that little group session taught me anything, it's that I need to fuck this adrenaline out of you. Hard and fast. Let's go."

Tweedle-Dee just made himself today's favorite.

CHAPTER TWENTY THREE

Lou-Lou

With his hand wrapped tightly around mine, Jameson pulls me down the steps of the library, and starts to maneuver us through the people still gathered in the court. It's not all that difficult. Not when you're Jameson Izaro, and the students part like you're Moses and they're simply the water in his path.

Rolling my eyes, I quicken my pace to keep up with him. I can barely feel the cool air as more adrenaline and excitement pumps through me. His last words bounce around in my mind, and all I can think about right now is him taking me home and fucking me until I'm exhausted. I don't even care if I get nothing to eat for lunch or miss classes, it'll all be worth it.

As we move toward the parking lot, I can see the truck in the distance, and Jameson releases my hand, making me almost pout, until he runs his hand under my coat, and beneath the casual t-shirt I'm wearing. I shiver at the contact of his fingertips skimming across the bare skin at my spine, and he keeps them there until we reach the truck. Leaving me even more desperate and needy than I was just moments ago.

I fumble for my truck keys as we come to a stop, quickly disengaging the alarm and swinging open the driver's side door. "Who's driving?" I ask, not even bothered if he wants to, I just need us to get back to the house as quickly as possible.

When he doesn't answer, I glance up at him, only to find him already staring down at me with his eyebrows raised. Jameson wordlessly takes my bag from my shoulder, and tosses it across the center console so it lands on the passenger's seat.

"Who said anything about driving?" He murmurs in response, and my heart quickens in my chest as my mouth dries. He can't be serious... Can he?

"What... I... What?"

My brain short circuits as I run my gaze over him, my pulse ringing in my ears as I stand confused before him.

Without a single word, he throws his bag in the truck beside mine, before opening the rear passenger door, and climbing in. He sits in the center seat, his dark eyes grazing over me from head to toe, and it feels like an eternity passes before his eyes reach mine again. All the while I continue to stand here, gaping at him in surprise.

"Get in, Ella," he practically purrs, before leaning forward and adjusting the front seats so there's more space in the back.

Trying to swallow past the lump in my throat, I glance over my shoulder as I see the court and the parking lot filled with people. Some will be heading for lunch while others could either be starting for the day or finishing early. Either way, I refuse to let them interrupt this for me.

My skin prickles with heat as I take a deep breath and climb in beside him, shutting the door behind me as I crouch, resting one knee on the seat next to him as I take my puffy coat off.

I turn my gaze to his after I place it on the driver's seat, and I watch as he wets his lips. "Are we really going to do this here?" I ask, nibbling on my bottom lip as excitement pools in my stomach.

Vince, and everything that happened only moments ago, feels like a distant memory as I look toward Jameson now. With a wave of his magical dick, he has erased the shit storm brewing outside of the truck. He's right, my adrenaline is still fiercely pumping through my body, and it needs a release, an escape. Now.

"Not with you fully dressed we aren't," he responds, a grin on his lips and a knowing twinkle in his eyes as he reaches out to run his fingers along the hem of my t-shirt.

Glancing around at the windows, I know they're all as tinted as possible, making it difficult to see in. I know the front windshield, by law, isn't as blacked out as the others, but someone's going to have to be close, and specifically trying to see in to notice us. Right now, even someone doing that isn't going to stop me.

I rub my thighs together, needy for the friction as I cross my arms over my body, grabbing the material of my t-shirt, and pulling it slowly over my head. I discard it over my shoulder as I look back at Jameson, his eyes devouring me without a single touch, and I try to catch a deep breath.

"Red really is your fucking color," he murmurs, reaching out to stroke his finger over my lacy bra, and my nipples instantly strain beneath his touch. "Now the jeans too, Ella," he breathes running his fingers from my collarbone to the waist of my jeans, and I nod in agreement, wetting my lips as I unbutton them, and slowly draw the zipper down.

I pause for a moment, trying to figure out how I'm going to get my jeans and boots off in this small space, but Jameson must see the concern on my face, because moments later, I'm being spun around and placed in his lap, with very little effort.

As I try to catch my breath, he taps at my thigh, making me frown, until he murmurs in my ear. "Lift." I lift my leg as he asks, and brace my foot on the back of the seat in front, before quickly untying my boot. I repeat the motion with the other before I move to shimmy my jeans down my legs, but he quickly grips my hips and holds me in place, thrusting the outline of his cock through his own jeans against my ass, and I groan.

Fuck.

It doesn't matter if these people can see or not, they'll be able to hear, especially when I can't control myself like this.

Jameson slips his hands into the waistband of my jeans, lifting me up slightly as his hands grip the globes of my ass, before he continues to drag them down my thighs. "Stand," he orders, and I can't help but comply, rising to my feet and hunching over while bracing my hands on the front seats to keep my balance.

When my jeans are pooled at my feet, I kick them completely off as Jameson strokes his fingers over the lace of my matching panties, and I shiver.

His hands fall to my hips again, his grip tight, telling me to remain in place as his teeth graze over my ass cheeks. He slowly gets lower with each pass, before he's pulling the lace to one side and stroking his tongue over my pussy.

"Lean forward, Ella," he says, his breath caressing my needy pussy as I swallow past the lump in my throat and do as he commands.

Bracing my hands on the center console, I try to keep my body low, especially since there are people walking past us casually, laughing and joking in groups, but no one seems to be paying any attention to us… yet.

With my top half leaning forward, my ass sticks up in the air, I sneak a glance over my shoulder, finding his gaze fixed on my core. He keeps the lace in place as he strokes his finger under the material from my clit all the way to my entrance, and my mouth falls open as I manage to keep the moan held in.

"You have such a pretty, pink pussy, Ella," he states as his fingers slowly repeat the motion, but he doesn't actually enter my core until the fourth pass, when I'm practically vibrating in his hands with need. The moment his two fingers thrust inside me, I jolt, catching my breath as desire ripples through me and a moan passes my lips.

Fuck.

"Please, Jameson, I don't want to come until you're deep inside me," I plead, glancing back over my shoulder to see his eyes widen with pleasure at my words.

"Say that again," he repeats, continuing to slowly thrust two fingers inside of me, making my skin break out in a pale flushed trail as heat consumes me.

"I don't want to come until you're deep inside me," I repeat, my jaw hanging loose as my body begs for me to release the groan I'm fighting to hold back.

At my words, he slips his fingers from my body, and I immediately whimper in protest, even though I know he's going to give me what I want. But I can't help it, I'm needy, desperate, and I want to feel it all.

Trying to turn around to face him in the cramped space isn't easy, but when I've finally got my feet planted on either side of him, and my body facing his, I find his jeans down his thighs and his thick, hard length on display.

I wet my lips, and waggle my finger at him as he looks up at me. "Not when you've still got your top and jacket on, Jameson," I purr, bracing one knee on either side of him as I straddle his thighs.

Slipping my hands inside his jacket, he leans forward just enough for it to fall from his body as I drag the arms down, and when I discard it at my side, his switchblade falls out beside it.

It wouldn't be Jameson if that blade wasn't nearby.

With a grin on my lips, I turn my gaze back to his to find his t-shirt long gone, and an array of tattoos on display as his hands stroke over my thighs.

"You're so fucking beautiful, Ella," he says, his eyes searching mine, but I have no idea what for as I inch myself forward, desperate to feel his cock against my pussy.

"I'll look even better with you inside me," I respond with a grin, and he matches it instantly as he unclips my bra effortlessly, letting my breasts fall free, before he grips the lace of my panties and tears them with ease, leaving me completely bare before him. In the car. In the middle of the campus parking lot. And I really couldn't give a shit.

"Hands on my shoulders, baby," he demands, not waiting for me to move them as he grabs my hands and places them exactly where he wants, and the move automatically edges me closer to his engorged cock.

Just looking at him makes my pussy clench, and excitement pools in my stomach as he drags me in close so we're chest to chest. One of his hands strokes gently down my spine as he presses his lips to mine, and I grind down on his cock, wanting to consume him as much as he's intoxicating me.

I feel a phone vibrate somewhere on the seats, but Jameson shakes his head instantly, speaking against my lips. "It'll be one of the others wondering where we are, and right now, this is about you and me."

I can agree with that.

With my hands on his shoulders, I rise to my knees as he lines his cock up with my entrance, and my blood spikes the second the tip of his length pushes against my core.

"Fuck," I groan, before slowly lowering myself on to

his dick.

I take my time, dragging it out perfectly so I can feel every inch of his stiff cock drag against my walls. When I'm fully seated, and completely filled, I let out a strangled cry.

"Shit, Ella," Jameson hisses against my ear as my hands tighten on his shoulders. He wraps his hands around my hips, jutting up into me slightly, and I know if anyone is near the truck right now they're going to hear me.

Wanting to control him, before he gets any ideas and continues to fuck up into me, I tilt my hips and grind against him, watching his eyes roll back in his head as I repeat the motion again and again. I love watching him crumble beneath me, his neck flushing pink like I'm sure mine is too.

I want to blow his fucking mind because I know I'm going to explode all over him in no time.

I drop my hand from his shoulder, rushing to grab what I'm looking for before he can force my hand back in place, and when I sit back up right, I watch as his eyes fall on what I'm now holding, and he gapes at me.

"What are you doing, Ella?" he asks huskily as I grind against him and flick open the switchblade at the same time.

"I'm fucking you, what does it look like I'm doing?" I purr back, continuing to grind against him as I brace myself with one hand on his shoulder, while the other holds the blade tightly as I tilt it toward my chest.

I'm not crazy enough to hurt myself, and I know my way around a knife, but watching his eyes widen as the silver glistens against my skin, the length of the blade pressed between my breasts, is like finding gold.

"Ella, you don't know what you're doing, it—"

"Jameson, shut the fuck up or I'll use the handle to get me off instead of you," I interrupt, grinding against him once more as my pussy clenches around him.

His jaw falls open further as he eyes me, and I can see the conflict in his gaze, he's turned on, but still worried about my safety.

Fuck it.

As I grind down against him on the next turn, I move the blade lightning fast, letting it press up against his throat. The blade is tilted so it won't cut him, but it's unreal watching his pupils completely blow as his grip on my hips tightens and he fucks up into me.

The combination of it all overwhelms me, and on the

third thrust I come long and hard around him, struggling to keep the blade held properly as my orgasm rips through me. The punishing grip on my waist gets tighter as I feel his cock pulse inside of me, and I scream in ecstasy.

When my eyes meet his, I drop the switchblade to the side as our lips crash together, each of us working off the frenzied desire still hurtling through us, until we're simply a pile of limbs.

"Holy fuck, Ella," Jameson croaks, as I cling to him, sweat dripping down my spine and mingling between us as I try to catch my breath. "That was the hottest thing I've seen in my entire existence," he admits, holding me tighter, and I grin.

Before I can utter my response, someone raps their knuckles on the front windshield, and I hear Jameson curse before I glance back over my shoulder to find Jagger glaring at us as he tries to squint through the tinted glass.

"I hope you motherfuckers are satisfied now," he grumbles as the driver's side door opens and I fall to the side of Jameson, trying to hide my body as Leo's face appears.

"Please, continue, I could hear your moans echoing throughout the court," he says with a grin, his eyes trailing over me, and he shakes his head. "As if I would open the door if anyone else was around, Lucy, what do you take me for?" he adds, and my eyes widen.

"It's fucking freezing out there, Leo. Shut the fucking door," I shout, swiping my hair back off my face as he falls into the driver's seat and closes the door shut behind him, while Jagger takes the seat beside him.

"What's going on?" Jameson asks, frowning at the pair of them, and I can hear the uncertainty in his voice, and when I glance back at Leo and Jagger, I can see the tension around their eyes too. Jameson's right, something is definitely going on.

Searching for my clothes, I freeze in place as Jagger answers his brother.

"Robbie called, he's announced what he wants in repayment for me fucking up the last fight."

CHAPTER TWENTY FOUR

Lou-Lou

The truck is quiet as we pull to a stop outside of the warehouse, Jagger already sitting idle on his motorcycle beside us as his words repeat in my mind again.

I've had better Thursday evenings than this one. That's for sure.

"Robbie has scheduled another fight for me, and this time I have to fake getting knocked out. Lose. Again. Only he's threatened Lola this time."

A wave of nausea washes over me again as I panic over Lola's involvement in all of this. I'm once again left understanding why the guys have done everything they have so far to appease Robbie. That motherfucker plays dirty.

The warehouse looks exactly as it did the last time we were here, but I feel completely different. Coming here last time opened the floodgates of secrets, and I cringe, remembering how I kneed Leo in the balls before running, but it led me to Lockwood, and all the secrets came to light from there.

Now, when I gaze up at the derelict looking building before me, I know exactly what I'm walking into, and exactly how to handle myself.

I also know that Robbie is going to be in there, in all his fucking glory, and again I'm still not going to be able to do anything to him. Fucker.

None of us move in the truck until Jagger swings his leg over the bike, pulling his helmet off as he stands beside his prized Harley Davidson. He looks hot as hell in a pair of combat boots, black combat pants, with a fitted, black sweater and of course a matching *black* leather jacket. Once he secures his helmet away, he runs his fingers through his long brown hair, pulling it back into a bun at the top of his head, and making me rub my thighs together in appreciation.

"Ella, you've got a little something there," Jameson murmurs, before leaning across the center console and slowly drags his thumb over the corner of my mouth. I frown in confusion, but when I turn my gaze to him I realize he's winding me up by the grin on his face, because he caught me drooling over his brother.

Sticking my tongue out at him, I hear him chuckle as I move to open the passenger door, but it's locked. Whirling around to glare at him, he swiftly shuts the driver's door. Fuck. Every time he's driving, he does this, and I can't even complain a little bit.

The first time he was angry, but it still felt romantic, and now, as I watch him stride around the front of the truck, I can't help but devour him just like I did his brother.

Jameson's white Dsquared hoodie, with a bright red emblem on the front, sits perfectly on him, molding around his shoulders as his tattoos peak out around his neck and wrists, teasing at what's hidden beneath. With his combat boots and denim jeans, he looks like a model, attempting to blend in, but the name-brand clothing instantly gives him away.

As he appears at my window, his brown hair a crumpled

mess on top of his head, and a five o'clock shadow, he looks fucking amazing, and he God damn well knows it, if the grin on his face is anything to go by.

Cocky asshole.

But *my* cocky asshole.

I hear the sound of the lock before my door swings open, and he stares down at me with a heated gaze. "I love it when I can feel your eyes raking over me. It makes me feel like a king," he murmurs quietly, reaching his hand out to help me down, and I take it.

As I stand beside him, his scent envelops me, and I just want to fall asleep beside him as his woodsy scent surrounds me.

"Jameson, you're hogging our girl again," Ezra grumbles, coming to stand beside us, and I grin.

Ezra, Jameson, and Leo have argued the entire ride here over where I'm spending the night and how the rest of my week looks regarding my sleep schedule, because apparently since Jameson fucked me in the truck, he's been stealing my attention.

Oops.

It's not my fault vying to be my favorite makes things good for them.

"And she promised to spend the night with you in your room tonight, Ez. I'm simply helping her down from the truck. Maybe you should be more gentleman-like," Jameson responds, and I shake my head at the pair of them as I turn to look at Ezra.

With his black-framed glasses perfectly in place, and his unruly brown curls sticking out in every direction, I instantly smile. He's dressed head to toe in a black tracksuit, to try and blend in with the security team here so he can do a little digging while the fight is happening. It seems weird seeing him dressed this way, instead of his usual jeans and tee combo, but I can't deny how fucking hot he looks.

"Sorry to break up the party, gang, but we need to head in," Leo says, rubbing his hands together anxiously as he stands beside Jagger.

If anyone catches me off-guard the most, it's definitely him. Dressed in a deep navy fitted suit, with a crisp white shirt, and no tie, he looks like he's had a busy day at the office and he's ready to unwind, which is exactly the look he's going for.

We don't know who Jagger is up against, a detail intentionally left out by Robbie, and we have no idea what he is threatening to do to Lola, so the plan is to divide and conquer. We need to be able to spread out and blend in on short notice if something is off and we need to get out the fuck of there.

I don't really understand why, this is all Jagger's idea, but I'm not going to argue with him when he has a fight to mentally prepare for. I'm just going to show up and roll with the punches because they have been tiptoeing around Robbie and his bullshit much longer than me.

Linking my arm through Jagger's, he looks down at me with wide eyes, likely wondering why I chose to walk at his side, and it's simple really; he needs me right now. He just doesn't know it yet.

The second he murmured that Robbie had threatened Lola if he didn't comply, I saw his walls go up and his tendency to push everyone away came out in full force. He's in preservation mode so I've given him space over the past three days, trying not to push too hard, while also showing him that I am here, no matter what, and we'll get through this *together*.

Jagger still stands behind those walls, regardless of my efforts, so I can't wait for them to come back down once tonight is all over.

As we head for the entrance, the same bouncer stands

by the door as last time, and he offers subtle nods as we pass through. I expect him to raise an eyebrow at how Leo and Ezra are dressed compared to usual, but he either doesn't acknowledge the change, or simply doesn't care. Either way, I feel like we overcame the first hurdle as we step into the hot, humid, and cramped warehouse.

People are filling every inch of the space as they shout over the music, jostling their drinks as they guess who is going to be up next, and where they want to place their money. Then there's the bimbos hanging off the big rollers like they're gods, and it makes me cringe at their desperation, but I force myself to keep my face neutral.

With the ring in the middle of the room, and bars set up around the perimeter of the warehouse, it looks exactly the same as when I was last here.

As if sensing the man himself, everyone in front of us turns to glance our way, their gaze instantly falling to Jagger's, and without a word, they part before him, creating a walkway through the crowded room.

I almost get goosebumps as I keep pace with him, and Jameson forces himself into the spot to my left so I'm guarded on both sides. As much as I don't need it, I'm not about to say no to being sandwiched between them. I'm just thankful they didn't leave me at home, but apparently I'll be safer here with them, even if they hide me away in a corner or something.

It's instinctive to want to look back over my shoulder for Ezra and Leo, but I keep my gaze fixed ahead, like I have no concerns with being here and I really couldn't give a shit. When in reality, my insides are desperately screaming for me to search out Robbie and kill him on the spot with a death glare.

I spy the door to Jagger's room, his little plaque on the door still, and it makes me laugh on the inside. The first time I came here, I thought that was cool as shit, to have a space just for him and a sign to confirm it. But now I hate it, just like I hate every other aspect of this fucking place because now I know what it all means.

Jameson steps in front, pushing the door open, but freezes as soon as he steps into the room. The hairs on the back of my neck stand up as tension ripples through my body and confusion crinkles my brows.

"What's going on?" I hear Ezra ask from directly behind me, but I shake my head subtly in response because I have no fucking idea why Jameson reacted the way he did.

I watch as he pushes the door fully open, Jagger immediately taking a step forward, and when I keep myself pinned at his side, I find Robbie standing before us.

Fuck.

No wonder Jameson paused. I don't think any of us expected him to be waiting for our arrival, not like this at least. But as I move further into the room, my heart stills when I see my mother and Lola sitting on the wooden bench behind him.

Double fuck.

My chest eases a little when I realize Lola is actually asleep in my mom's arms, even with all the noise outside she doesn't stir. No one says a word, until the door shuts quietly behind Leo.

Robbie sneers at the five of us as he casts his gaze around the room. In a pale gray suit and a worn, white shirt, he looks like a fucking wannabe mafia boss, or a has-been. Here, in the warehouse, he looks nothing like the man he's trying to portray to the media for his role as a councilman. He looks every inch the man in Nevada that I had long forgotten about.

"How nice of you to finally arrive, I was getting worried you wouldn't show and then poor little Lola would have to face the consequences," he starts in a condescending tone, making my fingers itchy to rip his throat out.

"Was there anything else?" Jagger asks gruffly, his body tense as he too tries to hold back, but it feels far too difficult right now.

"Yes, actually, Jagger, there is," Robbie replies with a grin, turning his back to my mom and Lola which eases me a little, but the way his gaze finds mine, makes my skin crawl, which tells me what he's about to say next involves me. I feel the energy in the room shift, like the guys can feel whatever comes next is going to be aimed at me too, and the tension rises to an almost suffocating level. "I think it would be an excellent idea for Luella to come and watch the fight with me and my friends," he says with a grin, and Jameson scoffs.

This guy is weird as fuck. One minute it seems like he's trying to pull me into the family in front of the cameras, but in moments like this he makes me want to scrub my skin off from the way he casts his gaze over my body.

"Over my dead body," Jagger bites out, and I squeeze his arm.

"It's okay, Jagger, I can go," I say with wide eyes as I turn to face him directly, praying that he too can see that if

Robbie is distracted by me, he's less likely to go near Lola, and we all agreed we would do whatever it takes here to protect her.

"Ohhhh, tension. I like it, who'll win," I hear Robbie chuckle from behind me as I flick my gaze to Ezra and Leo too, pleading with them to see the bigger picture as I do.

Leo clears his throat, swiping a hand down his face as he turns to Robbie. "Mind if I tag along? I was hoping to ask around about a couple of business positions, and thought this might be the place to do it," he lies, pointing down at his clothes, and Robbie rolls his eyes.

"Whatever, but Luella stays by my side at all times," he retorts, waving his hand dismissively as he moves to cut through us so he can get to the door.

Steeling my spine, I take a deep breath, ready to follow him, when Jagger's hand clamps around my arm and he spins me around to face him. His eyes are wild as he searches mine, and the tension in his jaw could cut ice.

"Luella, any discomfort or uncertainty and you defend first, we'll figure out the consequences afterward, but your safety is paramount," he whispers quietly, and I wet my lips as I nod in response.

"I'll be fine, Jagger. Do what you have to do so we can

get out of here safely. *All* of us," I add, looking behind him to see a sad smile on my mom's face as she looks down at Lola, and I truly see the scared and lost woman that she is.

Shaking my head, I focus back on Jagger as I offer him a reassuring smile, then I turn to Jameson who has moved in closer, and is just as tense as his brother right now.

"Take care of him," I murmur, and he nods once.

Jagger is the one to carry us all, at all times, but right now, the two girls who mean the most to him are in danger because of one man, and that one man is his goddamn father. I can't even bring myself to imagine how that must feel.

"Let's go," Robbie orders, the door swinging open and the music filtering in as I lace my fingers with Leo and follow him out.

A rock sits heavy in my stomach as I hear the door shut behind me, adding another layer of separation between us, and I really do want to be sick now.

"We're good, Lucy, I promise we'll all come out of here unscathed," Leo whispers as he presses his lips to my ear, and I nod in agreement.

Robbie only ever really sees the compliant side to us all as we try to toe the line, but fuck if we feel too threatened, then we'll just turn into destruction and chaos, and worry about the issues we may cause later. Just like the last fight. Jagger didn't give a fuck, because he was focused on getting to me, and that's what will happen again if Robbie tries to fuck with me or Lola.

We follow Robbie through the crowd, slowing as he approaches his table, and he's greeted by a few men dressed in their suits after a hard days work, and I want to scream. I bet every single man here thinks he's a gift to society in the day, which means they can become whoever they want at night.

I dread to think the shit these motherfuckers have gotten away with, all because they know the right people. I know my entire assumption of them is based on the fact that they can stand to be around Robbie, but I know I won't be far off the mark.

Monsters attract monsters, and that's what he is.

"Everyone, meet Luella, she's our family treasure," he says loudly so they can hear him over the dance track blaring through the speakers, and I tense at his words, gripping Leo's hand tightly as I offer a tense smile.

One of the men directly to Robbie's left takes a step forward to shake my hand, and I bite back every refusal as I place my free hand in his, cringing as his sweaty palm shakes mine.

"Pleasure to meet you, Luella. What a pretty name for a pretty girl. I'm Victor," he purrs as he leans in, and Leo takes a side step to put a little space between us.

There's something about the guy that just feels a tad familiar, and I can't quite put my finger on it. Dressed in a black suit, with his fair hair swept back off his face, his crooked smile makes me squint at him.

"Let's watch the fight, shall we?" I say loudly, rubbing Leo's arm in comfort as I point to the ring, getting ready for Jagger and his opponent to walk out so we can finally see who he has to fall to.

I don't wait for a response as I turn on my heel and face the ring, Leo doing the same as he places a protective arm around my shoulders.

"Tell me more about yourself, Luella. Do you go to college here at Emerson U?" Victor asks as he comes to stand on my other side, making my eyes widen in surprise as he doesn't back off.

Leo's grip on my arm tightens, but I wrap my fingers around his as I plaster a fake smile on my face, and turn to face Victor.

"There's not much to tell, but I am currently studying at Emerson U."

I hate that he leans in closer to hear me speak, but before he can respond, the music changes, and I instantly look toward the locker room, watching for Jagger because I remember him walking out to this exact song the last time I was here.

The only senses working right now are touch and sight. The touch of Leo's arms around me registers, but otherwise, the only things I see are Jameson and Jagger stepping toward the ring. They hold all of my attention as the crowd parts for them, the heavy bass from the song booming through the speakers, setting the perfect vibe for them even if the arrogance is a facade for tonight.

Both of them lock eyes with me as they reach the ring, and I raise my hands in the air, cheering him on and I chant Jagger's name with the other's in the warehouse as their voices filter through my brain.

Jameson offers a half grin, while Jagger glares at someone over my shoulder, who I can only assume is his father, but I ignore all that, focusing on my man. I hate that he needs to lose, but I understand the bigger picture.

As the music changes, signaling his opponent, I look

up to my right at Leo wearily and he plants a quick kiss on my forehead, before we turn to see who he's up against.

Fuck.

Dax.

It's Dax.

The leader of the fucking Vulture's Dax.

Is this all a joke?

It can't be a coincidence.

I gape at Leo who grinds his jaw, before I look back over at Jagger and Jameson, both wearing strained faces as they too try to piece everything together. None of it makes sense, but it never fucking does when Robbie's involved.

As I rise to my tiptoes to speak with Leo, I feel a hot breath at my other side, and I cringe, aiming my body toward Leo as I glance to find Victor all up in my personal space again.

"Emerson U is a good university for a solid future," he states, like my world isn't tilting upside down with everything that's happening in the ring right now. So much so that I even struggle to put a smile on my face as he continues. "My son goes there too. I'm not sure if you'll know him or not, his name is Vince, Vince Monroe?"

My pulse screams in my ears as my heart pounds in

my chest, the warehouse falling away as I only see Victor.

He's fucking joking, right?

He's Vince's father, *and* Jagger is about to fight against Dax, the leader of the gang we suspect Vince is connected to.

Fuck.

Fuck. Fuck. Fuck. Fuck. Fuck.

A tremble ripples through my body as I try to process all of this while remaining impassive, but it's far too difficult. My palms sweat as I try to swallow past the lump in my throat.

"What's wrong, Lucy? Why did you shudder and the color just drain from your face?" Leo asks in my other ear, but I don't know how to respond as my thoughts are interrupted with the referee ringing the bell to commence the first round.

Jagger has to make a decision here and we all know it. If he falls, for the leader of the Vultures, the rumor mill will go into overdrive, but if he doesn't, then Lola is in danger.

Robbie did this on purpose.

I already despised this motherfucker with every bone in my body, but now... I want to take Jameson's switchblade, carve him up and watch him fucking bleed out, drip by drip. I want to watch the life drain from his eyes.

He set Jagger up.

He set the Arrows up.

I refuse to let him get away with this.

Anger, rage, fuck… *chaos* bubbles inside me as I face the ring, hating the swirling emotion in Jagger's eyes from here. Dax grins, running his tongue over his lips as he takes a step toward Jagger, and I can see the decision before the next move is made.

He opens himself up, accepting the first blow from Dax, straight to the face, and like the protector he is, he falls down, refusing to move an inch as the crowd roars and cheers, while the referee counts him out.

My heart bleeds and soars for him all at once.

I didn't know if there were specifics to Robbie's order or not, too wrapped up in the disappointment overall, but to see him drop just like that kills me. But one thing is for sure, everyone present will see he didn't put up a fight.

The perfect sly dig at his father and his fucking rules.

The bell rings, echoing in my ears on repeat as I start moving toward the ring. Fuck Robbie and his little rules of staying with him, he got what he wanted, that prick doesn't deserve anything else.

I have no idea where Ezra is, but I pray he's ready to go, because I want Lola and Jagger out of here right this instant.

I watch as Dax laps up the attention, pounding at his chest like he's a beast, but he's just a fucking rat, they all are.

Jagger lost the fight. He lost it for love. For Lola.

If I thought he needed me before the fight, I wasn't prepared for the man I see lying on the mat still. That man needs me now more than ever, and I'll be everything he needs.

Forever at his side. Whether he likes it or not.

CHAPTER TWENTY FIVE

Lou-Lou

I wave enthusiastically at Lola even though it's dark and I can't see her through the tinted glass windows, but I know with all my heart she'll be looking back at me, and I want her to take only happiness away from tonight.

I mean, she slept through all the angst and disappointment, thankfully, but it must be confusing for a two-year-old to wake up in a strange place. Thank god the fire exit is right by Jagger's locker room.

My heart settled when Robbie practically dismissed us all without a word, leaving Jameson to take my mom and

Lola back to Lockwood in her car. I could feel words on the tip of my mom's tongue again, but as always nothing came out, and I refuse to let it irritate me right now when we have so much shit going on around us. She's not high up on the priority scale at the moment.

What a mess.

Just… what a fucking mess.

Swiping a hand down my face as I turn to Ezra and Leo, I sigh.

Jagger should be joining us at any moment, and with the truck and the Harley parked side by side, I know exactly where I need to be right now, but there's a few things we need to discuss as a group before we leave.

My head hasn't stopped spinning since we got outside, all the information overloading my brain as I try helplessly to piece everything together… the fall out, why Robbie set Jagger up, what will happen to the Arrows' reputation?

"What are we going to do about this?" I ask, referring to Dax in the ring with Jagger, my heart aching instantly at the memory. Jagger hates to look weak in front of anyone, including us, so to take a fall to the leader of their rival gang… fuck.

"He's probably going to push everyone away for the

next day or two. Jagger needs time to think, process, and then take action. This needs to have the least amount of impact on the Arrows as possible, but we'll face everything as it comes. I'm not really sure there can be any more secrets around us, but we'll get to the bottom of things, we always do," Ezra murmurs as he squeezes my shoulder in comfort, and I nod along, nibbling at my bottom lip.

It's in my nature to fix everything, with one touch or one hundred, I want to make it better, especially for my guys, my kings, my family, so it pains me to feel so helpless and lacking control.

There must be something.

"Oh fuck, I forgot to tell you," I blurt out, taking a step back as my eyes widen at the thought of Victor's words. Both Leo and Ezra look at me with confusion, but I shake my head. "There's got to be a connection, with everything we've had going on. I forgot to share, but Victor actually said something *very* useful in there," I state.

Leo takes a step toward me, tilting my chin up as he stares down at me. "Is this what caused your reaction during the fight? What did that motherfucker do, because I'm in the right frame of mind to go in there and fucking ruin him," he bites, and I smile up at him like a ridiculous bitch, but I love that he's willing to protect me like that.

Even if I don't need it.

"No, no, I promise it's fine. He was asking about Emerson U, and he casually mentioned his son attends there as well," I advise, and both of their eyes widening in surprise as I nod eagerly. "And I bet, out of the tens of thousands of students that attend Emerson U, that you can't guess which one it is."

Realization dawns on Leo's face first as Ezra runs his hand through his hair.

"Vince."

They both murmur it in unison, not as a question, but as a statement, and I nod in confirmation.

"The suspicious links between him and the Vultures, Dax showing up here tonight, and Vince's father being one of Robbie's close friends, this can't be a coincidence," I explain, and Ezra instantly pulls his phone from his pocket.

"I'm going to have to do some research because it's definitely not a coincidence. No way in hell," Ezra responds as the sound of the fire exit behind me slams shut, announcing Jagger's arrival.

I don't even need to turn around to see him there. My body can feel him behind me, even though there must be a couple of feet between us.

"What can't be a coincidence?" Jagger asks, his gruff tone forcing me to turn around as he stares at his bike in confusion, but he doesn't mention the fact that the second helmet is sitting on the seat. The second helmet for me. Whether he likes it or not.

"It doesn't matter for now," I say before either of the other two can speak, I can already feel the turmoil in his head, the glimmer of weakness he showed tearing at his insides. Not only that, he simply confirmed to Robbie that Lola is his kryptonite, leaving the door open for him to use her again and again to get what he wants to make Jagger submit to him.

He doesn't respond, not even a nod at my words as he moves to pull the helmet from the seat and place it on the gravel beside him, before pulling his own helmet out of the box and placing it over his head.

Leo reaches his hand out to take his duffel bag, and opens the truck to toss it inside as Ezra hovers awkwardly between the two vehicles. He can clearly feel the tension coming off Jagger in waves too, and doesn't want to get in the truck without making sure I'm safe first.

I lean over to grab the spare helmet, and I hear Jagger

scoff from above me. "Don't waste your fucking time. I want to be alone, and in case you're unsure what that means, Luella, I'll cut the bullshit and spell it out for you. Fuck. Off," he hisses, his words harsher than I expect, but I manage to keep my facial expression neutral as I simply stare at him.

Taking a deep breath as I pin my shoulders back I smile wide at him. "Unfortunately, kind, caring, and *listening* Luella isn't available right now. You're stuck with stubborn, determined, and sassy Luella instead. How would you like to proceed?" I watch as his eyes widen a fraction, surprised with my approach as I take a step toward him, placing my spare hand on the seat of his bike. "You have two options, climb on the bike and let me wrap my arms around your waist, or you can hold me as I pretend to know what the fuck I'm doing on there."

Silence falls over us for a moment, neither of us speaking but refusing to blink as we look at each other. *Bitch, I can do this all night, please try me.* I'm not leaving him, not like this. That isn't who we are or what we're about, and that's never going to change.

After what feels like an eternity, Jagger waves his hand dismissively at Leo and Ezra, I don't turn around to glance, but the sound of the truck doors shutting is all I need to know.

Placing my helmet on, I take a step back so he can lift his leg over first, and the second he's in place I climb on behind him, wrapping my arms around his waist so I can hold him to my chest. When he doesn't complain, kicking the bike into motion as it purrs beneath us, I relax a little.

The truck remains in place as we peel out of the parking lot, and I assume we're going to meet them back at the house.

I watch as we speed down the road, the trees, passing cars, and buildings flying past in a blur as Jagger tries to relieve some tension. It feels like hours go by as my legs go numb and we drive around aimlessly, and I have no clue where we are at all, but I'm here with him, and that's all that matters.

The constant push and pull between us has always been there, but I'm thankful that he's letting me in right now. He may not be speaking or even acknowledging my presence, but allowing me to be here speaks volumes all on it's own.

I think I could fall asleep, even with the noise and the vibrations, I feel relaxed and calmer than when we first climbed on. As if sensing my tiredness, I start to recognize where we are with the shops and buildings we go past as we slow, and a few minutes later we're pulling on to our street. A surge of sadness washes over me as I realize this small moment between us, him letting me into his safe bubble, is coming to an end, and as the garage door opens and he rolls us to a stop, it takes me a second to even attempt to stand.

On jelly legs, I chuckle at myself under my breath as I pull my helmet off and place it on the closest shelf, awkwardly standing around as I wait for Jagger's next move.

I don't want to leave, I want to stay with him, in his room, wrapped in his leather scent as he processes the bigger picture, and my heart soars when his fingers wrap around mine suddenly. Which means giving Ezra a raincheck, but I'm sure he'll understand.

Looking up at him in surprise, he rolls his eyes at me, before releasing my hand to pull me into his side, helping me walk a little as he opens the door that leads into the house.

I feel like I've had one too many drinks with how wobbly I am.

As we reach the bottom of the stairs, Ezra appears,

sticking his head out from the basement, eyeing us with uncertainty. "Want an update?" he asks, and I feel Jagger's body tense beneath my hand wrapped around his back, and I step in before he can speak.

"Could it wait until morning?" I ask, crinkling my nose as I wait for his response. I hate to put things on pause, especially with all of the things that happened tonight, but it's the right thing to do right now, and thankfully, Ezra nods in agreement too.

"Of course," he murmurs in response, moving toward us, and when he comes to a stop in front of me, I rise up onto my tiptoes and plant a kiss at the corner of his mouth, and he smiles down at me like I hung the fucking moon.

This feeling will never get old.

"Thank you, Ezra. We'll figure it all out then, alright?" I confirm, and he nods in response, squeezing my arm as Jagger remains silent. A slight touch in confirmation that he knows where I'll be tonight, I see it flash in his eyes.

The second Ezra takes a step back, Jagger starts to move again, slowly taking the stairs with me and my wobbly legs, and I grin.

He'll never admit it, but he one hundred percent just let me take charge of a situation, and it's the little things like this that make me feel like we're a family, a unit, the five of us together, and among all the shit, I can't help but smile.

Jagger silently opens his door, guiding me toward the bed, and I sigh in relief with the fact that he didn't just cart me back to my room in dismissal. He waits for me to take a seat before he heads for the bathroom, but he doesn't shut the door behind him as the sound of the shower turning on filters into the room.

I nibble on my bottom lip, considering what would be the best thing to do right now. I could sit here and wait for him to come back out, or I could join him in there, and let him see that I want to be his rock.

Fuck it.

I did warn him earlier that he was dealing with the stubborn, determined, and sassy side of me tonight, and he hasn't completely kicked me out because of it.

Yet.

Shrugging out of my jacket, I quickly kick my boots off, before stripping down to my underwear and slowly making my way toward the bathroom.

Seriously, how are my legs still slightly wobbly?

As I nudge the door a little farther open, I spy him just stepping under the spray in the large corner shower, and he must sense movement because he glances over his shoulder at me. I can see the defeat in his eyes, and before I can even catch up, my body is moving toward him. I pull the shower curtain open, and step under the water with him, still in my underwear, because this isn't about sex or desire right now, this is about being there for him in good times and in bad.

I want to remind him that we can weather any storm *together*, just like we have been doing.

He pulls his hair from the low ponytail he had going on from wearing the helmet, before tilting his head back under the water, and I watch as the droplets cascade down his body.

He's a fucking Greek god with all his muscles, dimples, tanned skin, and tattoos.

Reaching for the body wash, I lather the citrusy scent in my hands before I reach out and touch his stomach, watching as his muscles contract beneath my touch. He doesn't stop me from running my hands all over his body as I help wash the shitty night away from him.

It feels almost strange to be touching him without tearing at his skin to fuck me into oblivion. But it feels more intimate than we have ever been. When I've run my hands over every inch of his skin, he grabs the same bottle and proceeds to do the same to me, stripping the lacy material from my body before running his huge calloused hands over me from head to toe.

My body is practically singing with approval at his delicate caresses, and when he switches the water off and grabs a fluffy towel, wrapping it around my shoulders, I feel like I'm floating on cloud nine.

I follow his lead as he silently heads out into the bedroom again, and I rub my lips together nervously as he runs the towel over his body, quickly drying himself before he slips between the sheets naked, leaving the other side turned down for me to get in too.

Rubbing the soft towel over my body, I feel his eyes on me the entire time, and the moment I lie down beside him he pulls me into his side.

With my head resting on his chest, I feel every breath he takes as he tries to understand the weight of what happened tonight. It's hard trying to figure out what our game plan is when we still have no real information on what we're up against, but one thing is for sure, our two enemies just became one. Let's hope that makes it easier to tear them the fuck down.

"I love you, Luella," Jagger whispers so quietly I almost think it's in my head, but when I tilt my head back to look up at him, I find him staring down at me. With just the lamp on, I can see his eyes still swirling with a mixture of emotions as my heart pounds wildly in my chest.

"I love you too," I breathe in response as he strokes my hair back off my face.

"That's one of the few things I know right now. Among all the mayhem, I know it deep in my soul that I fucking love you with all that I am. I know we can figure this shit out. But even if we can't, even if I end up being one of my father's rats for the rest of my life, I know that I will still love you."

His words take my breath away as I look into his chocolate brown eyes.

"I won't ever let it come to that," I reply, referring to him forever being under his father's thumb.

We'll find a way. We always do, but fuck, I'd rather die than live trapped beneath Robbie fucking Izaro for the rest of my life. But then I still couldn't bring myself to give Robbie the satisfaction of knowing he sent me all the way to hell either.

CHAPTER TWENTY SIX

Lou-Lou

I open the fridge door, hoping for something to magically appear before my eyes and finally draw me in, but even the homemade chocolate fudge cake that Leo made yesterday doesn't entice me.

There's still a strange atmosphere in the house since the fight on Thursday night. When I woke yesterday morning, I found myself alone in Jagger's bed, and I haven't seen much of him since. I opted to avoid the usual party last night, hiding away with Ezra and all of my homework I need to get on top of.

I barely even recognize myself sometimes. Back in White River, I was the life and soul of every party, living my best life, always, and I thought I would really struggle focusing when I came to Emerson U. Even though I want this future for myself, I didn't think I would be motivated to get it, but with the guys and the constant drama surrounding us, I've never been more determined than I am now.

Shutting the fridge again, I turn around to find Leo sitting at the kitchen table, tapping away on his phone, just as he was when I got up to look for a treat.

It's a little after lunch, but for a Saturday I feel ridiculously antsy. I don't know what it is, but nothing seems to relax me, not even the thought of Leo fucking me over the kitchen island helps.

I'm sure it would if I actually threw the idea at him, he would definitely be all over it, but I just... fuck. I know what it is I want to do, it's been on my mind since Thursday, but I just don't want to admit it.

"Is there anything I can do, Luce?" Leo asks, placing his phone on the table as I drop down in the seat across from him.

I nibble on my bottom lip and twist my fingers together in front of me as I meet his gaze. He looks at me knowingly, like he can see in my eyes that I want to say or ask something, and I need a nudge to get me to talk.

I look anywhere but at him as I clear my throat. "Have you heard from Jagger? I'm trying not to smother him, but I have to admit I'm a little worried. I don't expect him to come up with a plan on his own, but I thought we would have sat down as a family by now and figured it out," I say, not speaking exactly what's on my mind right now, but something a very close second. Ezra caught us both up to speed yesterday morning, confirming the link between Vince and Victor, but apart from the fact that Vince's father runs a very successful business in the area, which I vaguely recall Vince telling me about, we've learned very little else. Which only seemed to piss Jagger off more.

"Honest answer or a flowery version of the situation?" he responds, making my eyes widen as I look back at him in surprise.

There's a reason he's fucking saying that, and I want to know why.

"Don't ever give me the flowery version, Leo Cooper," I shoot back shortly, and he grins at me, knowing that's exactly what I would say as he swipes a hand down his face.

"In this case, it might have sounded better," he mumbles, sighing as he spins his phone on the table. "Honestly, he stormed out this morning declaring he wouldn't be back until he had it all figured out, and none of us have heard from him since."

My jaw falls open as I process what he's saying, and fumble to quickly pull my cell phone from my pocket, unlocking the screen with my face before I try to call him. My heart pounds in my chest as I wait, and when I hear the phone ringing, excitement and hope zaps through me. "I don't want him to make decisions on his own, it's not just his burden to bear," I grumble, but my hope is short-lived when the line eventually goes to voicemail.

Fuck.

"I know it's annoying, Lucy, but this is just Jagger. It's how he operates. We need to give him space to think and put something together. He'll bring it to the table and then we can figure it all out then," Leo responds, trying to comfort me as he strokes his hand over mine, but I feel just as lost as I did before I attempted to call Jagger. "Now, how about you tell me what else is going on, and we can focus on that to distract you," he offers, a hint of teasing to his tone, but I can sense the seriousness too.

Rubbing my lips together, I consider my options, knowing just how stubborn Jagger can be, and reluctantly nod in agreement. If he's going to be out there somewhere trying to organize shit, then I need something to keep me busy, otherwise I'll be worrying the entire day. I need to trust their process when shit hits the fan, instead of trying to step in and take control. I'm a fixer, so letting them take the reins is a fucking nightmare on my mind.

"Can we go to Lockwood?" I ask, blurting it out before I continue to waste time considering it. I don't miss the way his eyes widen slightly, but he hides it well as he nods eagerly.

"For sure, we can totally go. Ezra and Jameson are downstairs in the basement. Do you want us all to go, or just the two of us?" he asks, far more casually than I was expecting. I thought I was going to get a full freak out.

I rise from the table, smoothing my hands over my long, black, sweater dress as I plaster a small smile on my face. "If they're busy I don't want to interrupt them, but I would never say no to being with all of my guys, or just my Leo," I respond, speaking the truth, and the megawatt smile he offers in return is enough to melt me into a puddle.

"I fucking love you, Lucy Carter," he says with a wink,

leaning across the table to kiss my forehead, before heading for the basement, leaving me to gape after him like a fool.

He hasn't really said those three words since the first time they passed his lips, but I've seen it in his eyes and felt it with his touch. The words just feel raw this time, especially after Jagger mumbled them to me last night too.

It makes my heart soar and my palms sweat as I realize I really do have a place I belong now. With the four people I thought were gone forever.

Swoon.

They're making me fucking soft.

Trailing after him, I make my way to the front door, not wanting to waste time by following him to the basement, and as I reach the bottom of the stairs, all three of them appear.

Jameson is the first to see me, a smile spreading over his face as sweat pours from him. In just a pair of gray shorts, with his abs on full display, he looks like he's been working out, and I'm almost sad I didn't get to see it.

"Give me two minutes, Ella, and I'll be ready to go," he murmurs, running his hand over my waist as he passes, taking the stairs three at a time in his hurry, and I shake my head.

I turn my attention back to the door under the stairs to find Ezra running his hands through his hair in frustration.

"Hey, you don't have to—"

"Oh, no, no, no, I'm not..." he takes a deep breath before releasing a heavy sigh as he moves toward me. "My brain feels like it's going to explode from looking over surveillance footage, documents, and other random shit to try and piece all of this mess together, and it's giving me a headache. I could actually use the distraction," Ezra insists, running his thumb over my cheek, and I shiver under the delicate contact. Relieved he's not feeling inconvenienced by me.

With him this close, I can really take him in, and the bags under his eyes tell me he didn't sleep much last night after we passed out from completing our assignments. Apparently all of this uncertainty is taking its toll on us.

"Are we good to go?" Leo asks, appearing from the kitchen door with a container filled with cupcakes in one hand as he fixes his hat in place with the other, and I raise an eyebrow in question.

"Since you're around, I've got to work my magic to make sure Lola still remembers I exist," he responds with a shrug, and I can't help but chuckle.

Before I can respond, Jameson comes barreling down the stairs, and his eyes immediately fall to the tub too. "Oh for fuck's sake, between the two of you, Lola's not even going to look in my direction today," he grumbles, flicking the brim of Leo's hat as he passes, and it only makes me giggle more.

"That means there'll be more of *you* for *me* later," I respond, and I watch as his eyes darken instantly, his tongue dragging across his bottom lip as he nods.

"Deal."

One word and my skin ignites, but not enough for me to put a pause on speaking to my mom. It needs to happen, and the way she's been biting her tongue around me, I know I need to take the situation into my own hands or she'll continue to stay muted.

Flashing the three of them a smile, I turn on my heels and reach for the front door. I'm going for answers, and I've got the drive over there to figure out what the fucking questions are.

The usual heat blasts me in the face as I step inside

Lockwood.

Fuck me, do they ever turn the damn thing down?

It's not in the rest of the building, just the entryway which is the worst, but it feels like my skin is melting.

I don't see the usual lady, Maggie, I think her name is, but Ezra doesn't wait around anyway. With his fingers laced through mine he leads me toward the room we usually go to. As we approach, I squint in confusion, slowing to a stop and almost making Leo step into the back of me.

"Is that a new door?" I ask, uncertainty swirling in my stomach.

"Yeah. Nothing happened, we just wanted to get a better door for them, one which included a peephole," Jameson responds as he comes to stop at my left, pointing at the little piece of glass, but my frown only deepens.

"Why would they need that?" I don't understand, especially since they've been living okay with a normal door for all of these years.

"We're just taking every precaution we can, since the Dax fight and Robbie being extra shady and using Lola as a threat. If things get worse, then your mom has an extra layer of protection to prepare if Robbie shows up… angry," Leo explains as Ezra steps forward and raps his knuckles on the wood.

I'm still left slightly confused as my mom opens the door, her eyes falling straight to mine as a nervous smile plays across her face. She's not surprised to see me, which means one of the guys must have given her a heads up.

She looks nice today, with her hair pulled back into a bun, in a pair of jeans and a sweater, she has complete soccer mom vibes going on.

"Where's my favorite girl? I brought cupcakes," Leo sings, stepping around my mom as the sound of Lola playing fills my ears.

Every time I hear the sound of her happiness it makes my heart soar and my body zing.

I offer my mom a tight smile as she steps back, letting the rest of us in, and I decide to give Lola my attention first because I still have no clue what I want to specifically ask my mom. The drive over didn't help settle the questions in my head either.

The second I step into the room, I'm slightly surprised again by how clean the place is, except for Lola's toys that she's been playing with, the space is actually well kept, a complete contrast to our childhood home.

"Le-la, it's Le-la," Lola shouts, her words slightly

muffled with the cupcake in her mouth. My eyes light up when I see her, and as she comes charging toward me I manage to lift her off her feet before she trips and falls.

She looks extra adorable today with her hair in pigtails, and there's the smallest bit of pink icing from the cupcake on her nose. She's just too adorable.

It's easy to fall into a rhythm with Lola. Letting her steer me around the room and having me play all sorts of games is as much fun for me as it is for her, and I know I made the right decision coming here today.

Even if I don't figure out what I want to say to my mom, I can at least spend time with my sweet and innocent sister.

As we drink yet another fake cup of tea from her little set, she yawns for the fourth time, and when I glance to check the time, I find Ezra, Leo, and Jameson watching us with huge grins on their faces, and I almost blush under their attention.

I can't imagine what it's like for them, to have uprooted their lives to protect my sister, *their* sister, as well as my mom, and now seeing me here with her too. I can't believe they kept her a secret from me, but I understand why now, and I know everything happens for a reason. This little girl was meant to come into my life exactly when she did; for the better.

My mom is sitting at the kitchen table, eyeing us, and I clear my throat, placing my plastic cup down again. "Is she due for a nap or anything?" I ask, and my mom nods, swiping her hands down her jeans before she rises.

"Yeah, she's twenty minutes late but you guys were having too much fun and I didn't want to interrupt," she responds, and although my face remains neutral, my insides are confused as fuck.

Who is this woman today?

The last time I visited and she threw her usual snarky comments my way, I knew where I stood; as far away from her as possible. But when she talks like this, all kind and considerate, it fucks with my brain.

My mom crouches beside us as she holds her hands out for Lola, who instantly rises to her feet and throws herself into her arms. "Come on, baby, nap time. Blow kisses to Le-la in case she has to leave before you wake up," my mom murmurs into Lola's hair, and she does just that, the sound of her lips smacking as she waves her hand at me, before she yawns again.

Silence descends over the room as my mom walks her

over to the door at the far right. Where's she going?

I glance back at the guys, and Ezra must see the question in my eyes because he's quick to explain.

"The bed near the door is your mom's. The night you showed up, Lola must have been having trouble sleeping which is why she was there. There's only one bedroom off of this room, and it's Lola's."

Ah, that makes sense.

Rubbing my hands together, I busy myself putting away the toys into the boxes, and thankfully the guys leave me to it, chatting about the latest Formula One Motorsports race that's on this weekend.

It's only a few minutes before my mom reappears, tucking a lock of loose hair behind her ear as she looks me over. "Want a drink?" she offers, and I nod.

"I'll take a coffee, please, if you don't mind," I respond, placing the toy teapot away before I move over to the kitchen table.

I take the seat across from where my mom has been sitting, and I have a great view of my guys from here. Each of them glancing in my direction subtly to make sure I'm alright, but they must be able to sense I need some time with my mom alone.

It's awkward as fuck, the sound of the coffee machine ringing in my ears as I rub my lips together, and when my mom finally places a drink down in front of me, she retakes her seat, staring at me just as I am at her.

An eternity passes, neither of us speaking as we stare each other down, trying to figure out where to begin.

"I have no idea how we got mixed up in all of this," my mom murmurs, blowing on her steaming mug of coffee as she looks at me, and my eyebrows raise in response.

"Really? You have no idea at all? Not a single guess?" I respond, a little harsher than I expect, but I roll with it, even though her eyes darken a touch with sadness.

"It wasn't a choice, Luella. I never asked for Robbie to… it doesn't matter, I won't ever regret it because Lola was a wake up call and a second chance for me to put right what I fucked up the first time around. I'm sorry about what I said the other week too, as soon as the words slipped off my tongue I hated myself. That's not me anymore, and I'm sorry I did that," she admits, and my eyes widen even more as I stare at her in surprise.

Well at least she knows she fucked up. It's never going to make it better, but the acknowledgment seems to relax my shoulders a little.

"Is there anything else on your mind at the minute? I feel like you've had something on the tip of your tongue the past few times I've seen you, but you never say a word," I state, speaking the truth and voicing what has been playing on my mind, the entire reason I'm here right now.

She nibbles at her bottom lip, her eyes scanning mine, but I don't know what she thinks she's going to find, I have no idea what to expect from her. "I was a shit mom, Luella, I am a shit mom to you still, I know that, but pushing you out of the door and away from the house every day when you were a child was the best way to protect you. I saw the way Jameson, Jagger, Ezra, and Leo looked at you, even then. The protection they offered you so willingly."

My heart beats faster in my chest as my eyebrows crinkle. Best way to protect me? What does that even mean?

"Protect me from what?" I ask, unable to stop myself, and I can feel Ezra, Leo, and Jameson glancing in my direction, but I force myself to keep my gaze fixed on my mom.

"Your dad was..."

Her words trail off as she looks into her mug, clearly trying to find the right words to say as I sit and wait patiently even though I desperately want to snap at her.

I know my father was a drunk, a cunt, and an all-round asshole, but the lingering fact that he's in prison tells me there's clearly more I don't know.

"He was always on call for Robbie in some way, shape or form. Always," she murmurs, flicking her gaze to mine, and I nod slightly, not entirely surprised by the fact, but I still had no clue until this moment.

What did that even involve? Why was that bad for us as kids, or worse for us, should I ask? I run my tongue over my bottom lip as I try to figure out how to word my next question when Jameson grunts.

"Fuck."

The shortness to his tone grabs my attention, and as I look over at him I see the tension around his eyes as he swipes his hair back off his face.

"What's wrong?" I ask, rising from the table and planting my hand on the wood as I try to remain calm, but I can feel the energy shifting in the room already.

"It's Jagger, he's back at the house, and it seems he's got a plan," he responds, but when his eyes meet mine, he doesn't look all that reassured either.

Fuck is right.

"We need to go," I state, standing tall as I feel everyone eye me wearily. My conversation with my mom clearly isn't over, but I need the guys to see that I know whatever is going on with Jagger right now is more important, and if I don't say we have to go, then they'll happily sit there and wait until I'm ready to leave.

"Are you sure?" Leo asks, flipping his hat around as he looks between my mom and me, and I nod once sharply, and he seems to get the message.

I sense the three of them rise from the sofa as I look at my mom. "We can pick this conversation up again soon, right?" I clarify, wanting her to know that I'm still interested in what she has to say, and she nods with a sad smile.

"Whenever you're ready, Lou-Lou," she responds, and my jaw falls open slightly when she calls me by the name I've always wanted. Apparently this woman does listen.

The only people to get a free pass are my guys, and that's simply because they're my kings in every sense of the word, but anyone else is to call me Lou-Lou.

"Before you go, I was wondering if you guys would like to come over for Thanksgiving dinner?" she asks, looking at me with pleading eyes, and I find myself nodding in response.

"Sure," I murmur as she stands from the table, almost inching toward me as if she's going to lean in for a hug, and I balk. Fuck. That. No way in hell.

Skirting around the kitchen table, I don't offer a backward glance as I feel the guys follow behind me and head for the door. If Jagger thinks he has a plan, then I'm all ears.

But why does my gut tell me I'm not going to like whatever it is he has to say?

WATCH ME RISE

CHAPTER TWENTY SEVEN

JAMESON

As I slow the truck in front of the house, tension falls even harder over us all, knowing Jagger is inside with some kind of plan is weighing heavier on us than I think we expected.

I know my twin, and I could sense the rash decision through the direct text message alone, and I know once we step inside, it's going to be all hell breaking loose especially between Jagger and Ella because they will instantly push back and forth against each other. That means Leo, Ezra and I have to sort through the bullshit and see what actually makes the most sense.

Jagger: When will you be home? I figured this shit out, and I thought you might want to know.

NOPE.

Nothing good is going to come from this.

Putting the truck in park, my hand instantly slips into my pocket, finding my switchblade as I twirl it in my hand. I wet my lips, looking to my right at Ella as I force a smile to my lips. "You ready to go in?" I ask, since no one has moved a muscle, and she nods nervously in response as she eyes the house.

The only way to know what's going through Jagger's head is to walk right in and ask him, he can be too impulsive for me to even guess what he's done.

I step from the truck, shutting the drivers' door behind me quickly as I hear the others do the same. Waiting for Ella to round the front of the truck, I instantly slip my arm around her shoulders as we head for the house.

No one says a word, but I can feel the uncertainty filtering from Ezra and Leo too. I know I'm going to end up getting caught in the crossfire for wanting to support my brother, while also understanding Ella's argument—

which is definitely going to come.

Leo steps in front, unlocking the door as I move inside, taking a deep breath as I grip the switchblade.

Ezra shuts the door behind us, making sure to lock it, as we move toward the kitchen instinctively. My heart pounds in my chest as I watch my twin pace back and forth in the kitchen, his body tense and rigid as he clenches and unclenches his hands. In a sweaty plain tee and shorts, it looks like he found a minute to beat the shit out of a punching bag before he rallied us all together.

"Jag," I call out, gaining his attention as we all just stare at him expectantly, and when his eyes find ours he looks like a caged beast, angry, filled with rage, and mad at the whole fucking world. Great. How can one person look both relieved and irritated to see you at the same time? It only confirms that we're not going to like what he's about to say, and Jagger fucking knows it.

"What's going on, Jagger?" Ella asks, taking a step toward him cautiously, and when she comes to stand toe to toe with him, he lets her place her delicate hands on his chest, but her touch does nothing to tame the beast warring under the surface.

He stares down at her for a moment, before dragging

his gaze over the three of us as we remain still.

"I've challenged him," he states. Three simple words and I feel my pulse quicken as I blink a few times trying to process what he's saying.

What the fuck *is* he saying? Challenged him? Challenged—

"Who?" Ella blurts, saying what was running through my mind, and likely Ezra's and Leo's too.

Jagger's jaw clenches as he refuses to meet everyone's gaze head on. "Dax."

Ah, shit.

I should have fucking anticipated something like this would happen. No wonder I can feel the tension a mile away.

Ella looks over her shoulder at the three of us, confusion in her eyes as she too tries to piece together the snippets Jagger is giving us.

Ezra moves closer, jumping up to sit on the counter top beside the two of them trying to remain relaxed and calm, but he fucking knows this is as crazy as the rest of us.

"What have you challenged Dax for specifically?" he asks, fixing his glasses as he raises his eyebrows at Jagger, who simply shakes his head in response.

"For it all, obviously," he grunts, still refusing to place his hands on Ella as she peers up at him.

"You're going to have to be a little more specific than that, Jagger," Leo states, edging closer too, but I can't join them, it feels like my feet are cemented to the floor.

"I'm going to fight him, in No Man's Land. Where it can't be overruled or rigged. Just the two of us. He fucking knows I had no choice but to take that loss, and if he wants the entire town of Emerson Grove, he'll need to win it fair and square." The determination in his voice is palpable, but I'm still too confused by it all to either nod and agree with him or tell him he's ridiculous.

Nobody speaks for a moment, until Ella scoffs, dropping her hands from his chest as she clenches her fists at her side. "Is this a joke?"

"Jagger's not a funny person, Luce," Leo mumbles, wetting his lips as he scans his gaze between the two of them. Ella glares at him for a split second before whirling her daggers back at Jagger.

"Please tell me this is actually a joke because I'm trying to figure out how you seem to think it's an excellent idea to *fight* some asshole for a town that likely means more to him than it does to you. Explain to me your fucking thought process here, Jagger, because I just don't get it," she bites, folding her arms across her chest as she puts a physical barrier between the two of them.

"I don't expect you to get it, Luella, but reputation is everything around here, and I've been the top fighter in The Grove since we arrived, which has only strengthened our rule as the Arrows. That's in jeopardy now, and Dax was already fucking pushing us. So, I either challenge him outright, and we figure this shit out between us, or I let him keep taking swipes at how things are run around here, and I won't fucking allow him to ruin our credibility."

His tone is harsh but determined, and I know we're not going to tell him any differently. Jagger's in the zone where he's blinded by his own perspective. He's not going to see the situation from our point of view, or likely understand the bigger picture, instead he's going to continue to push back again and again until something or someone gives.

Ella takes another step back, turning to glance over her shoulder at me as she wets her lips. "Jameson, please can you talk some fucking sense into your brother?" she grumbles, desperation thick in her blue eyes, and I groan internally at officially being brought into the conversation. I was quite happy standing back and not getting involved.

Clearing my throat, I reluctantly take a step toward the chaos as I shrug my shoulders and grip my switchblade like my life depends on it. "If this is what he wants, and he sees no other way, then I think we have to respect his decision, Ella," I admit. My heart pounds in my chest as I watch the shock wash over her face at my answer, before the anger sets in, making her jaw tick as she gives me an icy glare.

"So you're saying it's okay for your brother, your *twin* brother, to fight some fucking low-life out in No Man's Land for gang possession of Emerson Grove?" She spells it out slowly, but I don't take offense at her tone. I understand her being mad, I unfortunately have the middle ground and being Switzerland isn't all that fucking fun regardless of how I feel.

Neither Ezra nor Leo say a word, and I get that too, this isn't something I wanted to get caught in the middle of either.

"I'm saying if that's the decision he's chosen to make, then I will back him and support him with whatever he needs," I reply calmly as my grip tightens on the switchblade in my pocket.

"What? No, this is not okay, Jameson. Why can't you

see that?"

My feet are cutting the distance between us before I even realize it, and when I come to a stop in front of her, lifting my hands from my pockets and running them over her shoulders, she barely relaxes in my grip.

"Ella, it's his choice. Like you've told us in the past, you need to see the bigger picture, especially when Jagger can't. This is just like when you tell us you're the mighty independent woman that you are, pushing us to let you do things and stand on your own two feet, but now it's the other way around. So you may not agree with his choice but you have to respect it." I squeeze her shoulders in comfort, but it doesn't stop the disappointment from seeping through her eyes.

"I think you're wrong," she states, before turning her attention back to Jagger who still remains tense, and I can feel it in my gut there's something else he's not saying, but before I can question it, Ella continues. "There must be another way to take them down. What evidence do we have? We could take them all out in one sweep, Robbie included," she says, brushing her hair back off her face as she scrambles to find an alternative solution. This is what desperation to control the situation sounds like.

"Lou-Lou, we really don't have enough of anything, nothing that would stick with the friends he has in this town," Ezra responds quietly, clenching his hands in his lap as he feels her getting angrier.

None of us want to piss her off, but these are the kind of decisions we have to make sometimes, for the Arrows, and for ourselves.

Ella rubs her lips together, wrapping her arms around her body as she thinks. None of what we are saying is pacifying her, but she wanted us to be truthful and honest with her, and here it is.

"We could speak to Ryan, the guy who brought me here. He'd know exactly what to do, you guys, I swear," she says with pleading eyes, but Jagger is already shaking his head.

"Luella, the deal has already been made, I'm not going to go back on it now," he grunts, scrubbing his hand over his mouth, and I feel the wave of uncertainty wash over me once more. I hate it when he makes decisions on his own, he should know that by now, but apparently when he gets like this he only sees *his* version of an outcome.

"When is this happening?" I ask, hoping that will somehow relate to what has my insides itching at his stance.

"The day after Thanksgiving," he responds almost blandly, which only seems to irritate me more. That's in two weeks time, so it's not tomorrow, we at least have time to plan this out and train.

"Oh, so we're able to be thankful for your presence *before* you go and do something completely reckless," Ella grumbles sarcastically, which just makes Jagger roll his eyes.

Hating to continue being involved in their back and forth, I know there's still something he's not telling us, and even I need to know what it is. "Jag, what are you holding back?" I ask, hearing Leo clear his throat too, like he also feels something is missing here.

"We're fighting for Emerson Grove," he repeats slowly, as if trying to tell us what's going on without directly telling us what's happening.

"You've already told us that," Ella snaps, clearly agitated with the whole thing, and as I repeat his words over and over in my mind, it slowly clicks into place.

Fuck.

"You're fighting for Emerson Grove," I murmur, my heart pounding like crazy in my chest as I frantically search Jagger's gaze, and he nods once, knowing I've fully understood what it is he's saying.

Shit. Shit. Shit. Shit. Shit.

"What does that mean? Why are you just repeating the same fucking sentence?" Ella hisses, getting angrier at the situation, but fuck, I'm not going to be the one to tell her, no way in hell.

"Fuck," Leo mumbles under his breath, understanding finally dawning on him as Ezra scrubs his hands down his face, likely piecing it together as well.

"Somebody better fucking explain it to me. Right. The. Fuck. Now," Ella barks, and I swing my gaze to Jagger, conveying that he needs to be the one to fucking say it, and with a heavy sigh, he brushes his hair back off his face, pushing his shoulders back like he's ready for the fire to intensify with Ella.

"When you fight for The Grove, Ella, one on one, leader to leader, you fight to the death."

CHAPTER TWENTY EIGHT

Lou-Lou

I can see the professor's mouth moving, but I don't hear a word of what she's saying as she points animatedly at the board behind her.

I don't know why I even bothered showing up today. It's been like this all week, and I almost opted to stay in bed this morning. I only have a half-day anyway since it's Thursday, but Ezra somehow convinced me that going to classes was a good idea.

Everything back at the house, especially between Jagger and me is… hostile, to say the least, and even that feels like too tame of a word. The tension could be cut with a butter knife, but after he explained what it is he's actually signed up for with this fight, I fled from the room and vomited in my bathroom.

He's putting his life on the line.

His. *Life*.

No one else seems to understand the severity of that, or if they do, they're not as fazed as I am, and all that has followed since is silence. I can barely look at Jagger without instantly fighting the rage and pain bubbling beneath the surface of my skin as I take him in from head to toe. Wondering how much time I have left with him.

It's not about whether or not I think he can win, it's more about the fact that he merely opted for this outcome without consulting anyone first, like whether he lives or dies doesn't matter to anyone but *him*.

"Hey, Lou-Lou," Naomi murmurs, tapping my arm a few times as I jolt in my seat, surprised by her touch, but when I glance around the room I realize everyone's leaving because we've been dismissed.

Fuck.

I need to get out of my head.

Maybe, I should take one of the guys up on their offer

to train down in the basement, I really do need something to take the edge off.

Wetting my lips, I rise to my feet, offering her a tight smile in thanks for shaking me out of it. I desperately try not to search around for Leo, since this is one of the few classes where we don't sit by each other. But I can sense Naomi hovering beside me with something to say.

As I hitch my bag up on my shoulder, I flick my gaze back to her, to find her fidgeting with her dark hair and eyeing me nervously. Before I can say anything, she offers me a weak smile and clears her throat.

"Is everything okay with you? You've been distant lately," she says quietly, not drawing any attention to us as we instinctively walk side by side toward the door.

"I'm good, sorry, I just… have a lot going on at the minute," I murmur in response, zipping my coat up before I can feel the icy air coming from outside.

"That doesn't sound ominous at all," she replies, trying to keep the mood light, and I struggle to keep up the charade.

"I wish, far more boring than I'd like to admit," I manage to blurt out, ready to up my pace as I spy Leo by the door, but before I can get too far her hand curls around my upper arm.

Turning to face her, I try to take a deep breath and relax my body, but she must be able to tell that I don't appreciate her grabbing me like that, because she immediately releases me.

"Sorry, I just... wanted you to know that I'm always here for you, no matter what, where, or even when. If you need anyone, I'm here for you, Lou-Lou," she repeats, and I nod slightly, my lips tilting at the corners to pacify her.

"Thanks, I appreciate it," I reply tightly, before taking the few steps I need to reach Leo.

I can see the question shining in his gray eyes, but I simply smile, knowing now isn't the time to have that conversation, besides there's not all that much to say anyway.

"Hey, Luce, you miss me?" Leo mutters against my ear as we move toward the steps outside, and I shake my head at him as he pulls me tighter against his side, the cool air still swirling around my face as I try to keep warm.

"Like a hole in the head," I mumble in response, making him chuckle under his breath, and I appreciate that he's still himself, trying to be positive and make everyone smile, even when things really do feel like they're going to shit right now. "But I love you, so that counts for something right?" I add, tilting my head so I can look up at him, and he grins with pride shining in his gray eyes.

"It counts for everything."

Neither of us says anything else, not wanting to spoil those pretty little words as they make my heart soar. In sync, we make our way toward my truck. I know he has classes this afternoon, and Ezra will be at home, so one Prince Charming will escort me back to another Prince Charming, before returning to school.

Just call me a princess. A gang princess.

Save my queen status for my men.

It's unreal, completely ridiculous, but I understand the worry for everyone's safety at the moment, especially now that the fight has been set. The calm before the storm only causes me more stress.

Eight sleeps to go, and I'm nowhere near ready for any of this shit to actually go down.

I unlock the truck as we approach, desperate to get inside and out of the cold, and as I slip into the driver's seat, Leo immediately falls into the spot beside me. We've barely shut the doors before I'm starting the engine and kicking the heating on.

It really is fucking freezing compared to what I'm used to.

Slowly pulling out of the parking lot, I leave Leo to choose what song he wants to listen to, only because I like his choice in music more than the others, and within minutes we're turning on to our street.

As we near the house, irritation sits beneath the surface of my skin, and when we come to a stop, Leo must feel it too because he remains still for a moment, giving me a second to try and relax.

With a heavy groan, I swipe a hand down my face and look across the center console at him. "Are you using my truck to drive back?" I ask, and he nods, flipping his hat so it's backwards as usual, before climbing out of his side, and quickly rushing around to the driver's seat before I can even open the door.

He wastes no time wrapping his hands around my hips and pulling me against his chest as he drops me down from the truck. The feel of his chest against mine as he slowly lowers me to the ground gives me butterflies.

It's not difficult to be my favorite at the minute, unless your name is Jagger, but Leo just took the spot. "Want to watch a movie and camp out in my room tonight?" I ask, batting my eyelashes at him as he nods eagerly in response.

"You bet your sweet ass I do," he breathes in response, before crushing his lips to mine, and I let his body distract me for a moment, before he reluctantly takes a step back. Quickly leaning around me, he grabs my bag from the footwell, and places it over my shoulder.

Not wanting him to be late getting back to campus, I rise up on my tiptoes, offering one more brush of my lips against the corner of his mouth, before I head for the door.

Reaching the front door, I glance back over my shoulder, and offer him a quick wave, before I twist the door handle and step inside.

The awkward and lonely silence that I expect to greet me is far from the reality as I hear both Ezra and Jagger yelling at the top of their lungs.

How the fuck did I not hear this from outside?

I quietly drop my bag at my feet, careful to try and not make a sound as I strain to hear what the hell is going on.

"It's fucking bullshit, Jagger, and you know it," Ezra hisses, and the sound of Jagger scoffing in response quickly follows.

"I know what I'm doing, Ezra. I have enough shit on my plate with the fight and Luella's reaction, I don't need your crap on top of it as well," he bites back, and my heart starts to pound in my chest at the sound of my name on his lips.

"Maybe Lou-Lou is right to feel this way. Maybe you need to open your fucking eyes and see the bigger picture. We care about you, Jagger, and you know for a fact if you had brought this to the table we would never have okayed it," Ezra yells even louder.

Fuck.

I don't need these two at each other's throats too. Not that Jagger doesn't deserve it, but we need to be a unit now more than ever.

Shrugging my coat off, I let it fall to my feet, before I take a deep breath, steeling my spine and moving toward the living room.

The second I step over the threshold, Jagger's eyes zone in on mine, which causes Ezra to quickly glance over his shoulder.

Ezra is dressed in his usual jeans and a band tee, with his glasses framing his gray eyes perfectly, and his brown curly hair falling in every direction over his head. While Jagger is dressed in a pair of black sweatpants, no shirt on, and his dark hair pulled back into a bun at the top of his head. He's dripping with sweat, a sure sign he's just been training. Again.

"Why did you leave campus early? Does Leo or Jameson know where you are?" Jagger barks, putting me on the defensive instantly as I bite back the desire to growl at him.

"It's fucking Thursday, Jagger, my classes are finished for the day. Jameson is still in class and Leo just brought me home before heading back. Does that answer all of your questions, Izaro?"

His brown eyes darken as he glares at me, but I don't miss him spying the wall mounted clock out of the corner of his eye, showing him I'm right, and his tense shoulders lower slightly.

"Whatever, we're done here," he states, flicking his gaze between the two of us, and I shake my head in disapproval instantly.

"No, don't end it on my account. I feel like Ezra has some *really* valid points," I declare, folding my arms over my chest as I force a smile to my lips, trying to cover how fucking mad I am, but the backing I expect from Ezra doesn't come.

"Let's leave it, Lou-Lou, it's not worth the fight

anyway," he mumbles, waving a hand dismissively at Jagger, and I gape at him in surprise.

"It is fucking worth it. All of this is fucking worth it, *he* is fucking worth it, and that's because we care about each other, as a family. It's ride or die, and Jagger over here is not giving us any say on the dying part," I grouch, pointing my finger at the asshole in question.

"You're being dramatic, Luella."

"No, I'm really fucking not. We don't know what games they'll play, we don't know if we can trust them to follow through if Jagger wins. What are the rules for this fight?" I ramble, my words continuing to come out harsher as I let my anger take over. It feels good to air my agitation right at his face.

I can see Jagger's jaw tick as my questions run through his mind, but I don't back down. Ezra swipes a hand over his face, but doesn't interject again, clearly agreeing with what I'm saying.

"We're going to fight out at No Man's Land where Jameson raced. We're each allowed to bring members of our gang, but the unspoken agreement is that no one else gets involved," Jagger explained casually, like he's talking about popping into the grocery store, and it does nothing to console me.

"And what happens when someone fucking wins? You're telling me that the other gang members are all going to stand by and just clap before going home? Yeah, I don't think so," I stress as I clench and unclench my hands, my pulse rings in my ears, and no one offers me any kind of response. It's almost as if I'm fucking talking to myself. "Am I allowed to come and watch?" I ask, and I see Jagger's face balk immediately as he starts to shake his head.

"Fuck no. I either die or kill someone, and I'm not letting you see either of those outcomes," he retorts, taking a step toward me as my heart lurches in my chest. None of this is okay.

Wetting my lips, I tilt my gaze to stare deep into his eyes as I try to convey just how much all of this hurts. "I have so many memories I want to make with you, so much time I want us to catch up on, and you're just going to throw it all away," I state, feeling tears burning the back of my eyelids as my emotions get the better of me.

"I'm. Not. Going. To. Lose. Luella," he bites out slowly, coming another step closer as I feel Ezra inch in beside me too. "The Arrows are what protect us from

Robbie completely taking control of me, us, and I can't let that slip right now. We need that protection. In six months time I can have us all out of here, including your mom and Lola but I have to do this step first." His eyes plead with mine to understand. My fingers tremble at my sides as I try to take a calming breath, but it's useless.

"What are we going to do with Naomi? Vince? All of them?" I question as he comes to stop toe to toe with me, and Ezra plants his hand on my shoulder in comfort.

"None of them will be a problem when we wipe out the entire gang by getting rid of Dax, Luella. This will solve a lot of issues with one move. We won't be handling the little guys when we've crushed the leader," Jagger says, swiping his hair back off his face, and I shake my head.

"There's always someone else ready to take the leader's spot, Jagger, we all know that. And who is to say it won't be Vince?" I sigh, flicking my gaze to Ezra, but he's too busy watching us both with concern. "The Vultures will be over there having the same fucking conversation, Jagger, but we both know they'll be planning on taking everyone out instead of just one person. No survivors."

He pauses for a moment, rubbing his lips together as he tries to find a valid answer, but there isn't one. The worst part about it all is even if he hears what I'm saying right now, it's not going to change the outcome. Jagger won't go back on his word to the Vultures now, no matter what, which only fucking angers me more.

I can feel the flush creeping up my neck as I take a step back from them both, but lightning fast Jagger grabs my wrist, holding me in place so I can't take another step.

"This is bullshit," I mumble, my brain growing foggier by the minute as the anger and fear race through my body. Even getting this off my chest isn't easing the stress and anxiety building inside of me. I feel like a ticking time bomb, ready to explode.

"It's all bullshit, Luella, but I need you by my side. Always," Jagger mutters, his fingers flexing around my wrist, and I shiver at the contact mixed with the need in his voice.

Fuck.

I really am a hot mess right now. I feel like I did after I raced with Jameson; antsy as fuck with no way to calm myself. It's not even worth me asking someone to spar with me, because I know that's not going to help right now. Especially when it's a huge fight that's playing on repeat in my mind, causing all of these issues to begin with.

"Lou-Lou, tell me how to fix this for you?" Ezra asks, finally speaking as he grazes his fingers over my trembling ones, making Jagger zone in on them too.

"There's nothing to do, Ezra. I'm a minefield of emotions right now, and I would usually calm down with fighting, but that really doesn't seem like the right option with everything going on," I admit, and he nods in understanding as he runs his fingers through his hair.

I can see the desperation in his face, so I'm sure mine is just as visible.

Silence falls over us as Jagger, Ezra, and I continue to look at each other, waiting for a solution to miraculously appear, but that's never going to happen.

"Do you trust me?" Jagger asks quietly, and my eyes widen as I look up at him.

"What kind of question is that right now?" I ask, shaking my head in disbelief as he lifts his other hand to hold my chin in place.

"Forget about the fight, forget about the Vultures, fuck, forget about Robbie. I need you to see how much you mean to me, and how important you are, and I need it to calm you down because I might be a stubborn ass, but I can't bear to see you like this either," he states, and my heart lodges in my throat as I try to wet my lips, nodding ever so slightly in response.

When he puts it like that, there's no question over what my answer is. "I trust you."

The corner of his mouth lifts ever so slightly as his dark eyes swirl with relief, before he turns to Ezra. "That thing we were talking about last week? I think she needs it now," he states, all mysteriously, and I have no clue what he's talking about.

Ezra switches his gaze to me, looking deep into my eyes as his fingers lace with mine, before he glances back at Jagger. "If Lou-Lou trusts you, then I do too," he responds calmly, although I don't miss the way his pupils dilate.

Nope. We're not allowed to talk in little riddles, I want to know what he means by that.

"Someone better start exp—"

My words are completely cut off as Jagger smashes his lips against mine, the world pausing as he consumes me with his mouth.

His grip is still tight around my wrist as Ezra squeezes my hand, and as I finally part my mouth for Jagger's demanding mouth, I feel Ezra's lips caress against my temple.

Fuck.

I have no idea where this is leading, no idea what I just agreed to without any further information, but all I can feel right now is them, and the rest of my body willingly follows along.

My free hand strokes over Jagger's bare chest, his shoulder, and then up into his hair. When I get a good grip on his bun, I sink my fingers into it as I deepen the kiss. I feel Ezra slip his hand from mine, before his body presses up behind me, and my skin screams in delight as I find myself sandwiched between the both of them.

Home.

This is fucking home.

And I need Jagger to fucking feel this, see this, and understand this before he puts it all on the line next week.

"Upstairs. Now," Ezra grumbles from behind me, and without a word in response, Jagger grabs the back of my thighs and pulls me against his chest as I squeak in surprise, my legs wrapping around his waist.

We're moving toward the stairs before I can even process what's going on, and even though I pull my lips from Jagger's so he can see where we're walking, I grin mischievously as I spy the crook of his neck, leaning forward to sink my teeth into his skin.

"Fuck, Luella," he grunts beneath me, but it's not as angry as I expect, and that almost makes me pout. I want him to feel how fucking angry I am. Whatever is about to happen here won't change that.

I hear the sound of someone's bedroom door opening, and moments later I recognize Jagger's room, before I'm released, falling backward on the bed.

Ezra flops down on the bed beside me, leaving Jagger to shut the door behind us, and I wet my bottom lip, already out of breath from doing absolutely nothing but feeling absolutely everything.

"Grab the lube from my top drawer, Ezra," Jagger orders, making me gulp as I eye him. He's orchestrating this whole thing in his head already, I can see it in his eyes, and as much as I want to bite back, argue with him every step of the way, I'm also far too eager to see where this may lead.

I don't pull my gaze from his as I hear the pull of his nightstand drawer opening, and moments later the lube drops onto the sheets beside me.

"Good, now strip our girl down," he demands, and fuck him for making my skin tingle as Ezra leans over me, his own heated gaze matching mine.

"Would you like that, Lou-Lou?" Ezra murmurs against my ear as he trails his fingers over the V neck sweater I'm wearing, and I moan in response, goosebumps rising at his touch.

"Yes," I breathe, confirming that I want all of the things with them, and he grins down at me, a glimmer of deviousness in his eyes, making me raise my eyebrows, but he doesn't explain what they've already said.

"There's nowhere near enough stripping going on right now," Jagger grunts, placing his hands on his hips as he stands beside the bed, glaring down at me as he fixes the hair tie holding his bun, but my gaze is fixed on the red, raw, bite mark I left, and I grin like a menace.

Shuffling to sit up, Ezra moves with me, and immediately grabs the hem of my sweater and pulls the pale pink material over my head with a grin, before instantly finding the waistband of my leggings.

I can feel Jagger's eyes watching every move we make, and I decide he deserves some teasing. As I lean back for Ezra to pull my leggings over my ass, he quickly pulls my Vans off too, before discarding everything off the end of the bed, leaving me in just my mint green panties and bra.

Ezra faces me, and keeping my eyes fixed on his, I rise to my knees before him, placing my hands under the material of his t-shirt as I slowly drag my fingertips over his abs, lifting his band tee with the movement.

"I don't recall giving you permission to undress him, Luella," Jagger states, and I shrug, still not turning to look at him as Ezra lifts his arms up above his head, his teeth sinking into his bottom lip as he tries to hold back the grin teasing his lips. I lift the material over his head, his soft curls bouncing with the movement as he adjusts his glasses, and I groan at how fucking hot he looks with his jeans hanging low on his hips, revealing the deep V desperate for my tongue to run along it.

"Lie back on the bed, Luella," Jagger orders, and I can't help but lean forward and press my lips to Ezra's before I follow his little command.

As I sink back into the pillows like he says, an idea pops into my mind, and I try and test my luck. "Kiss," I blurt, nibbling on my bottom lip as they both turn to look at me as they step out of their pants, leaving me to drool over the outlines of their cocks through their boxers.

Jagger laughs first as Ezra grins, and I think my excitement has instantly been squashed, when Ezra finally speaks. "Lou, what do you think we're doing here?" he says deeply, the tone of his voice hitting me straight at my core as my eyes widen and flick between the pair of them.

What the fuck does that mean?

I'm too stunned to voice the words playing in my mind, but when Ezra turns to his left, looking up at Jagger with a knowing smile playing on his lips, I almost die when their lips meet in the middle, and a whimper falls from my lips.

Oh. My. Fucking. God.

Yes. Yes. All of this. Yes.

Their kiss doesn't deepen, both of them testing the feel which starkly shows me that this is something they've never done before, but they're putting on a little show… for me, and if they're into it, I sure as fuck am too.

We'd only been playing around a few weeks ago about what—

Wait… this isn't… we're not… are we?

Excitement buzzes through me as I move toward them, but Jagger must see me out of the corner of his eye and wags his finger at me.

"If you want us to have fun, Luella, you'll do well to listen to what I'm telling you to do," Jagger states, pulling back from Ezra, who takes that as his cue to crawl up the bed toward me with his eyes dancing with heat, and I almost come on the spot.

I'm not going to survive this. There's no way in hell, but I can't think of a single better way to go. Well, unless Jameson and Leo were here. I cannot imagine this being their scene, but it's most definitely mine.

Not wanting to miss out on the opportunity, I sink back to my elbows on the pillows as I did earlier, and I gasp when Ezra trails his finger over the outline of my panties.

Fuck.

"Ask her, Ezra," Jagger murmurs, running his thumb over his bottom lip as he watches where Ezra touches me, and a shiver shoots down my spine.

Before I can open my mouth to ask what he means, Ezra looks up at me with his gray eyes fixed on mine. "How much do you want to see Jagger fuck me, while I'm deep inside of you, Lou-Lou?" he asks, his breath fanning over my pussy, and my mouth and eyes widen at the same time.

"I think I might die from excitement," I mutter, trying to swallow past the lump in my throat. "Is that answer enough?" I add, my hands fisting in the bedsheets beside me as I look between them both.

Instead of nodding or speaking his agreement, Ezra leans forward and rakes his teeth over the lace of my panties, making a moan fall from my lips.

This is definitely one way to help distract me right now, and it one hundred percent beats sparring. "I'm still going to be mad after this you know," I manage to say as Ezra's teeth drag across the lace covering my clit, and Jagger grins.

"I wouldn't expect anything less, but you wanted memories, so here we are," he replies, his eyes searching mine, completely opposite to his words, and it somehow settles me even more. "Now, keep Ezra busy while I stretch him," he proceeds to add with a wink, making my heart leap again as Jagger pulls at the waistband of Ezra's boxers.

"How am I supposed to... ah, fuck," I moan as Ezra tears at my lacy panties, tossing them over his shoulder before he grips the globes of my ass and leans in to drag his tongue over my pussy.

"You're going to let me feast on you, Lou-Lou, by the time you're coming all over my face I'll be ready for him," Ezra murmurs, his lips brushing over my clit, and I sink farther into the bed as my back arches up off the bed.

That's a timeframe I can definitely get behind.

Ezra runs his tongue from my clit to my core, and my fingers instantly make my way into his curly hair as I grind up against him. Holy fuck. My eyes squeeze shut with the sensations, and when he slowly thrusts two fingers into my center, I tilt my hips up to meet him.

My other hand grips the sheets like my life depends on it as he works me over, and I want to scream with pleasure when the slightest bit of stubble on his chin grazes across my clit. It's the sweetest kind of pain, and I'm desperate for it.

"Fuck," Ezra groans, making my eyes blink open immediately, and when I manage to focus on him, my jaw hits my chest.

As Ezra licks, sucks, and plays with me, he has his ass up in the air as Jagger slowly works a second finger into his hole, and my core clenches at the sight.

"Oh fuck," I murmur, repeating Ezra's words as I feel my skin prickle with heat and desire courses through my body.

"No one's fucking until you come on his tongue, Luella," Jagger mumbles, his dark eyes blown just as much as mine are as he watches me writhe beneath Ezra.

"Yeah, Lou-Lou," Ezra adds, a sparkle of mischief in his eyes as he sucks my clit into his mouth, and I try to tighten my thighs around his head, but he moves his hands from my thighs to my legs to hold them in place.

Shit.

Holy fuck.

As if he's spurred on by Jagger's moves, Ezra thrusts his fingers deeper inside of me, twisting and running his pads against my walls, and a cry falls from my lips as I fight to keep my eyes open.

The click of the lube bottle opening jolts my senses, making me focus on Jagger as he pours it over Ezra, and as Ezra moans, his lips vibrate over my clit, and that's the tiny extra sensation I need for my body to come crashing all at once.

"Ahhhh," my body tingles from head to toe as I climax, melting under Ezra's touch as he laps at my release. Wave after wave crashes through my body as Ezra continues to slowly thrust his fingers inside of me, but when he removes his mouth I whimper, until I force my eyes wide open, and see what's coming next.

"How do you want us, Lou-Lou?" Ezra asks, moving to hover over me, my orgasm glistening on his lips, and I push up on my weak arms to press mine to his, tasting my release on his tongue, and I hear the both of them groan.

Moments later, another pair of lips are dragging between ours as Jagger joins us. We're a complete mess of tongues and lips, but it's so fucking hot I can't bring myself to pull away.

"Answer the question, Luella," Jagger mumbles, his hand gripping my throat and tilting my head back so he can look down at me, and my body pulses with desire again.

I don't know how I'm supposed to stay mad at this fucker, but I force myself to remember his stubborn asshole-ish ways.

"I thought you were the one giving the orders," I say with a quirk of my eyebrow, and he rolls his eyes at me.

"Have it your way," he responds, leaning forward as if to kiss me, before dragging his teeth along my jaw, and I have to bite back yet another groan.

As if sensing the pleasure building within me, he releases his hold on me, before moving to the foot of the bed. Lifting myself up onto my elbows, I watch as Ezra shuffles down the bed so he's the perfect height for Jagger, and my pussy sparks with need.

Jagger wraps his arms around Ezra, his large hand

instantly covering Ezra's cock, and he groans in response, his head falling back onto Jagger's shoulder, and I gape at them together.

Before I can follow them, Ezra grabs my ankles and drags me down the sheets until I'm perfectly positioned with my legs on either side of him, and Jagger releases his hold on Ezra's cock, letting it graze against my core, and I gasp, trying desperately to wet my dry lips as I raise my hands to his hair.

I almost think this is a dream, until I watch Ezra's head tilt back and a moan falls from his lips as Jagger teases him, and in one swift move, Ezra nudges his cock at my entrance. Lifting my hips ever so slightly, I gasp for breath as he edges inside of me, and when he's fully seated, he thankfully gives me a second to adjust.

"How good does she feel, Ezra?" Jagger asks, his voice gruff as his gaze meets mine, and Ezra nods eagerly.

"Like a fucking dream as always," he bites out as he braces his hands on either side of my face, and I can tell by the gleam in his eyes that Jagger is nudging at his entrance too.

Holy fuck. This is happening. It's actually happening.

I think I'm going to come again already as my pussy

clenches Ezra's cock desperately, and he moans, leaning forward to press his lips to mine.

"Relax, Ezra," Jagger murmurs, his hand grabbing my calf as he connects the three of us as he slowly works himself inside Ezra.

"Fuck. It never felt this good, not without you heating my cock, Lou-Lou," Ezra rambles, sweat beading along his forehead as his lips caress my cheek.

His words only set me on fire even more, and as I feel him relax above me, I can tell when Jagger is deep inside of him, because the slight thrust has Ezra thrusting into me too, and the three of us groan together.

"Holy shit," I gasp, my eyes widening as Ezra's roll to the back of his head.

"Both together is just… I'm just… shit," Ezra stutters as Jagger tightens his other hand on Ezra's waist, pulling out slowly before thrusting forward, and creating a domino effect as Ezra does the same.

"Grab her other leg, Ezra, I want you to fuck our girl and yourself on my cock," Jagger orders, and my pussy jolts with excitement.

I want to feel every touch, but I wish I could have a better view of the two of them.

Ezra takes a second to grab my thigh while rising up on his knees a little better as Jagger continues to fuck him slowly. Every brush of Ezra's cock, knowing that the movement and pace is being set by Jagger, only heightens the pleasure dancing through my body.

"Do it, Ezra," I murmur as I look at him, smiling at his blown pupils and damp hair, and he slowly tilts his hips back, retreating from my core as he impales himself on Jagger's cock, and my mouth falls open. Hell yeah.

All too quickly he's slamming forward, thrusting deep inside me as only the tip of Jagger's cock remains inside him.

"Oh, shit," Jagger bites, as turned on as I am at the sight, and as Ezra ups his pace, none of us can seem to speak a full sentence. We're a jumble of moans and cries as we all chase the one goal; ecstasy.

"You're... so fucking... beautiful, Lou-Lou," Ezra mumbles, and it almost feels like a cry as his chest and neck prickle pink as he flushes.

Sinking my teeth into my bottom lip, I undo my front fastening bra, letting my breasts spill out, and he groans in delight as he eyes me. I drag my thumb over my pebbled nipple as I slowly stroke my other hand down to my clit, wanting to give him a show too.

"Fuck," he hisses, just as Jagger thrusts forward, taking back control of the pace, and Ezra falls above me again, managing to brace himself as Jagger practically fucks the pair of us. "I'm… I'm gonna… fuckkk."

Ezra's whole body tightens as ecstasy ripples through him, and I circle my clit, my eyes meeting Jagger's above Ezra's head, I find myself following swiftly after him as a sharp orgasm practically paralyzes me and I scream.

My pulse pounds in my ears. I can't hear either of them, but I watch as Jagger's face contorts, his orgasm tearing through him as he falls against Ezra's back and grinds inside of him in long thrusts.

We're a pile of panting limbs as we try to catch our breath, and I shiver as Ezra pulses inside me one last time. My eyes close, my body exhausted from all the emotions from today, and I throw an arm over my face as I continue to try and catch my breath.

I don't register either of them moving until Ezra slowly slips from my core, and I whimper as I feel completely empty, but moments later there's a warm cloth stroking against my skin, and I peer up to see Jagger cleaning me up.

All I see in his eyes is love and pain, just like mine.

He's made this bed for us all to lie in, and we just have to trust he really does know what he's doing because I can't live without him. I can't live without any of them.

I hear the sound of the shower turning on in the distance, and I assume it's Ezra taking a minute to clean up as Jagger rubs his lips together. "Tell me what you need, Luella," he states, not a question, not a plea, a calmly spoken demand, and I sigh.

Looking around the room, my eyes settling on my panties which sit in complete tatters, again, and I do the only thing that will calm the atmosphere between us. I channel my inner Leo and defuse the situation.

"I need new panties. At the rate you guys are going, I'm going to have none left," I murmur, pointing in the general direction where they lie, and a small, relieved smile takes over his lips.

"I'll buy you some the day after Thanksgiving," he answers, raising his eyebrow at me, and I nod, understanding exactly what he's insinuating.

"You better."

WATCH ME RISE

CHAPTER TWENTY NINE

LEO

My hand leisurely strokes Lucy's thigh, drawing circles as we sit side by side in the back of the truck, leaving Jameson to drive and Jagger to sit shotgun. I can see her hand laced with Ezra's as he sits on her other side as we all remain silent, letting the radio fill the space around us.

Nothing says Happy Thanksgiving quite like a tense car ride.

Lucy looks fucking stunning today, with a black rollneck top tucked into a deep purple checkered mini-skirt, a pair of tights and heeled boots. Her blonde hair is piled up on top of her head as large hooped earrings dangle from her ears, and my dick has been eager to rub against her since she walked down the stairs.

The past week has been beyond tense, the five of us moving to the stage of pretending like shit isn't going to get ugly tomorrow, but the elephant has been in the room every day.

Now, with tomorrow evening looming over us all, I can feel everyone getting edgy again, even though we were supposed to be relaxing and enjoying the atmosphere of Thanksgiving.

Jameson turns into the driveway for Lockwood, and I watch as Lucy rubs her lips together. I was surprised when her mom asked if we would like to come over for Thanksgiving and she said yes, but any progress is progress, and it's nice that we get to spend the holiday with Lola too. I want her to have all of the love around her. I know her mom is a bitch, but she really is much better than she used to be, but the uncertainty will always stick to her now. Her past is always tainting the future.

As long as I have my queen at my side, I don't really care where we are.

The truck comes to a stop, and we silently pile out, my heart warming when Lucy takes my outstretched hand, letting me help her down. My arm instinctively wraps around her shoulder as we move as a unit toward the entrance, the clear sky making a nice change to the weather we've had lately.

I reluctantly drop my arm and lace my fingers with Lucy's before we step through the rotating door together, and I see the peek of a smile on her lips when I rub my thumb across her knuckles. This girl loves every little passive touch and lingering kiss, and it makes me feel like a king when I put a smile on her lips.

The usual heat hits us the second we step through into the lobby, and Maggie greets us immediately as I brush my lips at Lucy's temple.

"Happy Thanksgiving!" she shouts cheerily, running toward us with her arms wide open, and it catches me off guard when she moves for Lucy first, wrapping her arms around her neck casually, like she's done it a million times before.

Lucy wraps her free hand around her in response, but I refuse to let go of her hand to give her the ability to respond with both arms.

"Happy Thanksgiving," I murmur in response as she moves to me next, before quickly making the rounds with the other guys, all of which mumble a Happy Thanksgiving as well.

"We've been cooking all morning. I'm not saying June is excited to have you all here, but… well, she is," she says with a grin, running her hands down her usual uniform. She doesn't even slip into her own clothes, even on a special occasion, but I can't imagine her without the usual outfit I'm used to seeing her in.

I catch Lucy's eyes widening in response, but she doesn't say a word, letting Maggie lead us down the hall excitedly as the rest of us trail behind.

"Don't think you can keep Ella all to yourself for the entire day, asshole," Jameson grumbles from behind me, and I roll my eyes as Lucy grins over her shoulder at him.

She fucking loves us fighting over her. It's never actually negative or aggressive, but the underlying tone is there, and I can see her eyes sparkle with glee every time she sees how much we fucking love her.

"Make yourself my favorite and I might just let you," she mutters to Jameson, before turning to face forward again, leaving Jameson to grumble something about the challenge being accepted.

Maggie doesn't bother to knock since the door is slightly ajar, and the second we step inside, the little squeal and the tiny footsteps of Lola charging toward us sounds out.

"Turkey day, it's turkey day," she sings, clapping her hands with giddiness, and I reluctantly release Lucy's hand as she crouches to catch Lola as she throws herself at her big sister. Their embrace warms my heart, while making me feel guilty for keeping them separated for so long, but I have to remind myself that everything happens for a reason, and they weren't meant to meet until they did, under the circumstances that they did, so Lucy could see and feel the rawness for herself.

Lucy twirls Lola in her arms, her cute little red festive dress floating around them, and it makes me smile.

Drawn to the love blossoming around the two of them, the four of us instinctively circle around, almost protectively as we wrap our arms around them both.

"Group hug!" I shout, making Lola giggle as a calmness washes over us, the tension building only minutes before quickly drifting away, as Lola's mere presence relaxes us all.

I'm glad we got out of the house today and did this, it's exactly what we needed. Especially if we're going to embrace tomorrow head on, a moment to have for ourselves first is paramount.

As we all step back, Lola does her grabby hands in my direction for me to give her a hug too, and Lucy hands her over to me with a soft smile, moving toward her mom as Lola's arms tighten around my neck.

"Hey, sweetie, have you been a good girl?" I ask as I hear one of the guys shut the door behind us properly, but my gaze remains on Lucy as she embraces her mom, and hope fills my veins.

If we can get through this mess, we can get through anything, I think as Lola leans back to meet my gaze, nodding frantically in response as she grins at me.

"I'm always a good girl," she states, her voice getting clearer every time she speaks, and I ruffle her blonde hair before Jagger steps up beside us with his arms outstretched for his turn, and she goes willingly.

Patting Jagger on the shoulder, I swoop past them, heading for my girl as she helps carry a few trays of food over to the dining table.

"Does anyone need a big strong man to help?" I ask,

flexing my muscles as I waggle my eyebrows, and both Lucy and her mom chuckle at me as Maggie shakes her head, not surprised at all with the shit that comes out of my mouth, but if it makes my girl smile, I don't care.

"I think we've got it, big man, how about you get the silverware?" Lucy responds, and I salute her, making her wave a hand dismissively at me after she's placed the casserole dish down.

My stomach grumbles with excitement at the spread before us. We haven't really eaten since breakfast, now it's almost four in the afternoon and I'm starving. It's killed me to leave the food in someone else's hands for the day so I'm more than ready to tuck in. Turkey, mashed potatoes, green bean casserole, cranberry sauce, pumpkin pie, corn, asparagus, and even a salad that no one will touch, fills the table.

It's nothing like it was at Robbie's place a few weeks ago, where everything was grand and over the top. It's… homey, and exactly what we need. This is the kind of setting I wish I could look back on as a child and remember, but there's nothing I can do about that. Although we're here making it happen for Lola, and that's just as important, and makes up for the time we lost.

Reaching for a slice of turkey, my stomach getting the better of me, my hand is slapped away just before I can reach it. I look up in surprise to find Maggie staring at me expectantly with her eyebrows raised, and I pout, but it only makes her face get even sterner, and I know I have no chance of tasting anything before she's ready for us to sit down.

I stick my tongue out like a petulant child, which definitely doesn't help my case, before I glance around the room to see what I can distract myself with, when I find Lucy grinning at me as she tries to cover it with her hand.

Her.

I can always distract my hunger with my girl.

Is there somewhere we could sneak off to now so I could get a taste of her on my lips?

The thought has barely crossed my mind when she reaches out and playfully slaps her hand against my chest as she rolls her eyes.

"Leo Cooper, I have no idea what you're thinking, but based on your facial expression I know it means you're up to no good. You have to stop," Lucy says with a giggle, before rising up on her tiptoes and running her fingers through my hair.

I smile at her, my hand finding her waist before she places a soft kiss at the corner of my mouth and steps away.

Fucking tease.

"How long are we waiting to eat, June? I'm starving," I groan, trying my best to put on some puppy dog eyes as I look at her, and she shakes her head while tossing a dish cloth over her shoulder.

"Sit your ass down, everything is pretty much ready to go, but don't you dare touch a single thing until we've said grace," she says sternly, and I nod agreeably as I drop down into the nearest seat, not caring to make sure everyone else is ready.

"Where does the little princess want to sit?" Ezra asks as he carries Lola toward us, and she points right at her highchair at the end of the row on my side, and Lucy immediately rushes to the spot beside her before anyone else can take it.

I almost try to move over a chair so I'm beside her, but Jameson beats me to it, and I bite back my groan as he looks at me with a smug as fuck grin on his face.

Motherfucker.

Jagger takes the seat across from Lucy, while June takes the one facing Lola. Leaving Ezra to take the seat beside Jagger, and Maggie to take the seat at the end to my right.

We're a bizarre bunch to find sitting around a table, but fuck, it's as close to family as we're getting, and I'm thankful for that.

Maggie wordlessly places a bottle of water in front of each of us before she takes her seat, and we all look to Lucy's mom for her little grace speech she wants.

Clearing her throat, she tucks her hair behind her ear before smiling at Lucy. "I thought we could say grace, but maybe a little different, like we all could go around the table and say something we're thankful for," she murmurs, nervously twisting her fingers together as she waits, seeking Lucy's approval, and although her eyes widen in surprise at the request, she does nod in agreement and her mom smiles wide.

"I'll go first," Maggie interjects, and June's shoulders sag in relief as some of the pressure is taken off her. "I'm grateful for the five of you showing up and making this a fun occasion for us all, especially Lola, but also us. Our list of visitors is short, so seeing your faces always brings me joy," she announces with a smile, and everyone smiles at her.

Assuming we're going clockwise around the table, I take a deep breath, glancing at everyone around the table as I try to decide what it is I'm thankful for.

"I'm thankful for… uh, nope, I can't say that," I quickly stutter, remembering there are little ears present as well as parents, and I can see Lucy blush from here, knowing my dirty mind drifted.

"Idiot," Jagger grumbles under his breath, and I stick my finger up at him in my head as I think.

"Okay, I'm thankful for time. The time I get to spend with Lucy, when I thought it would never happen again, makes me glad to be alive," I state, and everyone's eyes widen in surprise at my seriousness, and I shrug in response.

"How am I supposed to follow that?" Jameson grunts as Lucy smiles softly at me. "Fine, I'm thankful for switchblades and the spacious backseat in the truck," he states, not caring who's present, and Lucy's face turns pink as she kicks him under the table.

"I'm thankful for the universe bringing me here, and that I took the opportunity for a fresh start when I could have stayed where I was. Things may be crazy right now, but I wouldn't change a single thing now that I get to be here with you all. Especially this little princess," she adds, bopping Lola on the nose and she chuckles in response.

"Okay, my turn," June murmurs, sitting taller as she clears her throat, and focuses her gaze on Lucy. "I'm thankful to see my beautiful eldest daughter again. I'm thankful for the kind, spirited, yet fearless woman she has become, and the fact she's even sitting here, willing to offer me a second chance. I'm thankful to have her little sister too. Everything happens for a reason, and I'm just..." her words trail off as tears fill her eyes and she waves her hand in front of her face quickly. Lucy leans across the table to squeeze her mom's other hand, offering her silent support.

I'm beyond fucking proud of the woman she is, June definitely got that right.

"June, why do you have to go so big like that before me, huh?" Jagger grumbles, making June grin and calm down a little as he takes a deep breath, his dark eyes zeroing in on Lucy, and it makes me grin that we're all fucking thankful for her. Fuck Thanksgiving, let's just have a Luella Carter appreciation day.

Jagger's mouth opens, but before a single word can fall out, a siren blares around us, and I jump to my feet in an instant.

What the fuck is that?

My wide eyes glance to Maggie who stares in shock at everyone at the table, her mouth moving but nothing comes out as she tries to process what's going on.

"What's the siren for?" Lucy asks, standing from the table with her palms flat against the wood as she looks at everyone.

"It's… it's the… I set the door triggers once you get in like I always do… I don't know what…" Maggie doesn't need to say anymore.

Someone is here, uninvited.

Fuck.

"It's probably Robbie, here to ruin our day," June states, as she nervously stands from the table too, her hands trembling slightly as she places herself at Lola's side, and I wet my lips as I glance at the other guys.

"Jagger, stay here with the girls, the three of us will go and see what's going on and do a perimeter check. Do you have access to the security cameras on your phone, Ezra?" I ask, losing my joking persona as I focus on the here and now.

"I do," he replies, rising to his feet and moving toward the door immediately. "I can access that while I take the back with one of you, the other should do a check of the lobby."

"I'm on it," Jameson states, his switchblade already in his hand as he beats Ezra to the door, looking through the peephole before he slips out.

I can't believe we didn't consider bringing more weapons. A gun or two maybe? But we stupidly thought this would be a casual family day. Not… this.

"Uh, I'm not going to just fucking sit around, assholes," Jagger grunts, completely forgetting about swearing in front of Lola. He fists his hands at his sides while trying to remain as calm as possible in front of Lola, but I shake my head.

"No one can take care of the girls better than you, man," I state, and his shoulders sag, knowing I'm right as I race for the door behind Ezra.

"Be safe," Lucy calls out, and I grin over my shoulder at her, trying to be as calm as possible, but it falls flat as my heart pounds in my chest.

My gut tells me it can't be as simple as Robbie showing up.

As I step out into the hall, I slam the door shut behind me, and my hand turns to lock it, but it's a key lock and I don't have the key, so I quickly slam my fist against the wood. "Lock it," I yell, before rushing to catch up with Ezra who takes the fire exit door to the right as Jameson continues forward, heading for the lobby.

Fuck.

"What can you see?" I ask Ezra as I step outside with him, trying to close the fire exit without it actually locking, but it's impossible, and the sound of the slam rings in my ears along with the siren still blaring everywhere.

"Three guys in hoodies, but they don't seem to have stepped into the building, it looks like they threw a brick through the lobby glass door, triggering the alarm before running around the back," he advises as I run my fingers through my hair, my body itching to find the fuckers and make them pay instantly.

"Take the right, I'll go left," I order, not waiting for a response as I keep my eyes focused on my surroundings. Around the back of the building is filled with trees and greenery. I'm sure it was once a nice space attached to Lockwood, but no one's really cared for it enough to keep it's shine, so everything is overgrown and in disarray.

Keeping to the exterior of the building, I see nothing out of the ordinary, and when I press myself up against the wall to peer around the side, I still see no one there.

What the fuck is going on?

I turn down the side, staying alert as I up my pace, but as I reach the other end, I stumble into Jameson, and both of us frown in confusion.

"No one's here," he mutters, and I nod in agreement, I haven't seen a fucking soul.

Is this some sort of game?

"Let's go for Ezra," I say, swiping my hand over my face as I spy Ezra standing confused in front of the entrance.

"Ez, what's going on?" Jameson grunts as Ezra rushes to us, his phone in his hand as he frowns down at it.

"I have no clue at all, the security feed is glitching. Look," he mumbles, turning the screen to us, and it's like an old DVD disc where it's scratched so it keeps freezing.

"Ezra, is someone fucking with the system?" I ask, my heart sinking as I take off for the door, my heart telling me to get back inside to the others, but as I approach the usually revolving doors, I stall.

It's barricaded.

Fuck.

I feel Jameson and Ezra slow at my side as they see what I see, and realization dawns on me.

"I think it was a distraction."

WATCH ME RISE

CHAPTER THIRTY

Lou-Lou

I have no idea what the fuck is happening, but as soon as the guys left and Jagger clicked the lock, I've felt like my soul is splitting in two.

"Mama, Mama," Lola cries, confused with what is happening around her, and I feel frozen in place, unsure of what to do or how to help.

I have no idea what is going on out there with Leo, Jameson, and Ezra right now, and that's only adding to my stress and anxiety.

My eyes meet Jagger's, and he flicks his gaze to Lola's

bedroom again, hinting for me to take them in there, and I sigh, nodding as I place my hand at the base of my mom's spine and guide her toward Lola's room.

Lola clings to Mom, feeling the anxiety building around her, and Maggie rushes in front, understanding that we need to get out of the way from the windows and doors just in case.

I barely register any of her bedroom as my mom takes a seat on the bed, and Maggie puts the television on, distracting Lola with one of her favorite cartoons.

I can't stay in here, not being able to help. I'm already going crazy as it is. Jagger's just going to have to deal with it.

"I need you to stay in this room until one of us comes to get you, okay? Prop whatever you can against the door for now. We need to keep her safe, even if it's absolutely nothing," I state, leaning forward to run my thumb over Lola's cheek delicately as my mom nods in response.

Wetting my lips I reach the door, and as I move to close it behind me, Maggie is right there to do as I said. "Be safe," she murmurs, a tight smile on her lips, but it doesn't reach her eyes, and I don't have the strength to try and return it.

As the door clicks shut behind me, my gaze instantly goes to Jagger as he paces in front of the door. I understand the decision to have him stay behind, but it'll be eating him up inside to be here, feeling as useless as me, even under the guise of protecting Lola, Maggie and my mom.

Jagger glances down at his phone, tapping away before bringing it to his ear, seemingly trying to call someone, but after a few moments he lowers it, his face getting redder as he gets angrier.

"What's going on?" I ask, moving toward him, and his dark eyes flick to mine as his jaw tightens.

"I don't fucking know, Luella. No one is answering their phone," he grinds out, fisting his hands at his side. "But, I told you to go in there with them," he adds, and I give him a pointed look as I put my hands on my hips.

"Jagger, and I mean this with all of my heart… fuck off," I reply, ready to go to bat with him on this because I can't do it. I need to be near at least one of them right now.

A bang sounds from outside the room, making me jolt in surprise and my spine stiffens as I jump, and before I can even process what's happening, Jagger is heading for the door.

"Fuck this shit. I'm not waiting in here, I'm going

to see what's going on," he hisses, peering through the peephole as panic settles over me.

Rushing to keep up with him and hold him back, I manage to place my hand on the door before he unlocks it, but when his gaze meets mine, I know he's not going to hear a word I say.

"Jagger, please," I murmur, knowing my words aren't strong enough to keep him in place, and he lifts his hand to my chin, tilting my head back so he can look down at me properly.

"Luella, I'll be quick, I promise. Do not step out of this room, do you hear me? I will be thirty seconds max, but I need to know what that noise was, and I have to check that my brothers are alright," he states, his brown eyes pleading with mine to understand as dread sits heavy in my stomach.

"I'm fucking holding you to that," I reply, before he presses his lips to mine in a demanding kiss that is over far too quickly.

With one final nod, he twists the key in the lock, looking through the peephole, before he swings the door open and steps out. Before I can even say his name the frame is rattling as he slams it shut behind him, and I rise up onto my tiptoes to see through the peephole.

I can see the back of Jagger's head, his hair falling loose from his bun as he lifts his hand to swipe it down his face. It feels like my heart is in my chest as he takes a step down the hall, but he instantly pauses, his body freezing as he widens his hands at his side in a show of surrender.

What the fuck is he doing?

I can't see around him, all I can see is the back of him as he slowly raises his hands.

"I don't know what the fuck you want, but whatever it is, not her," he states firmly, and I press up against the wood as I desperately try to see around him.

What are you doing, Jagger? Come back inside! I scream internally to myself, not wanting to actually make anything worse by yelling.

Silence falls around me, and I wrap my hand around the door handle, considering whether to open it or not, when the sound of a gunshot rings in my ears, making my body lurch and I watch in horror as Jagger stumbles back a step, hitting the door between us.

"Jagger! Jagger!" I yell, terror coating my skin as I slam the palm of my hand against the wood beneath my touch as I feel the door handle rattle from the other side. "Jagger!"

As he slumps back, he dips below the peephole and I catch a glimpse of a guy dressed head to toe in black, with a hat on, his hood up, and a scarf covering the rest of his face, but more importantly, I spot the gun aimed in our direction.

Jagger's direction.

No.

No, no, no, no, no.

"Jagger!" I scream, as the door handle wiggles again, and my eyes widen as I try to turn it, but it doesn't budge. What the fuck? How did he lock it? I frantically look out of the peephole again, watching as the person lowers the gun, and I hear Jagger's soft words.

"Not her. Not her," he repeats, his hand gripping the door handle from the other side as I pull on it manically, but I can't get the door to open.

"Jagger," I shout, my throat burning as the words rip from my chest. "Jagger."

Slapping the wood repeatedly as I still try to work the door open, I notice the guy slip out of the fire exit, and my movements become even more urgent as I yell for Jagger.

"Jagger, open the fucking door. Jagger! Jagger!"

Tears prick my eyes as he doesn't respond, and as I

try to force the knob, it doesn't move an inch, because it's fucking locked.

Stepping back, I wipe at my eyes as I try to think, and that's when I see it, the red trickle of blood seeping under the door, and my heart lodges in my throat.

Fuck. No.

As I take a step back toward the door, I hear a slight bang, and when I peer through the hole, I find Jagger slumped to the side.

He needs me. Jagger fucking needs me and he locked the fucking door.

Anger and pain burns my soul as my face reddens, and I take two steps back from the door before charging at it, and throwing my entire body into it.

It moved slightly but it wasn't enough.

It needs to be enough.

"Jagger, I'm coming to help you. I swear, I'm fucking coming," I cry, my tears a mixture of fear and rage as I take four steps back and launch myself again.

Fuck.

It's still not enough progress.

Doing the same again, I aim more of my body at the top half of the door, and as I make contact with the wood, it splinters down the middle from the force.

Holy shit.

Panting, I swipe my hair back off my face, before I grip the door frame and raise my heeled boot at the broken wood, and my body sags in relief as the hinges remain in place, but all of my efforts on the other side have the wood ruined down to where the lock is.

Kicking it a few more times, it creates a hole in the door, and I scramble to climb through it, my tights snagging on the wood, but it doesn't stop me as it tears through the material, likely grazing my skin too, but I'm running on adrenaline and feel nothing.

I can't place my foot safely on the floor, so I toss myself through the gap, his name raw on my lips. "Jagger! Jagger!"

Lifting my hand, my face pales as his blood is smeared across my palms. Looking him over from head to toe, he is slumped in an awkward position, his neck tilted at a weird angle as blood pours from his abdomen.

Oh, God. No, please no.

Tears stream down my face as I panic, not knowing how to move him or make it better, but I cup his cheek as I swipe my bloody thumb across his skin. "Jagger," I murmur. "Jagger, can you hear me?" I say calmly as I use my other hand to search for a pulse at his neck.

The relaxed facade lasts mere moments when I feel nothing.

Nothing.

My eyes widening in terror as I feel my heart break in my chest and my soul shatter into a million pieces.

"Somebody help me!" I scream in desperation. My voice cracks on the final word and my fingers tremble against his skin as I try to cover the wound with my palm.

No, he can't be, no.

No, no, no, no, no.

I only just got him back, he can't leave me.

Not yet.

He fucking promised.

AFTERWORDS

This motherfucking bitch of an author can literally suck my dick.

Does she get off on leaving us here?

HELL FUCKING YEAH SHE DOES

Hahaa!

Sorry not sorry lol

But for real, my alphas will tell you, I wrote the last words to Chapter thirty and sobbed. My heart is aching!

I love you guys for not sending death threats, it means a lot

Roll on April 29th <3

THANK YOU

Michaelllllll I love you, you know this. I know this. Everybody knows this. Thanks for putting up with my weird and crazy ways!

To my precious babies! I love how we still happy dance and rock out to the playlists even though you have no real clue what's actually going on.

To my awesome bubble squad who accept my cheer squad moves and obscene organization attempts, I love ya!

Nicole, Jeni, and Tanya. You three together should come with a warning sign, Haha. Thank you so much for your time, help, support, and GIF's that get me through the day.

Thank you to my awesome betas on this book, who always yell, cry, and laugh along with me.

Thank you to BellaLuna as always for making my babies look so damn beautiful! You make me cry and say thank you so much that you hate me for it, but you know I won't stop. Haha.

ABOUT KC KEAN

KC Kean is the sassy half of a match made in heaven. Mummy to two beautiful children, Pokemon Master and Apex Legend world saving gamer.

Starting her adventure in the RH romance world after falling in love with it as a reader, who knows where this crazy train is heading. As long as there is plenty of steam she'll be there.

ALSO BY KC KEAN

Featherstone Academy

(Reverse Harem Contemporary Romance)

My Bloodline

Your Bloodline

Our Bloodline

Red

Freedom

All-Star Series

(Reverse Harem Contemporary Romance)

Toxic Creek

Tainted Creek

Twisted Creek

(Standalone MF)

Burn to Ash

Emerson U Series

(Reverse Harem Contemporary Romance)

Watch Me Fall

KC KEAN

Watch Me Rise
Watch Me Reign

Printed in Great Britain
by Amazon